Praise for the novels of Michelle Major

"Major's charming small town is packed with
salt-of-the-earth people readers will embrace,
and each sister's journey is beautifully imagined."
—*Publishers Weekly* on *The Wish List*

"A dynamic start to a series
with a refreshingly original premise."
—*Kirkus Reviews* on *The Magnolia Sisters*

"A sweet start to a promising series,
perfect for fans of Debbie Macomber."
—*Publishers Weekly* (starred review)
on *The Magnolia Sisters*

"*The Magnolia Sisters* is sheer delight,
filled with humor, warmth and heart....
I loved everything about it."
—RaeAnne Thayne, *New York Times* bestselling author

"This enjoyable romance is perfect
for voracious readers who want to dive into
a new small-town series."
—*Library Journal* on *The Magnolia Sisters*

Also by Michelle Major

The Carolina Girls

A Carolina Promise
Wildflower Season
A Carolina Christmas
Mistletoe Season
Wedding Season
A Lot Like Christmas
The Front Porch Club

The Magnolia Sisters

A Magnolia Reunion
The Magnolia Sisters
The Road to Magnolia
The Merriest Magnolia
A Carolina Valentine
The Last Carolina Sister

For additional books by Michelle Major,
visit her website, michellemajor.com.

MICHELLE MAJOR

The Christmas Cabin

CANARY STREET PRESS

CANARY
STREET
PRESS™

Recycling programs
for this product may
not exist in your area.

ISBN-13: 978-1-335-43066-3

The Christmas Cabin

Copyright © 2023 by Michelle Major

A Carolina Song
Copyright © 2023 by Michelle Major

This is a work of fiction. Names, characters, places and incidents
are either the product of the author's imagination or are used fictitiously.
Any resemblance to actual persons, living or dead, businesses,
companies, events or locales is entirely coincidental.

For questions and comments about the quality of this book,
please contact us at CustomerService@Harlequin.com.

Canary Street Press
22 Adelaide St. West, 41st Floor
Toronto, Ontario M5H 4E3, Canada
CanaryStPress.com

Printed in U.S.A.

CONTENTS

This one is for all of us who believe in the magic of Christmas and the wonder of this special season.

THE CHRISTMAS CABIN

CHAPTER ONE

"THIS PLACE SUCKS."

"Don't say *sucks*." Lauren Maxwell drummed a nervous finger on the steering wheel of her Jeep Wrangler with the front bumper bungee-corded to the frame.

Her daughter, Hannah, huffed out an annoyed breath from the passenger seat. It was unbelievable how much an angry sixteen-year-old could communicate simply by drawing air in and out of her lungs.

"But it does suck," Hannah complained.

"If you're trying to annoy me, it won't work," Lauren answered, leaning forward to gaze through the rain-splattered front windshield.

It wasn't as if she could see very far in the darkness of the early December evening. Her headlights managed to illuminate enough of the gravel driveway that led into Camp Blossom, situated on an inlet of the North Carolina coast, that she wasn't worried about driving into a ditch.

At least not totally worried.

"It feels like this is where axe murderers hang out." Hannah crossed her arms over her chest. "Like maybe your beloved summer camp switches gears in the winter, and it's a home for horror movie villains. Maybe they're in the middle of a round of thumb wars trying to figure out who will be the lucky one to maim and dismember the dummies fool enough to encroach on their safe haven."

Lauren blinked several times as she stopped the car to turn to her daughter. "Explain how you got a D in English last semester when you seem to be a font of creativity."

"Font," Hannah repeated. "That's like a twenty-five-cent word, right? Should I be impressed that a bartender can talk fancy?"

"Can we make the best of this?" Lauren pleaded with a sigh.

In most areas of her life, she was deemed witty and clever. The regulars at the bar where she worked loved her brand of sarcastic humor. She could use it either as a way to connect or to shut down an overserved patron quick as a wink but she knew there was no sense trying to argue or engage in banter with her daughter.

One of the few things other than her phone Hannah seemed to enjoy was verbally ripping her mom a new one every chance she got.

"Aunt Kayla said Grandpa probably wouldn't mind if we stayed at his house."

Lauren turned her attention to the road again. She hit the gas a little too hard at those words, and the back tires skidded on the wet gravel.

"We're not going to my father's house. And Kayla isn't your aunt. She's my stepsister. There's no blood relation between us."

"She sends me awesome birthday and Christmas gifts." Hannah shrugged. "That makes her a good aunt in my book."

"Maybe Jim Lowery missed the message that we were arriving late tonight," Lauren said, unsure whether she was talking to herself or her daughter. There was no point discussing her stepsister or their nonexistent relationship now, let alone their father. "I don't see lights on in any of the cabins."

"Because the serial killers are hiding in the woods."

"Enough, Hannah." Lauren held up a hand. "Let's remember why we are here two weeks before winter break starts. It's because of your DUI and the toppled flagpole in the high school parking lot. For the record, Magnolia has no serial killers, and this camp is magical. You *will* love it. I don't want to hear another negative word out of your mouth, young lady. If you don't have anything nice to say—"

"Then I guess I'm becoming mute." Hannah clamped her lips together.

"One could hope," Lauren said under her breath, then snapped to attention. "There it is."

She pointed through the darkness to a structure on one side of the path. "Cabin number six. It's the one I reserved. I stayed there every summer when I was a camper until I switched to one of the counselor cabins."

A smile curved her mouth as something loosened in her chest. She didn't have a lot of sweet memories from childhood, but most of the good ones involved Camp Blossom. "Back in the day, the Lowerys didn't lock any of the cabins. Let's check it out. You can get settled while I connect to Wi-Fi and reach out to Jim to see if he has any instructions for our arrival."

She glanced at Hannah, whose jaw was clenched tight. She could tell her daughter struggled not to bite off a snarky response.

Lauren didn't know how long this silent treatment might last, but she wouldn't complain.

Hannah took after her mother in that she couldn't keep her mouth shut for long. Lauren couldn't remember any report card—either hers or Hannah's—that didn't include a comment about talking too much.

"We can make a run for the porch and grab our bags after the rain stops."

"If we're still alive by then," Hannah muttered.

So much for the silent treatment.

Lauren counted to three, and they bolted from the car and up the uneven steps. The screen door opened with an eerie squeak, and Lauren had to remind herself there was no basis for Hannah's axe-murderer musings.

She tried the door and whispered a prayer of thanks when it opened. It took her a second to find the light switch, and another moment of gratitude was in order when a dim overhead lamp flicked on.

"Oh, hell, no." Hannah's tone held the same note of disbelief that Lauren felt.

"Maybe Jim wanted us in a different cabin."

"Or he's a Santa-themed serial killer."

"No one is going to kill you but me," Lauren told her daughter. "It's simply a mix-up with the reservation."

At least, she hoped that might explain why she was staring at a cabin full of Santa Claus decorations in all shapes and sizes. There were lawn Santas made of plastic with beady black eyes and painted beards, plus ceramic statues and totes overflowing with wreaths, quilts, and a myriad of other types of Christmas decor, all featuring fat and jolly St. Nick.

It was creepy as hell.

A horn sounded from outside the cabin.

Hannah yelped and darted behind Lauren, grabbing fistfuls of her sweatshirt as she ducked.

"Are you using me as a human shield?"

"You distract the axe murderer while I go for help out the back door," her daughter answered, her voice shaky.

"How do you know there's a back door?"

"There's always a way out."

If only that were true. Lauren should know about ways out. She was an expert at walking away when things got tough. She'd quit jobs, boyfriends, and just about everything in her life except her daughter.

For Hannah, Lauren would always stick. She might not be on the short list for any mothering awards, but she never faltered in her love for her girl.

"I'm sure it's Jim coming to check on us, but no matter what, I've got you," she said with as much confidence as she could muster. For good measure, she grabbed a Santa nutcracker from a nearby table and held it aloft like a sword.

"Are you going to clobber him with Claus?"

She heard the nervous laughter in her daughter's voice. Even though this was not how she'd planned to reconnect with Hannah, Lauren would not look a gift axe murderer in the mouth.

"Jim, is that you?" she called after the engine died and a door opened and closed.

No answer. She took a step back, and Hannah held on tighter.

"Maybe you want to look for that way out," she whispered to her daughter.

"I'm not leaving you," Hannah said like it was an obvious fact of life.

Lauren should be used to her daughter's ability to shock her. It happened often enough but not so much in a positive way lately.

She'd been shocked when the high school principal had called her late Saturday night to report that Hannah had driven a car—Lauren's car—into the flagpole in front of the school. Before calling Lauren, Mr. Moody had phoned the local cops, and Hannah was being charged with a DUI after she failed an on-site breathalyzer.

Suddenly, her daughter's trouble seemed manageable in light of the fear for their lives pounding through her.

"I'm armed," she shouted as the screen door released its demented squeak.

"Naughty list for defiling Santa that way," Hannah said.

"Shush." Her heart hammered in her chest.

"Lauren, is that you?"

She whipped the nutcracker out of her hand as soon as the broad shape appeared in the doorway, then immediately wanted to take back the throw as she realized she recognized the deep voice.

Ben Donnelly let out a muttered curse as Santa clattered to the ground and splintered into a dozen pieces.

What in the world was Ben doing there?

"What the hell?" he demanded.

"The serial killer knows your name." Hannah released her grip on Lauren's sweatshirt, then popped out from behind her. "Yeah, I don't think this guy's an axe murderer. He's hot."

"You can't say that." Lauren grabbed her daughter's hand. "He's old enough to be your father."

"That's creepier than the Santas."

"You realize I can hear you talking about me, right? Ben shook his head as he stepped over the pieces of the broken nutcracker and into the cabin's tiny front room. "Why are you doing in Magnolia, Lauren?"

"I'm here for my brother's impending nuptials, and we're staying at the cabin."

"No, you're not."

"You're not the boss of me, Ben. You never have been."

"Wow, Mom. Real mature."

"Trust me." Ben's hazel eyes narrowed. "I am well aware I'm not the boss of you."

Unfortunately for her equilibrium, which was already teetering on a razor's edge, the years had been kind to Ben Donnelly. He was tall, dark and incredibly handsome with a chiseled jaw, broad shoulders and those damned soulful eyes that used to spark when he looked at her.

They were fiery now, but for an entirely different reason.

"It seems like you guys go way back, and this is a fun reunion." Hannah's assessing gaze darted between Lauren and Ben. "But can we get out of this potential horror movie set before an actual axe murderer shows up?"

"There are no axe murderers in Magnolia," Ben said without missing a beat.

He and Lauren had always been on the same wavelength. She resented the hell out of him for it.

"Where's Jim?"

"Bingo night. I'm picking him up—" Ben checked his phone "—in a half hour."

"You work for Jim Lowery?"

"In a manner of speaking. Do you have a problem with that?"

"I do if you're the person who messed up my reservation."

"You don't have a reservation, Lauren. These cabins aren't for rent."

"That's not what the Camp Blossom website said."

Ben pressed two fingers to his temple. "I told the kid who set up the website for Jim to take it down."

"No one took it down. My credit card payment went through. My daughter and I are staying in cabin number six."

"Oh, no." Hannah took a step closer to Ben. "Not cabin number six. I'm not staying here with all these fat old men leering at me."

"Santa doesn't leer," Lauren insisted.

Ben flicked a finger at the plastic Santa with beady eyes. "That one's sketchy. Give me a minute."

As he tapped his phone screen, she had a moment to study him. When she'd known him as a teenager, he'd been lean and lanky with a thick mop of honey-colored hair that was perpetually in need of a cut.

That part hadn't changed, which charmed her more than it should. But he'd grown into his height and his hair had darkened to the color of thick maple syrup. He wore a canvas jacket over a plain white T-shirt, but his muscles were evident and caused unwanted desire to pool in her belly.

It had been a long dry spell, mostly self-imposed. Ben wasn't the guy she'd break it with—not on her life.

Hannah gave Lauren a nudge and wiggled her eyebrows in Ben's direction. Her daughter loved playing matchmaker, misguidedly believing that finding a partner for Lauren might be enough of a distraction so she would leave Hannah to her own devices.

Fat chance.

He looked up after a few moments, and the force of his steady gaze almost knocked her off her feet. Odd, because as a teenager, his calm balance had been her anchor when emotions and uncertainty battered at her heart like an ocean squall.

"I thought Brody was getting married on Christmas Eve," Ben said.

"He is," Lauren acknowledged. "I'm here to help with planning." She wasn't sure if Ben believed her lie, but he didn't challenge it.

He didn't need to. She could manage to fight with herself and come out the loser on either end.

"You could stay with your father," he suggested quietly.

"Yes." Hannah clapped her hands together. "That's a great idea. Why didn't I think of it?" She glared at Lauren. "Oh, wait. I did."

"No." Lauren forced her gaze to remain on Ben even though she wanted to look away. She might have been able to run from her past, but there was no way to hide from Ben and how well he knew her.

Something passed between them, a sliver of connection and understanding that hit her harder than any sort of desire. *Danger*, her brain screamed. *Home*, her heart countered.

"Fine." Ben ran a hand through his rain-soaked hair. "I'm in the caretaker's cabin. There's an extra bedroom. The two of you can stay there overnight, and we'll figure out what to do about your reservation in the morning. I'll get you settled, then pick up Jim."

Lauren wanted to decline the offer, but she didn't have the energy to find an alternative. One night. Not a big deal. She'd paid for lodging, after all. This was business.

Sure.

"I'm getting weird vibes again," Hannah announced.

"Ignore them," Lauren told her. "We'll follow you to the cabin," she said to Ben.

He nodded and glanced out into the darkness. "The rain stopped, so that's a plus."

"How did you say y'all knew each other?" Hannah asked as she followed Ben out the front door.

"From camp," Lauren said quietly, but not low enough that Ben didn't hear.

He glanced over his shoulder, his changeable eyes no longer calm. They blazed with an emotion Lauren didn't want to name. "Your mother never mentioned me?" he asked Hannah.

"Slipped her mind," Hannah answered.

Lauren willed him not to say the words, but they came anyway in that smoky, rich voice that still made shivers erupt across her skin.

Ben looked directly at Hannah as he said, "I'm your mom's ex-husband."

CHAPTER TWO

BEN MADE HIS escape from the disastrous reunion with Lauren in order to pick up Jim Lowery from bingo night at the retirement center and spent the entire drive castigating himself for revealing his former relationship with Lauren to her daughter.

He'd spoken without thinking about the consequences, something he never did. But, damn, seeing Lauren Maxwell again after all these years had been like a sucker punch right to the face.

He felt dizzy and disoriented—and if he had to admit the truth—still angry as hell. The woman he'd loved with all his stupid, naive heart had not only left him behind, but he didn't even get a mention to her daughter.

For most of his life, Ben had kept such a tight rein on his emotions that it was almost as if he'd lost the capacity to feel anything deeply. He knew better than most people the perils of losing control. His father had done that far too often when Ben was a kid.

He could still feel the burning embarrassment of his dad showing up drunk to a game or some school event—making a public spectacle of himself or getting in a fight with another parent.

Ben prided himself on his stability and control. He never lost it, except when Lauren Maxwell was involved.

Her daughter, who was the spitting image of Lauren as a coltish teenage girl with thick mahogany-colored hair and piercing blue eyes, had been quiet after his announcement. If she took after her mother in personality, quiet was a red flag.

Lauren had let her finger do the talking, flipping him the middle digit as he walked past.

He'd almost expected her to get in her car and drive away, but she'd followed him to the caretaker cabin he'd moved into three months ago when he'd had to sell his house to afford to pay the taxes Jim owed on the Camp Blossom property as well as a down payment to reserve Jim's one-bedroom apartment in the independent living facility near downtown Magnolia.

He'd thought Jim Lowery would immediately transition to the retirement home where he spent so much time during the day, but there had been a delay with his apartment. As a result, the older man remained at camp with Ben.

"So little Lauren Maxwell is back in town?" Jim asked in his gravelly voice.

Ben blew out a breath as he turned off the coastal road leading to the camp. Across the darkness of the truck's interior, he smiled at Jim Lowery, a man who had been a father figure to him growing up, hoping he couldn't read Ben's emotions the way he'd been able to years ago.

"She's five-nine, Jim. Not exactly little."

"You know what I mean. That girl hasn't stepped one foot into Magnolia since the big kerfuffle your senior year. I still can't believe she managed to smuggle three hogs into the school. I thought her daddy was gonna blow a gasket."

"She made a lot of people angry with that prank," Ben said as he slowed over a bump in the driveway. "Those animals made a hell of a mess."

"The fact that she numbered them one, two and four, which had the principal and teachers searching for hog three for hours, is the best part. She's a legend from how I've heard the young people speak about it over the years."

Yeah, Ben's ex-wife was a legend. It was on the heels of getting caught, facing expulsion from high school and her father's wrath, that Lauren had proposed marriage.

They'd been hot and heavy at that point. Ben had a scholarship to the University of South Carolina, and there was no way for her to go with him unless they qualified for married housing. He'd agreed without a second thought.

Then his dad needed help, finally committing to getting sober, and Ben had to make a choice. Lauren believed he'd chosen Magnolia, his duty and his father over her.

Their marriage failed before it had a chance to succeed. Most people in town hadn't even realized what had happened, but he'd known. Her family had known. His father had taken it as another sign that Donnelly men were bound to be chewed up and spat out by a cruel world and cruel women.

"I don't see why she can't stay with her father." Although Ben knew better than anyone that was wishful thinking.

"Robert Maxwell is an egotistical ass," Jim said, slapping a hand against his thigh. "Just remembering what that man put Lauren and you through makes me rethink this whole property deal."

"You're selling Camp Blossom to me," Ben reminded him. "I'll take care of the land."

"By partnering with Maxwell Enterprises," Jim countered. "I know everyone wants it to go through. You're depending on me for the profit from the sale. And I need the money."

"You need to live someplace that isn't so much work." Ben pulled to a stop in front of the cabin where Jim was staying until his efficiency apartment was available. "You'll have access to bingo and game night. Your friends are there. There's someone to cook for you."

"I need the money," Jim said with a harrumph. "Don't deny it."

"We're paying off a lot of Nancy's medical bills. I want you to have a break from financial stress, Jim. It's been a long few years. You've earned a break."

"Maybe I don't want a break."

Ben's stomach clenched, but he forced himself to remain calm. "We have less than a month before the sale is final. Are you telling me you're going to pull out now because you remembered you don't like Robert Maxwell?"

Ben had leveraged everything to make this deal a reality. If Jim decided not to sell, all of Ben's hard work would be for nothing. If Jim decided not to sell because of Lauren…well, that was unconscionable.

"I never forgot my feelings for Robert." Jim unclasped his seat belt. "But I know letting go of Camp Blossom is the right thing to do, and I trust you, Ben. I wish you'd found a different partner for this development, but I'm not going to change my mind."

"Thank you." Ben nodded. "I promise I'll keep Robert Maxwell in line."

"Good luck with that." Jim laughed softly. "And with Lauren. Are you okay having her and the daughter at your place? They're welcome to the couch in my cabin. I'm not sure any of the others are in solid enough shape for guests at the moment. We can work on that tomorrow morning."

"They'll be fine with me." Ben shrugged. "Both of them looked like they were running on fumes when I left. Chances are I won't see them until morning."

Jim nodded. "I'll be over for breakfast."

"Do me a favor and don't mention the sale of Camp Blossom."

Jim's hand stilled on the car door. "You don't think Lauren knows?"

"She doesn't speak to Robert or Kayla, and I doubt Brody would have mentioned it. He's smart enough to try to keep the peace between his sisters."

"Hmm. This could end up being one hell of an interesting holiday season."

"That's the truth," Ben agreed. "Sleep well, buddy."

The cabin was dark when he parked in front of it a minute later, and Ben breathed a sigh of relief. After seeing Lauren, he needed more than one night to regain his equilibrium and would take whatever reprieve he could get.

But as soon as the door clicked shut behind him, a lamp flicked on in the cabin's small family room, illuminating Lauren, who sat rigidly on the plaid sofa.

"Why did you do that to me?" Her voice was as frigid as the Atlantic Ocean in winter.

He didn't pretend not to understand the question. "You don't think she would have heard now that you're back?"

"I didn't think that far ahead." She tapped her foot on the colorful braided rug that covered the distressed pine floor.

Lauren was always in motion, like a butterfly flitting from blossom to blossom. The only time she was still had been when he'd held her in his arms. The first time they'd been together was the night before camp shut down the summer before senior year, and they'd spent the night in a sleeping bag under the stars.

Ben had been ruined for camping after that.

Now he dropped his keys on the counter and took the seat across from her in a worn leather chair that might have been original to the cabin.

"I'm sorry," he said softly. "It was a shock to see you. I lashed out. I shouldn't have brought your daughter into our problems."

"Do we have problems?" she asked like she was genuinely curious. "It's been nearly seventeen years."

He felt his mouth drop open. "You're saying you have no hard feelings about how things ended between us?"

"I'm saying I don't have any feelings where you're concerned."

He would have believed her, but she reached up and squeezed her earlobe between two fingers. That had been Lauren's tell when she was hiding something since the day he'd met her, but he didn't call her on it.

"I guess you're a better person than me," he said, and she laughed.

"We both know that isn't true."

"Why are you here now, Laur?"

"Because Brody needs help with his wedding."

He placed his hands on his jeans-clad legs and forced himself to remain relaxed. He had a tell, too, and wasn't going to take a chance on Lauren suspecting how much she still affected him.

Her hair was as dark as he remembered, swirling over her shoulders and making her appear young, like the girl he'd once known.

But there were faint lines of worry bracketing her mouth, and her eyes held shadows that seemed at odds with her devil-may-care personality. Her gaze had sparkled with light and passion as an angry and rebellious teenager. He didn't like the wariness he saw there now. He didn't want to think what had caused it or how much she'd been through to extinguish her light.

"Do you think Brody wants or needs your help?"

She wrinkled her nose, and he wanted to lean forward and find the freckles that dotted the bridge of it.

"He might not know it, but he does," she answered. "He told me Kayla's back, so at the very least, I'm not letting her take over. She and my dad will bully him into riding in on a horse or some other highfalutin nonsense."

Ben felt his lips twitch. "I think riding in a Rolls-Royce would be considered highfalutin. A horse sends a different message."

She rolled her eyes but flashed a smile that seemed genuine. "I wouldn't put it past Dad to rent a car for the occasion."

"You haven't talked to him or your sister?"

"She's not my sister, and I'm sure Hannah has texted Kayla. She does it to annoy me."

"Or maybe they have a connection. Maybe Kayla wants to be close to her niece."

"Hannah is not Kayla's niece."

"Kayla is your sister in all the ways that count."

"We're not related by blood. Stepsisters aren't the same, even though my dad would have loved it if I'd been more like her."

It was a distinction he'd heard from Lauren countless times. He still wondered who she was trying to convince that the younger woman didn't mean anything to her and why it was so important.

"It doesn't matter," Lauren said dismissively before he could answer. "We're here to help Brody. I'm also surprised you work for Jim."

"He needed some help," Ben said, which was the truth. "And this place means a lot to me." Also the truth, just not the whole of it.

"I'm sure you'll be able to turn it around."

"Do you really want to stay out here while you're in town? Your dad's place would be much more comfortable, or a short-term rental in a central location would be more convenient."

She bit her bottom lip as if uncertain how much to reveal. He shouldn't want to know Lauren's secrets, but he did.

"This place means a lot to me, too," she said finally. "I'll admit it's not easy being back here and thinking about everything my daughter could be exposed to with regard to my old life."

"I'm sorry I said anything to her," he repeated, really meaning it. He'd known about her daughter, just like he knew she was divorced from the girl's father, but he hadn't considered that he would be a part of Lauren's past she'd never mention. How could he be so easily put aside when it felt like she was still part of him?

Lauren shook her head. "I'd like to say your little revelation is going to be the worst of it, but I don't think that's true. She only knows Kayla through texts so far. Brody is a part of our lives when he has time, but he always comes to Atlanta for visits. My dad hasn't shown interest in knowing his granddaughter. I don't know that our proximity is going to change anything. Camp Blossom might not be the same as it used to be, but I still believe it's special."

"Yes," he agreed. "It is."

"I want Hannah to see that. I want her to know something about me other than the fact I'm her annoying mom who can't hold down a job and has a dysfunctional relationship with my family. I don't mean dysfunctional in a fun way."

"You're fun, Lauren."

"Nope." She straightened from the couch and stepped toward him. "I gave up fun long ago, and my daughter is well aware of that."

He stood as well but didn't allow himself to reach for her, no matter what his body wanted. "Cabin number three had guests this past fall. It's clean enough, and the heat and water work. We can move you there tomorrow morning. I live on the property, but I'm away most of the time." That wasn't exactly the case, but it might be while Lauren was there.

"Do you have a plan, Ben? This place needs a lot of attention if it's going to be viable again. It deserves to be honored and respected."

"I have a plan," he said, purposely not revealing the details of it.

It was unlikely to think Lauren wouldn't find out about his partnership with her father. He might not be able to keep it from her but wouldn't be the one to reveal the details.

He shouldn't care about her opinion, especially when she'd told him she felt nothing toward him. But she'd be upset about the changes coming, and he'd face that soon enough.

"Have you been happy?" he asked, feeling as shocked by the question as she looked.

"Yes," she answered with a furrowed brow. "My daughter makes me happy even when she's also making my blood boil."

It didn't feel like the entire answer, but once again, he didn't pursue more.

"You should go to bed. You look tired."

She barked out a laugh. "Somebody's lost their charm. Don't you know you're not supposed to tell a woman she's a hot mess?"

"I didn't say that."

"It's true, and there's no point in either of us denying it."

He wanted to tell her that even with dark circles staining the delicate skin under her eyes and the hunch of her shoulders and lines of worry that he wanted to smooth away, she was the most beautiful woman he'd ever seen. He wouldn't say those things either.

"I'm going to bed." She turned and then glanced back over her shoulder. "Thank you for letting us stay here tonight. I bet it wasn't an easy offer to make."

The simplest thing he'd done in ages, no question.

"Hannah looks like you," he said, suddenly not wanting this moment to end. The quiet cabin felt like a safe place for them to let down their guard. He had a feeling the morning would change that, her prickly defensiveness and his bitter hurt blooming with the sun like flowers turning toward the light.

It had been years since Ben craved the darkness, but if it meant a truce with this woman, he'd gladly linger in the shadows. "I can tell she has your spirit."

"God help her," Lauren muttered.

"I meant it as a compliment."

"The ex-husband comment aside, you always were too nice for your own good, Ben Donnelly. I'll see you tomorrow."

And he stood there and watched her walk away, just like he had seventeen years ago.

CHAPTER THREE

KAYLA MAXWELL SUCKED air in and out of her lungs as she jogged against the wind on the beach in front of her childhood home. Random gusts blew bits of whirling sand into her face.

She'd seen her neighbor go out the back door of his house a half hour earlier, and she knew that Scott O'Day normally ran for forty minutes every day. The man was a creature of habit, and Kayla was a woman who appreciated discipline and following the rules.

It was how she'd managed early on to navigate the choppy waters of being raised by a single mother who was on a mission to look for security for the two of them—even after she'd found it in a marriage to a powerful, egotistical, mercurial man.

Robert Maxwell.

Kayla had been schooled by her mom in the art of being pretty, helpful, agreeable and quiet. They were lessons that served her well with her stepfather but made an enemy of the daughter from his first marriage and later turned Kayla into a doormat for everyone from men to friends to her bosses to use for their own devices.

Maybe she was being used even still—out here in the sharp morning light and rasping wind, trying to worm her way into the good graces of her neighbor, who wanted nothing to do with her.

The alternative was checking off the next item on her to-do list—going to see her stepsister. She needed to figure out why Lauren had come back to town with Hannah and what she was doing out at Ben Donnelly's soon-to-be-acquired property.

She pressed three fingers to the stitch in her side, about to give up, when a lone figure appeared at the far end of the beach.

Unlike Kayla, Scott was now running with the wind at his back. His long strides ate up great gulps of wet sand. As he got closer, she could see the ropy muscles in his legs and the sweat beading on his forehead. She wasn't sure she'd ever seen him in anything but baggy athletic shorts since she'd arrived in Magnolia three weeks ago.

She'd been given the assignment of convincing him to sell his property to her stepfather. She'd done her research and knew Scott owned forty acres of prime real estate that butted up to the Camp Blossom boundary. Having both would ensure her stepfather could develop the area into the exclusive waterfront resort he envisioned.

Scott didn't need the money. He could buy and sell most of Magnolia a couple of times over with the reported profit he and his late partner had made from selling their restaurant delivery app to a multinational corporation.

As far as she could tell, he hadn't invested in another company or taken on any sort of new work-related challenges. He ran in the morning and then worked on his house for a few hours after lunch, the hammering and sawing driving her stepfather to distraction. If the weather cooperated, in the afternoon he'd paddle into the sound on a longboard or sometimes in a kayak if the water was choppy.

He was always moving, much like her stepsister. Kayla envied him because she felt stuck, like her sneakers had been dipped in cement. She slowed her pace, both because of the cramp and the fact that she was in front of the steps that led up to Scott's house. She knew the moment he noticed her because his gait faltered for a second—the footprints he left in the sand no longer evenly spaced.

"Great morning to work up a sweat," she said as he got closer, trying for a casual tone but sounding more like the voice of the artificial intelligence device that sat on her father's gleaming granite countertop in the kitchen.

Sometimes Kayla peppered the AI mechanism with conversational questions just for fun. A pitiful version of fun, but it got lonely being in her father's big house when he spent most of his time locked in his study. She would not reflect on how pathetic that made her.

It was easy enough to focus on Scott, especially when he scrubbed a hand over his scruffy jaw, because darn if the scratchy sound didn't make her shiver.

"Yeah, you look like you're enjoying yourself."

"I sure am." Kayla had attended enough exercise classes in studios with mirrored walls to know what she probably looked like at the moment. Red cheeks, limp hair and chapped lips, not to mention the dried sand she could imagine dotting her face like grimy freckles embedded into her skin.

It wasn't pretty.

She was the kind of woman who looked good in a business suit—being buttoned-up gave her confidence. Gazing up into Scott's smiling face made her feel fluttery and nervous, like a schoolgirl asking her crush to the Sadie Hawkins dance after he'd said no several times.

"What are you doing out here, Max?"

He'd bestowed the nickname on her after she introduced herself the first time, shortening her adoptive father's surname—the one she signed so proudly even now because it meant she belonged to a family.

But she also liked the way the syllable Max sounded in Scott's measured voice. No one had ever given her a nickname before, and it was a different feeling of belonging.

"I'm just being neighborly."

"The answer is still no."

"I haven't asked a question."

"You're an attorney, Max. I know your type. You don't have to say the words out loud. Your longing to close the deal is written all over those gorgeous brown eyes of yours."

She drew in a breath. He thought her eyes were gorgeous?

"I'm not that easy to read," she insisted.

He came to join her on the step, folding his long frame to fit next to her. Their legs didn't touch, but she could feel the electric charge and heat of his body. Hers reacted immediately, and while she should be wary of the hum of attraction sparked by his nearness, she couldn't bring herself to feel anything but intrigued.

"You must be very close to your father to do his bidding so willingly."

"My stepfather," she clarified.

Even though Robert Maxwell had adopted Kayla shortly after marrying her mother, she still felt the need to point out the distinction. "For the record, I didn't stay in town to work for him. I moved away but recently decided to make a change in my career. I'm helping him while I have some free time. I'm the one doing him the favor."

"He doesn't seem like the type who would appreciate favors. I know men like your stepfather. They're a dime a dozen in California. Men who think that money and power give them the right to take what they want without thinking about how their choices affect other people."

"My stepdad is well aware of how his choices affect others." Kayla didn't bother to add that Robert simply didn't care. That seemed obvious enough. "You don't know him. You don't know me."

"Let's change that," Scott said suddenly. "Have dinner with me?"

She blinked. "That doesn't make sense. You won't consider a business proposition but you want to ask me out on a date? You are talking about a date, right?"

He flashed a boyishly handsome grin. "Sure, we can call it a date if you're the kind of person who likes labels."

Kayla's whole life was based on labels. Good girl. Orphan. Dutiful daughter. Sucker.

"Labels aren't important to me," she lied. "It just doesn't make sense."

"I like you, Max. Let's spend some time together. You don't have to overthink everything."

Oh, but she did.

"Fine. I'll go to dinner, but while we're there, I want you to give me fifteen minutes to make my pitch for why this land deal makes sense."

"And what if I say no to your condition?"

"Magnolia might be a small town, but word travels, even down here on the water. I'm sure there are plenty of single ladies and maybe a few who don't care if they aren't technically available. Women who'd be happy to share a meal and more with you."

Scott stood and looked out toward the water, which was calm now that the wind had settled. "How silly to assume that you or any woman might like to spend the evening with me on the basis of my sparkling personality and potential for witty dialogue."

"I didn't mean to offend you," she said, although Kayla had offended plenty of people over the years. She wasn't exactly known for her gregarious personality. She was socially awkward and lacking in the ease that her sister had to turn strangers into friends.

"Ten minutes," he told her, and she quickly stood.

"Really?"

"I believe a night with you will be worth it."

She hadn't expected that. "Okay, then."

They stood in silence for a moment. His hair was tousled from the earlier breeze, and she wanted to reach up and smooth it. Not that he didn't look good rumpled. She simply wanted to touch him way more than was appropriate, so she made a show of glancing at her watch.

"I need to go. My stepsister just got to town."

"Big family reunion?"

"Definitely not. She hates the fact that I exist. We might hug it out with Christmas coming and all that, but I doubt it."

Scott blinked and tried to hide a smile. "I look forward to hearing more about your dysfunctional family over dinner."

"It should be a treat. Have a nice day," she said, and quickly walked away. Why had Kayla shared that tidbit of information? She needed the upper hand if she was going to convince him to seriously consider the deal.

If she could do this thing for her stepfather, it would prove she was the woman he'd raised her to be. A woman worthy of being his daughter—worthy of his love.

NERVES DANCED AROUND Kayla's midsection as she pulled her Audi to a stop behind her sister's Jeep in front of the ramshackle cabin at Camp Blossom an hour later.

These nerves were different than the fluttering she'd had with Scott. These were more like a battalion of invisible anxiety warriors stomping through her, leaving the destruction of her equilibrium in their wake.

She couldn't believe the sight of Lauren's ancient Wrangler could turn her into a quivering mess of uncertainty. How in the world was that old beast of a vehicle still running?

She remembered the day her stepsister had proudly driven it home. The used Jeep had been purchased with the money she'd made as a counselor at Camp Blossom the summer before her junior year.

Their father had bought Lauren an adorable red convertible for her sixteenth birthday in July of that year. But there'd been conditions. She would have to quit her counseling job and break up with Ben Donnelly in order to start the job Robert had procured for her at the nearby country club.

He'd told her it was for her own good—that she needed to start hanging out with people who were more like her. Lauren had literally thrown the keys back in his face.

The red convertible had been taken away the next day, only to reappear on Kayla's sixteenth birthday. By then, Lauren was long gone. Kayla had worked at the country club during the summer and on weekends until she'd left for college. She'd also driven the shiny red sports car that never felt like it truly belonged to her.

The Jeep must be three decades old by now, and she knew it wouldn't have any of the bells and whistles of her luxury sedan. Heated seats and steering wheel plus a fancy touch screen. The Audi could practically drive itself, a treat of sorts after her first year as an associate when the prestigious law firm in Charlotte had given her a year-end bonus.

She'd been so proud of buying something for herself. Something shiny and new. The rust corroding the Jeep's back bumper made her feel tarnished.

"I am successful out of the shadow of my sister."

She repeated the affirmation she'd created after listening to several audio books on overcoming birth order issues. She shouldn't define herself on being a middle child or the younger sister of a strong personality like Lauren.

Brody was Kayla's half-brother, just as he was Lauren's. She shared no blood relation with her father's daughter.

As she stepped out of the car, the door of the cabin opened.

"Aunt Kayla?" a hopeful voice asked, and she smiled

around the shock of seeing her niece in person for the first time.

Hannah had texted photos since reaching out two years earlier, so she knew how much the girl looked like Lauren. Kayla still felt the invisible urge to shield herself against whatever verbal tirade might spew from that familiar mouth.

"Oh, my gosh, you came. Thank you." The girl, whose thin frame was clad in baggy sweatpants, a Pink Floyd hoodie and rubber Birkenstocks, ran from the house and gave Kayla a tight hug.

"You've got to get me out of here. I want to go to Grandpa's house. I want to meet him. Mom says no, but she's not the boss of me."

As constricted as Kayla's lungs felt, she managed a laugh. In her mind, Lauren was the boss of everyone. Not even their father, with his blustery temper and manipulative affection, had been able to control her. Why on earth would Hannah think Kayla could stand up to her sister's strength of character?

"Where's your mom now?" she asked quietly, her eyes darting to the front of the cabin like Lauren might burst forth at any moment.

"She's helping Jim Lowery in one of the other cabins. That guy has a weird obsession with Santa Claus."

Kayla relaxed slightly. "When I was little, he and his wife decorated the camp with thousands of lights and outdoor Santa decorations. It was ten dollars for a carload to drive through. For years, I thought this place actually transformed into a Carolina outpost of the North Pole each December."

"Mom really likes the old guy."

"He really liked your mom back in the day. Not in a creepy way," she felt the need to point out.

"Is there any other way but creepy when he's got a cabin full of Santas?" Hannah took a step back and mock shivered. "I don't see why people make such a big deal about Christmas anyway."

"Your mom loves Christmas."

"No, she doesn't."

Kayla mulled that over in her mind for a few minutes. As kids, the only time Lauren ever called a truce in her resentment and animosity toward Kayla was in the weeks leading up to Christmas.

Even when they no longer believed in Santa Claus and Lauren seemed to want to make it her personal mission to end up on the proverbial naughty list, she still got caught up in the magic of the season and would let her annoying little stepsister into her life for a few brief happy moments each year.

Maybe Kayla had wondered if that might be the case this year.

"You aren't welcome here," her sister called as she appeared on the trail that led through the pine trees to the rest of the cabins.

So much for the magic of the season.

"I invited her." Hannah turned like a pint-sized sentry.

Kayla put her hand on her niece's shoulder. "It's okay, Hannah. Hello, Lauren. Nice to see you."

"You're blocking my Jeep."

Kayla took a step to one side and pointed to the clear path in front of the vehicles. "I've never stood in your way."

Lauren breathed out a laugh. "That's right. You were

always too busy off to the side, sucking up to my dad, to have time to get in the way."

"She's going to take me to Grandpa's house," Hannah announced, although Kayla had agreed to no such thing. "I want to meet him. You might not get along, but that doesn't mean I won't."

Lauren fiddled with her earlobe as she walked forward. "If your grandfather wanted to know you, Hannah Banana, he would have made an effort at some point during the past sixteen years."

"Unless you made it clear he wasn't welcome to be a part of your life," Kayla couldn't help but point out to Lauren. "The same way you did to me." She wasn't quite the mealy-mouthed wimp she used to be. "You're not the boss of me anymore, Lauren."

Okay, maybe not mealy-mouthed, but she still needed to work on her maturity.

Hannah gasped when her mother stuck out her pink tongue. Good to know Kayla wasn't alone in her regression.

"Why are you even here?" Kayla asked as Lauren drew closer.

"I'm helping Jim get ready for Christmas the way I used to. Just like I'm going to help Brody with his wedding."

That smarted. "I told Brody I can handle preparations with Avah." She wasn't thrilled about their younger brother's shotgun wedding to a woman he'd only known a couple of months, but Brody was determined to do the right thing. So Kayla was going to make the day as perfect as it could be. She wanted to believe in love for someone even if she didn't believe in it for herself. "I'm organized and an expert with details."

"Also about as creative as a roof shingle," Lauren said.

Kayla rolled her eyes. "That's not even an expression. Roof shingles aren't creative."

"My point exactly, sis." Lauren only claimed a familial relationship when she wanted to get under Kayla's skin. "I think Brody and Avah should get married here."

Kayla didn't like to reveal emotion to her sister but couldn't help jerking back. "This place isn't habitable."

"Now that Hannah and I are here, we're going to change that."

Didn't Lauren know the camp was being sold?

"Doesn't Hannah have school?"

"It's online," Hannah explained. "I'm really smart. Online classes are a piece of cake."

"Not smart enough to avoid that pole when you were drinking and driving," Lauren said to her daughter.

"Everyone makes mistakes," Kayla offered, and Lauren realized her daughter must have confided in Kayla.

Lauren snorted. "Name one you made." She turned to her daughter. "Your step-aunt does not make mistakes."

It had been a mistake for Kayla to believe things could have changed with Lauren in the years they'd been apart. A stupid mistake that caused her heart to pinch and made her hate herself for her weakness.

"Does Ben know you're here?" she asked before she thought better of it.

"Yes, please." Hannah threw up her hands. "Let's talk about the husband I knew nothing about."

"You never told her about Ben?"

Lauren pulled on the end of her long braid, looking uncharacteristically flustered. "Why would she need to know about Ben? He was a blip on the radar of my life."

Kayla only stared, unsure how to call her stepsister out on the enormity of that lie.

"I always appreciated that about you, Lauren." Ben's voice filled the silence of the sunlit clearing. "There's no question where someone stands." He'd come from the other direction, and apparently none of them had noticed his approach.

Kayla had seen Ben Donnelly off and on over the years. He was always nice to her, just like he'd been when he and Lauren dated and then…well…were married for a hot minute.

If possible, Lauren looked even less happy to deal with Ben than she was to have to see Kayla. But she didn't look angry the way Kayla would have expected in light of the news about Ben's partnership with their dad.

Which meant Lauren didn't know.

Kayla felt her heart skip a beat. Who needed Christmas lights when the fireworks destined to erupt when her sister discovered the plan would set the whole town ablaze?

CHAPTER FOUR

LAUREN'S STOMACH TIGHTENED with dread as she turned onto the fashionable street that led to her father's house later that night.

Shivers shimmied across the back of her neck the moment she drove through the ornate gate that marked the entrance of the upscale community, and she'd cracked the driver's side window. The cool air and smell of the ocean should have relaxed her, but her jaw remained locked, and her knuckles had turned white as she gripped the steering wheel.

This was stupid. She wasn't a rebellious, recalcitrant teenager anymore, the girl who liked to fancy herself the victim—albeit a privileged one—of her father's dictatorial style and narcissistic manipulations.

Robert Maxwell didn't hold sway in her life any longer. There was nothing he could do to her.

"You seriously grew up here?" Hannah asked, her tone filled with disbelief and wonder.

"I've told you before, I lived with my mom in Europe for a few years after the divorce," Lauren said matter-of-factly. "My father didn't agree to take me until she went completely off the rails. Even he couldn't have known the downward spiral would lead to her death."

Although she didn't take her eyes off the mansions they drove past, Lauren could feel her daughter's eye roll. "Sucks about your mom, but you went from living on the beach in Greece to living on the beach in a mansion. Not exactly a hardship."

Lauren bit down on the inside of her mouth until she tasted blood. She'd made a purposeful decision not to share the details of her childhood with Hannah.

What was the point?

Lauren might not be in the running for mom of the year by traditional standards, but she put Hannah first always. Without guilt trips, histrionics, or bellyaching about what a hardship it was to be a mother.

Sophie Lavigne had been a waif-like model whose star was rising when she'd met Robert Maxwell at a club in Miami Beach.

He'd already been a successful developer, ten years her senior, and their love affair had been the stuff of legend—fiery and hot. It had also ended as quickly thanks to Robert's need for control and Sophie's independent streak and unwillingness to curb her bohemian lifestyle. They'd both wanted to be the center of attention and butted heads on every subject imaginable the way Lauren's mother had told the story.

They'd gotten married after Sophie became pregnant and managed to stay together until Lauren's first birthday. At that point, Robert bought the house on the water without consulting his wife.

Sophie had thought that she wanted the life of a stay-at-home mother, but by then she'd changed her mind and filed for divorce, much to Robert's chagrin.

With her body back to its pre-pregnancy litheness—thanks in large part to an eating plan of mostly celery, sugar-free soda and diet pills—and a baby with dark hair and glacial blue eyes, Sophie had realized that Lauren was portable and even a benefit on some of the photo shoots.

At least, that's what Sophie convinced herself. Robert had been too consumed with building his real estate empire on the East Coast to concern himself with a flighty ex-wife or the daughter he didn't care about getting to know.

"An address doesn't hold a person's value, Hannah. What matters is feeling happy and loved wherever you are."

"Yeah, right." Her daughter turned, and the look she gave Lauren spoke volumes. "I'm pretty sure that's just a line you fed me so I didn't complain about our crappy apartment."

"Our apartment isn't crappy," Lauren argued. "It's cozy, with plenty of room for us. Living in a smaller place allowed me to put money in your monthly college fund. You're going to thank me for that someday."

This time Hannah didn't hide the eye roll. "Admit it, Mom. It's easier to be happy when you're rich."

Lauren rubbed her tongue over the chewed flesh on the inside of her mouth. She knew about being rich and poor and could say with certainty that the first didn't lend itself to happiness—just different problems.

"It's easier to feel rich when you're happy," she answered, giving herself a mental pat on the back for that pearl of wisdom.

"Ah, the old chicken and egg argument. You've been listening to self-help podcasts again."

"I should be listening to how-to-parent-sassy-teenager podcasts."

The bantering with her daughter had taken Lauren's mind off her nerves or at least settled them slightly. She was her own person now, and even if Hannah didn't understand or agree with her choice to walk away from her father's wealth, Lauren didn't regret the decision. Robert Maxwell's affection came with far too many stipulations.

There were things she regretted, of course. Seeing Ben again after all these years had brought most of them to the forefront of her mind and heart. She was surprised at the memories that had risen to the surface and wanted to know how to sink them again.

However, avoiding her dad's house for the most recent half of her life counted as a win.

"Oh, my gosh." Hannah spoke the words in a reverent whisper. It was only then that Lauren realized they'd pulled into the driveway of the house she'd grown up in. Muscle memory had gotten her this far.

"I'm staying here," her daughter announced.

Lauren understood the desire. The house was two stories, custom-built with exquisitely detailed millwork, oversized windows, and a balcony that ran the entire length of the second floor. There were panoramic water views from almost every room upstairs and a meticulously manicured lawn.

"You will stay with me at the camp," Lauren announced as she pulled under the porte cochere outside the front entrance. "It's not up for discussion."

"Maybe Grandpa will invite me to stay."

"It doesn't matter what your grandfather thinks. I'm saying no, and I'm your mother."

Hannah slumped back in the seat with an exaggerated huff. "Maybe I'll call Dad and spend the holidays with him, so I don't have to sleep on the Santa Claus horror movie set. That would show you."

Lauren heard the catch in her daughter's voice and didn't bother responding. They both knew the holidays with Hannah's father wouldn't happen. "Dad is on the road until the new year. He's going to fly you out to LA after the holidays."

That probably wasn't true either.

The chances of her ex-husband remembering the promise he'd made during the phone call with his daughter on her sixteenth birthday two months earlier were slim to none—a trip to California and VIP tickets to Disneyland.

Tommy had a friend who worked in the front office, or so he claimed. He'd made similar promises over the years and followed through on very few. Lauren doubted this one would be any different, but that was a hurdle for another day.

"I'm going to post this house all over Snapchat," Hannah said, rubbing her palms together. "All those losers in school think I'm being punished, but—"

"You don't have your phone," Lauren reminded her. "You *are* being punished."

"Well, I'm sure you'll give it back to me at some point."

At this rate, that would be some point in the next century.

They climbed out of the car and stood together, looking up at the house. Lauren wasn't sure what her daughter saw when she took in the luxury of the structure. Could she recognize anything beyond the beauty and opulence? Would she see the dysfunction that resided behind the heavy wood door?

Lauren imagined the gabled windows looking down on her, sighing as they remembered the nights she'd snuck out of her second-floor bedroom and shimmied down the trellis at the side of the house to meet Ben or her friends. There were late-night swims and other late-night adventures courtesy of her first love.

The scent of the ocean was strong here, tickling her senses. Because of the fence surrounding the backyard, there was no ocean view from here. Once inside, the large family room with floor-to-ceiling windows offered breathtaking vistas of the water.

If Hannah was impressed now, she would be blown away once she got a glimpse of the vaulted ceilings, bright breakfast room, chef's kitchen and media room with a huge fireplace. Lauren almost wished she'd waited another hour for darkness to settle over the neighborhood.

The house would be impressive illuminated on the outside by the rows of Christmas lights her father paid a local landscaping company to hang. A picture-perfect sunset over a mansion on the beach could impress even the most jaded teen. Lauren refrained from mentioning that the crashing winter waves foreshadowed the arguments they were sure to encounter inside the house.

She didn't blame Hannah for wanting to stay, but Lauren wouldn't let her. It was as easy to be happy when you were poor versus wealthy, and things of beauty on the outside often hid an ugliness deep inside that could corrode everything around them.

She would not risk exposing her daughter to that influence. She was here for her brother. Nothing more.

Her heart beat faster when Hannah reached out and took her hand. "It's okay," Lauren said, understanding the gesture without Hannah speaking. "It's just a house.

Just money, despite what my father will tell you. Money doesn't make people who they are, Banana."

"I wish I'd worn something nicer than ripped jeans and beat-up Converse," her daughter admitted in a conciliatory tone Lauren barely recognized.

Lauren would not have this. She would take teenage attitude all day long instead of anxiety over how judgment might be meted out.

She squeezed her daughter's fingers and stepped in front of her, blocking Hannah's view of the house. "You are smart, gorgeous and perfect just the way you are. Even your eye rolls are perfect. I want you to know that, Hannah. I want you to feel it deep inside yourself. Channel whatever emotion you can muster to keep the fire lit inside you. Your anger at your father or me."

She dragged in a shaky breath and tucked a limp lock of hair behind Hannah's triple-pierced ear. "I don't care how much your grandpa pays in utilities for this place or how many perfect fires he has burning in the fireplace. The inside of this house is cold, girl. You have to bring the warmth, and you have to be your own—"

"Okay, Mom." Hannah tugged away. "No need to be dramatic. This isn't the theater department."

Lauren swallowed the emotion in her throat and turned away v. She wasn't being dramatic. She offered a reminder they both needed, whether Hannah realized it or not.

"You're perfect," she said again. Before she could say more, she heard the soft whoosh of the door behind her opening.

"Well, well. I wondered what it would take to bring you back here."

She turned to face her father, wondering how he

looked older and yet exactly as she remembered. He was over six feet with a muscular build and eyes a few shades darker than Lauren's, with salt-and-pepper hair as thick as it had been seventeen years ago.

"You've stayed away too long, Lauren. You've kept me from my granddaughter too long." He offered Hannah a welcoming smile. "Now things have changed."

Nothing had changed as far as Lauren was concerned. Her father's voice was not only familiar, but it also echoed the sound of self-recrimination in her head. The voice that told her she hadn't lived up to her potential. The voice she'd tried to tamp down in her soul for seventeen years.

Robert held out his hands in a gesture of impatience she'd seen a hundred times in her life. "Don't just stand there like you're casing the place. Come in and introduce me to my grandchild."

She took a step forward, because what else could she do? There was no chance of turning and running the way she wanted to. Showing weakness only gave Robert Maxwell power, and his money and influence offered more than enough.

"Hey, Mom?"

She glanced over her shoulder, tears stinging the backs of her eyes when Hannah winked.

"You're not perfect," her daughter whispered, "but you're okay just the way you are."

Right now, okay was more than enough.

CHAPTER FIVE

"What are you doing?"

Kayla glanced up at her stepsister, then returned her gaze to the gleaming marble floor of her father's study as Lauren stared at her. "Breathing."

"You look like you're in labor," Lauren commented dryly, and Kayla hated to admit how much she liked being noticed, even in such an ungracious manner. As a kid, she'd craved Lauren's attention. Confident, crass and magnetic Lauren, who was everything Kayla wasn't, specifically the daughter who carried Robert Maxwell's DNA.

"It's called box breathing. A therapist taught me the technique for when my anxiety spikes. I can teach you if you'd like. It involves breathing in for four beats, holding your breath for the same amount of time, then breathing out and holding the breath again. My therapist said navy SEALs use it to stay calm and improve concentration. Not that I'm comparing myself to them, but…" She shrugged. "It helps."

"Your therapist?" Lauren gave a dismissive shake of her head, and Kayla realized she'd revealed too much. "What kind of problems could you—Miss-Perfect-In-Every-Way—have that would warrant a therapist?"

Kayla had forgotten that displaying any weakness in front of her sister was akin to blood in the water. Lauren wouldn't want to believe she had anything in common with her father, but she took after him in more ways than made Kayla comfortable.

"It's not important," Kayla muttered, because making herself small had always been the quickest way to deflect Lauren's harsh criticism. "We should get back to the kitchen with Dad and Hannah. Brody will be here any minute. I texted, and he said he's on his way."

Lauren held up a hand and continued to stare intently. "Answer my question. Why do you see a therapist?"

Kayla blinked. Lauren's tone didn't exactly make it sound like she cared about the challenges Kayla might be dealing with, but at least she'd asked. They'd grown up in the same household for most of their lives, so it couldn't come as a huge shock.

"You know, the usual childhood stuff. My mom died suddenly under tragic circumstances. Dad was…well, you know how Dad was."

"Not your real dad?" Lauren suggested, and Kayla inhaled sharply for an entirely different reason than the box exercise. Sometimes when she held her breath, Lauren's jabs didn't hit as hard.

"Never mind," Kayla said.

"I'm sorry." Lauren ran a hand through her long hair and looked around their father's imposing study, glancing out the large windows to the dark beach like she was remembering what it had been like to live in this house. "He's your dad, too. He adopted you. I shouldn't keep bringing it up. For the record, I'm not an insecure little girl anymore."

"You were never insecure," Kayla said with a laugh, refusing to believe the admission from her larger-than-life sister. "You were a badass from the day you walked into this house and commanded me to give up my bedroom for you."

Lauren's lips curved at that comment. "It had the window seat, and I was older. It wasn't personal."

Everything between them was personal. Or at least that's how Kayla had always felt.

"How often do you talk to Brody?" Lauren asked. "Is he..." She paused midsentence, shoulders going stiff when their father's laughter rang out from the kitchen. "You're right. We need to get back in there. I'm not leaving him alone with my daughter for any length of time."

Kayla followed her sister out of their father's inner sanctum and through the dining room, then passed the formal living room with the uncomfortable furniture they weren't allowed to sit on unless guests were over.

"I'd like to get to know Hannah," Kayla said, finding it easier to make the request to her sister's back than face-to-face.

Lauren stopped and spun on her heel. "You know her plenty. You certainly seem to know what she wants for her birthday and Christmas every year. I know you also have a regular text exchange."

"Do you read her messages?"

"Do I look like the type of mother who would read my daughter's messages without her consent?"

Kayla felt her mouth open, but no words came out. Finally she said, "I don't know what type of mother you are because I don't know you. You won't let me. But to be clear, you don't know me either. That's not something I need my therapist to confirm."

Lauren's eyes narrowed. "Fair enough. Again, I apologize. I'm not shaming you. Mental health is important.

It's good you're taking care of yourself. Also, stay away from my daughter."

She turned and stalked toward the kitchen again. Was that progress?

Kayla hadn't ever imagined hearing multiple apologies out of Lauren's mouth, other than when she'd screamed she was sorry Kayla had been born or their parents had ever met.

She trailed a hand over the antique sideboard table in the foyer. This house had felt like a museum when her mother, Marcie, first ushered Kayla through the front door to meet Robert, her new fiancé.

Kayla had been a preschooler at the time, but her mother had made it clear that she was to be on her best behavior. They'd been living in her grandmother's basement, which smelled like wet towels and stinkbugs even in the dead of winter. "This is our shot, baby," Marcie had said. "I'm going to make a better life for us. Robert Maxwell is going to help me do it."

Maybe those words made Marcie a gold digger, but Kayla quickly realized that her mother also adored Robert. He'd been intimidating, gruff and loud, but his smile was kind, and he treated Kayla's mother like a queen.

Kayla had believed she'd lucked into the role of princess until later when Robert had gone away for a week and returned with Lauren.

Marcie, pregnant with Brody at the time, tried to make the best of it.

She'd told Kayla that she was getting an older sister, but it wasn't the sibling relationship Kayla had longed for and imagined. There was no *Little Women*-type of closeness. She was the outsider, the interloper, the one who didn't belong. Lauren made sure she knew it.

She returned to the kitchen to see Lauren, hands on hips, in an apparent standoff with her mini-me daughter. Kayla had the sudden realization that she wasn't the only outsider in this house any longer. Most people would say she was now the daughter who belonged.

Yes, she'd left behind her partner-track job at the law firm in Charlotte to be here helping her dad with his legal affairs. He'd hinted at making her Maxwell Enterprises' in-house counsel in the new year, especially if she could ensure the deal with Camp Blossom went through and convince Scott O'Day to sell his property.

She'd toed the line her father expected and had cemented her place as his dutiful daughter.

Lauren would probably call her a lackey, but Kayla had learned the art of making herself useful early.

"I'm staying," Hannah said with a mulish tilt to her chin that was 100 percent reminiscent of her mom.

"No."

"Lauren, be reasonable." Robert's voice was placating with the slightest tinge of impatience. Lauren probably didn't even register his annoyance, but Kayla was finely tuned to other people's emotions.

The easiest way to smooth the water was never to let the ripples start.

"I'm being plenty reasonable," Lauren shot back. "I booked a cabin at camp for a month, and I expect my daughter to stay with me."

"The cabins are gross," Hannah complained. "Grandpa invited me to stay here, and that's what I'm going to do."

"You're both invited," Robert clarified. "We have plenty of room. Right, Kayla?"

"It's a big house," she answered, "but if Lauren already—"

"Don't be ridiculous," Robert muttered. "We all know that camp is a dump. There's no point in anyone living there."

Kayla snapped shut her mouth. She hated being reprimanded by her dad and had always carefully chosen her words and actions so it wouldn't happen. Once Lauren left the summer after her senior year, Robert hadn't raised his voice to Kayla.

She'd made sure never to give him a reason to find fault with her. The news of her leaving the firm had shocked him, but she'd spun the situation so that Robert believed her motivation for going was to be more involved in the family business.

Always the good girl.

Unlike Lauren, whose creamy skin had turned blotchy pink as her glare shifted between Robert and Kayla.

Kayla willed her heart to stop racing. She didn't want to experience the emotions pounding through her. She felt admiration for Lauren for never backing down and sympathy for Hannah because the girl didn't understand what she was getting into by stepping in between her mom and grandfather.

Then there was Kayla's suppressed resentment toward her father for expecting the world to cater to his whims and her self-recrimination for capitulating.

A door slammed at the front of the house.

"What's for dinner?" Brody called, appearing in the kitchen entrance a few seconds later. Long enough for Lauren to drag in what Kayla hoped was a calming breath. Robert moved toward the wine chiller under the massive island.

"Hi, Uncle Brody." Hannah smiled and waved. Her

hand dropped as she took in the scowl of the woman following her uncle into the room.

Avah Michaels was tall, blonde and beautiful. According to Brody, his fiancée was a model, but Kayla thought of her more as a low-level influencer, touting a slew of products on her social media platforms. According to Brody, she also had no paid endorsements. Did that simply make her an avid shopper?

Brody stopped short, with Avah nearly bumping into his back. "Tell me you aren't fighting," he said, glancing at Robert and then Lauren. "What's the problem?"

"Your sister is being unreasonable," their dad answered immediately. "Nearly two decades away, and nothing has changed."

"Dad is an overbearing ass." Lauren crossed her arms over her chest. "He'll never change."

To his credit, Brody ignored them both. "Hey, kid," he said to Hannah, opening his arms wide for a hug. The teenager approached like he was the last life raft on the *Titanic*. "Good to see you. Don't mind your mom and grandpa. Bickering is their love language."

"Whatever," Lauren mumbled while Robert let out a disgusted snort, but they kept their mouths shut.

Brody, with his wavy blond hair always in need of a cut, wide smile and boyish good looks, had that effect on every member of the family. He expected them to fall in line in his presence, and for the most part, they did.

"Avah, this is my oldest sister, Lauren, and her gorgeous and too grown-up daughter, Hannah."

Avah held out her elegant arm. "Nice to meet you both."

Hannah and Lauren took turns shaking her hand.

"Congratulations on your engagement," Lauren said. "And…everything."

"The baby," Brody said in a stage whisper. "She's talking about the fact that you're pregnant."

"I'm excited to have a cousin," Hannah offered, then bit down on her lower lip when Avah only stared at her. "Um, I can babysit and stuff."

"That's awesome, kid." Brody beamed while Avah continued to look stiff and uncomfortable. "Your mom and aunt used to fight over who got to babysit me back when I was an ankle biter."

"Lauren made everything a fight," Robert said under his breath.

"Do I smell lasagna?" Brody asked before Lauren had a chance to respond. "Let's get some food and catch up."

"And discuss wedding plans," Kayla added, inclining her head toward Avah. "I have some ideas about a venue on short notice. I've called around and—"

"My parents won't pay for the wedding," Avah blurted, covering her face with her hands. "They don't agree with us getting married under the circumstances."

Lauren shot Kayla a look, communicating that, for once, the sisters were on the same page. Why would Avah's parents have a problem with their daughter marrying Brody—their unborn grandchild's father?

Brody got his coloring from their father and was tall and handsome with a movie-star smile and piercing blue eyes that were always laughing. He was the human equivalent of a golden retriever—happy, energetic and ready for fun. Everyone loved Brody. People were drawn to him.

He'd been the only passenger in the car that had

killed his mother, a year-old baby who miraculously survived. Kayla and Lauren might not have agreed on much, but they'd been devoted to Brody's happiness and united in making sure he grew up knowing he was loved.

It hadn't been difficult with his sunny personality. Every nanny and housekeeper their father had hired fell in love with him, even the ones who'd treated the sisters like dirt—and there had been several of those. Strangers in stores and restaurants approached in droves to coax an easy smile from the boy.

Kayla had been half-afraid that Brody might be kidnapped and taken from them. He had a magnetic personality and the uncanny ability to stay detached from their father's emotional machinations.

Perhaps there were deep, uncharted depths to Brody, but Kayla had never seen them.

He was simply happy and easygoing.

"They'll come around eventually." Brody looped an arm over Avah's bony shoulder. "I'm extremely lovable."

Avah swiped at her cheeks. "But they won't pay," she insisted. "How am I supposed to have the wedding day of my dreams—one worthy of posting—on such short notice *and* a shoestring budget?"

"Maybe you two should have thought of the consequences of your actions," Robert said into the silence that descended on the room. "An unwanted pregnancy changes your whole life."

Kayla felt the immediate shift in Lauren's demeanor. It was as if a wall came down around her sister, either keeping her safe or imprisoned in her thoughts—it was hard to know which.

Lauren's mother had married Robert because she'd been pregnant, and Lauren had done the same thing before Hannah was born. But Kayla couldn't imagine that Lauren had ever made her daughter feel like she wasn't wanted or had been a burden, like their father had.

"Unexpected," Brody clarified, his voice uncharacteristically tight. He pulled Avah closer. "Not unwanted. Let's be clear on that. I'm excited to be a father, and I'm going to be a damn good one."

"First, you need a wedding." Robert ignored the unspoken message in his son's words.

"We can go to the courthouse," Brody countered, earning a soft gasp of protest from his intended bride. Avah didn't seem like the type of woman who would be satisfied with a low-key wedding, let alone an unassuming trip to the courthouse.

"You'll get married at the country club." Robert pulled out his phone and began thumbing out a message on the screen. "I'll confirm an available date with the front office."

"It has to be Christmas Eve." Avah's cheeks colored when Robert raised a brow. "My dream is to be a Christmas bride."

Robert's jaw tightened, but he nodded. "I've spent enough on events over the years. They can figure it out."

"We'll make it perfect," Kayla offered, imbuing her voice with an enthusiasm she didn't feel. Avah wasn't the type of woman she'd expected her brother to choose. It wasn't any of her business, but—

"Not the country club." Brody met their father's gaze across the room, and Kayla felt something pass between the two men, although she couldn't understand what.

"We won't take your money for the wedding. This is on me."

She glanced at her sister for clarification, but Lauren was frowning, clearly just as confused at Brody's refusal to accept their father's financial assistance. Brody seemingly never cared about details as long as he didn't have to deal with them.

"This is not the time to grow a spine," Robert advised. "I know you, Brody. All fun and no savings. How will you fund a wedding without someone else bankrolling it?"

"I'll figure it out," Brody said.

"I think your dad is being very generous," Avah said with a syrupy smile for Robert.

"I think you should have kept your legs closed," Robert told his intended daughter-in-law, his tone casual given the appalling rudeness of the message.

Avah looked shocked, Brody growled low in his throat, and Lauren let out a long sigh. The comment was crass, even for Robert.

Kayla knew their father had expected big things from his only son, but unlike Kayla, Brody hadn't been willing to kowtow to his father's desires. Despite her years of pandering, she got very few kudos or recognition from her dad. It hadn't stopped her from trying.

"Turns out I'm not in the mood for lasagna," Brody said evenly, then pointed a finger at his father. "Or your crap. Get it together, Dad, or you won't be invited to the wedding."

He reached out and tousled Hannah's hair. "I'll see you soon, cutie." Then he switched his gaze to Lauren. "I appreciate you coming back for this. I know it couldn't have been easy."

"I wouldn't miss your big day for anything," Lauren assured him. "It's going to work out, Brody. I'll make sure of it."

"*We'll* make sure of it." Kayla shifted so that her back was to their father. "I'll support the two of you with whatever help and support you need. Avah, you're going to have the wedding of your dreams."

"I told you my sisters were the best, babe." Brody dropped a kiss on his fiancée's head. She still looked unsure what to make of the scene Robert had started and Brody's reaction to it.

"I like lasagna," she said in a small voice.

She couldn't possibly think Brody's comment was about the food, could she?

Kayla watched her brother's sparkling eyes close for a long moment, and she noticed the fine lines fanning out from their edges for the first time. Brody was twenty-eight and an avid outdoorsman, so the effects of years of being in the sun shouldn't come as a surprise, but Kayla thought of him as the little boy she'd always coddled and adored.

He was a grown man about to marry and become a father. In truth, Kayla didn't even know if Brody had a steady income at this point. He and Avah had met when he was working for a charter operation at the nearby marina. How did he make a living in the off-season, and what did it say about her that she didn't know?

"Let's go to town for dinner," he told Avah. "There's an Italian restaurant with a lasagna that will make you see God."

"The same lasagna that's in the warming drawer of this kitchen," Robert said with a scoff.

"Il Rigatone has better ambiance," Brody shot back.

"I'll text you two tomorrow," he told Lauren and Kayla, and with a wave, led Avah from the room.

"What's ambiance?" Kayla heard the woman's baby doll voice ask.

Their father muttered a curse. "I knew my son wasn't the brightest bulb in the drawer, but I can't believe he's going through with this."

"Let's go, Hannah." Lauren crooked a finger at her daughter. "I'm not in the mood for lasagna either. Dairy and smug condescension upset my stomach."

"Fine." Robert threw up his hands. "Run away like always."

"I want to stay," Hannah said. "And not just for dinner."

"We've got plenty of food and room." Robert flicked a glance at Kayla. "Take the salad out of the refrigerator, and then you can show Hannah the guest bedrooms."

"I said no," Lauren whispered.

"If you want to spend the next few weeks at that rundown camp, be my guest," their father taunted. "It's the last chance you'll have to wallow in the past. You always had an unnatural connection with the Lowerys. It's obvious my granddaughter is smarter than her mom."

"Hannah, I mean it." There was something in Lauren's tone that Kayla had never expected to hear. Desperation.

"You don't have to decide tonight," Kayla told her niece. "It's an open invitation. Go with your mother and—"

"She wants to stay now," Robert interrupted, and Kayla swallowed down the familiar need to keep the peace. This wasn't her fight, anyway. Why should she stick up for Lauren? Despite everything, she loved her sister. But there was no way to win against their dad once he set his mind to something. It was less painful to give up.

"Kids stay with their grandparents all the time." Robert began to open a bottle of wine, his movements sure and fluid, like they were discussing the weather.

"She doesn't even know you," Lauren said through gritted teeth.

"Then let her get to know me," Robert shot back. "Unless you're worried about her liking it here too much."

"Mom, you can stay, too." Hannah crossed her arms over her chest. "We can pick up our stuff tomorrow."

"I'm leaving, Hannah," Lauren said in a tone that brooked no argument. "Are you coming with me or not?"

The girl's chest rose and fell in uneven breaths, but her voice was sure when she answered. "Not."

"Be careful what you wish for, Banana. Things aren't always as good as they seem."

Then Lauren spun on her heel and left the room.

"Would you like a glass of wine?" Robert asked Hannah conversationally like tension wasn't oozing from the walls of the room.

"She's sixteen," Kayla said, placing the salad bowl on the granite counter.

He gave her a blank look. "In Europe—"

"We're not in Europe. No wine. Don't push it."

Kayla never spoke in that kind of tone to her adoptive father, but apparently even she had a line in the sand that could not be crossed. Taking care of her niece was it.

"Hannah, sodas are in the main fridge's bottom compartment. Help yourself. Grandpa will get the lasagna out. I'm going to talk to your mom before she leaves."

"I don't care about my mom," Hannah said with more attitude than conviction.

"Crack open a soda," Robert said with a laugh, "and we can toast to that."

Kayla ignored his bad behavior as par for the course and hurried down the long hall to the front of the house.

Lauren had just opened the oversized cherry door.

"Wait."

Her sister turned, and the pain of rejection in her eyes stopped Kayla in her tracks.

"Want to gloat?"

"No. I want you to know I'll look after her while she's here."

Kayla had expected some cutting remark in response, but Lauren gave a barely perceptible nod. "Thank you." She started out the door and then turned back. "What do you think of Brody's fiancée?"

If Kayla were honest, would her sister use it against her and rat her out to Brody so Lauren could position herself as the supportive one?

She shook her head at the thought. Despite all the ways she and Lauren hadn't gotten along when they were younger, the two of them had never used Brody in their petty little war of death by a thousand cuts.

There was no reason to believe that had changed now. Some things were sacred, or at least Kayla wanted to believe that.

"Avah would not be my choice for him."

Lauren sighed. "Me neither, but I like that he's standing up to Dad."

"It's weird to think of Brody as a man." Kayla offered a smile. "I know he is, but I still consider him our baby."

"Yep." Lauren looked down at the thick antique French Aubusson rug like it was the solution to all her problems. "Will you text and let me know how she's doing?"

"Or you could stay, too," Kayla suggested, earning a frown from her sister. "Fine. You go. I'll text you. We can all meet at Sunnyside Bakery in town for breakfast."

Lauren's mouth twisted into a scowl. "I don't want her to think I want to see her so badly after just one night. Just text me."

Before Kayla could respond, her sister had closed the door behind her. Kayla would have said it didn't make her weak to show her daughter she cared.

But what did Kayla know? She wasn't a mother and hadn't had one since she was a girl.

"Kayla, come on," her father bellowed from the kitchen, and she started through the house. What did she know about anything?

CHAPTER SIX

BEN HAD SEEN Lauren return to camp a half hour earlier, the Jeep she'd been driving since she turned sixteen bouncing over the bumps and divots in the gravel road.

He'd stood inside his cabin waiting for her to come storming up and shouting at him for partnering with her father. Maybe he was a fool and a coward for not telling her himself, but he hadn't wanted to see the disappointment or anger he knew he'd find in her gaze.

They were nothing to each other at this point, and Ben had done what he needed to make his way in the world and find contentment in the town of Magnolia, which Lauren had left behind right along with him.

But she hadn't come to confront him, and curiosity finally got the better of him. No lights glowed from the windows in the cabin where she and Hannah were staying, although he didn't think the power was out.

He grabbed a flashlight and sauntered toward her place, breathing in the chilled air. It was difficult to admit how much Lauren's return affected him.

Buying the land and partnering with Robert Maxwell made sense—or at least it had until Lauren's arrival. Her father was one of the most prominent real estate developers on the Eastern Seaboard and a massive player in the Carolinas.

Their plan for the property on Blossom Sound was

to create a luxury coastal living experience that would enable residents to enjoy the charm of small-town living surrounded by the beauty of the water and forests that made this area special. It would also prove beyond a shadow of a doubt that the Donnellys were more than generations of ne'er-do-wells and slackers.

It wasn't as if anyone had charged Ben with the responsibility of reinventing his family's tarnished reputation. Still, he'd grown up feeling the preconceived notions about him like a weight on his shoulders.

He'd had friends with ordinary families and carefree lives who didn't have to think about a mom who deserted him and a father who drank away most of his meager paycheck each week.

Those regular parents wouldn't let their kids come over to the ramshackle double-wide where Ben had lived, not that he would have invited them. As he'd gotten older, any whiff of trouble always had people looking in his direction. Someone vandalized the school—he had to be involved. A bike was stolen out of the Thompsons' backyard—check behind the Donnelly trailer.

It had taken years of keeping his nose clean and helping this community for people to trust he wasn't like his father and uncles. His father's long-term sobriety had also added to the rehabilitation of their family name.

But Robert Maxwell had been a holdout. The man didn't believe Ben was good enough for his daughter when Ben and Lauren dated. He'd seemed to hold a grudge against Ben for their short-lived marriage, ignoring the fact that Lauren had left town and served him with divorce papers.

After Ben earned his general contractor's license, her

dad went out of his way to make it difficult for Ben to get a foothold in the residential construction business. It felt as if he were being punished for Lauren turning her back on both of them, even though Robert had ruined their relationship without any help from Ben.

Finally, after the death of Jim's wife, Nancy, Ben had realized how dire the Lowerys' finances were due to the financial burdens they'd taken on during her years of cancer treatments. Jim hadn't necessarily wanted to sell the camp, but he'd needed a way out of the staggering debt he'd accumulated, so Ben had committed to finding a means to help.

Then Robert had approached him about a potential partnership as if everything that came before hadn't mattered. Their history hadn't counted enough to make Ben refuse to work with Robert. It was only business, after all. But with Lauren back, it felt like more. It felt like a mistake, and Ben prided himself on being too much of a perfectionist to make mistakes.

He knocked on the door to her cabin, surprised when it immediately opened and more surprised to see Lauren, half-empty wineglass in hand, her eyes red-rimmed, standing on the other side.

"What are you doing?" he asked.

She held up her glass in a mock toast. "Having dinner."

"I thought you were going to dinner at your dad's." He was careful to keep his tone neutral.

"I lost my appetite for the crap he was dishing out," she said, and turned away.

She'd left the door open, so Ben walked in, more confused than ever. He couldn't remember a time when Lauren and her father weren't at odds, but she didn't seem angry at Ben for his part in it. Did the land deal have anything to do with her current mood?

He stepped into the small space and paused. "Why are you in the dark?"

"Saving Jim money on electricity."

"If you're that concerned, I'll bring over a few candles." Ben flipped on the light switch next to the door, surprised at the change in the cabin in just one day. He'd cleaned out one of the smaller two-bedroom bunk cabins of extra furniture and boxes when it became evident she was determined to stay. Somehow Lauren had turned a grubby and grimy interior into something warm and cozy in less than twenty-four hours.

The pine counters and floors of the small kitchenette area gleamed like they'd been cleaned with wood soap, and the paneled walls were just as bright. An ancient vacuum cleaner sat in one corner, and he guessed she'd used it on both the rugs and the old chenille sofa, which had been covered by heavy drop cloths but now had a bright quilt folded over the back.

"This place looks great."

"It's not rocket science," she said, draining her glass and pouring more yellow liquid into it. "Elbow grease and some suds in a bucket. Even someone as flighty and irresponsible as me can handle feathering a nest."

"I didn't say you were irresponsible," he answered. "Nor did I think it. You're a mom."

She laughed, but it held no humor. "So was mine, and she was bad at it."

"You're not a bad mom."

"You don't know that."

"I know you, despite what you want to believe."

She gulped down another slug of wine and hiccupped. "Then maybe you can explain why my daughter chose to abandon me for my father's mansion after I've devoted the past sixteen years of my life to her. After she gave me…"

Lauren yanked at the hem of her sweatshirt, revealing a flash of pale skin, and for a moment, Ben had trouble keeping track of the conversation or even remembering his own name. "She gave me stretch marks, Ben. And just ditched me. She picked him."

Stretch marks. Ben blinked. He couldn't see anything with Lauren halfway across the room. But he would have gladly fallen on his knees in front of her and more closely examined every inch of her perfect body if that would help.

He shook his head and tried to focus—not on her skin, which had disappeared from view when she'd let go of her sweatshirt.

"Why did Hannah decide to stay with your dad?"

"She claims the camp is gross and creepy."

"It's not gross," he clarified. "But as homey as you've made an empty cabin, this place has seen better days. If someone offered me the option, I might choose to stay at your dad's house."

She laughed, then snorted, and her chin wobbled slightly, sending pain lancing through his heart.

"You wouldn't choose him over me," she said in a small voice.

She couldn't know about his deal with her dad yet. There was no other explanation.

"Hannah loves you, but she's a kid." He ran a hand through his hair. "She doesn't understand the complicated relationship you have with your dad. Hell, I never quite understood it."

"It's simple." Lauren straightened her shoulders. In addition to the bulky sweatshirt, she wore black leggings and thick argyle socks. She looked too adorable for Ben's own good. "He's a narcissistic ass, and I hate him. He hates me for not being perfect like Kayla."

"Don't say that. It isn't true."

She was about to take another drink but placed her glass on the scuffed counter as she considered his words.

"Which part?" she demanded quietly.

Ben inclined his head. "Without question, your father is a selfish ass. That's a fact, not an opinion. But he doesn't hate you or wish you were your sister."

"She's not my—"

"Stop." He held up a hand. "She's your sister, and she loves you. She's always craved your approval. She was nervous as heck at the thought of you coming back here."

"How do you know that? Are you and Kayla close? Is there some flawless-person connection between the two of you?" Her chin jutted out like she was posturing for a fight.

There were plenty of things Lauren could say to hurt or rile him, but subtle jealousy over his relationship with Kayla was merely amusing. "We're friendly. She's like a little sister to me. You have nothing to worry about in that regard."

She scoffed. "I'm not worried about *you.* I'm worried about my daughter being brainwashed by her grandfather. I'm worried about Jim Lowery and this camp. He can't keep taking care of it, and without someone interested in running it…what happens now?"

"Why does it matter to you? You haven't been a part

of Jim's life since you left. We were bits of gravel and dirt thrown up behind your tires when you peeled out of town."

Her eyes narrowed. "I thought you were going with me."

That claim elicited a reaction. Ben felt regret and bitterness crawl over his skin. They clung to him like a cobweb he'd walked through, sticky and disorienting as he tried to bat it away.

"Let's not go there again. You know why I couldn't leave when you wanted me to and refused to wait."

"I would have been waiting forever," she said with a snort. "This town has its hooks sunk into you too deeply."

He took a step closer and noticed she did as well. It made him smile. Lauren never backed down from a challenge.

"I was going to come after you." He felt more than saw the catch in her breath.

"What do you mean?"

"Once my dad got out of rehab, and I felt like he was in a good place—solid enough that he wouldn't slip back into his old habits right away—I was planning to come to Atlanta. It was nearly Christmas, and I had a stupid fantasy of a grand holiday reunion—the magic of the season and all that."

Emotion swam in Lauren's eyes before she blinked it away. "But you didn't come." The words felt like an accusation.

"I saw Kayla in town the night before I was pulling out, and she told me you'd gotten married again."

"I was pregnant with Hannah."

"This time to a musician," he continued like she

hadn't spoken. "Your sister was so excited because he was in a band that had a popular single on the radio."

"A one-hit wonder," Lauren muttered.

"She said you were designing album covers and doing marketing for him. She was proud of you."

Lauren looked away and let out a sound that sounded more like a wheeze than laughter. "That's what I told her; it wasn't a complete lie. They had a viral single and booked a few gigs as an opening act for a couple of chart-topping bands. I stepped in to help because their manager was an idiot. I was having a baby…we were having a baby. That meant needing to pay bills and buy supplies. My baby needed a mom and not the kind I had."

"I think your mom loved you despite everything."

"She loved me enough to leave me with random people on photo shoots while she worked or partied. I wanted to take care of my baby, so I needed her father to make some money. That never really happened, but I wasn't about to let Kayla or my dad in on that."

Ben's heart pounded. He'd spent the past seventeen years harboring the belief that the girl of his dreams had thrown him over and moved on to someone more exciting and worthy of her than he could ever be. He hadn't doubted Kayla's version of the truth for a second.

It was too late to do anything about it now, and there was no way to return to the past.

But if he'd known Lauren was struggling…

"Are you sure I can't tempt you?" she said, holding up the nearly empty wine bottle.

She tempted him all right.

"No, thanks." He reached out and touched a finger to her cheek, tracing the tip across the soft skin down to her jaw before forcing himself to pull away. "Do you remember being a teenager?"

"I remember certain things with great clarity." Her tone had taken on a husky resonance.

"Do you remember wanting to challenge your dad on everything?"

She jerked away. "You need to take Billy Joel's advice and leave a tender moment alone, Donnelly."

"Hannah reminds me of you in so many ways, and her need to test boundaries is only one of those."

"I'm not like my dad." She wrinkled her nose. "Please tell me I'm not like him."

"You aren't a narcissist, if that's what you mean."

"But…"

"But you're strong, and you're raising a strong daughter. There's no denying you get some of that strength from your father."

"Being strong and being a bully aren't the same thing."

"Wanting to push a parent's buttons isn't learned behavior. It's built into kids' fabric once they hit a certain age."

"You never did that. You never rebelled."

"In my family, being good was an act of rebellion."

She acknowledged the truth in his statement with a small smile. "How's your dad?"

It sounded like she genuinely cared.

"Sober," Ben said, which seemed like the most critical piece of information. "He never returned to the bottle or drugs after that last stint in rehab."

"So picking him over me was the right choice."

"That's not what I did."

"It's what it felt like."

"I had responsibilities I couldn't turn my back on, but you were always my first choice, Lauren. My best choice," he added before thinking better of it.

He'd revealed too much, and she could use it against him if she wanted, but he refused to pretend. Not now. Not at this moment.

She stepped into him, their bodies not touching, but almost. Close enough that her citrusy scent curled through him, and he could feel tendrils of awareness sparking along his skin. He couldn't deny the attraction. How could either of them deny it?

No amount of time, distance, hurt or anger could dampen his desire for this woman. She was as much a part of him as the blood running through his veins.

"You always did know how to make things better," she said, and pulled her pink lip between her teeth.

His knees just about buckled.

"Thank you for giving me hope that I haven't completely lost my daughter. Now, what are we going to do about Camp Blossom? Jim needs our help, Ben. I don't want to see this place sold off or swallowed up by developers."

Developers. That word rattled through the thick haze of his need with all the subtlety of a hockey buzzer going off in the middle of a yoga class.

"What makes you think Jim cares about keeping the camp? He'll be set for the rest of his life if he sells the land."

"Money isn't everything, and you know it. This place is important to him. It's important to me, and I assume it is to you since you work for him."

Heat crept up Ben's neck as he tried to think of how

to respond. That was the thing about Lauren—nothing was ever simple, not even wanting her.

"You wouldn't know this," he told her, "but before Nancy died, my dad and I went to the Lowerys' every year for Thanksgiving. She fussed and made us feel like we were a part of their family. Losing her after over fifty years together was a profound blow for him."

"Everyone loved Nancy Lowery," Lauren said quietly.

Ben didn't acknowledge the comment. He wasn't interested in everyone. "I've hosted the holiday meal for the past few Thanksgivings," he explained. "Once Nancy got too sick to handle it, I took over. That first year, Jim insisted I carve the turkey. I was thirty-one years old and carving a damn turkey for my father and the person who'd been like a father to me when mine couldn't. It made me feel more like a man than anything I've done in my life."

He drew in a breath, but the clean scent of polished wood and the cool air of the cabin did nothing to ease the agitation churning inside him. "Of course I care about Jim. My memories of this place are some of my best, but time moves on. Things change."

"More than I'd realized." She turned away to survey the cabin's interior. "I'm going to find a way to make this place better for Jim."

A strange sort of desperation clawed at Ben's chest. He didn't want Lauren here. He didn't want her to get involved or make him care about what his partnership with Robert meant for this land.

The Donnelly legacy mattered to Ben. His reputation as someone with influence in this community was a critical aspect of his identity. This development was a way to solidify both.

"At the very least," she said, "I'm going to ask Jim if Brody can get married at camp."

"Why would your brother want to get married here?"

"Why not? He needs more help than I realized. I came back early because he's stressed out. His fiancée's family isn't happy, and they're saying they won't pay for the wedding. Who knows if they'll even attend? My dad wants to have it at the country club, but that's not like Brody. He doesn't want Dad involved, so—"

"You're going to insert yourself into his life."

She took the step away that he'd been unwilling or unable to.

He simultaneously wanted to pull her back and push her farther from him. "Are you doing this to get under Kayla's skin? When I talked to her last week, she said she was excited to help Brody."

Lauren's blue eyes flashed with temper. "This isn't about Kayla. It's about my baby brother marrying a woman I don't think he loves because he's trying to do the right thing. I know what that can do to a person, and I don't want it for Brody. I want him to be happy."

"He's responsible for his happiness."

She rolled her eyes, and Ben wondered if she realized how much she looked like her daughter. "Pump the brakes, Dr. Phil. I gave you credit earlier, but enough with the pearls of wisdom."

"Think about what you're trying to do, Lauren. You don't know—"

"*You* don't know what it's like," she snapped, "when there's a baby in the picture. A baby changes everything."

"You're right." He nodded slowly. "Maybe I don't know you either. I do know you should have something for dinner besides alcohol. Otherwise, you'll have a wicked hangover in the morning."

"Thanks for yet another piece of unsolicited advice. But I'm going to take some action here. Talk is cheap, just like the nightly rate of these cabins. You get what you pay for."

"I'll remember that," he told her before walking out into the crisp night and stalking back to his cabin.

He refused to admire the stars on his way or appreciate the quiet and peacefulness of the camp. He also did his best to disregard the disappointment he'd seen in Lauren's crystal-blue gaze when he'd refused to go along with whatever idea she had about helping Jim.

Ben's future had seemed straightforward days ago. Now it felt like he was trying to surf the winter waves at midnight with Lauren as the moon—the only light to guide him to safety. The rise and fall of both his plans and heart were undeniably controlled by a woman who didn't even realize her power over him.

CHAPTER SEVEN

THE FOLLOWING DAY, Lauren walked down the sidewalk of Magnolia's main street with nerves fluttering in her stomach that she would have denied if anyone had asked her about them. Without thinking about what she was doing, she began counting her breathing the way Kayla had mentioned and found the method actually relaxed her a bit.

The town had changed considerably, with new shops and restaurants and a revived energy that was undeniably appealing. Businesses seemed to be thriving, and every storefront was decorated for the holidays with cheery boughs of garland, greenery and giant bows. A colorful banner positioned above Main Street welcomed people to the Christmas on the Coast Festival.

Lauren wondered if anyone would recognize her. After leaving, she'd cut all ties with her friends from childhood. She didn't want anything or anyone to remind her of how life had let her down.

But true to her word, Kayla had texted early this morning with a report that Hannah's night at the big house had been uneventful and that the girl had chosen Lauren's old room to stay in.

Kayla once again suggested they meet at Sunnyside Bakery for breakfast and to discuss the living arrangements. Neutral ground and a ton of coffee and a few pastries couldn't hurt.

She needed something to soak up last night's over-indulging. Ben had been annoyingly correct in his pre-diction that she'd wake up with an enormous headache. How hard would it have been to add some chips and salsa or a few slices of cheese and crackers to the menu?

Leftover lasagna would hit the spot, and Lauren thought about asking her sister to bring her a slice. But that was too much to ask, silly as it might seem.

She would make nice with Kayla for Hannah's sake but refused to budge in any other way. She hadn't needed a pesky sister when she'd been a kid and cer-tainly didn't need one now.

"Lauren Maxwell, is that you?"

She automatically cringed but turned, only to feel her body relax at the sight of Lily Wainright—who she understood was now married and went by Lily Dawes—approaching. Lauren met Lily her first summer as a counselor at Camp Blossom. Lily had been a skinny car-rottop with freckles and knobby knees, but she'd grown into a beautiful woman with a creamy complexion. She wore a long-sleeve white T-shirt under baggy overalls paired with sturdy-looking work boots.

Her red hair was piled on top of her head in a messy bun, and although her face appeared free of makeup, her skin was creamy and her blue eyes bright.

"Hey, Lily." Lauren stopped in front of the bakery's window. She wondered if her daughter was watching from inside and reached out and pulled Lily in for a hug, just in case.

Lauren didn't blame the other woman for being surprised but appreciated that she easily returned the embrace.

Lily's grin was wide as they stepped away from each other. "I was telling my husband about you the other day."

"Why would you tell him about me?" Lauren was genuinely curious. "Also, congratulations on your marriage. Is the lucky guy from around here?"

Lily shook her head. "Garrett and I met when I was still living in California."

"That's right," Lauren said with a nod. "You were going to be an actress."

"I've settled for appearing in a couple of plays at the regional theater. I've started directing, too." Lily's pale skin went pink.

"Good for you," Lauren said, happy for her former camper.

"I'm also involved in the campaign to raise money for a new fine arts center and school here in town."

"Wow. That's big-time for Magnolia." The town's revitalization was obviously more than red bows and garland.

"Yeah, the community has grown and changed quite a bit. It's exciting. It wasn't my plan to return, but my dad got sick and needed one of us to take over the hardware store. Anyway, that's why I was talking to Garrett about you. The changes planned to the area around Blossom Sound made me nostalgic for all those summers at camp. You were the best counselor, Lauren."

"Thanks, Lily. That's sweet."

"It's true. Your encouragement to take part in the talent show my first summer sparked my love of acting. While my big dreams of stardom didn't amount to much, I met my husband in LA. Now I get to spark that same enjoyment in other kids from this area. You made a real difference in my life."

Lauren felt tears sting the back of her eyes. She'd left Magnolia believing she hadn't left an impression beyond her family's disappointment and the mutual heartbreak of her divorce from Ben. She never dreamed anyone would think of her or that she'd made a positive difference in someone's life.

Lily seemed to understand the power her words had on Lauren. She offered a self-conscious smile as she squeezed Lauren's arm. "I didn't mean to hit you with all this when you're on your way to Sunnyside. I'm like the Lauren Maxwell Fan Club president geeking out over my hero."

"You're the sole member of that club." Lauren laughed. "I'm meeting my stepsister and my daughter for breakfast. Hannah and I are in town because my younger brother is getting married."

Lily nodded. "I heard that—not about you being back but that Brody is getting married. I'd really love to meet your daughter

"Sure," Lauren agreed, still somewhat dazed by the interaction. It was hard to believe she'd had that much of an impact on another person, let alone a positive one.

"Wait," she said when Lily started to turn away. Something scraped at the edge of her brain, making it past her shock. "What were you saying about the changes on Blossom Sound? I'm staying at Camp Blossom, and Jim didn't mention anything to me."

"You're staying at camp? I didn't know anyone was there other than Jim and Ben."

"It was a bit of a mix-up, but I'm giving my daughter a real adventure. I only saw Jim the first night. He's supposed to be back later today, but he went away for a couple of days to visit his grand-niece."

"I'm pretty sure she's the one who had a baby last fall," Lily said. "Reconnecting with family helped Jim deal with his grief at Nancy's passing. It's good to have something positive to focus on. But I'm surprised Ben hasn't said anything. He's the one who bought the camp."

Lauren felt her mouth drop open as she thought about the conversation she'd had with Ben. Why hadn't he mentioned that pertinent detail?

"I don't understand. I thought Ben worked for Jim as a caretaker. Isn't that why he's staying there?"

Lily looked as confused as Lauren felt. "Not exactly. The way I understand things, Ben leveraged everything he had to buy the land,"

Lily's tone implied that she couldn't understand how Lauren wasn't aware of that, which made two of them. "He and your dad are working together on a new luxury housing community."

"My dad and Ben Donnelly?" Lauren clarified, shocked she could speak when it felt like she'd just been punched in the gut.

"Your Ben."

"Not mine," Lauren corrected her. Not even a little bit at this point.

"Oh, I see," Lily said, but how could she? None of this made sense. "Ben's making quite the name for himself around here."

"Sounds like it." Lauren had a couple of names she'd like to call Ben and her father. Her gaze flipped to the bakery window. "I don't want to keep Kayla and Hannah waiting."

"I hope to see you soon. Stop in at the hardware store. I'd love to give you tickets for the Christmas show. It will be at the high school this year, but hopefully, by next year, we'll have our own local theater."

"That's great, Lily." Lauren struggled to keep her voice even. "Happy holidays."

Wasn't that what people said when they were being civil and friendly? She didn't feel either of those things. She opened the door to the bakery and nearly plowed into a mother-and-daughter duo on their way out.

"Someone's in a hurry for a muffin," the woman said with a smile. She was tall, thin, and blonde, and although she was dressed casually in an oversized sweater and dark jeans, Lauren guessed the woman would fit in perfectly at one of her father's country club parties.

"Or an apple fritter before they run out," her daughter added, looking up at Lauren with wide blue eyes that matched her mother's. "Do you like fritters, ma'am?"

Ma'am. Lauren hated that she was old enough to be considered a ma'am.

"I like all sorts of baked goods." Lauren realized her voice held a reedy thread of impatience when the mother's gaze flashed.

She was unpracticed at being social with strangers in the way that felt expected in a small town. Anonymity fit Lauren's personality and mood a lot better.

"Let's leave this *nice* lady alone, Margo," the woman said, her gaze measurably cooler than it had been moments earlier. "Try a fritter," she advised. "It's difficult to be in a bad mood once you take that first bite."

"No offense," Lauren answered. "But I'm not sure all the fritters in the world could help my mood right now."

"Been there." The stranger nodded and placed a friendly hand on Lauren's arm. "I found screaming into my pillow helped. That and my friends. Good luck."

Lauren watched the two for a moment. This place was something else. At least the brief exchange with the stranger had taken the sharpest edge off her anger, enough that she felt in control to the degree that she wouldn't start screaming at her stepsister in public. She'd save it for her pillow.

"Hey, Mom," Hannah said as she approached the table where she and Kayla sat. There were three cups in front of them. "We got you a chai tea latte."

"And a chocolate chip muffin," Kayla added. "I remember that being your favorite."

"I like apple fritters," Lauren said. "And I don't like being lied to. Hannah, grab a box for your pastry from the counter. We're not staying."

"Wait, what?" Hannah's feathery brows lowered over her cornflower-blue eyes. "I didn't lie about anything. I thought we were having breakfast and talking about stuff. Aunt Kayla said—"

"Things changed," Lauren said. "I'm not arguing this morning, Hannah. Get a box or leave your breakfast. Either way, you're coming with me. Now."

"I don't want to go back to that stupid camp," her daughter complained. "The bed at grandpa's house was so comfy, and I have my own bathroom there."

"Not up for debate." Lauren clenched her teeth. "Don't force me to make a scene, Hannah. I'll do it."

Her daughter made a disgruntled sound but got up

and slunk toward the counter for a to-go box. "This isn't fair."

No, it wasn't, Lauren agreed. She didn't want to return to Camp Blossom now that she knew Ben had lied and misled her. It wasn't as if he owed her anything, but the sharp pinch of betrayal lodged in a place just below her ribs like a stitch in her side from running too fast.

Kayla looked genuinely confused. "I think it would be better to sit down and discuss the living arrangements. Hannah was no trouble, and Dad actually—"

"—is going to build a luxury neighborhood on the camp property?"

"Ben told you." Kayla blew out a huge breath. "I'm glad he finally said something." She looked relieved, which sparked Lauren's temper once again.

"Ben didn't tell me," Lauren said slowly. "Dad didn't tell me, and neither did you."

"It wasn't my business," Kayla offered quickly.

"But you knew about it." Lauren glanced toward where Hannah stood near the bakery's display cabinet, waiting for her box, then back to her sister. "Are you telling me you aren't involved in the project? It seems a bit of a coincidence that you would come home around the same time Dad's company might need local legal counsel."

Color bloomed on Kayla's cheeks as she looked away. "I'm helping push some papers through and read contracts." She fiddled with the edge of her napkin. "I didn't want to rock the boat."

"The boat capsized," Lauren said as Hannah returned to the table.

"I don't see why you're so mad about me staying at

Grandpa's. Just because you want to sleep on a lumpy mattress in a cabin that smells like raccoon poop."

"You don't know what raccoon poop smells like," Lauren told her daughter. "You've never smelled raccoon poop."

"Aunt Kayla, tell her—"

"Go with your mother," Kayla said quietly. "She's right. You shouldn't be at the house without her permission. I was wrong to let it happen." She looked at Lauren. "I was wrong about a lot of things. I'm sorry."

"Don't be sorry," Hannah pleaded. "She's bullying you. I know how she operates."

"We'll discuss how I operate later," Lauren answered, her voice cracking on the last word.

She didn't want to cry or break down, but after the initial surge of anger, sadness and betrayal took over.

They were emotions she thought she'd hardened her heart against years ago, especially concerning her father. She blamed motherhood. Having Hannah stay at her grandfather's last night caused a shift inside Lauren, a crack in her controlled facade that would not be glued back together so easily. That much was clear.

"Fine. I'm coming. You always get your way." Hannah followed her out of the bakery. At least that was a small win.

Lauren squinted against the bright sunlight of the morning as she tried to process this new turn of events without completely losing her composure.

"This town is over-the-top with the holiday decorations," Hannah observed. "Now I see why that guy is so into the Santas. I guess he's not the only one with a weird fixation on Christmas. Aunt Kayla said you used to be obsessed with Christmas. I told her she had to be thinking of the wrong person. We hardly have any decorations at the apartment."

"I used to help at camp each year during the holiday season," Lauren explained, memories buffeting her from all sides. She wanted to shrink under their power. She wanted to run and not look back. "Jim and Nancy sponsored a Christmas carnival that was a big deal at the time."

"I'm sorry that camp you loved sucks, but it does. I don't see how that old guy will get any people willing to stay there if he doesn't clean it up. Nobody will come just to see a cabin full of old creepy Santa Clauses."

"You're right," Lauren agreed, "and apparently, I'm the only one who still cares about the camp. Ben and your grandfather are tearing it down to build fancy houses."

"Nobody mentioned that before you paid the money to book a cabin? That's messed up, Mom."

"The money isn't even my concern." Lauren reached out and tugged on Hannah's braid. "But I appreciate any concern I can get from you."

"Grandpa's house is nice, and it's huge," Hannah said far too casually for Lauren's liking as they walked toward the car. "I doubt you'd even have to talk to him if we both stayed there."

"I'm not staying at Grandpa's, and I think we're done with this conversation."

"Aunt Kayla was nice, too."

"She's nice enough," Lauren admitted. "But…"

She stopped herself, thinking of Ben's words. The comment he'd made about Kayla being her sister in all the ways that counted was true, despite how much Lauren hated to admit it.

"I don't know what happens next, Banana. This business about Grandpa buying the camp has thrown me for a loop." She blew out a long breath as she climbed into the Jeep.

"Are you sure it's that?" Hannah asked as she fastened her seat belt. "Or is it the fact that Grandpa's hanging out with your old bae?"

"My bae?" Lauren grunted. "Remember, your mom doesn't have a TikTok account. Use words I understand, girl."

"Ex-husband, if we're being precise," Hannah amended with an exaggerated sigh. "Ben, the hottie. It's been a while since you dated anyone, Mom. Maybe—"

"Are you trying to rile me up, so I send you back to the high thread count sheets and million-dollar ocean view?"

"He has one of those fizzy water machines built into the fridge. It's pretty cool. And being on the water is nice."

"I've raised you wrong if the ocean is behind a carbonated water device on your list."

"I might find the ocean more impressive if I stayed there longer."

"Fine," Lauren blurted as she took a turn toward camp. "We'll drive back over to Grandpa's later tonight."

Hannah let out a squeal that made Lauren cringe on the inside. "Seriously, Mom? Just like that, you're willing to agree after fighting me so hard?"

Lauren glanced over at her daughter and smiled, then quickly looked back to the road when she felt her mouth tremble at the edges. "I'm sick of fighting."

"I'm okay if you want your old room," Hannah said quickly. "There's another guest bed—"

"I'm not staying at Grandpa's." Lauren gripped the steering wheel more tightly. "I know the house is impressive, and it feels like the lap of luxury to you. To me, it's still a gilded prison. I didn't belong there, and I wasn't happy."

The word sounded foreign on her tongue. "I want you to be happy, Banana. But I want that for myself too."

"Fizzy water might make you happy," Hannah suggested quietly.

"I'll buy a six-pack of sparkling water at the grocery if I have an inkling for it."

She could handle buying groceries and managing her own life. But discovering she'd been lied to by the man she used to love, and that he still had the power to hurt her... Lauren would find a way to deal with Ben Donnelly. No one was going to have that kind of power over her. Not again.

CHAPTER EIGHT

KAYLA SAT AT the end of the boardwalk that led from her father's house later that afternoon and watched the winter sun descend toward the horizon.

The sky was pale gray with a watercolor swath of translucent orange along the bottom edge. It was mediocre as sunsets went and suited her mood perfectly—flat and nearly despondent. After all the years of being ignored, criticized, rejected and judged by her sister, Kayla shouldn't care what Lauren thought.

But the disappointment in those blue eyes that morning seemed different from everything that came before. It felt as though Lauren was the injured party, and Kayla didn't like that anymore than she wanted to be seen as a victim.

How embarrassing to admit she'd relied on that role in the past—a born people-pleaser bound to be taken advantage of or cast off by the people she cared about the most.

At least as a girl, she'd been able to take comfort in the fact that she hadn't done anything to warrant her sister's animosity.

When she'd brokered a breakfast between Lauren and Hannah that morning, Kayla believed it could be a new start. Hannah would be the bridge that finally brought the Maxwell sisters together. The idea of it had been ruined before it started because Kayla was too big of a wimp to tell Lauren about the deal between their father and Ben Donnelly.

To that end, she still didn't understand why Ben hadn't said anything, although maybe both men believed Lauren already knew.

Robert Maxwell was just that self-centered to assume his estranged daughter kept tabs on him. At this rate, they'd be lucky if Lauren stayed for Brody's wedding, let alone help with the planning.

Kayla didn't want her sister to leave again so soon. They might not have much in common, but Kayla couldn't stop hoping for something more. She pulled the edges of her thick cardigan sweater more closely around herself as tiny sand tornadoes swirled in front of her.

The biting wind hadn't even registered when she'd first walked from the house. She'd spent the whole day ruminating over what she should've done differently and how she could fix things. Now she thought about reaching out to Ben, but there was no chance she would risk incurring more of Lauren's ire.

She looked down at her fingers, which were turning a somewhat alarming shade of purple at the tips. Her body felt frozen in place, although the sting of the cold on her cheeks was welcome.

"Do your big plans for tonight involve turning yourself into a human popsicle?"

Her head snapped back, and she looked up to see Scott looming over her, his dark brows furrowed. She'd been so consumed by her own thoughts that she hadn't seen him approach, and he was practically shouting to be heard over the howling wind.

"What?" Her voice sounded rough, and she cleared her throat. "What are you talking about?"

"Kayla, you're freezing out here."

"It's refreshing," she said in the snippiest tone she could manage.

He reached down and covered her hands with his bigger ones. The heat of his skin against hers stung, and she yanked away her hands, balling them into fists and shoving them into the open flaps of the cardigan.

She didn't want his comfort. "I am not good company." He had to lean down to hear her.

"Is that why you're putting off going out with me?"

"You don't want to be around me, Scott. I'm not good for you. I'm not good for anybody at the moment. Trust me on that."

"I think you can trust me to judge who I want to spend my time with." Scott rubbed his hands together. "As much as I want to spend time with you, I'm not interested in turning myself into a freezer pop to do it. It would be best if you also went back into the house, invigorating as the wind might be. Then you should go out with me."

Stubborn but not stupid, Kayla stood, her limbs stiff from the cold. Her father had gone to Charlotte for the night on business, and she honestly did not want to spend the evening alone in the big house.

"Fine," she said, her voice nearly lost as a gust of wind carried it away.

Scott leaned in, close enough that she could see the golden flecks at the edges of his eyes. She could easily get lost in his gaze if she let herself. "Is that a yes?"

"Yes," she said, suddenly shy, making her feel defensive. "I'll have dinner with you, but I warned you about being bad company, so don't expect too much."

"I won't expect anything other than the pleasure of your company," Scott said, and the way he looked at her made her cheeks feel hot despite the cold. "I'll pick you up at seven."

Kayla nodded, then headed back to the house, glancing over her shoulder once to see Scott jogging down the beach toward his home and the forty acres that bordered the Camp Blossom property.

His agreement to sell the land was integral to her father's master development plan, and in her heart, Kayla did not want to be a part of convincing Scott. She'd made so many decisions, consciously or not, because she wanted to please Robert Maxwell. And that included choosing a boring, egotistical and upwardly mobile boyfriend.

Look where that had landed her—a woman in her early thirties humiliated by her cheating boyfriend so choosing to start over in her career and holed up in her childhood bedroom. She felt pathetic, just like Lauren thought her to be, but she wasn't confident she had the courage to change. It was easy to do what other people expected because then she wouldn't have to risk failing at her own dreams.

She walked into the house, and her fingers began to tingle as her circulation returned. Frostbite was not a good way to handle her troubles. She took the hottest shower she could tolerate, relieved when the feeling returned to her limbs.

Her phone dinged as she was getting dressed: a text from Hannah that Lauren had agreed to Hannah continuing to stay at the Maxwell house for the duration of their visit.

Hannah was going to spend one last night at the cabin with her mother and get dropped off in the morning if that was okay with Kayla. Funny that the girl's grandfather didn't seem to factor into her decision when Kayla had spent most of her life framing her actions by whether or not they'd make Robert Maxwell happy.

It was more than okay for her niece to stay, although Hannah made no mention of her mother coming with her. Kayla responded to the message, assuring the girl she was welcome as long as she wanted and could go back and forth between there and the cabin without committing to one or the other.

She pulled up the contact information for Scott O'Day, and her fingers hovered over the home screen, ready to send a text canceling again. It would be easier to avoid all interaction with him, but that wasn't what she wanted.

Then another notification sounded—a message from her father.

Saw you talking to Scott as I pulled out. You've got this. Couldn't do it without you. Proud of you, K. Glad to have my girl home.

Her skin started to tingle again, and not because of the heat or cold. When was the last time her father had told her she made him proud? Maybe when she'd graduated first in her class from Duke law school, but even then his words had been something more along the lines of, "That a girl. You're a chip off the old block," as if his DNA was so powerful it had impacted hers.

She knew rationally that his message said more about him than it did her, but her little girl's heart still reacted.

She craved Robert's approval as much as she yearned for Lauren's. Right now, it seemed out of reach to believe things would get better with her sister.

Brody loved everybody, but he'd be married soon. Kayla had tried her best to make a connection with his fiancée, but she and Avah were not going to be friends beyond the help Kayla could offer with wedding planning.

If she lost her father's approval, she'd have no one—no family and no close friends. More than anything, the thought of being alone terrified her.

So she got dressed in black jeans and a pale blue sweater that she knew made her eyes pop. Normally she would wear a camisole under the deep V-neck, but tonight she chose to reveal a bit of skin, trying to convince herself it wasn't simply so that she could persuade Scott to sell his land.

Women made an effort with their appearance when they went on dates, so why shouldn't she try for Scott? Kayla groaned, realizing she was gaslighting herself. But that knowledge didn't entice her to change clothes.

Five minutes before Scott was scheduled to pick her up, she walked downstairs and entered the kitchen, then let out a startled scream.

Brody, who was standing at the counter shoveling leftover lasagna into his mouth, shouted in response.

The bite of lasagna halfway to his mouth dropped off the fork and tumbled down the front of his gray sweatshirt onto the pristine granite counter.

"Are you trying to give me a heart attack?" he yelled.

"I could ask the same about you," she shot back,

pressing her open palm to her chest. "Maybe you could've let me know you were here."

Brody grabbed a wad of paper towels to clean up the lasagna. "I heard your music coming from upstairs. It sounded sad. I figured you were having a moment. That sad-girl guitar music usually meant you were on your period or upset about a guy."

Kayla felt her mouth drop open. "Lauren and I did not raise you to be a chauvinist pig, Brody Maxwell. My music doesn't say anything about me other than I have good taste. What are you doing here, anyway?"

"What are you doing in that sexy sweater, sis?" Brody ran a paper towel under the faucet for a few seconds, then swiped at the front of his sweatshirt. "That does not look like the outfit of someone having man trouble."

"I'm not having man trouble."

He shrugged. "It looks like you're having man adventures. Are you about to go on a date? Good for you, Kayla. Seth was a prick. He didn't deserve you."

"Now you tell me," she said, rolling her eyes. "And for the record, I do have a date tonight." The words felt fizzy on her tongue like those packets of candy from childhood with exploding rocks zinging around her mouth. "Where's Avah?"

"She's at the apartment." Her brother's brow puckered. "It's weird living with somebody, you know? We need to get a bigger place. I know that was the plan before the baby comes, but we need it sooner. Avah says I'm smothering her."

Kayla moved closer as he placed the foil over the lasagna tray and carefully folded the edges. It was unlike Brody to be careful with anything.

"I get that we're living together in a one-bedroom apartment, and she likes her space, but do you think it's unreasonable to expect to make and eat dinner together?"

"She doesn't want to have dinner with you?"

"Mostly, she wants to eat chips and salsa while watching reality TV shows."

"You don't have a television." Brody had never cared about television, video games, or any indoor activity.

She knew his apartment wasn't fancy, but a nice living space wasn't a priority for free-spirited Brody. His home was more a glorified storage unit or place to lie down in between adventure trips.

"I bought one when Avah moved in. She watches a lot of shows, and even when she's not, she keeps it on like it's a white noise machine, no matter what we're doing. Anyway, a little more space is what she needs. Me too, if I'm being honest."

"Are you sure about this wedding?" Kayla asked gently.

"Yeah." He nodded. "This baby deserves to grow up with a mother and a father. You and Laur did a bang-up job with me, but I didn't like all the women Dad hired because he couldn't be bothered to act like a father."

Shock reverberated through Kayla. It was the first time she'd heard her happy-go-lucky brother refer to his childhood as other than halcyon memories.

"You don't have to be married to give a child a good life, Brody. Plenty of people co-parent kids even when they aren't together."

"I hated not having two parents."

"This isn't the same thing," Kayla told him. "Mom

died. She would have never left you—us—on purpose, and Dad did his best."

Brody inclined his head, and once again, he reminded her of a floppy-haired retriever, his eyes gentle and guileless. But she read the confusion and pain in them. "Do you believe that?"

"I want to. I want to believe—"

She didn't get to finish her thought, not that she was exactly sure how to, because the doorbell rang. A wide grin split Brody's face, the sadness vanishing so quickly that Kayla wondered if she'd imagined it.

"Your date is coming to the door like it's high school. This is going to be great. Does Dad have a shotgun I can pretend to clean?"

"Not funny, Brody. You are not meeting him. Stay here. Stay," she repeated.

Like most fun-loving creatures, Brody completely ignored her command and raced to the door.

She ran after him. "Brody, do not answer that. It isn't what you think. It's also none of your business."

He opened the door as Kayla skidded to a stop behind him. Scott's whiskey-colored eyes widened as he looked between them.

"Good evening, young swain," Brody said, sounding remarkably like their father when he was trying to intimidate someone.

Kayla grabbed her purse from the table in the center of the foyer where she'd left it. "My brother was dropped on his head multiple times as a baby."

"Hello." Scott stuck out his hand. "I'm Scott O'Day. I live next door."

"The restaurant app nouveau Richie Rich." Brody

glanced toward Kayla and wiggled his brows. "He's an improvement over Seth."

"Hush, brother. For the record, you sound like Dad and you're being super rude." Kayla tried to push him out of the way, but her brother was extremely strong for someone so loose-limbed.

"What are you doing, Brody? Let go of his hand."

Brody released the grip. "It's just a friendly shake, but I want an answer to that question. What are your intentions toward—"

"Oh, my gosh." Kayla placed her hands over her eyes for a moment. "Ignore him, please."

"It's a fair question." Scott sounded oddly appreciative of Brody's antics. "I intend to buy her dinner and ask questions and hopefully not bore the life out of her."

Brody seemed to consider that. "I accept your answer."

"Then go away," Kayla muttered.

Brody pulled her in for a quick half hug. "I will. Just know this one is special even if she doesn't realize it."

Kayla's cheeks were flaming by this point, but she appreciated her brother's concern. When was the last time someone acted like they cared that much about her?

"There's ice cream in the freezer," she said and could finally push her brother back a few steps—only because he let her. "Next time, text before you come over, and I'll have dinner with you. Any night you want."

"Thanks, K," Brody said. "Nice to meet you, Scotty."

"Oh, my gosh." Kayla repeated under her breath. "Don't say I didn't warn you about going out with me," she said as they walked down the cobblestone path through the front yard toward a black 4Runner parked at the edge of the manicured lawn.

"I like your brother. He's the one getting married, right?"

She sighed. "Yes."

He waited for her to say more and seemed to understand why she didn't. "That was a more weighted yes than I expected." Instead of demanding an explanation, he opened the passenger-side door for her and smiled as she got in.

It was a small gesture but sweet in a way Seth had never been. Fiercely independent, Lauren probably would have told Kayla she was being foolish to appreciate it. Women were undoubtedly capable of opening their own car doors. But it was the thoughtfulness that had Kayla's stomach dipping.

"Do you believe in love?" she asked when he started to pull out of the driveway.

"In general or specifically for myself?" he asked with a soft chuckle.

"Either, I suppose. Have you ever been in love?"

"I don't think so." He glanced over at her. "Have you?"

"I thought so, but I was wrong." She placed her hands on her legs and spread her fingers wide. At one point, she'd expected to wear an engagement ring on her left hand but now realized she was glad Seth had cheated and undermined her at the firm.

Not exactly glad, she supposed, but it would have been a mistake—another thing she did because it looked good on paper and was what her father expected.

But she wouldn't have been happy.

Kayla wanted to be happy.

"I believe in love," Scott said, and she noticed his neck had gone pink like he was embarrassed admitting it. She was charmed by his honesty despite his apparent hesitancy to admit it.

"I do, too," she told him. "I want that for Brody, and I'm not sure getting married right now will give that to him."

"But you're going to let him make his own decision because he's a grown man."

"Is that a question or your advice?"

"Call it an observation," Scott said with a shrug. "I hope your brother finds what he's looking for. It's clear he adores you, so I have no doubt you'll support him no matter what."

Kayla blew out a long breath. For whatever reason, that reminder took the edge off her worry. "I will." She smiled and reached over to squeeze Scott's hand.

"I'm glad you saved me from freezing on the beach *and* didn't take no for an answer for tonight."

"Me, too," he agreed, and turned his hand over so he could link their fingers together.

Anticipation danced through Kayla, and she put aside troublesome thoughts about her family. She would allow herself to enjoy a night with Scott no matter where it led or what came next.

This moment and the hope it gave her were enough for now.

CHAPTER NINE

BEN WALKED UP the steps to Jim's cabin later that week, Lauren's words about being stewards of Camp Blossom embedded in his brain like a thorn in an animal's paw.

He had a myriad of projects to keep him busy from well before the sun rose to late at night. His company had three custom houses they were building currently, plus paperwork to push and emails and voice messages to answer. Once the land deal was finalized and things got rolling on the new housing development, he'd have to scale back his work in other areas.

But Ben didn't fully trust Robert Maxwell, so he didn't want to let his foot off the gas in building his client list and risk falling behind if Robert decided to screw him over.

Not for the first time, he wondered about the wisdom of partnering with a man he didn't particularly like or trust. Robert was the most prominent player in residential development in this part of the country, so Ben had a lot to gain if things moved forward as they were scheduled to.

He put in countless hours and more energy than he had to achieve his current success. When Ben first got his general contractor's license, the biggest hurdle was attracting clients. He had plenty of ideas and good intentions but also the shady reputation of several generations of Donnelly slackers to overcome.

It had been a couple new to the area who'd hired him for his first big job. He'd built a vacation home on the water that exceeded their expectations and came in well below budget, waiving his fee because he needed the reference more than he needed money.

They'd sung his praises, and slowly he'd built a solid pipeline that allowed him to hire his own crew and work with some of the best subcontractors in the area. There had been a few lean years, and he'd gotten used to living on ramen and peanut butter sandwiches and working around the clock to build the business.

He'd done it. He'd supported his dad through a successful stint in rehab and then cleaned up his family's tarnished name and image in the community. Now he risked everything to make his mark with Robert Maxwell's newest venture.

Until Lauren called him out on it, he'd been able to ignore the bothersome tug on his conscience, whispering that he was compromising his values for material gain.

He knocked on the door and then opened it after Jim called a hearty "Come on in."

Since he'd moved into the caretaker's cabin, Ben did his best to stop by and visit with the older man every few days. But it had been a wet fall, so his crews were behind on a few projects, and he was once again working around the clock to stay ahead and on budget.

"I brought you an apple fritter from Sunnyside." Ben paused as he took in the state of the cabin. Decorations were strewn about the family room, which was already cramped with the various pieces of furniture

Jim couldn't part with. Jim sat at the head of the kitchen table, tufts of silver hair sticking up in all directions, making him look like a lumberjack version of Albert Einstein.

"What's going on?" Ben asked. "Why does it look like you've taken out everything that we put into the empty cabin to be donated?"

"Oh, I'll get rid of it eventually," Jim said, "but not yet. Thanks to little Lauren Maxwell, we've got a shot at one more big to-do at the camp."

What the hell had *little* Lauren Maxwell done now? Ben wondered as Jim beamed like Santa had promised to bring everything on his wish list.

"It's going to be the best Christmas carnival ever. I've got my old plans for where things went for the light displays. I hope the electrical panel has enough oomph left to handle the event. If not, I might need your help getting it back up to snuff."

Ben drew in a calming breath. He felt anything but calm. "Jim, we're not fixing stuff at the camp. All of this will be torn down once the sale goes through. You know that. You agreed to that. It's the right decision."

Ben wasn't sure whether he was trying to convince his friend or himself.

Jim smoothed a hand over the large sheet of paper that looked like a map of the camp buildings. "You've been good to me, Ben. You were good to Nancy, too, before she passed. In a lot of ways, you're the son we never had."

Ben's heart ached at those words. "I care about you." He didn't want that ever to be called into question.

"I know you do, and that's the only reason I agreed to sell. There's no way I would let Robert Maxwell anywhere near this land if you hadn't assured me you would do the right thing by it."

Jim didn't understand he would not have had a choice about selling, because Ben had protected him from that.

"I'm going to do the right thing," Ben repeated, even though at this moment, he wasn't sure what was right. "What does Lauren have to do with any of this?"

Jim smiled. "She talked to the gal who runs events and whatnot for the town. They started that Christmas On the Coast holiday festival a few years back."

"I'm familiar with it." Frustration made Ben's head throb. "The festival activities and events take place downtown."

"They're expanding this year, and Camp Blossom is going to be part of it. We're doing a light display again to get people out here to enjoy camp. Lauren wants a hot chocolate booth, craft projects for the kids, games, and a big snow maze. Not with real snow, of course, but you get the idea. We'll have kids at camp again, Benny."

Ben's stomach felt like it dropped to his toes. "Jim, you haven't actively run anything out of the camp for years."

"Six years," Jim confirmed. "We stopped after Nancy got diagnosed, and we had to focus our time and energy on getting her well."

He swiped a hand over his wrinkled cheek. "The chemo and radiation weren't supposed to last as long as they did, taking that much out of her. Or me. I didn't expect cancer to take her, but it did. She was the heart and soul of this place, and after she was gone, I couldn't imagine hosting events without her at my side."

"And now you can?" Ben ran a hand through his

hair, imagining he'd look as wild as Jim by the end of this conversation.

"Yup. I want to do it up right one more time for Nancy—to honor her memory. Lauren helped me remember what a difference this camp has made to people. We used to be a big part of the community."

"Times have changed," Ben said gently.

Jim didn't seem to hear him. "Lauren said Lily Wainright Dawes was inspired to become an actress because of her participation in the skits and talent shows we used to put on here."

"Lily isn't an actress anymore. She runs her family's hardware store."

"I know that, but she's also involved in community theater because she wants to give back and inspire kids just like she was inspired during her summers at camp. We have a legacy to consider."

Ben wondered if it were possible to actually grind teeth to dust. "Are those your words or Lauren's?"

"Now, don't get your britches all twisted," Jim told him. "Lauren knows this is the last hurrah for the camp. She might have bigger long-term plans, but I made a commitment to you. I'm going to honor it, no matter what."

"No matter what," Ben repeated stonily. "This is what you wanted. You were going to sell this land one way or the other." *Lose it* was closer to the truth than *sell it*, but he still refused to frame it that way. He wanted to protect Jim's pride as much as his bank account.

"Without anyone to help you with the day-to-day operations, the work was too much," he reminded Jim. "You know the shape these cabins are in. I don't think—"

"Lauren looked at the long-range forecast. The activities she's planning can be done outside. She said we'll even have the money to bring in some porta potties so we won't have to mess with the old plumbing out here."

Ben's jaw ached just like his head. "It sounds like Lauren's thought of everything."

"She can't do it alone." Jim pointed toward Ben. "I want you to help her, son."

Hell no, Ben thought, then answered, "Even if I wanted to involve the property in the town's festival line-up the way you're suggesting, I can't. I don't have the time or the bandwidth to take on something else. I've got my own projects to finish, and I'm neck-deep in getting permits and approval for what needs to be done to keep the development plans on track once the sale goes through."

"It's going to be a shame to see this place torn down," Jim said with an exaggerated sigh.

Point taken.

"Where's Lauren now?" Ben asked.

"She's working on sorting out the lights in cabin five, seeing what still works and what doesn't. I kept things pretty organized, but I'm sure there's going to be plenty of strands and decorations that need to be replaced."

"Who's going to pay for that?"

"I've got money."

"You know that money is earmarked for your living expenses at Shady Acres."

"It's fine. I already called and explained the situation."

The situation was that Jim was supposed to move as soon as his apartment was ready. There had been delays, but the retirement community's manager had assured Ben that Jim would be in by the new year.

It had taken a lot for him to ensure all the moving parts would line up to fall into place without a hitch. With a few stubborn intrusions, Lauren had knocked his master plan off the rails so entirely he wasn't sure he'd be able to right it again.

He tapped one hand against the kitchenette counter when he really wanted to put his fist through a wall to release the tension threatening to boil over inside of him. "I'm going to check on Lauren and see if she needs help like you said."

"I knew I could count on you." Jim offered a grateful smile that was like a kick in the gut. "Lauren didn't believe me, but I knew you'd understand why this needed to be done."

"I'll bring dinner over for you later," Ben said. "I made chili last night."

"You and that girl have always thought alike. She brought me a whole pot full of turkey chili this morning and some homemade chocolate chip cookies. You know how I love cookies."

"I do." Ben sighed. After promising to check in later—chili or not—Ben left the cabin.

He knew how much Jim loved cookies and Camp Blossom. He also understood the precarious edge on which the camp's finances were teetering in a way the older man didn't. In a way Lauren Maxwell couldn't.

It was time for the two of them to have a serious conversation. Ben was not the villain in this situation, just like he hadn't been years ago, despite what she wanted to believe.

Lauren needed to understand what was at stake for all of them.

He stalked through the camp, paying no heed to the

rain or wind. He did notice the board of one step of cabin five was missing and thought about the potential hazard of that as he climbed over it.

Lauren had no right to do this, no right to make Jim sentimental about camp or to complicate Ben's life or make him feel so much. He always felt too much where she was concerned, and this was no different.

He yanked on the screen door with so much force that it broke off the hinges, frustrating him even more.

If Robert Maxwell had his way, this place would have been foreclosed upon months ago, and the deal done. Ben was the one who stepped in and sank every bit of his savings into making sure Jim could sell the camp on his terms with enough money to cover his living expenses at the retirement home for as long as he'd need.

Ben's frustration mounted with every ragged breath he dragged in, and he pushed open the door and stepped through as it banged against the side of the cabin.

"What the heck?"

Lauren's yelp pierced his angry haze, and he rushed forward as she started to topple off the rickety stool she stood on. He caught her just before she hit the ground and then stumbled under the force. He couldn't tell whether the panic lurching through him at the thought of her being injured or the feel of her body against his sent him off balance.

She was so familiar and yet different from the girl he'd first held in his arms. She grabbed hold of his shoulders, then squirmed to be released.

"What is wrong with you?" She smoothed shaking hands over her faded jeans.

"Me? I'm not the one standing on tiptoe on the

stool that looks like it could barely hold the weight of a feather."

"It's plenty solid," she maintained, and they both looked to where the now three-legged stool was on the ground, one spindle popped out from where it was held together by...

"It's held together by duct tape, Lauren. What were you doing up there anyway?"

She pointed to the corner of a piece of paper peeking out from a crack under one of the beams that stretched the length of the cabin.

"This was the girl counselors' cabin," she said. "Maren, Izzy and I left notes that final summer."

He hadn't heard the names of her two best friends from camp spoken out loud in years. "Notes about what and to whom?"

"To ourselves—our future selves. The plan was to come back and meet up in ten years and see how much of what we'd written had come true."

"I had no idea." Ben kept his gaze on the ceiling, wondering how many other things he didn't know about the confounding woman standing before him.

Not just who she'd become since leaving but the intricacies of who she'd been back then and why she'd been able to walk away after making what was supposed to be a lifelong commitment to him.

"That was the summer before senior year," he said as if she didn't realize it. Anger still ran through his veins, but curiosity diluted it.

She nodded.

"Have you spoken to the others? Did you keep in touch with your friends?"

She frowned. "I didn't keep in touch with anyone. At

our tenth anniversary, I was busy being a single mom. The thought of coming back here—"

"You could have returned for a visit." He wouldn't let her get away with lame excuses although he didn't mention that she'd also missed Nancy's funeral. That felt like too low a blow even for him.

She nodded. "Izzy reached out," she said quietly.

"That's not a surprise." Izzy McFarland had been the one who would have cared the most about keeping their trio together.

"What about Maren?"

"She sent a one-line email that she was on assignment in Italy for a month that summer. *Ciao, bellas*, was pretty much all we got."

"Yet you're willing to risk life and limb to pull down the old notes?"

"I didn't get them, obviously."

Ben felt his mouth pull up in a half smile. "I know what the hand behind your back means."

"Fine. But I don't even know which one I grabbed," she said, and shoved her hand with the piece of paper into her pocket.

He wanted to be the man she would share her deepest secrets with, but he hadn't been, apparently even when he'd loved her with every fiber of his being.

That thought brought reality back enough that he could refocus on the whole purpose of coming to find her. "The situation with the sale of Camp Blossom is not what you think."

She blinked, and the vulnerability he'd read in her eyes vanished. "I'm well aware of that, because I thought my father was behind all of this. Then I found out you're partnering with him."

"Who told you?"

"You should have told me."

"Kayla?" He could have guessed as much

"No, but she should have told me as well."

"Why?" he demanded softly. "Why should your sister show you any regard? Why should either of us concern ourselves with your not-so-tender feelings? You certainly didn't show us the same amount of respect."

"You don't get to say that to me."

"Who's going to stop me?"

"Are you doing this as an act of revenge? Are you willing to screw over Jim because you know it would hurt me?"

"I'm not screwing over Jim." Ben didn't bother to hide his frustration.

He moved to the small kitchenette on one side of the cabin and gripped the Formica counters to steady himself. "Nancy was sick for a long time. Cancer took a toll on both of them."

"I know," Lauren said, "and I know how heartbroken Jim was when she died."

"What you don't know is that this place is in the red so bright, he wasn't going to get out—not without a huge influx of cash. Even then, he would have needed somebody to run it…somebody willing to devote their life to making it great again. Who was going to do that, Lauren? You were nowhere to be found, for all your talk about caring for him. Your father had made arrangements with the bank to foreclose on the property. If that had happened, by the time the debts were paid, there would have been nothing left for Jim to live on."

"It couldn't have been that bad," she argued, but her voice was uncertain.

Ben knew the truth, and Lauren needed to know as well.

"Jim and Nancy didn't have insurance. I don't know how or why they let it lapse." He shook his head. "That's not true. I do know. The year before her diagnosis, the water heater broke a few weeks before campers arrived. They didn't want to disappoint anyone, so instead of paying their insurance premiums, they paid for the repairs and never got caught up again. Medicare covered some of the expenses, but they tried several treatments for her, some experimental and others not covered at all."

"And my dad was going to take advantage of that? This place was like a second home to me," she said. "He knows that."

"It means just as much to me, Laur. They were like the parents neither of us had. I'm not the bad guy. You can believe I am if you want, but it's not true."

It had never been true, but he didn't say that. The past was the past, and it was better left there.

"But you're still tearing down camp," she said, like the decision had been easy for him.

"And taking care of Jim in the process." He scrubbed a hand over his face. "I didn't see another way." He held up a hand when she would have argued that point. "I don't want to fight with you, Lauren."

"Then help me," she countered. He was about to say no when she added, "One more Christmas. For Jim and Nancy."

Ben closed his eyes for a moment, and her voice found him as if across the miles.

"Let's do this for everything this camp meant to both of us. I believe in Christmas and the magic of the season. I'd forgotten how much it means, but I want to remember. I want to show Hannah how special it is. We were part of something that touched people's lives, Ben."

How was he supposed to say no to that?

"Fine," he agreed with an exhalation. "Let's give Jim one last Camp Blossom Christmas and honor Nancy's memory."

"Thank you," Lauren exclaimed and threw her arms around him.

He hadn't expected the embrace, but it felt right. Lauren fit in his arms the way she always had. Perfectly, as if she belonged there.

"We've got a lot to do." She pulled back almost reluctantly, and he noticed her cheeks were tinged pink. She lifted a hand to her earlobe, then lowered it again, but he knew what the almost-gesture meant.

She was as discombobulated by the connection between them as he was.

The holidays were a time when anything could happen. If Christmas magic did exist, there was no doubt it would be found at Camp Blossom.

CHAPTER TEN

LAUREN FELT AS though she were walking on air as she left the planning meeting with Avery Atwell at town hall the following Monday morning. She'd spent most of the weekend preparing camp for visitors and updating the website and social media accounts.

Maybe it was silly to work so hard on the holiday event when there was no future for the camp she loved, but she wanted a do-over on the mistakes she'd made.

Returning home reminded her that she hadn't lived up to her potential. Or, more accurately, the fact that she'd amounted to very little, the way her dad had warned she would if she didn't follow the path he set out for her.

There was no sense regretting her decisions as she had no way to change what had come before. She'd done what she needed to for her daughter's sake. Hannah might be going through a sullen, rebellious teenage phase, but the girl was the brightest spot in Lauren's world.

Hannah was exceptional, and Lauren would give up her dreams all over again if it meant paving the way for her daughter's to come true. It might not feel like the two of them against the world any longer, but Hannah still held her heart.

She wanted the girl to be proud—or at least marginally impressed—as she seemed to be when it came to Kayla. Lauren had heard more than enough about her younger sister's accomplishments since Hannah had been dividing her time between camp and the house on the beach. From fancy degrees to partner track at a prestigious law firm, Lauren had nothing that could compare to her sister's achievements.

She was proud of the artwork and promotional graphics she'd done for Tommy back in the day, but there had been no future for her work or their marriage. Instead, he'd blown every chance the band had for something more with his penchant for drugs and reckless behavior.

As a single mom, she'd taken whatever kinds of jobs she could find to pay the bills and allow her to spend as much time as possible with Hannah. When Hannah was a toddler, their sweet elderly neighbor had watched her during the day in exchange for light housekeeping and meal prep.

Lauren had done everything from restaurant work to tending bar to remote call center customer service, where disgruntled customers phoned in throughout the night across several time zones to complain about things Lauren had no control over. It had been a job she could do while Hannah slept, fueled by coffee and a desperate need to provide for her child.

She hadn't been able to volunteer at the elementary school like some of the other moms. Instead, she'd taken a weekend job working overnight at a local hotel with a waterpark connected so that she could host birthday parties and end-of-year events.

It had given her at least a smidgeon of cool-mom cachet. She couldn't compete with Kayla's accomplishments, but the sacrifices she'd made had ensured that

Hannah had access to at least some things that she would not have otherwise.

Lauren had experienced feeling like a burden at times with each of her parents and understood what it did to a kid to feel like an encumbrance on the life her mom and dad wanted. She hadn't realized what it might do to a mother to feel unappreciated.

So whether Hannah appreciated it or not, she was still happy with her decision to help with the Christmas festival. Another benefit would be that the camp would be at its shiny best, so if Brody and Avah wanted to have their wedding there, she could give them that, too.

Maybe Kayla would suggest something fancier, but Lauren wanted to prove she could contribute. She deserved a place at the Maxwell table, or at least an invitation that she could decline.

She glanced around the empty parking lot at town hall, scanning for her sister's car. Hannah had spent the night at the beach house, so Kayla was bringing her into town.

They needed to rehearse what they would say to Brody and Avah about planning the wedding—a united front, Kayla had suggested.

Tomorrow they were taking the bride to Raleigh to look for wedding dresses, even though Lauren had found a designer option that could be perfect in A Second Chance, a secondhand boutique in downtown Magnolia. The shop was owned by Mariella Jacob, who had formally been one of the most-sought after wedding dress designers in the world.

It wouldn't take much effort to make the already gorgeous Avah into a stunning bride, but she'd rejected the idea of wearing something from a consignment store.

Although most of Lauren's wardrobe had been thrifted, she'd tried not to take offense at Avah's attitude. Every bride had a right to pick her own gown but given Brody's insistence on paying for the wedding himself, Avah's options were somewhat limited by their budget.

Even Kayla had agreed the local dress was perfect, but Avah refused to consider it, and Brody didn't want to cause her any more stress, but the potential of starting married life racking up debt to pay for the wedding was clearly weighing on him

Lauren turned at the sound of a car door shutting and inwardly groaned as her father accompanied Hannah across the parking lot. She'd managed to avoid talking to him since the night they'd exchanged heated words and mentally cursed her sister for not telling her that he was the one coming into town.

She felt her phone vibrate in her purse and realized it was on mute. She waved and pulled the phone from her purse with the other hand.

Did you get my message? Dad is with Hannah. I thought you'd want to know.

Okay, so much for blaming Kayla.

"Thanks for dropping her off," she said to her father, hoping to keep this interaction short and sweet.

"We're going to head over to the hardware store," she told Hannah. "You can meet Lily, and then we'll pick up a few strands of replacement lights."

"What is this nonsense about you fixing up that ragtag camp you love so much?"

"Well, Dad," she said with a tight smile, "I think

you've hit the nail on the head. I'm fixing it up for the holidays."

"It won't change what will happen to that place."

"I'm not trying to change anything. I'm trying to give Jim a happy memory of his last Christmas at Camp Blossom. Have you heard of happy memories?"

Her father sniffed. "I'm familiar with the concept."

"To be honest, the Santa Clauses that Jim collects didn't look quite so creepy once we started putting them out on the paths and in the common areas around camp," Hannah said, crossing her thin arms over her chest when Robert blasted her with one of his patented glares. "It's going to be cool, Grandpa."

Lauren noticed the incredulous expression on her father's face.

"That's the first time you called me Grandpa."

"Is that bad?" Hannah asked, sounding genuinely curious. "Do you prefer something like Big Papa, or I could call you Robbie? What about Robo Pop?"

Lauren grinned. For all the potential she hadn't reached, she'd raised a firecracker of a kid. She wished Kayla were here to see Hannah teasing their father. To her knowledge, no one had the nerve to mock the all-powerful Robert Maxwell.

He cleared his throat. "Grandpa will do," he said as if he were some Regency-era duke speaking to the poor street urchin he'd adopted.

But Hannah didn't need a wealthy benefactor because Lauren would always provide for her daughter. No matter what material success or conventional social status she lacked, Lauren had survived and thrived in her own way and on her terms. She could accept Hannah forging a relationship with her grandpa but wasn't about to let Robert call the shots.

"I understand what's going to happen to the camp in the New Year," she told him. "I also trust Ben to take care of Camp Blossom's legacy."

"But not me? Your attachment to that place is as off-putting now as it was years ago."

"Why does it bother you so much that I liked it there? I was out of your hair and doing something productive when I went to camp. They appreciated my help."

"You had a home and family."

"Not one that cared about me," she countered. "Not the way Jim and Nancy did. They liked *me* without a constant pressure to change or be better."

She let her gaze stray to the naked live oak and magnolia trees that lined the edge of the town hall property, feeling as empty as the winter branches devoid of their summer leaves when she thought about how she'd felt growing up in her father's house.

"Besides, you sent me to camp that first summer."

"You had an overabundance of energy and needed an outlet for it."

"And I found a place where I belonged. I still feel that even with the camp looking a little worse for wear."

Robert rolled his eyes, and for a second, she saw herself and her daughter in his passive display of disrespect. "That's an understatement."

"Jim had other priorities than building maintenance the past couple of years. I think you would empathize with his grief. Despite everything, I know it wasn't easy on you when Marcie died."

Robert swallowed and looked away, like the mention of his late wife's name still caused him pain.

"Mom used to call me Tigger." Hannah spoke into the awkward silence that fell between them. "Because I was so bouncy when I was little. I take after her in that way."

"I loved your energy," Lauren said, feeling protective of her daughter even if Hannah didn't need defending.

"Excess energy or not, this whole Christmas bit is a waste of your time," Robert insisted.

"Good thing it's my time to do with what I wish. Wasting it making people happy over the holidays floats my boat. You have nothing to say about it."

"Lauren, I'm not going to argue with you. That never amounted to anything for either of us."

She shrugged, making it look nonchalant. "Then I guess we also have nothing to say to each other."

"If that's how you want it," her father agreed, inclining his head.

Her heart pinged, but she ignored it. It was challenging to be as detached as she pretended. Did any child give up on a parent's love, or was it a loss a person felt no matter how many years passed?

"I'm here because I have a favor to ask," her dad said.

For all her skill with a quick retort, Lauren was left speechless for a moment. "What kind of favor?"

Hannah's attention was focused intently on the asphalt parking lot, and Lauren knew whatever her dad wanted wasn't going to be good.

"I need you to talk some sense into your brother."

She felt herself go numb. "What does that mean, Dad?"

"This marriage business, of course. He can't go through with it."

"I don't think you or I can make that choice for him."

"You know better than most, just like me, that a baby won't bind two people together the way he thinks. It's obvious he and that woman aren't a match."

"Her name is Avah."

"I know her name," Robert said, frustration darkening his tone. "A baby is a stupid reason to get married. Look what happened to your mother and me. Take your life as an example. You didn't learn from my mistake, but I'd hoped Brody would have taken a clue from both of us."

Lauren darted a glance toward Hannah, whose face had gone as pale as the gray sky above them.

"I don't think you can compare Brody to you or Tommy," Lauren answered. "He wants to do the right thing and be a good father."

"The boy doesn't understand the responsibility involved."

"He's not a boy, and I think he understands more than you realize. Just because my marriage didn't work out—"

"Neither of them," her father interjected.

"Neither was a mistake," she confirmed, a familiar ache lodging behind her rib cage as she thought about Ben. "They were the right decision at the time."

"I refuse to discuss the farce of you and Ben shackling yourself to each other. But the marriage to a low-life, no-talent musician with a cocaine habit was a new low, even for you."

"Why do your judgment and condescension not surprise me? For the record, Tommy got clean a couple of years ago. He lives in Los Angeles and teaches music at an after-school program when he's not on the road. He's doing well."

"Does he see his daughter? Does he support her financially?"

Lauren tipped up her chin. "I've never asked for money from Tommy, and we don't need it."

"Hannah said your apartment would fit into my family room."

Great. She could only imagine what else her daughter had said out of anger and frustration.

"I know that to you, size matters," Lauren muttered.

"Mom, we should go," Hannah said before Lauren or her father could lob any more verbal bombs at the other. "Thanks for the ride, Grandpa."

"Remember, sweetheart, as soon as you get your license back, I'll have a car waiting for you."

Lauren glared between her father and her daughter. "You are not buying her a car."

"She needs her own set of wheels, and I'm not sure that junk heap you drive is street-legal."

"Street-legal, Dad? This is none of your business. If I want Hannah to have a car, I'll buy her one."

"With what—your good looks? How much—"

Lauren held up a hand. "This is not up for discussion. I'm her mother. You will *not* buy her a car."

"I'm *your* father, and I'll do what I want."

"It's okay," Hannah said quickly. "We don't have to discuss this now."

"You're right," Lauren agreed with a tight smile. "Because there is no discussion." She headed across the parking lot, unsure whether she wanted her daughter to follow.

"Mom, he only offered." Hannah hurried to catch up to her. "It's not a big deal."

"Is that what this was about? Is that why you're

spending time with him and calling him Grandpa? Because you want something? I taught you better than that, Hannah."

"Did you?" her daughter shot back. "I distinctly remember your rent-is-due sweater."

Lauren felt herself blush. It was true. At one point when her finances had been precarious, she'd purposely worn a low-cut sweater every time her slightly lecherous landlord came looking for the monthly rent.

"I did that for *you*." She gritted her teeth. "It's not the same thing."

"I didn't ask Grandpa for a car, and that's not why I went to stay there. Whether you like it or not, he and Aunt Kayla are family. I don't have a relationship with anyone from Dad's side. I want to know your family. Sue me."

"Sue you? You've already been spending too much time with your attorney aunt. Come on, Banana. I don't want to fight."

She thought about Ben saying the same words to her.

"I can't speak for Grandpa, but Aunt Kayla doesn't want to fight with you either. She thinks you're something special. She talks about high school like you were the queen bee."

"It was a fairly small hive," Lauren said. But she had felt on top of the world at camp. "I think it's nice that you want to get to know them, even if it also bothers me. But no car. Grandpa's gifts come with too many strings. You might not realize it yet, but you will."

They'd made it to the hardware store. Lauren walked in, the tight knot in her gut uncoiling slightly as Lily offered a genuine smile.

The former camper introduced herself to Hannah and gushed over Lauren's role in her life.

She was amused by the look of incredulity on her daughter's face. Lily read it too, because she assured Hannah that she may not realize it, but her mother had been the coolest girl in all of Magnolia back in the day as far as Lily was concerned.

Lauren had also been uncomfortable in her own skin until she fell in love with Ben. When she was with him, everything seemed to slip into place.

They'd been like two sides of a magnet that had finally found their match. While Hannah and Lily talked about the holiday musical at the high school, Lauren found the supplies she needed.

Although Ben had offered to pay for everything, she didn't want to rely on him, so she charged the items to her credit card. Some things didn't change. She still wasn't good at letting people take care of her.

After Lauren finished her purchase, they walked into the ice cream shop next to Sunnyside Bakery.

"I thought I'd find you here," Kayla said, entering the shop just as the teenage boy behind the counter handed Lauren a scoop of cookies and cream in a cone. "Your mom always craved ice cream when the weather was cold," she explained to Hannah.

"She still does," the girl answered. "One time, there was a freak snowstorm in Atlanta, and we had a whole carton for dinner."

"We also had celery with that dinner," Lauren reminded her daughter. "It's all about balance."

"Do you want to join us for ice cream before we start talking wedding plans?" she asked her sister.

"Really?" Kayla looked genuinely surprised, and

Lauren felt a twinge of guilt over how she had treated her younger sister over all these years.

She didn't have to be such a bitch. It was habit at this point.

"My sister will have a chocolate malt," she told the gangly kid and glanced toward Kayla. "Is that still your favorite?"

"Yeah." Kayla nodded, then grinned at Hannah.

"I told you she doesn't totally hate your guts," Hannah assured her aunt, and Lauren smiled despite herself.

Being home for Christmas was turning out to mean more to her than she'd expected, and not all of it was awful. In fact, parts of this holiday season were more fun than she'd had in ages.

CHAPTER ELEVEN

KAYLA SHIVERED AS a gust of air whooshed through a giant gap in the passenger side door of Lauren's Jeep. She'd woken that morning to gray skies, a dismal light rain and concrete-colored skies. Not exactly a cheery day to take their brother's fiancée wedding dress shopping, but here they were.

"Remind me again why we had to take your car on this errand," she said through chattering teeth.

"The Jeep is awesome." Lauren patted the faded dashboard of her beloved vehicle.

Kayla rubbed her hands together and blew on her fingers. "I don't think the heat works, Lauren."

"You're too spoiled. Learn to toughen up, K."

How often had Kayla heard some version of that admonishment from her older sister?

The accusation of being spoiled, which may have been true although irrelevant in most cases, had been how Lauren convinced Kayla to do most of their chores and hand over half her lunch money every week. Lauren wielded her skill at making Kayla feel bad for being the perceived favorite like a knife.

Despite their constant bickering, Robert adored his spunky daughter. Before she'd died, Kayla's mother encouraged Lauren's brashness, telling Kayla she could learn something from her confident older sister.

The lesson Kayla had learned was how to stay out of people's way and do and say the right thing so as not to make waves. She might be spoiled, but she was also expendable, the exact opposite of Lauren.

There was no way for Kayla to change who she was at her core—certain habits were too ingrained to overcome. She considered herself a work in progress; some things had evolved in her personality from when they'd been kids. The need to defend herself against baseless criticism was one of those.

"I don't drive a nice car because I'm spoiled."

"You sure about that?"

"I'm also sure if you wanted a vehicle upgrade, Lauren, you'd find a way to make it happen."

"Oh, my God, Aunt Kayla." Hannah pushed hard on the back of Kayla's seat. "You're so right. One of my friend's dads is the manager at a dealership. He told mom he would find a car for her after this thing broke down when we were on the way to school. It always breaks down, but she loves it too much to trade it in."

"It doesn't *always* break down," Lauren insisted. "Jeremiah Jeep is doing fine today."

Other than the rattling in the dash, the nonexistent heating system and a muffler that sounded like it had seen better days. Kayla chose not to mention any of those minor issues.

"It's probably why I wrecked," Hannah continued.

Kayla glanced over her shoulder and tried to communicate a silent warning. *Danger, Will Robinson.* Although she imagined the argument made sense in her niece's myopic teenage mind.

Lauren snorted. "You got a DUI and wrecked my car because you had a fake ID and were driving drunk."

"Fine." Kayla heard Hannah's put-upon sigh as she flopped against the back seat.

"Oh, cool. You had a fake ID?" Avah asked from where she sat next to Hannah. "One of my old boyfriends used to make fake IDs. I helped with the laminating. Did the cops take yours?"

"Yeah," Hannah answered quietly.

"I've still got his number if you want me to call him and see if he could make a replacement for you."

Seriously? Kayla bit back a cackle. Brody's fiancée was as big of a fool as Hannah.

"Bad idea," she and Lauren said in unison.

"Oh look, the Jeep's stereo system is working again," Hannah deadpanned.

Kayla wanted to tell her future sister-in-law that it wasn't a great idea to mention helping with an illegal ID ring so casually but prolonging the topic wouldn't do any of them any good.

She gazed out the window. "I love the way the frost shimmers on the tips of the pine needles," she said. It had rained heavily overnight, and the temperature was hovering just below freezing, so at the random times the sun peeked through the clouds, the light filtering across the evergreen trees sparkled like diamonds.

"Brody can tell you why that happens," Avah said. "He knows all kinds of useless information about trees and bushes and the forest and stuff."

Lauren's knuckles turned white on the steering wheel.

"He *is* a wildlife biologist." Kayla turned to smile at Avah. "At least, that's what his undergraduate degree is in. He's got a master's in environmental management. I'm sure you knew that, right? You guys haven't dated long but—"

"Yeah, I knew that." Avah nodded. "He got accepted into the fud program at Chapel Hill, but he had to say no since we've got a baby on the way."

"Do you mean PhD?" Hannah asked, sounding as incredulous as Kayla felt.

"Is that how you pronounce it? Weird. I thought it sounded like it spells."

Kayla felt her mouth drop open as she tried to absorb this new information and the way Avah spoke about it.

"Just to make sure I understand," Lauren said casually, "our brother was accepted into a UNC doctoral program?"

"Yeah," Avah said, "although he'll probably make more money working for Ben. Plus, he gets to wear a tool belt, which is super hot. If we have a boy, I'm gonna get him his own little tool belt and toolset. If it's a girl, I can do the same thing. I don't want to be sexist. Hers will be pink."

Kayla smiled. "Pink will be cute," she said woodenly, although Avah didn't notice.

"At first, I wanted to be surprised by the sex of the baby," she said. "But now I think I want to know, because how am I going to decorate and buy a bunch of clothes if I don't? I hope it's a girl. I hope she's just like her cousin Hannah."

"Wow," Hannah said with a choked laugh. "What a compliment. Thanks, Avah."

"You can call me Auntie."

"We might wait on that," Lauren said, then glanced out the windshield. "Ladies, here's the first shop."

Kayla took in the elegantly converted house with the whitewashed brick and manicured planters on the porch. There were mannequins in the shop windows dressed in designer wedding gowns, and the sign on the door read By Appointment Only.

"Oh." Avah sounded overwhelmed. "I didn't realize it was going to be so fancy."

Lauren shot Kayla a look that clearly said *I told you so*. "This is Raleigh's most exclusive bridal store," Kayla confirmed. "You said this is where you wanted to shop."

"It is. But now…do you think I'm dressed okay? How expensive is this going to be? I guess it doesn't matter," Avah said before Lauren or Kayla could answer. "Because your dad said money was no object."

Lauren pulled to a stop in a loading zone in front of the small boutique store. "Dad isn't paying for any part of this. At least, that's what Brody wants. The whole point of having the wedding at Camp Blossom is to make it…well, it will be beautiful but affordable."

"I know what Brody said." Avah sounded petulant. "But your dad talked to me separately. He said he'd buy my dress and pay for our honeymoon and that Brody didn't need to know it was him. We could tell him that my parents contributed."

"I thought your parents weren't sure if they were coming to the wedding, let alone funding it." Kayla closed her hands into fists.

"True, but that can be our secret, too, for now. It would hurt Brody's feelings if he knew."

Kayla felt her temper flare. "You can't start your marriage off on a lie. It's not right."

The woman sighed dramatically. "I just want to look beautiful for your brother."

"He thinks you're beautiful," Lauren said, rolling her eyes.

"I want to be good enough for this family."

"This family is a train wreck," Hannah said.

"That might be overstating it," Lauren told her daughter.

Kayla reached out to place what she hoped was a comforting hand on Avah's knee. She'd make this better, for Brody's sake. No matter what. "I asked Mariella at A Second Chance to hold the dress Lauren found for you."

"You did?" Lauren asked.

"Sure. It's a gorgeous gown, and I think Brody and Avah can have a beautiful wedding at any price point."

"But how, if it's not perfect?" Avah whined . "I want it to be perfect."

"Okay." Lauren tightened her hands on the steering wheel. "I know another place. It was a long time ago that I tried on wedding dresses, but maybe it's still there. I ended up buying one at a discount store, but this place…"

Lauren's voice shook with emotion. "Kayla, look it up. It was called Something Borrowed."

Despite everything, Kayla didn't like seeing her stepsister so worked up. "I'll look for it. We'll find the place."

She quickly punched in the name on her maps app. "I've got it. It's still there, and it's got over two thousand reviews with a four-point-eight average."

"That's pretty good." Lauren let out a shaky laugh. "There's always one complainer. You can't satisfy everybody. Am I right?"

"Mom, are you okay?" Hannah asked from the back seat.

"Yeah, I'm good."

Kayla didn't think her sister sounded okay, or anything like her sister, for that matter. "Maps says it's seven minutes away. We can pop in and then grab lunch."

"I want chicken nuggets, nachos, and cheesecake for dessert," Avah said.

"Do you want to add a vegetable to the menu—maybe a side salad?" Hannah suggested. "Have you tried Aunt Kayla's roasted broccoli? It's really good."

"High praise," Lauren confirmed, and Kayla felt an inordinate amount of pride.

"I don't eat anything green," Avah said. "But I take prenatal vitamins. The gummy kind."

"That's just perfect." Lauren jerked the Jeep back onto the street. "Moving on. Something Borrowed, here we come."

They were mostly silent on the short drive. The shop was crammed between a Chinese restaurant and an auto parts store but was adorable, with boughs of holly draped around the front door and pretty gowns hanging in the display window. It also looked much more welcoming than the first shop, although Kayla couldn't say precisely why.

"We're going to drop Hannah and Avah off in front. Kayla will stay with me to find parking."

"Mom, there's an open space across the street."

"That won't work." Lauren turned and glared at her daughter. "I don't want to risk the Jeep getting sideswiped."

Hannah choked out a laugh. "Seriously?"

"The sign in the window says they're doing free wedding cake samples today," Kayla offered before Hannah could respond. "I'm sure you'll get the cake from Sunnyside, but it doesn't hurt to try some different flavors."

Avah sighed. "I love cake."

"As long as it's not green," Hannah added.

"Yuck," Avah agreed.

"Thanks, Banana," Lauren said, reaching through the seats to squeeze her daughter's leg.

"Don't be too long," Hannah said. "I hope you find a spot that's close."

Lauren nodded. "We will."

"Did anyone go with you to look for a wedding dress?" Kayla asked when they were alone in the vehicle.

Lauren frowned. "No. Why do you ask?"

"I would have," Kayla said, willing her sister to understand how badly she wanted them to have a better relationship.

"You didn't know about the wedding."

"You could have trusted me."

"Maybe I should have," Lauren admitted as she turned the corner at the next street on the right. "It was easier to make you the enemy along with Dad. I hated being compared to you because I always fell short."

"That's funny, because I only wanted to be like you."

"I'm glad you weren't." Lauren parked next to the curb. "But as fun as this visit from the Ghost of Weddings Past might be, I need your advice on a current matter."

"Um…okay." Kayla couldn't hide her shock.

"Dad asked me to try to convince Brody not to go through with marrying Avah."

"Dad asked you? Why didn't he ask me?"

"K, come on. This isn't about you."

"I know. I'm sorry." Kayla understood, but at some level, she was still hurt by the fact that she was her father's most loyal daughter, yet when he needed something important, he turned to Lauren.

It was always Lauren.

"What did you tell him?"

"What do you think? I basically told him to sit and spin." Lauren tugged on her earlobe.

This must be really upsetting her. Typically that gesture of anxiety was saved for when Ben was around.

"But I feel bad," Lauren said.

"For getting in a fight with Dad?"

"Keep up, Kayla. I feel bad because I kind of agree with him, and I haven't felt the same way as Dad on a subject since they canceled *Veronica Mars*."

"Are you going to talk to Brody?"

Lauren looked over, her gaze filled with uncertainty. "Do you think I should? Have you talked to him? Would you?"

"No." Kayla shook her head. "We have to trust him to make his own decisions even if he makes a mistake. People shouldn't go through life afraid of making mistakes."

"But marriage is a big deal. I know how hard it can be to get over if it doesn't work out."

"Are you talking about Ben or Tommy?"

Lauren thumped her head on the steering wheel. "I'm in my early thirties and twice divorced. Pathetic."

"If it makes you feel better, you're thirty-four. That's officially the mid-thirties."

Lauren laughed. "Were you always like this?"

Kayla blinked. "Like what?"

"Funny, snarky…" Lauren shrugged. "Easy to be around."

"Yes, definitely," Kayla confirmed. "You missed out."

"I think you might be right," Lauren murmured. "Okay, so I'm not warning Brody."

"Do you think it would help?" Kayla asked, then answered her own question. "I think it's going to make him more determined. We think our baby brother is this easygoing, good-time guy—"

"Are you saying he's not?"

"I'm saying there's more to Brody, and we don't give him enough credit. You and I both went through the tragic loss of our respective mothers, but he doesn't even remember Mom. What do you think that does to a person?"

"He had us," Lauren countered.

"It's not the same. I wonder if there are uncharted depths to him—still waters and all that. Avah might not be who we would have picked for Brody, but we don't get to make that choice. Lord knows I've got no room to talk in the relationship realm."

Lauren's gaze took on an inquisitive glint, and Kayla realized she'd said too much.

"We should get into the shop. I feel bad for sending Hannah off on her own with Avah."

Before Lauren could say more, Kayla exited the Jeep and closed the door. Wishful thinking that her sister would leave the subject alone.

"I thought you were dating some muckety-muck at your law firm," Lauren said as they started across the parking lot. "That's what Hannah told me. The way she described the relationship made it sound like you two were a real power couple."

At Kayla's surprised scoff, Lauren shrugged. "She googled you regularly and forced me to look at a bunch of photos from various fundraisers and whatever."

"He was cheating on me with one of the paralegals at the firm," Kayla said, surprised at how easily the words rolled off her tongue and the fact that her heart didn't even clench. "I called them out, and there was a big HR to-do. I decided to resign instead of pushing the matter."

"That's not right. You should sue. Isn't that what lawyers do?"

"I'm a contracts attorney. I don't sue, nor would I in this case. The attention on me would be too much. Besides, it helped me see that Seth wasn't much of a catch in the first place and that I don't want to work at a firm that would sweep that kind of behavior under the table."

"And he's still living his best cheater life?" Lauren placed her hand on the door to the shop to keep Kayla from opening it.

"I guess. I haven't checked up on him."

"Do you want to egg his car?"

Kayla started to laugh, then realized Lauren was serious. "No, of course not."

"Fine, but know I'm available to ride shotgun if you change your mind. We'll take your car."

"Why would you offer that?"

Lauren cocked her head like she didn't understand Kayla's question. "You're my sister."

"Step," Kayla clarified.

"So I've reminded everyone for years. Maybe we have more in common than I realized, and maybe my daughter was smarter than me in wanting to get to know you. Either way, we *are* family, even if I denied it for too many years. I can be mean to you, but your loser ex can't. You deserve better than that, K."

Kayla's heart stammered as they entered the shop and found Avah and Hannah chowing down on cake samples. She'd said those words to herself a thousand times, but they were easier to believe coming from Lauren.

CHAPTER TWELVE

BEN SENSED LAUREN'S approach before she'd said a word. Even with the crisp afternoon breeze, her citrusy scent floated to him, teasing his senses.

Since she'd been back, it was as if she left orange blossoms in her wake. Everywhere he went around camp, he could smell her, and it was driving him to distraction.

But it was more than her perfume, lotion, or whatever scented her skin. It was her effect on him. His body tingled whenever they were close, and his fingers itched with the physical need to touch her.

His reaction to her, and the fact that he had no control over it, felt ridiculous. He was a grown man, and it wasn't as if he hadn't had relationships over the past seventeen years, not that any of them had stuck. After the heartbreak of his impulsive marriage and dealing with his father's sober recovery, Ben hadn't felt like he had a heart to give anyone else. It had splintered into a million pieces when Lauren walked away.

But now, during their few encounters, the heart he believed irrevocably broken was beginning to mend, as if she was the only one with the power to heal it. In too many ways to count, his heart would always belong to her, but he needed to keep that knowledge to himself until she left town.

He never dreamed he'd willingly take up the mantle

of the tortured hero. That seemed more straightforward than risking being hurt by her again.

"Did you get all this done today?" she asked.

He turned from the sawhorse where he was cutting wood to build the sides of the gingerbread house. "We're only doing a facade, so it isn't like it had to be perfect."

"But it is perfect," she said. "You have no idea how much I needed that this afternoon."

"Wedding dress shopping didn't do it for you?"

"Avah burst into tears on three different occasions— and not happy tears. She tried on every dress in the store, but it was like shopping with Goldilocks. Nothing was right. It feels like she's determined to be unhappy, and I don't know how to fix it."

As he studied her, she pressed her lips together. "There's something else you're not saying," he told her.

She held up her hands. "You don't know that. I'm not fiddling with my ear lobe."

"What else?"

"It's hard to imagine happy-go-lucky Brody settling down with someone like Avah. She told us that they had to order a bed frame when she moved into his apartment because he still just had a mattress and box spring on the floor."

"Your brother has never struck me as the kind of person who gets wrapped up in material possessions."

"Exactly, which is why I'm not sure Avah is right for him. She has champagne tastes, and they're going to be living on a light beer budget."

"Brody will do okay." Ben stepped away from the sawhorse to face her fully. "He's only been working for me for a couple of months, but he's smart, talented, and always makes an effort. I was thinking of promoting him to a project manager role once we begin the new development."

"You don't have to do that because of our history together," Lauren said.

"I'm not." Ben shook his head. "Brody will have earned a promotion because he's done a good job, and I trust him."

"Thank you for telling me," Lauren whispered. "I'm used to him smiling and joking, but he's so serious when he talks about the wedding."

"Is that such a bad thing?" Ben asked.

"Not necessarily, but I know how it can weigh on you to marry for the wrong reasons, and—"

"Ouch." Ben pressed two fingers to his chest.

Lauren shook her head. "I don't mean you, Ben. You can't possibly think I'm talking about us. I married you because I was head over heels in love with you."

"Really?" He forced his voice to remain even. "I thought it was because you were desperate to get out of town, away from your dad, and going to college with me was the quickest way to make that happen."

"I wanted to get away, but I wanted to get away with you."

"Yet when I couldn't, you left anyway. You left me."

"I was scared," she admitted after a moment. She came closer and tucked a strand of dark hair behind her ear. "I understand your honor and loyalty. It's one of the things I like best about you. If your dad needed you, it wasn't going to be a temporary delay. You'd stay. Making it in this town felt different for you than for me, and I loved you so much. It terrified me that if I didn't leave right then, I wouldn't be able to. All my dreams about the big life I was going to create by putting Magnolia in my rearview mirror would be for nothing."

"I wanted to be more important than your need to leave," he told her honestly.

"My mom loved my dad," she said out of nowhere. "Even after they broke up, she held him close in her heart. I think missing him is what drove her to lose herself in some of the bad habits. She didn't know another way to numb the pain of that heartbreak. She used to tell me that she wished she'd never met him. That, of course, meant I wouldn't have been born. As a kid, I didn't know how to separate the two. I figured maybe she wished I'd never been born. She hated and loved him at the same time. I didn't want that. I didn't want my heart to be imprisoned by my love for you, and the only way I knew to make sure that didn't happen was to escape. Unlike my mom, I didn't regret our time together. I could never regret you, Ben."

Something shifted in the air between them. The spark of awareness and attraction that typically burned bright had deepened, different from the first crackling flames of a new fire. This heat could sustain a person even on the coldest nights.

He saw it in her gaze and knew his own eyes mirrored the same. Lauren must have sensed the change and realized its power because she took a step away, nostrils flaring.

"My marriage to Tommy, on the other hand… I don't regret being with him because it brought me Hannah. She's the best part of me—the brightest thing I've ever done, more than I could have imagined. But I shouldn't have tried to bind myself to him. That was never going to end well."

And what if she hadn't? What if Kayla hadn't told Ben that Lauren had married again just before he'd planned to leave town? Would he have truly gone after her?

He didn't even hesitate to answer, at least to himself. He would have found her and fallen to his knees, begging for another chance, promising they would run off together the way they'd planned, only with her baby added to the mix.

He would have said anything to convince her, but he knew it couldn't have worked out for them. His dad had been doing well, and Ben intended to stay in his hometown and single-handedly repair his family's reputation. He was determined to prove that he was more than everyone thought.

That goal, while he'd achieved it, had cost him the only woman he'd ever loved.

And what about now? Yes, he'd agreed to help with the Christmas event in camp, but once the lights were taken down and the decorations put away, he planned to bulldoze the setting of his happiest memories.

He felt like a fool, but he'd come too far now and invested too much. This was his dream, like it or not. He was going to make it come true no matter the cost.

"What did you write in your camp letter back in the day?" he asked. She blinked, then smiled.

"That was the summer before senior year—before everything changed. I wrote that in ten years, I would be Mrs. Ben Donnelly, and you'd have your own engineering firm. I'd be a schoolteacher."

"A schoolteacher?" He started to laugh, then quickly covered it when Lauren sent him a death glare.

"I would have been a great teacher. I love kids. I

loved working with them at this camp. Who knows? Maybe I could have run a summer camp wherever we lived." She flashed a smile. "It was Vermont, by the way. We were going to live in Vermont because I wanted to be in a place with snow."

"You like snow?"

"In theory." She smiled again. "Hannah and I drove up to Vermont over winter break one year."

"Did it meet all of your expectations?"

She made a face. "It was cold, icy and not as charming as Magnolia. Turns out I'm terrible at skiing."

"You didn't love the adrenaline rush?"

"Not as much as I hated feeling not in control."

"Yes, control." Ben blew out a long breath. "I remember how much you like control." The hair at the nape of his neck stood on end when she stepped forward, her gaze on his mouth.

"You made me feel out of control, Ben Donnelly. In the best way possible."

He reached forward and placed his hands on either side of her waist, unable to resist touching her.

"That doesn't have to be past tense." What the hell was he saying? Getting involved with Lauren in this way—in any way—would be a huge mistake.

But he couldn't seem to stop himself from drawing her closer.

"I want to kiss you," he said, recognizing the longing in his own voice.

One side of her mouth tilted. "What's stopping you?"

"Good sense," he murmured.

"Overrated," she shot back, and rose on tiptoe to press her lips to his, deciding for him.

And praise the Lord she did, because the featherlight

contact sent his heart into overdrive, slamming against his rib cage as heat pooled low in his belly. How was it possible that Lauren tasted the way he remembered but at the same time completely new?

He wanted more…so much more. Angling his head, he deepened the kiss, their tongues mingling.

She let out a soft moan that made his knees go weak, then tightened her hold on him like she wasn't certain she could stand on her own.

As profoundly as the connection rocked him, Ben would support her for as long as needed. Her arms wound around his neck, nails grazing his skin and driving him wild.

He suddenly felt as out of control as he had when they were teenagers, wanting nothing more than to lead her back to his cabin, peel away her clothes—all the layers that separated them—and feast on her beautiful body.

But as much as he wanted her, he also wanted to savor this moment and the glorious feeling he got from holding Lauren.

He forced himself to slow down and concentrate on the pleasure of it. He wanted the joy of rediscovering how they fit as if they were made for each other.

When they heard the sound of car wheels on the gravel driveway, he pulled back. Whatever this was—a fleeting moment or the start of something new—they were in it together, at least for now.

Lauren's palms rested against his chest, and even through the heavy weight of the canvas jacket, it felt like she was branding him, although it wasn't necessary. He had always belonged to her, as much as he wanted to deny it.

"It's Kayla," he said, and she jumped away like she'd touched her finger to a hot stove.

"I need to go," Lauren said. "She can't see me here."

"You live here," he reminded her." I don't think she's going to assume—"

"She'll know," Lauren insisted. "She's always been too perceptive for her own good. I'm going to go down by the shore and work on the luminaries. Give me a minute, and then you can send her that way."

He nodded, and she hurried off before he could say anything else. Before he could tell her he wanted more. He returned to work like his entire world hadn't just shifted.

After parking in front of the big cabin, Kayla approached.

"You're really getting into this," she said. "Is that a faux life-sized gingerbread house?"

"It was your sister's idea. She can be very persuasive."

"I know." Kayla studied him. "I thought I saw her standing with you when I pulled up."

"Yeah, she went down toward the sound to check on the luminaries. It takes a lot of sand to ground those things with the winds we get this time of year."

"Sand," Kayla repeated, like the word meant something different than he realized.

"I'm sure she'd appreciate your help if you stopped by to lend a hand."

Kayla produced a thin manila file folder from a tote bag Ben hadn't even noticed her carrying. "Your dad wanted some changes to the contract."

Ben felt the fizziness from the interlude with Lauren rush out of him like a helium balloon that had just been popped with a sharp pair of scissors.

"I told him no more changes. This is the fifth revision he's sent over, Kayla, and each one asks for something more. He is slowly switching this from a partnership to him being in control."

He thought about what Lauren had said earlier regarding control, and it left a bad taste in his mouth. He didn't want to believe that she had anything in common with her father, although he knew part of the reason they butted heads so viciously was because of how they were alike. Kayla bit down on her lower lip and looked toward the water, where small ripples played across the surface.

The sound was protected by the marsh on one side and the dry land of camp on the other, so the winter winds didn't whip up the waves as they could at the beach. But it still looked cold and dark, exactly how he felt when he thought about what he risked by going into business with Robert Maxwell.

"He's worried about your commitment to the project," she said after a minute.

"What is that supposed to mean?"

"Your loyalties," she continued. "Now that Lauren is back—"

"She doesn't have anything to do with this."

"I know," Kayla said quickly, "and I don't want her to find out I'm doing more of Dad's bidding. Please, Ben. She was nice to me today."

He laughed. "She was nice to me, too."

"Is something happening between you? I'm getting a vibe. Are you catching feels for her again?"

"No." He could say that with certainty, because feels

for Lauren weren't something that he needed to catch. She was a part of him whether he liked it or not.

"You guys could get back together. Stranger things have happened."

"Are you sure about that?"

"You two were good together. Like Barbie and Ken."

"Hardly, and you can't do both. You can't advocate for your dad and your sister. That is an inherent conflict of interest."

"So that you know…" Kayla looked to the ground momentarily before lifting her gaze to his, eyes shining. "If I had to pick, I'd choose Lauren. I want you to know that I'm not like my dad."

He believed her, but he wasn't sure she'd have a choice with her loyalties, just like he didn't have a choice.

He'd already secured Jim Lowery's apartment in the independent living community. He'd had to sign a contract for two years and pay the first six months of rent up front. That was how in demand the apartments were. Ben had also taken care of Jim's medical debt with the sale of his house. They'd both be in big trouble if this deal didn't allow him to recoup the money he'd spent.

"I'm not like your dad either, K. We're in this together."

"You can't tell Lauren that I'm helping Dad. Promise me."

"I promise," he said without hesitation. Lauren wasn't planning to stay in Magnolia, so in a few weeks, this wouldn't matter. At least, that's what he told himself.

If only he could believe it.

"I'll read over the changes tonight, but I'm not promising anything. We have a signed contract."

"Dad is threatening—"

"I'm not interested in your father's threats. It's not complicated. There's no reason he shouldn't honor the current contract—the one we agreed on. I'm helping with the camp Christmas carnival. Nothing else changes."

Except Lauren and his wanting her. That changed everything.

Kayla looked like she believed his words as much as he did. "I'm going to see if Lauren needs help."

"You better not let your dad find out," Ben muttered, then shook his head. "I'm sorry. That was uncalled for."

"You're right, though. He'll take it as a personal attack if he finds out I pitched in around here. I'm going to take my chances. She's worth it, you know?"

He sighed. "I do."

She flashed a meaningful smile. "I thought as much."

"It's nothing, Kayla," he called as she walked away.

"Keep telling yourself that," she answered. "Maybe you'll believe it."

Despite everything, he returned to the project with a new lightness in his heart. Maybe it was the magic of Christmas or this place, but despite his denial, Ben could almost believe in second chances.

CHAPTER THIRTEEN

"WHY CAN'T I read them?" Hannah asked, dancing around Lauren as they took care of last-minute decorations at camp two days later.

"Because they don't belong to you," Lauren answered. "Help me put up this last strand of lights. I want to make sure people are impressed and awed tonight."

Tonight was the soft kickoff of the Winter Wonderland Carnival at Camp Blossom, and she had high hopes for attendance. There would be a fake snowball toss, a hot chocolate booth, a station for making maple taffy on ice shavings, the gingerbread house where Santa would make an appearance every night, and a host of holiday-themed games for kids.

They were doing a preview evening for family, friends and business owners from the area so they'd have time to make tweaks or deal with any snafus before the first big weekend.

Jim was thrilled at the prospect of the camp being full of people again, and more than anything, Lauren didn't want to disappoint the man who meant so much to her.

Guilt clattered around her mind and heart like an unwelcome houseguest since her return to Magnolia. She should have kept in touch with Jim and Nancy over the years, but her affection for them had been so intertwined with her love for Ben that it hadn't seemed possible. Brody had told her on his occasional visits to Atlanta how close Ben remained with the Lowerys, and Lauren had never gained the emotional distance to separate how she felt for him with what this place meant to her.

Hannah had been dividing her time between her grandfather's house and camp. She liked the creature comforts the mansion on the beach offered—soft sheets, dependable hot water, a housekeeper and strong Wi-Fi for her online classes.

But to Lauren's surprise, her daughter also came to camp daily to pitch in. It seemed that by giving her a little space, Hannah had decided her mom wasn't such an ogre.

Lauren had returned to the cabin where the notes to their future selves had been hidden and pulled out the ones Maren and Izzy had written.

She'd been thinking a lot about her former friends recently and felt a good bit of regret for not keeping in touch with them.

Hannah was tracking down contact information for both of them, and Lauren mulled over the idea of reaching out—or at least mailing off their notes. It had meant a lot to her to revisit the past, remembering the sweet moments along with the difficult memories.

"I don't think they'd mind," Hannah said. "Maybe we should look at the notes to ensure there's nothing weird or creepy in them. Like one of them planned to become a serial killer."

"Neither Izzy nor Maren would have planned a life of crime." Lauren held out her hand. "Give me your phone again. I want to see that photo of Izzy. She looks the same as she did when we were teenagers."

"What about Maren Barrish?"

Lauren thought about her brash and prickly friend. "I wouldn't have pegged her as a contender for 'America's sexiest weather girl.' She was always beautiful, but when we were younger, she was serious about being a scientist. She loved being outside at camp and had a weird fascination with the weather."

"Maybe it was more exciting to be famous."

"I guess." Lauren wasn't convinced. She thought she'd known Maren well, and the girl she'd known wanted to change the weather world, not have social media fan accounts posting photos and breaking down her style choices.

"I still haven't found current contact info for Izzy," Hannah reported, tapping a finger against the screen. "It looks like she quit her job as a social worker last month, but I can't find anything else about her. No social media accounts, nothing on the White Pages app."

"That's kind of strange, right?" Lauren asked with a frown. "Not that I expect you to go super sleuthing, but in this day and age…"

"I could call the agency where she worked in Boston," Hannah suggested. "Tracking down your friends is way more fun than World History questions."

"School is more important." Lauren smoothed a hand over her daughter's shiny hair. "The most important."

Hannah made a face. "It's weird when you talk like a mom."

"I am a mom," Lauren reminded the girl. "Your mom."

"You're not like other moms," Hannah countered, and Lauren felt a pang of insecurity shoot through her.

"Does staying with Grandpa make you wish I was more conventional? I could have found some nice man to marry and given you a stepdad with a steady job to take care of us the way Kayla's mom did."

Hannah pocketed her phone then turned. "We did okay, I guess. You and me against the world."

"Really?" Lauren felt heat radiate through her chest. "I've been getting the distinct impression you consider me a failure in almost every way. Your exact words after *you* wrecked the Jeep were, 'This is your fault.'"

"That obviously wasn't true." Hannah let out a sheepish laugh. "I knew it, but it was easier to blame you than take responsibility." She chewed on her bottom lip for a moment. "You know, Mom, I thought you were exaggerating when you talked about how difficult and annoying Grandpa can be, but he's just like you said."

"Wow, that didn't take long." Lauren scrubbed a hand over her eyes when tears threatened.

"What's wrong? I thought you'd be happy that I agree with you about him."

"I won't deny it feels like sweet vindication, but I don't want you to go through any of what I did. Maybe now you're ready to stay overnight at camp with me?"

"He has a steam shower and one of those fancy ice makers on the counter that makes tiny ice."

"Is tiny ice worth his emotional manipulation and gaslighting?"

"I'm not going to let him do that to me," Hannah answered. "You raised me to be stronger than that."

"Oh." Lauren reached forward and pulled her daughter into a tight hug.

"But I also really like the steam shower. I'm not quite ready to give that up."

"Fair enough."

"I like getting to know Aunt Kayla, too. I'm sorry if that upsets you."

"It doesn't." Lauren touched a finger to her earlobe. "I never meant for you to grow up not knowing any family besides me. You and me against the world is a fun sentiment, but I get that family is important. I shouldn't have tried to keep you away from them for so long—even Grandpa, although my intentions were good. I didn't want him to have an opportunity to hurt you the way he did me."

"You would have protected me," Kayla said, so sure in her belief that it made Lauren's eyes sting again.

"I hope so, but I didn't trust myself either, and I made my sister—"

"You didn't use the word *step*," Hannah said with an exaggerated eyebrow wiggle.

"It was implied," Lauren lied. "I made her into a bad guy, too, because it was easier than facing the fact that my dad loved his adopted daughter better than he liked me."

"If it makes you feel any better, I don't think he's been particularly easy on her." Hannah shrugged. "She's also not as good at standing up to him as you. I think it's because she was adopted and afraid of being sent away."

"He would never have done that," Lauren said, then took another long breath. "Who knows what he would have done? I'm fine with you getting to know her, and you should enjoy that steam shower while you can. After Uncle Brody's wedding, it's going to be back to pathetic water pressure for you."

Hannah looked momentarily chagrined, then said, "Maybe we could find a place with better water pressure. Even a little house or condo that we owned instead of rented. I want a home that belongs to us, although I guess I'll be going to college after all. I'm pretty smart."

"You are when you apply yourself."

"Now you *totally* sound like a real mom."

"I am a *real* mom," Lauren insisted and hugged her daughter again. "Now be a real kid and go finish your homework. World History doesn't wait for anyone."

Hannah made a face but nodded. "I'll keep looking for your friend Izzy. I'm into doing this sort of work like I'm on one of those detective shows. Maybe I'll work for the FBI."

"You need a college degree to be an FBI agent," Lauren said, "but you can do anything you set your mind to."

"Thanks, Mom. I love you."

"I love you, too, Hannah Banana."

Lauren watched Hannah make her way down the path, relieved and overwhelmed by the changes in her daughter since they'd arrived in Magnolia. It felt as though Camp Blossom still held its same enchantment, and every day it became more difficult to think about saying goodbye.

Why couldn't the magic of Christmas last forever?

IF LAUREN FELT on top of the world after her conversation with Hannah, she was absolutely over the moon when the last of the guests pulled out of the camp parking lot later that night.

"Well, little Lauren, you did it," Jim said, wrapping an arm around her shoulder. They stood with Ben, Hannah, Brody and Kayla as the camp emptied.

"It wasn't just me. The gingerbread house and the hot chocolate stand were all Ben."

"You're right." Jim gave a big thumbs-up in Ben's direction. "The two of you make a good team."

Lauren felt her face heat at those words.

"Everyone pitched in to help, and I appreciate it." Jim smiled at Hannah. "You've got a way with the kids, just like your mom did when she was a counselor here."

"It was fun," Hannah said. "Way more fun than I thought."

"That's high praise." Jim laughed.

"Maybe if the cybersecurity thing doesn't work out, I'll be a teacher."

Lauren felt pride warm her heart.

"Cybersecurity?" Kayla frowned. "What's that all about?"

"Just trying to track down a couple of old friends," Lauren answered. "Jim, do you remember Maren and Izzy?"

"How could I forget? There was way too much squealing when the three of you were together."

"Mom was a squealer?" Hannah laughed and then glanced at Ben. "That was a rhetorical question."

"Oh, my, Hannah." Lauren shook her head. "Inappropriate."

"I like how you operate, kid." Brody gave Hannah a high five before turning to Lauren. "That was pretty great. You made this place feel as festive as the North Pole. As a bonus, I had a chance to talk to Kayla's new suitor, Scott O'Day. He seems like a decent guy and has a lot of ideas about what he might want to do next. Most of them involve something that will benefit the environment and his bottom line. I appreciate a businessperson who cares about his impact on the world. Quite a change from some people I know."

Lauren saw Ben fidget, and without thinking, took a protective step closer. "He's talking about my dad, not you," she told him.

"And Scott is not my suitor," Kayla said. "He's Dad's neighbor."

"He's also Camp Blossom's neighbor since a big parcel of his land borders us," Jim said. "Robert would love to get his grubby hands on that property."

"But it's not for sale, right?" Ben asked. "We talked to Scott at the start of this, and he wanted to keep his acreage wild."

"Yeah," Kayla said, but Lauren heard something in her voice she didn't like. "Dad knows Scott doesn't want to sell."

Knowing and accepting were two different things for Robert Maxwell.

"All that fun wore me out," Jim said. "I'm going to head back to my cabin. Ben, will you shut off the lights before you call it a night?"

"You bet, Jim."

Lauren placed her hand lightly on the older man's arm. "Camp Blossom still has the magic. After tonight, we're going to get so much traction from word of mouth and the photos Avery is planning to upload to the Magnolia social media accounts. We'll be flooded with visitors on opening weekend. It'll feel like old times."

Jim rubbed a hand against his hip. "Other than my achy joints and missing Nancy. She would love to see this." He hugged Lauren. "Thanks, sweetheart. You made an old man really happy."

It took her a moment to answer around the ball of emotion lodged in her throat. "This place makes everyone happy, Jim. It's my pleasure to help."

"I can walk you back to your cabin," Kayla offered.

"What do you think?" Lauren asked Hannah. "Do you want to stay at camp tonight?"

"Maybe another night, Mom. Uncle Brody and I are in the middle of an intense *Call of Duty* battle."

"Are you staying at Dad's house?" Lauren asked as she glanced between Kayla and Brody.

"Just for a couple of nights," he said. "Avah has a few friends in town for a bach… I mean…they're just visiting her."

"A bachelorette party?" Lauren looked at Kayla. "Did you know about this?"

Kayla shook her head. "I guess we didn't make the cut. Brody, you and Hannah can walk Jim to his cabin with me then I'll drive us home. Looks like Lauren and I will be taking you out for a bachelor night instead."

"I think I'm supposed to do that," Ben murmured.

"I remember my bachelor party." Jim gave a devious laugh as he started down the path. "The fellas and I went down to Myrtle Beach for the weekend. I don't remember much of it."

"I'm planning to remember," Brody said.

"Can I come, too?" Hannah asked.

"You bet." Brody inclined his head. "Because nothing makes for an awesome bachelor party like it being hosted by a guy's two older sisters and his niece."

"Don't forget your boss," Ben reminded him.

Brody made a face. "This is going to be a wild time."

"It's going to be epic," Lauren confirmed as Brody, Hannah, Kayla and Jim walked away, ignoring the pit in her stomach when she thought about her brother's impending nuptials.

"You can't say anything," Ben whispered in her ear.

"I'm not planning to, but what kind of woman doesn't invite her soon-to-be sisters-in-law to a bachelorette weekend? Also, how much of a party can she have when she's pregnant? She kicked my brother out of his apartment and then didn't bother mentioning it to Kayla or me."

"Maybe a woman who can tell you don't approve of her for your brother," Ben suggested.

Lauren scoffed. "She doesn't know that."

"People know these things. Women sense them."

"Even if she can feel the shadow of subtle judgment rolling off me, Kayla is not like that. She's nice. She's a better person."

He turned to face her and threaded his fingers through her hair. "You're a good person. You care about the people you love, and you've raised a strong, funny, smart-as-a-whip daughter—"

"Who's finishing up the semester doing online school because of getting in trouble."

"Kids make mistakes. You're going to make sure she stays on the right track. I know who you are, and you won't give up on her."

"Like I gave up on us?"

She expected him to pull away even though it was the last thing she wanted. Why did she even mention their past? Why couldn't she let it be? But she couldn't or wouldn't.

If Ben was going to be with her—and based on the heat in his gaze, he wanted her as much as she wanted him—if they were going to be together, he would choose the woman she was now, not some halcyon memory of what they'd shared a lifetime ago.

"I was angry then," he said, leaning in and kissing her. "You broke my heart."

"Ditto," she said, and nipped at the edge of his mouth. He sucked in a breath but didn't release her. "Are you still angry?"

"Mostly, I'm regretful. I regret letting you go."

"No." She pulled back at the sound of her sister's car. Although Lauren knew they couldn't be seen from here, it was an innate reaction.

Ben frowned, but before he could follow her lead and step farther away, she reached up and cupped his face with her hands.

"No regrets," she clarified. "For either of us. Not from then and not now." She loved the warmth of his skin, the way his stubble tickled her cheek.

His mouth kicked up. "Is this the part where I ask my cabin or yours?"

"Yours," she said. "You have a bigger bed."

"And you think you're going to need more room to stretch out?" He lifted her hand and gently kissed her knuckles.

"You never know," she said, feeling cheeky and flirty and like the weight of worry had disappeared, cast to the dark shadows of her heart.

"Then I can't wait to find out." As he kissed her, she felt her resistance breaking apart like shards of a glacier. Then Ben took her hand and led her down a path lighted by solar lamps. In the stillness of the night, with only silence and the beauty of this place surrounding them, Lauren found herself believing in the magic of Christmas. This season could renew a person in both big and small ways.

Maybe it didn't matter if she deserved another chance at happiness. Christmas wasn't truly about stockings full of toys or lumps of coal. It was about faith and hope; for the first time in many years, Lauren wanted to believe in both.

CHAPTER FOURTEEN

KAYLA FACED OFF with her father two days later, inwardly trembling at the potential consequences of standing up to him but keeping her outward appearance placid like the tranquil doll he expected her to be.

Except dolls didn't have backbones, and Kayla was doing her best to use hers.

It wasn't easy. Acting as the equivalent of a human doormat was familiar, a rut in a dirt road the wheels of her heart seemed to find over and over.

"This is a slap in the face, Kayla. You're not only undermining my plan for the land. You're undermining me personally."

"I'm helping to serve hot chocolate at a Christmas carnival, Dad." She crossed her arms over her chest. "Do you think you might be overreacting?"

"I was in town yesterday for a meeting with Dylan Scott. He's one of the main real estate developers responsible for Magnolia's resurgence. He told me how excited his wife and her sisters are about the revival of Camp Blossom."

"He's married to Carrie Reed, right?"

"Yes, the daughter of Magnolia's most famous resident. Although he was critically panned, Niall Reed's paintings were always a huge commercial success. Now the girl is making a name for herself as an artist."

"I think Carrie would be considered a woman, and she's quite talented. But what does that have to do with anything?" Kayla was genuinely confused. "I know she helps with the holiday festival every year along with her sisters, but who cares?"

"*I* care if some sentimental do-gooder decides to take up the camp's land as a project. It's bad enough for your flighty, irresponsible sister to beat the save-the-camp drum."

"She isn't either of those things," Kayla felt compelled to point out.

"She has the time to take almost a month off work and put together a Christmas carnival to indulge a man whose days as Camp Blossom's owner are numbered. What kind of responsible adult can do that?"

"The kind who has flexibility in her schedule," Kayla shot back. "One who is committed to caring for her kid when that kid needs her."

"Even Hannah understands that Camp Blossom is awful. Why do you think she spends most nights here?"

"Maybe she's trying to get to know her grandfather. Would you rather she didn't?"

"Of course not, although Lauren has managed to raise a daughter just as frustratingly independent and headstrong as her."

"I'm sure Hannah would take that as a compliment."

"Lauren never rubbed off on you that way, thankfully." He considered her for several seconds. "Or at least she didn't until now."

Kayla's phone pinged, and she picked it up from the counter. A message from Scott. Her gaze darted to the window facing his property without thinking about the audience. "I've got to go."

"Was that Scott who texted?" her father demanded.

"What makes you think that?" she asked, hoping she sounded casual.

"You're blushing."

"I'm hot. Standing in my coat while you lecture me really makes me sweat."

"Answer the question."

"Yes, Scott is going out to camp with me."

"You're still working that angle." Robert nodded. "You didn't tell me."

Because she hadn't wanted her father to know how much time she'd been spending with their solitary neighbor. Time that had nothing to do with a land deal and everything to do with her feelings for the man.

What wasn't to like about Scott O'Day? Handsome, funny, thoughtful…he was the whole package. But what Kayla appreciated most was that he seemed to like her not because she could offer him something, had the right job, wore nice clothes, or was the kind of woman appropriate enough to bring home to his parents.

She couldn't explain it, but he liked her; no bells and whistles needed. In fact, he seemed to be amused when she got worked up about something inconsequential like she was a puppy trying to get his attention by running in circles when all she needed to do was calm down.

"It's not an angle. Scott has said no to selling. He's helping out to be nice and have fun."

"Selling hot chocolate at a lame Christmas carnival isn't fun for a man like him. He must want something, possibly in your pants."

"Dad, stop."

Robert held up his hands. "No judgment here, Kayla.

You're an adult, and despite my best efforts, it doesn't sound like Seth will take you back. If Scott—"

"Your efforts," she interrupted, feeling the aforementioned color seep from her cheeks. "What is that supposed to mean?"

"You know."

"I don't. Tell me."

"I called him. Sometimes decisions are made in haste. You two were good together."

"No, we weren't," Kayla countered. "I wanted us to be, but he cheated. There's nothing good about that."

"Wild oats." Robert flicked his hand in the air like he was dispelling an annoying puff of smoke.

When Kayla returned to her hometown after her life had so spectacularly fallen apart, she'd been excited by her dad's suggestion that she do some work with his business.

For most of her life, she'd wished to be seen as legitimate enough to play a vital role in her father's life. Lauren and Brody had rejected Robert in their own way. But despite her loyalty, Kayla felt like her dad didn't see her as worthy of a place at his side.

That hadn't changed. He didn't want her at his side; he wanted her under his thumb. Was that future worth the price she would have to pay for it?

"I'm going, Dad. We can talk about this later or not. Preferably not."

"You might want to put on lipstick before you leave," he suggested. "Your mother always took so much pride in her appearance."

Kayla felt his words like a blow to the gut, but the knockout punch was still to come.

"Lauren has it easy," he continued, "with her coloring and that dark hair. Some women look good without makeup, but others—"

"I get it, Dad." The words felt like spikes on her tongue, but she spoke them without emotion. "Thanks for the insight."

"I'm trying to help," he said, holding his hands up like he needed to protect himself against her overreacting. "Everything I do or say is for your own good. You know that, right? You've always been the one who understands how things are."

"I do understand," she said and forced a smile. Always amenable and compliant. "You should come out to the carnival. Hot chocolate on the house."

He scoffed. "Not a chance."

"Your loss." She turned and hurried away, trying to swallow back the tears that clogged her throat.

She got in her car and took a few calming breaths before heading next door to pick up Scott.

It was a lovely property, although the house felt as cold and impersonal as her dad's. She wondered what it would look like on the inside. Scott had invited her in several times, but she'd made excuses. Now she second-guessed why. Was it because she knew if things went further with Scott, she would end up using their relationship to try to advance her father's agenda?

As angry as she was, that didn't stop her from taking out a tube of lipstick, smoothing a layer over her lips, then rubbing a fingertip on it so that she could dab a little color onto her cheeks.

What a fool she was. Always a fool.

Scott opened the car door and got in a moment later. "Big question. Are we using mini marshmallows or regular size?" he asked as she shifted into Drive. "Because I have strong feelings about marsh—"

He broke off and turned in his seat to face her. "What's wrong? What happened?"

"Nothing." She shook her head, pulled a tissue out of the glove compartment, and swiped it across her mouth. "Mini marshmallows in hot chocolate. The big ones are for roasting."

"You're good at that." He studied her as she pulled out onto the beach road. "Better than me, and I'm an expert."

"At what?" she asked, even though she didn't want to know.

"Acting like nothing is wrong. My partner was good at it, too. But Pete jumped off the edge of a bar on the fifty-fourth-story of a Manhattan skyscraper, so the gig was up. No pretending at that point."

"I'm not going to jump off a building," she said. "There aren't buildings higher than two stories around here. It's a county ordinance."

"Kayla."

"That was terrible. I'm sorry. I can't imagine what it must have been like to lose your business partner."

"He was also a friend, which made it even worse. I thought the business was important. I thought it defined Pete and me. Losing him defined me more than any app, success, or money ever could. You understand that you are more than your résumé, job title, or what your father wants you to be, right?"

"Sometimes I feel like I either have to resign myself to being less or prepare for a lifetime of trying."

Scott reached over and took her hand from her lap.

He linked their fingers together. "I hate to ask, but does this have anything to do with me and my land?"

"I told him you wouldn't sell, and I was done asking." She hadn't exactly said those words to her father but hoped they were implied.

"He isn't going to give up."

She shook her head. "No."

"Do you want me to sell to him?"

Kayla sucked in a breath and tried to tug her hand away, but Scott held fast. "Don't ask me that."

"Why?"

"Because I can't be trusted when it comes to loyalty. Ask my sister."

"I thought you and your sister were getting along now. I'm excited to meet her."

"When we were younger, she was busy butting heads with our dad, and I did my best to take advantage of it. I'd show off another school honor or an A on a paper for every detention Lauren got. I was a complete suck-up. A fat lot of good it did me."

"You were a kid. Give yourself a break."

"Did you manipulate your parents when you were younger?"

"I tried," he said with a laugh. "My mom never fell for it."

"Because you had so many brothers and sisters?" Kayla guessed. Scott had told her he was the youngest of seven kids.

"Because she had a nose for crap. You remind me of her."

"That's a compliment I don't deserve," she said quickly.

"You aren't great at taking compliments."

"Sure I am," she argued.

He squeezed her fingers again. "You look beautiful tonight."

"Wait until you meet my sister. Lauren's mom was one of the most beautiful women in the world—a literal supermodel. Lauren looks like her."

"For the record, that's not how you accept a compliment."

"Oh." Kayla hadn't noticed her natural tendency to deflect praise until Scott pointed it out. "I guess I'm not used to receiving them."

"You should be."

"I'll let you tell me how good I am at serving hot chocolate when we get to camp."

"Not the same thing. I want to compliment who you are, not what you can do."

She laughed, but it sounded like she had something stuck in her throat. "You're venturing into unfamiliar territory."

"I don't like that."

"If I'm being honest, I don't either."

"I like your honesty."

Kayla opened her mouth, a self-deprecating remark on the tip of her tongue, then shut it again. "Thank you," she said simply.

"Was that hard?" Scott asked, not like he was making fun of her but as if he genuinely wanted to know.

"Kind of," she admitted. She pulled to a stop just as they turned onto the winding driveway that led to Camp Blossom. "So that you know, I put up all the greenery on the sign." She pointed to the wooden sign that had welcomed visitors to camp for as long as she could remember. "In case you'd like to notice my innate sense of Christmas style, which is different from a competence at hanging pine boughs."

"I do." To her surprise and delight, Scott leaned over and brushed a kiss across her lips. "In case you were wondering, I like noticing almost everything about you."

The kiss made her feel like a champagne cork had been popped inside her chest. Her insides were fizzy and light, and even though she wouldn't allow herself to believe that anything serious could come of this easy flirtation, she refused to let those thoughts overtake her happiness in this moment.

Kayla spent far too much time being realistic and practical, trying to make others happy. People like her ex-boyfriend and her father. None of her efforts had given her the kind of effervescent joy she got from being with Scott, not to mention his sweet kiss.

"Wow, this place is incredible," he said as they drove into camp a few minutes later. "My land butts up against the camp property, but it's not like this. How long have the current owners been running the camp?"

"The Lowerys have owned this place for at least three generations," she told him. As familiar as Kayla was with the landscape from her time as a camper and more recent visits, today, with the sun shining through the fir trees and the holiday decorations giving the whole place a sense of wonder, she saw it through new eyes.

"From what I understand, the family was deeded the land from the church organization that owned it. Even back then, having this kind of property on the water would have been special, so that fact it's lasted this long as a summer camp and retreat center is exceptional."

"It reminds me of the kind of summer camp experience my mom used to talk about." Scott leaned forward as the first glimpses of the cabins came into view. "She went to some place up in the Poconos and always told us it was the highlight of her year to get out of the city and into nature. I swear she would nearly shed a tear thinking of her happy memories from childhood."

Scott had shared how much his mother's death when he was a junior in high school and the last kid still living at home had impacted him.

"Did you ever go to summer camp?" Kayla asked softly, not wanting to intrude on his thoughts but curious about his reaction to Camp Blossom.

"Not really. There was a day camp at the local Y she'd send me to, but there wasn't extra money, and my dad, who'd never left Philadelphia, didn't see the point of it. He said we could have as much fun running around the woods behind our house." He shrugged. "We had plenty of fun, but I imagine it wasn't the same. You came here every year, right?"

"Yeah." She rolled her lips together, then smiled as Jim waved at them from the porch of the main cabin. "I hated it. My sister was a legend here. She probably still holds records for earning the most badges in one session. I was the kid afraid to fall asleep because my bunkmates would dip my hand in warm water."

She parked the car around the back of the main cabin and turned off the engine. "That was a long time ago," she said with a laugh that felt forced. "I can remember the good things now."

Scott stared at her with a confused look clouding his gentle brown eyes. "Why warm water?"

"You don't know the old 'dip your hand in warm water to pee' trick? It's a camp classic."

"That's mean."

"People can be mean. Kids especially."

"I don't like the thought of anyone being mean to you, Kayla."

The sincerity in his voice made that fizzy feeling inside her shimmer again. As they got out of the car and headed toward the cabin, Kayla reminded herself that her father would survive if Scott didn't sell the land to him.

And that Scott would be just fine if he agreed to it.

The question was how involved she wanted to be in the arrangement, and the truth of that was less and less the more time she spent with Scott. Somehow it felt as though her father would punish her for her disloyalty, even if she hadn't done anything to act on those feelings yet.

Like Robert Maxwell had some kind of magic mirror hidden in the depths of that big house where he could see Kayla's doubts about whether to keep pushing Scott.

What would that tiny rebellion cost her if her father discovered it?

She introduced Scott to Jim, Ben and her sister. He and Hannah did the strange fist-pump greeting they'd devised the first time they'd met.

Their arrival was timed a couple of hours before the carnival was scheduled to start to help with last-minute preparations. Lauren seemed uncharacteristically nervous, and Kayla noticed that Ben found small excuses to brush his hand across her back or lean into her as if he were trying to settle her anxiety.

To Kayla's shock, her sister didn't bristle or push him

away. She seemed to like it. That was an interesting turn of events and one Kayla hadn't expected.

"I can't imagine this place as a bunch of McMansions crowded together," Scott said as they readied the drinks at the hot chocolate stand in the clearing next to the big cabin. "It's a damn shame."

"That's not how it's going to look," Kayla countered, feeling oddly defensive, especially since she'd had the same thought when her father first explained the plan. "It's going to be a community with plenty of character."

He raised a brow, making his doubts known without saying a word.

"You've met Ben. Even if you don't trust my father, it should be obvious that Ben is a stand-up guy."

"I like him," Scott agreed. "Not as much as I like you. You're special, which I want to focus on right now. You and hot chocolate. Thanks for inviting me out here, Kayla."

She was about to tell him he'd better be careful what he wished for but instead whispered, "You're welcome."

That simple statement felt like it meant something. Scott meant something to her. For the first time in her life, Kayla was putting what she wanted before what other people expected of her. The change felt scary and exhilarating, and she couldn't wait to see where it led.

CHAPTER FIFTEEN

THE FOLLOWING MORNING, Ben let himself into his father's small apartment behind a strip mall about ten miles south of town. "Dad, I've got your groceries. You awake?"

"Did you get the red licorice this time?" Bart Donnelly called from the bedroom.

Ben rolled his eyes as he placed the bags on the scuffed kitchen counter and listened to the sound of his father's cane on the hallway's hardwood floor.

"One bag," he confirmed as Bart came into the kitchen.

"I need at least two to get me through the week."

"Dad, we had this talk before. Your doc has told you to cut back on sugar. Your last labs showed that you're in the pre-diabetic range. That's serious."

"I'm an old man and an alcoholic who hasn't had a drink in over sixteen years. You and the docs expect me to give up sugar, too? It's too much, Benny. I need some pleasure in life."

Ben put the meager assortment of staples his dad required weekly in the cabinets. "The pleasure is in waking up every day, which will be much less so if you end up with type 2 diabetes. You're sixty-five, buddy. Not exactly one foot in the grave if I have anything to say about it." He pushed the bag of red vines across the counter toward his father. "Besides, if you want some-thing different at the grocery, you can buy it yourself."

Bart's eyes narrowed. "Dragging around this cane? I don't want people to see me like this and know how pathetic I've become."

His fingers gripping the corner of the counter, Ben tried not to show his frustration. Getting angry at his father wouldn't do any good, but he hated how small Bart's life had become, especially since a fall a couple of years earlier had left him using a cane for mobility.

"You aren't pathetic."

"You keep telling yourself that. Want a piece?" his dad asked after tearing open the bag of licorice.

"Sure, why not? It's ten in the morning. A perfect time for licorice."

"Exactly my point." Although Bart didn't directly ad-dress Ben's sarcasm, he tossed the bag with more force than was necessary. "Why not enjoy life? Why can't I enjoy more than one bag of licorice a week?"

Ben had half a mind to stalk out of the house, drive back to the grocery and buy every damn licorice bag on the shelf to end this argument once and for all.

He drew in a slow breath. "I think you'd enjoy life more if you left this apartment."

"I leave sometimes."

"Other than when I force you out to a doctor's ap-pointment, name a time."

"I have a big window," Bart hedged, then shoved an-other bite of licorice into his mouth and chewed. "What more do I need to see?"

They'd had this argument repeatedly as Bart had slowly stopped venturing into the world. Consumed by the day-to-day grind, Ben hadn't noticed it at first, but something had changed. Although Ben was happy his dad hadn't returned to the drinking, fighting and general bad behavior that had been a hallmark of Ben's childhood, he wished his dad took more pleasure in his current life.

Maybe part of that was Ben's fault. Bart had relied on him so heavily when he'd first gotten sober, but once he'd been stable, Ben had transitioned his focus to the legacy he was trying to create in town. Repairing the damage to his family's reputation had become his only priority.

In his compulsion to rectify that, he'd managed to remain oblivious to the changes in his father—the low-grade depression and health troubles that signaled his pulling away from the outer world.

His slow recovery from the fall had been, in many ways, the final nail in the coffin.

Bart found little reason to participate in community activities, and he hadn't bothered to renew his driver's license, constantly complaining about how his leg ached if he got behind the wheel. That had shrunk his world further, but again, Ben had been dealing with his own life, so he assumed things would get better without his intervention.

But they hadn't, and he didn't know how to fix it or if it could be remedied.

"I'd like you to come to the grand opening of the Christmas carnival this weekend at camp," he said, forcing a smile. "We had a soft launch last night."

"What's a soft launch mean? Did you have a waterbed as part of the entertainment?"

"No waterbed at a family Christmas carnival." Ben massaged a hand over the back of his neck. "We invited friends and family from around town to check things out and make sure it all went well."

"I'm family."

"I asked you about the event last week, Dad," Ben reminded his father. "You said no."

"Is this where you and Robert Maxwell get out your fancy house plans and try to finagle people into giving you money?"

"I'm not finagling anybody, and Robert has nothing to do with the carnival. Nothing will happen as far as plans for the development until after Christmas. I've promised Lauren."

"Lauren's back in town?" his dad asked. There was something in his tone—a level of interest Ben wasn't sure whether or not to like.

"I'm pretty sure I mentioned that to you."

"I'm positive you didn't, son. How's it going between the two of you? Does she still hate you and me in equal measure?"

Ben immediately thought about Lauren coming apart in his arms late last night when she'd snuck into his cabin after camp had gone dark and quiet. He could say with certainty that she didn't hate him, although how she truly felt or would feel after he bulldozed the structures around the property remained to be seen.

"She never blamed you," he told his father. That much was true. "All of her anger was directed at me, and rightly so."

"If I hadn't needed your help, you wouldn't have had to stay."

"I was happy to help, and you know I'm proud of you for staying sober all these years."

"How's she doing?" his dad asked, ignoring Ben's

words. Bart did not like to talk about the disease that had cost both of them so much or his path to recovery.

"She's good. She has a sixteen-year-old daughter. Hannah looks just like her and has as much spunk as her mom."

"That doesn't surprise me." Bart scratched his chin. "It didn't take her long after you to find somebody new."

"No, it didn't." Ben had never shared with his father that he'd considered going after Lauren. What purpose would that serve when nothing had come of it?

"Maybe I *will* venture out to camp, so long as you promise I won't have to talk to Jim Lowery."

"Isn't it time you let go of your resentment toward Jim? He never did anything to you. He never did anything but help take care of me."

"Ain't that the point? I was your daddy. I know your mom left, but we were doing fine. Jim didn't need to butt in and pretend he was better for you than me." Bart inclined his head. "Even if that were true. A man has his pride, you know."

Ben nodded, thinking about everything he'd done and how hard he worked to feel proud of carrying the Donnelly name. "Yeah, Dad. I know what you mean. The carnival opens Friday night and will go for the next three weekends."

"Up until right before Christmas Eve?"

"Exactly. Do you want me to pick you up?"

"Nope, I don't think so."

Ben blinked. "I thought you said you were willing to attend. You can't drive."

"I don't know if it's such a great idea after all. I guess I want to do the mature thing, Ben, and I don't want to intrude on—"

"I invited you. You're not intruding." He didn't want to admit how the sick feeling in his stomach brought back memories of all the childhood activities his dad had never attended, using one lame excuse after another for his absence.

"I'll tell you what," Bart said with a shrug. "I'll call you if I change my mind."

"Are you sure? I promise it will be—"

"I said I'll call you." Bart made a show of checking his watch. "They're playing *It's a Wonderful Life* on TV this morning. You want to stick around and watch?"

Ben shook his head. "I wish I could, Dad, but I've got to get back to work."

"I know how important you are," Bart said without sarcasm.

Ben's neck grew hot anyway. "It's not about me being important. I have commitments."

"Go." His father waved a hand. "Thanks for the licorice, even if it was only one bag."

"I WAS SURPRISED to get your call," Lauren told Bart Donnelly as she helped him into the Jeep Friday afternoon, then placed his cane in the back seat.

"I like that you still drive this old hunk of junk, kid," Bart said instead of answering. "It suits you."

Lauren choked out a laugh. "Apparently, it wasn't the alcohol that prompted you to offend half the town back in the day."

"I can offend people just as easily sober. Ben deserves way better than me."

"That's something we have in common." Lauren bit down on the inside of her cheek as she pulled away. "Did he give you my number?"

"Nah, I got it from Jim. Ben's gonna be mad as a hornet when I show up with you."

"What the…" She jerked on the steering wheel before righting it again.

"Try not to kill us both on the way there," Bart said as he grabbed the door handle.

"Listen, Bart. I don't need another reason for your son to be mad at me, and I don't appreciate being used as a pawn in whatever's going on between the two of you."

He made a noncommittal grunt, then said, "I'm more curious about what's going on between the two of you, which is part of why I want to attend this carnival shindig, even though it goes against my nature. I'm not sure if Ben mentioned it to you, but I don't get out much anymore."

Ben hadn't told her anything about his father, and she silently berated herself for not asking.

"Why tonight?" she asked quietly, her fingers gripping the wheel. "Tell me you aren't going to embarrass Ben. I don't want anything to do with that, Bart."

"You serious?" The older man sounded genuinely confused. "I thought that would be right up your alley."

It had been years since she'd had a conversation with Bart Donnelly. During the time she'd been friends with and then dated Ben, she'd kept away from his father, known in town for his drunken antics and bad temper.

She hadn't feared her father's ranting, but Bart terrified her. She had a feeling he didn't approve of her for his son just as much as Robert wasn't a fan of Ben as a partner for Lauren.

They'd been young and in love, and perhaps thwarting both of their fathers had been part of the appeal.

"Why would I help you hurt Ben?"

"Because you hate him," Bart suggested conversationally. "Don't you?"

She shook her head.

"What about me?"

"I don't hate you."

"It was my fault Benny couldn't leave with you."

"Your son made a choice. I never blamed you."

"You should."

"Maybe," she conceded, then pulled over on the shoulder of the two-lane road that led up to camp. "Tell me you aren't going to cause a scene tonight. Promise that Ben has nothing to worry about, because he's got enough on his plate without you acting up."

"Are you lecturing me, girlie?" Bart growled.

Lauren's stomach fluttered, but she didn't relent. "I'm protecting your son."

"He's done okay without you," Bart shot back.

"Better than okay. Ben has made something of a name you did your best to destroy." She shook her head. "This was a mistake. I thought… It doesn't matter what I thought. I'm taking you back. I won't be a part of—"

"I'm sorry, Lauren." Bart reached out and placed a calloused hand over hers on the gear stick. "I won't sabotage or embarrass Benny. I promise. Don't turn back now."

Somehow Lauren felt like his words had a deeper meaning than just for tonight. "What's your endgame?"

"Nothin' underhanded. I wanted to see you and attend the carnival because my son asked me."

"Why would you care about seeing me, and why wouldn't you simply ask him to drive you?"

"Because I'm a burden to him in almost every way

these days," Bart admitted, his voice hoarse. "I just wanted to do something on my own, and despite how I acted back in the day, I liked you, Lauren. I like you for my son—always did."

"That's a shock," she muttered.

"Well, as much as I liked anything besides liquor at that time. I was hell-bent on pissing off anyone who came into my line of sight when the alcohol had its hold on me."

"You've stayed clean, Bart. That's an accomplishment."

"Sure. Part of the program is making amends, you know. I also wanted a chance to apologize to you privately. I'm not much for public declarations, and despite all the good Ben has done around here, I know what people think of me." He sighed. "They're not wrong. My son is a better man than I could ever hope to be."

"Your son is amazing," she confirmed.

Bart drew back his hand. "Look at that. You and I agree on a couple of topics—at least where Ben is concerned."

Lauren glanced over at him and winked. "I think we agree on plenty. We agree that you were an unmitigated ass back in the day, as you call it."

He laughed. "Do we also agree that you were a fool to walk away?"

"He let me go," she said in her own defense, even though it didn't feel like much of one any longer. Returning to her hometown and finding the connection with her sister and Ben, wishing she could do the same with her dad despite everything, made her realize that she had been a fool—naive and immature.

What would she have given up for the chance to

have the relationship with her dad that Ben had forged with his? She'd always wanted Robert's approval, even though she thwarted his control at every turn. What would she do for it even after all this time?

She might not be able to answer that question, but she could admit she'd been too harsh on Ben. Not that it made a difference at this point. They'd gone their separate ways. He had a life that didn't involve her.

It couldn't involve her, given that he was both partnering with her father and tearing down the place that meant the most to her in the world.

But she wouldn't judge him for that. She'd let it be and walk away when the time came, so she didn't have to watch the camp's destruction and think about what it said about Ben's priorities and how she no longer had a right to believe they should include her.

She smiled at Bart as they bumped up the gravel driveway. "I'm glad we had this talk."

"Me, too, sugar. I'm glad you finally came back."

"So we're clear, I didn't return for your son."

"But he's here. You're here. He's unattached. You're—"

"A single mom with no intention to stay," she reminded him.

"From what Ben says, you're the catalyst behind this Christmas spectacular."

"Carnival," she clarified. "*Spectacular* might be pushing it, given the state of the camp."

"I don't know about that. I may not socialize much these days, but this looks spectacular to me."

She glanced around at the lights and decorations, her heart squeezing with pride and anticipation. It did look spectacular.

She'd done it. Ben, Kayla, Hannah, and Brody had all pitched in, and she loved working with each of them.

Avah had shown up once or twice, mainly to give her opinion on how things should be placed for the carnival that would also work for her wedding.

Lauren pulled around to the back of the caretaker's cabin, and Ben came out to greet her. His smile faded as he realized his father was in the car with her.

"I didn't think this far ahead," she muttered, inwardly chastising herself for not realizing how Ben might react to seeing her with his father.

"It'll be fun." Bart patted her arm. "Look, Benny, you managed to convince me to leave my natural Scrooge tendencies at home for the night." He reached for his cane after exiting the Jeep. "You did nice work up here, son. The town is gonna enjoy coming back to camp for Christmas."

"I'm glad you decided to check it out," Ben said slowly, glancing between his father and Lauren. Her stomach tumbled under his scrutiny. "Although I'm surprised to see the two of you together."

"That was the idea," Lauren said brightly. "I hope it's a happy surprise."

Ben's forehead wrinkled. "I guess that remains to be seen."

"Bart Donnelly!"

Lauren cringed as Jim came around the corner. "I did not expect to see you on my land," the older man called.

"I assume that ban from twenty years ago doesn't still apply," Bart answered in a booming voice so different from the one he'd used with Lauren on the way over.

Tension hung in the air like a jackknife, and Lauren wondered if she'd made a mistake that would cost her whatever this new connection she and Ben were forging turned out to be.

She could lie to herself all day long about not expecting anything or wanting a long-term situation, but she wanted that connection now.

She wanted more.

"I'm glad you're here, Bart," Jim said finally. "Maybe you'll take me up on that invitation to bingo night out at the retirement home."

"I don't like old people," Bart answered without hesitation.

"You're ten months older than me," Jim reminded him.

"Never said I was a big fan of myself."

"Dad, please." Ben looked like this moment was costing him.

"Come on, old man." Jim beckoned Bart forward. "I've got a bad knee to match your bum hip, so neither of us will be winning any land speed races, but let me show you around."

Lauren studied Ben's face as the two older men walked away. "Say something. Please. I'm sorry, Ben."

"For what?"

"I don't know exactly. I thought I was doing the right thing. You mentioned that you had invited your dad out here."

She shook her head. "I guess I wasn't thinking. Maybe I was putting my nose in where it didn't belong. I'm sorry for upsetting you. I didn't mean for that to happen."

"Are you sure about that?"

She felt her temper flare.

"What reason would I have other than trying to be helpful?"

"I don't need your help, Lauren."

She did her best not to wince, but his words stung. "I'm aware of that."

Ben could push her buttons with more accuracy than anyone else. He got to her because she cared about him. She cared about his opinion even now—after all this time. She would have thought her emotions were worn down by now, like stones under rushing water, but he made her feel as sharp and jagged as ever.

Only when Ben held her did she feel safe enough to let down her walls. But she wasn't the same angry teenage girl she'd once been.

"I'm glad he called me and relieved to know your dad doesn't hate me."

Ben laughed softly. "I would think it's the other way around. You hate him."

"I don't," she said without hesitation. "I never did." She took a step forward, loathing the distance between them. "The mistakes we made were ours."

"You're right, but I thought hearing you say it would feel more gratifying. I have so many regrets, Lauren."

"Ben."

He looked past her to where the parking lot was quickly filling with cars, then shrugged. "My emotional pity party can wait until later. We have an event to run."

"No." She stepped in front of him when he went to move past her and placed her hands on his broad shoulders. So strong, solid, and willing to hold up the weight of what everyone needed and expected from him without asking for anything in return. "My sister can handle it for a minute."

"Your sister can barely handle making hot chocolate because she's too busy flirting with her neighbor." Ben inclined his head. "I can't decide whether she likes him or she's trying to manipulate him because she's doing your dad's dirty work, as per usual."

Lauren gripped him more tightly. "Stop trying to distract me. Why are you having an emotional pity party?"

He sighed. "I'm glad my dad is here. I am. And for some bizarre reason, I'm glad you've made peace with him. I want to believe he's here because he cares about me."

"Your dad doesn't seem like the Christmas carnival type, so why else would he be here?"

"Old habits and worries die hard," Ben said like that was an explanation, but when Lauren didn't respond, he continued, "My dad has a propensity for destroying things that make me happy. He gets sick when I have an opportunity to go on a trip or gets sober when…"

"You're about to leave town with your new wife?"

"Yeah. He and I are doing okay and have been for a while. I hate that I still think anything out of the ordinary—even a simple conversation with Jim—could set him off." He tipped his head forward until their foreheads touched. "It's strange because all I wanted as a kid was for Dad to show up, and now I feel like an ass because I don't trust him."

"You're a lot of things, Ben Donnelly. An ass is not one of them. People are entitled to their feelings no matter what they are. You matter."

"Thank you." He lifted his hands and threaded his fingers through her hair. "Thank you for understanding, making peace with my dad, and bringing him here. I mean it. I don't know what comes next, Lauren, but what is happening now is—"

"Hey, Mom!" The two of them jumped apart like they'd been electrocuted.

"Gross." Hannah made an exaggerated gagging motion. "Are you guys swapping spit?"

"There was no spit being swapped," Lauren told her daughter. At the moment, she declined to add.

"I don't want to know about other bodily fluids. No wonder you're in a better mood, Mom. I noticed you were all blissed out. I get it."

"You don't," Lauren insisted.

"I don't think anyone in their right mind would describe your mother as blissed out," Ben said from behind Lauren.

"I'll feel a lot of bliss when I elbow you in the ribs," Lauren shot back.

He only chuckled. "I'm going to go check on Jim and my dad. I want to make sure they aren't going after each other."

"The second old guy is your dad?" Hannah shook her head. "He keeps randomly ringing bells and talking about angels getting their wings."

"This I have to see." Ben took a step away, then turned back. "Hannah, I want you to know I respect and care for your mom, and it would never be my intention to gross you out."

Lauren stifled a laugh as Hannah's eyes rolled toward the pale sky. But her daughter was smiling, which was a good sign. "Just get a room next time, okay?"

"Hannah, stop," Lauren implored.

Ben only nodded. "Fair enough," he agreed. With a wink at Lauren, he jogged down the path.

"Now I see why you don't mind me staying at Grandpa's." Hannah crossed her arms over her chest, arching a brow.

"Don't go there." Lauren shook a finger at her daughter. "I want you to stay here with me anytime. All the time."

"Not ready to give up the steam shower," Hannah answered. "What's the deal with you and Ben?"

Lauren mulled over that question and answered honestly, "I have no idea, but if you have a problem with the two of us, I'll end it now."

"Really?"

"One hundred percent."

"I don't mind him," Hannah said, scrunching her nose. "I'd mind him less if you gave me back my phone."

The nerves that had been fluttering through Lauren's chest settled. "This has nothing to do with Ben," she said. "But I think you've earned your phone privileges. I'll grab it from the hiding place tonight after the carnival."

"In the back of the bedroom closet?" Hannah grinned. "I can go ahead and grab it now."

"Cheeky Banana," Lauren murmured, then held out her arms. She wasn't sure how her daughter would respond, but Hannah came forward and accepted the hug without complaint.

From a distance, Lauren heard the faint sound of bells ringing. She wasn't sure if it meant an angel got its wings, but she decided to take it as a sign of things to come.

CHAPTER SIXTEEN

K<small>AYLA SAT OUTSIDE</small> the dressing room in Mariella's private office in the back of A Second Chance on Saturday afternoon, exchanging meaningful looks with her sister as they listened to Avah's conversation with the boutique's owner, Mariella Jacob.

"Do I look fat?" Avah asked, her voice a plaintive whine.

"You look beautiful," Mariella assured her from inside the fitting room where Avah was trying on bridal gowns. "That silhouette is a classic, and the ivory color flatters your skin tone. No one, especially your groom, will be able to take their eyes off you."

Kayla saw Lauren nodding like she was silently encouraging Mariella and felt like doing the same. This was what Avah needed—someone to assure her that everything would work out for the best.

The curtain opened to reveal their brother's fiancée wearing the gown Lauren had noticed in the shop window two weeks earlier and Kayla had asked Mariella to put aside. The dress was strapless with an A-line shape and a lace overlay with floral appliqués that gave the gown a fairy-tale feel.

"It's gorgeous," Lauren said with a smile. "You're gorgeous, Avah."

"Do I look sexy?"

Kayla tried not to react as Hannah, sitting beside her, covered her laugh with a cough.

"You look beautiful," Lauren answered deliberately.

"And not pregnant," Hannah added, "even though you are."

Avah huffed out a harsh breath and glared at Hannah. "It's kind of rude to remind me of that right now."

"Sorry," Hannah mumbled and stared at her lap.

"What color and type of flowers are you thinking?" Mariella asked in the awkward silence that followed. "Red and ivory will complement the dress and play into the whole Christmas theme."

"I always thought I'd have a spring wedding," Avah complained, picking at one of the tiny pearls sewn into the bodice.

"You still could," Lauren offered, inclining her head toward Kayla, a silent communication Kayla understood all too well.

"That's true," Kayla assured her soon-to-be sister-in-law. "There's no hurry."

"I'll be as big as a house in the spring," Avah complained as Mariella rubbed a hand over her back. Kayla appreciated Mariella's grounding presence. She clearly had experience with emotional brides. "Plus, I was a preemie, you know. If I go into labor early and we're not married, my baby won't have a daddy."

"Brody loves you," Kayla countered. "A piece of paper isn't going to change the fact that he's committed to you. Or that he's the baby's father."

Avah's eyes darted to Kayla's in what could only be described as a look of pure terror followed quickly by guilt.

Guilt.

Kayla could only think of one reason her comment would make Avah appear guilty.

"Mariella, could you give us a minute?" Lauren asked, her voice deceptively even as she fiddled with her earlobe.

"Absolutely." Mariella nodded. "I'm going to check on things in front. Call if you need anything. Hannah, would you like to meet my daughter, Heather? She's working the register today and is only a few years older than you."

As outs went, it was a lame one, but Hannah hopped off her seat like she'd been offered front-row tickets to a Taylor Swift concert.

"I'd love to meet her."

As they disappeared from the room, Kayla watched Avah's expression morph from fear to defensiveness. "Forget I said anything. The dress and the Christmas Eve wedding are fine. Easier and all of—"

"Is Brody the father of your baby?" Lauren asked bluntly.

"I see where your daughter gets her manners," Avah muttered.

"Answer the question, Avah." It wasn't often that Kayla utilized an attorney's commanding tone, but this situation warranted it.

"I'm feeling triggered and bullied right now," the woman said. "I told Brody that the two of you like me less than you like each other, and that's saying something."

Kayla thought about denying the Avah's words. That was her typical modus operandi when someone was upset with her. It's why she focused on contract law in the first place, primarily wills and trusts. She had a natural tendency to soothe ruffled feathers. However, it had backfired when it came to her own life. But this wasn't about her or Lauren or their complicated relationship, even though she had a feeling Avah was purposely trying to distract them.

"I like my sister plenty," Lauren said. It wasn't exactly a resounding show of emotion, but the fact that Lauren had defended their relationship in any manner warmed Kayla's heart.

"That's not what Brody has told me," Avah said with a loud sniff. "He said—"

"This is not about Lauren and me." Kayla stood and began pacing. "Is Brody the father?"

"You have no right—"

"Answer the question," Kayla repeated.

"He should have been, but no." Avah wrapped her arms tightly around her midsection like she needed to protect her unborn child from a physical assault. Kayla's stomach tumbled, but she needed an honest answer.

"He knows the situation," Avah said finally. "I'm not deceiving him. I'm not lying or trying to pull one over. As you said, he wants to marry me. He wants to be a father."

As firm and decisive as Kayla had felt moments earlier, Avah's tacit admission left her speechless.

"Our brother is a good man," Lauren said quietly, almost as if she were speaking to herself.

Avah sniffed. "He is, no thanks to your father. He tried to pay me off, you know? He said he'd done the same thing with the guy you were involved with in high school."

Avah pointed a finger at Lauren, and Kayla gasped. She had to be referring to Ben, but there was no way he would have allowed himself to be bribed by their father. Of all the manipulative things Robert had done over the years, Kayla thought this was a particularly low attempt at controlling Lauren. And the fact that their dad had shared it with Avah felt like an acute betrayal.

It was hard to know what Lauren thought. Although the color had drained from her face, her expression gave away nothing. But Kayla got the impression her sister's legendary devil-may-care attitude was teetering, and there was no way Kayla would let Avah realize her words had made a dent in Lauren's control.

"Avah, Brody is an adult—"

"Even though none of you treat him like one," Avah protested.

The accusation stung, but it wasn't entirely baseless.

"Old habits are hard to break," Kayla conceded. "But we're trying. We'll try harder. Whatever the circumstances, he's asked you to marry him. You are a part of this family now, dysfunctional as we may be."

Avah turned her gaze to Lauren.

"You're a part of this family," Lauren confirmed.

"But it's time to step up," Kayla continued.

Avah moved away like she'd been shoved in the chest.

Kayla ignored the look of outrage. "This isn't about you."

"I'm the bride," Avah reminded them.

"You're also going to be a mother." Lauren leaned forward in her chair, her eyes blazing. "Christmas Eve or a perfect Saturday in spring…the dress and the flowers—it's all fluff. You are having a baby and have a responsibility to do right by him or her."

Avah's feathery brows furrowed. "Her," she whispered. "I'm having a girl. We're having a girl," she quickly amended. "I haven't told Brody yet. I think he wanted a son."

"He's an amazing uncle to Hannah," Lauren said. "He seems destined to be surrounded by women."

Kayla nodded. "He'll be a great girl dad. I used to make him play Barbies with me. He was more into it than he let on and weirdly good at doing Barbie hairstyles."

Lauren laughed.

"I guess that's good to know." Avah smoothed a hand over the lace of the dress. "Thank you for introducing me to Mariella. At least I'm going to be able to tell my friends that my dress was designed by somebody famous, even if it's used."

"Gently worn," Lauren clarified. "Who among us isn't?"

"Why don't you get dressed, and we'll take you out for lunch?" Kayla attempted a smile. Given everything she learned today, having lunch with Avah wasn't her first choice, but as they said, she was now part of the family.

Avah smiled. "Awesome. I have been craving the eggplant lasagna from Il Rigatone again. I'm going to order two slices. I mean, you guys are treating, right?"

"We sure are," Kayla confirmed.

When the door to the dressing room clicked shut behind Avah, Kayla turned to Lauren.

"Don't say it." Lauren held up a hand.

"Of course I'm going to say it. There is no way Ben took money from Dad. The guy married you. He didn't run away."

"I always wondered how they afforded the private

rehab facility for Bart," Lauren murmured, tugging on her earlobe. "It doesn't matter. What's done is done."

"You have to talk to Ben. I know it matters to you, and I don't believe it's true."

Lauren closed her eyes as she drew in a deep breath. Her gaze was unreadable when she opened them again. "Can we focus on Brody and Avah right now?"

She shifted her gaze toward the office door and lowered her voice as she asked, "What are we going to do, K?"

Kayla blinked. "Um, plan a Christmas Eve wedding and keep Avah happy, as difficult of a task as that might be?"

"It's not his baby," Lauren whispered.

"He's made a choice, and we have to honor it." Kayla swallowed and then continued, "A child doesn't have to be biological for a parent to love her. Or him. Her in this case."

"Also in your case," Lauren pointed out. "But this isn't about you."

"Or you." Kayla felt her temper start to simmer. "It's what Brody wants."

"Why didn't he tell me? Tell us," Lauren clarified.

Maybe because their younger brother knew the information would not be received well. Kayla couldn't imagine what their father would think of this turn of events.

"We're taking our almost sister-in-law to lunch, helping her plan a wedding and staying out of it," Kayla told Lauren.

"You always were a pushover." Lauren stood, looking thoroughly unconvinced about staying out of it.

"You always think you know best."

"Because I do. I'm the oldest."

"Not the wisest," Kayla cracked.

"I'm starving," Avah announced as she flung open the door. "Do one of you have a credit card I can use for the dress? I forgot my wallet."

"How convenient," Lauren said under her breath.

"I'll take care of it," Kayla offered, making her voice chipper even though that was the opposite of how she felt.

"That's right," Lauren agreed when Avah handed over the dress. "Kayla will take care of everything just like she always does."

Kayla ignored Lauren even as her heart felt like it might beat out of her chest.

She paid for the dress, shaking her head at Hannah's questioning glance. After speaking to Mariella for a few minutes, the four of them left the shop and headed around the corner toward the restaurant. Too bad Kayla had lost her appetite.

LATER THAT NIGHT, Kayla lay on a lounge chair on Scott's patio, wrapped in the comforter from her childhood bedroom, gazing up at the stars, when she heard footsteps approaching.

"My security company thought you were a burglar," Scott said, pointing to a camera hidden under one of the home's eaves. He wore loose jeans with a dark green sweater, and even though she couldn't see his eyes in the darkness, she suspected they were sparkling.

She hadn't thought about the fact that he would have security cameras around the property but supposed it shouldn't have surprised her. Most of the homes in this neighborhood were fully outfitted, including her father's.

"It's too cold to care about breaking in," she said, her teeth chattering as if to emphasize a point.

Scott's easy smile disappeared in an instant. "What are you doing out here anyway? We need to get you inside."

Kayla hoped the smile she flashed was indulgent, although it felt half-frozen. "The cold air was refreshing at first, but somewhere around the time I stopped being able to feel my toes, that stopped. You might have to leave me here." More chattering. "I'm not sure I can move."

Scott bent and scooped her into his arms without missing a beat. As surprised as she was, she still registered his sinewy muscles.

She wasn't frozen enough for that part not to register. She pressed her hands against his chest. "You don't need to carry me. I was joking about being frozen."

She'd been joking—sort of. "Seriously," she said more sternly when he didn't break stride on his way to the French doors that led to the house's kitchen. "I can walk on my own. You can let me go."

"There's no chance I'm letting you go."

That provided some instantaneous warmth. Kayla might be a pushover, but she was no fool, so she buried her face into the crook of Scott's neck and held on tight.

She'd never been the type of woman a man would stride across the moors to rescue. If she were being honest, she'd never even been the type of woman a man would walk across the street for. She was more the giver type.

She'd learned that from her mother early on—do

enough for a man or friend or anyone in your life and they were less likely to shut you out. It hadn't always worked. She'd never felt entirely secure in the Maxwell family despite trying her best to be the daughter her adoptive father wanted and *not* be the things that annoyed Lauren.

Kayla had tried to help her mom when she was pregnant with Brody. She'd kept the house clean and gotten good grades, but none of it had made a difference after her mom died in the car accident. Bad things happened no matter what measures she took to guard against them.

She was tired of trying and failing. Today had been the icing on the craptastic cake of her current life. In the process of trying to be what other people wanted and expected, she'd done potentially irreparable damage to her own identity and self-esteem, not to mention her relationship with Lauren.

Her fingers and toes began to sting as the circulation began to normalize moments after they entered Scott's warm house.

"You didn't answer my question," he said as he lowered her onto the sofa in the family room that opened to a spacious open-concept kitchen. "Why were you hanging out alone in my backyard?"

"Your house was dark, so I figured you weren't home, and I didn't want to be at my dad's when he got home. Where were you tonight?"

"I grabbed a burger with some friends and watched the game." He ran an agitated hand through his hair as he studied her. "Your lips look a little blue. Are you sure you're okay? Do you want tea or a hot shower?"

"Are you offering to take it with me?" she asked,

then immediately regretted it at the look of shock on his face. They'd been hanging out regularly, but he hadn't taken things further, much to Kayla's disappointment. "Forget I said that. You have friends in town?"

He blew out a laugh. "I don't think I can forget that offer, and yeah on the friends. I met some guys at the marina when I first moved in. They invited me to join a local basketball league, so…" He shook his head. "Why are we talking about my social life right now?"

"Because I don't have one," she answered, wiggling her toes, which burned like she was being stung by a dozen bees at once. "I grew up here and didn't keep in touch with anyone from childhood. Even when I see people I know, it's weirdly awkward. I'm awkward." She sighed. "And now I'm jealous of you for having friends."

"You and I are friends," he told her.

"Are we?" It hadn't started that way. She'd sought him out because her father wanted her to, and she wanted to make Robert happy.

She liked Scott. More than liked, if she admitted the truth. But that didn't change who she was on the inside—an insecure girl who would do almost anything to win her father's favor.

"You're not having the greatest day," Scott said, clearing his throat. "And you came to my house."

"Lucky you," she muttered.

"I agree." He moved closer to her on the sofa. He peeled away the two ends of the blanket and took her hands in his, transferring some of his precious heat to her. "What's going on, Max?"

"My dad is not a good person," she said quietly.

One side of Scott's full mouth kicked up. "You're just coming to that realization?"

She felt her eyes go wide. "I guess I didn't want to believe it. I know he's tough and controlling, but I've always thought his intentions were good."

Scott laughed. "That's funny, because my partner used to say, 'The road to hell is paved with good intentions.' I think Pete and your dad might have gotten along. That's not a compliment."

"But Pete was not only your business partner," she pointed out. "He was your best friend. You loved him."

"Yes, but something changed with the money and the power." Scott looked pained. "I didn't handle it any better in my own way, so I didn't realize the toll it was taking on him and the measures he was taking to anesthetize himself from the pain."

"I don't think my father has enough self-awareness to feel pain," Kayla admitted. "I'm afraid I might take after him more than I care to admit."

"Tell me what happened."

"He tried to bribe my brother's fiancée to break things off before the wedding. He's always wanted to control each of us. I'm starting to understand why my sister felt like she had to leave town and break all her connections here."

Kayla tugged slightly on her hands, but Scott didn't release her. The truth was she didn't want him to.

"It seems to me your dad is throwing crap at the wall to see what sticks because your brother is standing up to him. Brody understands his worth. That's impressive given his age and, more importantly, having a domineering father in his life."

She turned her hands until their palms were facing, and she felt the tiny calluses of his hand against her smooth skin. It was oddly comforting. "I think part of why Brody is committed to marrying Avah is because it's a different kind of escape, not exactly running away. But if he has his own family, then I wonder if he thinks our father won't play as big a role in his life."

"Your brother strikes me as capable of handling whatever decision he makes."

"I think we've underestimated Brody," Kayla said, hating that the admission made her feel like she'd let down her mother. "At least, I have."

"Is it possible you've underestimated yourself as well, Max?"

She shook her head. "No. I've told myself that because I moved away and joined a firm in a different town, I was forging my own path. I was the one able to strike a balance and earn our father's respect without having to either walk away or purposely flaunt his expectations. But here I am with no more autonomy than I had as a scared kid afraid to be sent away. I'm still afraid."

"If it makes you feel any better, you don't seem afraid from where I'm sitting. You seem strong and sometimes vulnerable but committed to showing up and doing your best. That counts. You have no idea how much."

"You're too nice, O'Day. It's one of the many things I like about you."

One thick brow rose. "There's a list?"

It was his turn to tug, but not away. He pulled her closer, and she didn't resist. "Tell me more."

She knew what he meant, but she found herself wanting to share that her father had claimed he'd also bribed Ben Donnelly years ago. Not that the past would matter to Scott. He knew Ben as the man he was now. Kayla also wanted to believe Ben was honorable and honest, committed to being a good steward of the precious land the way he promised.

Somehow, the information Avah had revealed today shook Kayla's faith in the man she considered a big brother. What would enable him to hold steady now if he had caved to Robert's influence years ago?

And what would that mean for the Camp Blossom property and its legacy? What would that mean for her sister?

But she didn't voice those concerns, not with Scott's warm gaze making her forget that she'd almost turned herself into a human popsicle.

She wanted him, even though it was a terrible decision. Kayla didn't make bad decisions, not on purpose anyway. Maybe her body temperature was still too low because she couldn't think clearly when it came to Scott.

Her hand lifted to his chest of its own accord, but instead of putting distance between them, she gripped his sweater and yanked him closer. So close that she could see the gold flecks dancing in his eyes and the way his breath hitched.

Their lips brushed gently, and she wasn't sure which of them initiated the kiss. But she melted into him, her body heated to the core.

Kayla typically didn't trust things that came easy, but she lost herself in Scott's kiss, falling without fear because she did not doubt he'd catch her before she hit the ground.

CHAPTER SEVENTEEN

"So now it's okay to be seen in public with me?" Lauren asked with a laugh as she and Hannah walked toward the hardware store after having breakfast at Over Easy later that week. "I told you I'm a cool mom. If only you would have believed me earlier."

Her daughter groaned dramatically. "Don't ever use the phrase 'cool mom' again. It's embarrassing for you."

Before Lauren could react to that bit of sass, Hannah continued, "It's also gotten weird at Grandpa's house. I don't know what's going on with Aunt Kayla, but since we did that dress fitting with Avah, she's been acting differently. I can tell Grandpa doesn't like it."

"Different how?" Lauren asked, even though she had a fairly good idea.

"Like she doesn't ask how high when he says jump. Honestly, Aunt Kayla is a bit of a suck-up."

Lauren choked out a laugh. "A bit of one?"

"Mom, come on. Be nice. I think she was trying to keep the peace."

"And now she's not?"

"Now she'll barely talk to him. When I was getting my stuff yesterday, he commented under his breath about her staying out all night and how she better make good use of her time. Like she was a teenager or something. I didn't understand what he meant, but it was obvious she did and got mad about it."

Hannah shrugged. "I think maybe it had something to do with Scott."

"Your aunt has always put my father first. That's a lot of pressure, but I think she felt like she had to be especially loyal—"

"Because she's adopted," Hannah supplied. "You both make such a big deal about that, and she's told me all about how she could never compare to you. But it didn't seem to bother her before yesterday. I wonder if Grandpa did something extra skeezy."

If he'd tried to bribe both Avah recently and Ben years earlier, Lauren knew her highly moral sister would consider that extra skeezy. Yet she was afraid to ask Ben about it.

It had been simple enough to steer clear of him last night since Hannah had come back to the cabin to stay with her, but she couldn't avoid him forever. How would she handle knowing that part of the reason he let her go was because of a financial payout from her father?

"Your aunt needs to stop letting Grandpa take advantage of her. I hope she's standing up to him for the right reasons."

And not because Kayla had some weird sense of loyalty to Lauren. Lauren didn't need anybody to come to her defense. She could take care of herself. She'd been doing just that for a lot of years without any help.

"Did you finish the English paper?" she asked Hannah as she opened the hardware store's door. She didn't want to spend more time thinking about her dysfunctional family. She wanted to enjoy a day in town with her daughter.

"Yes, Mom." Hannah's tone made it clear what she thought about her mother checking in on homework progress. "I even turned in the extra credit for math. Does that make you happy?"

Lauren looped an arm around her daughter's shoulder. "It makes me happy to see you trying, Banana. You're a smart kid, and watching you work so far below your potential killed me."

"Are you speaking from personal experience, Mom?"

"What's that supposed to mean?"

"You've done a lot since we've been in Magnolia, and I guess I wonder why you didn't try harder before?"

Lauren felt her mouth drop open. She'd tried and succeeded in raising her daughter with no financial support from anyone else. Didn't that count? As a single mom, where would she have found the time for volunteering, Christmas carnivals, or anything other than survival?

But she didn't say any of that because…she hadn't found the time. It was easier to use her life as a single mother as an excuse than to put herself out there in any way that could have meant failing or being rejected.

She'd had enough of that in her life.

"It's not a big deal," Hannah amended as if reading Lauren's reaction. "You don't have to get all bent out of shape about it."

"I'm not bent." Lauren concentrated on breathing without hyperventilating from the panic beating through her like a drum.

"Sure, Mom. Anyway, I like it here. I think you do too. Maybe enough to stay?" Hannah wiggled her brows suggestively, which looked ridiculous. "I bet Ben would be happy if you stayed."

"I don't make my decisions with Ben Donnelly in mind," Lauren told her daughter.

"That's true," Ben's voice said from behind her. "Your mother has never considered anyone else when deciding what was best for her."

Ouch. Although maybe she deserved the remark given her comment. She didn't bother to turn around.

"Thanks for holding the door, sis," Brody said, patting her back. "I'm going to take Hannah back to the free popcorn machine, and maybe you can try to extricate your foot from your mouth?"

Ben gave her a little nudge with his hip, and she quickly walked toward the far side of the store in the opposite direction from Hannah and Brody. She didn't need to wonder if Ben was following her. She could feel the heat and frustration radiating from him.

She turned to face him. "You don't need to take that personally, and I do think of someone else when making decisions. I think of Hannah. I'm raising a daughter, and I want her to know how to be independent and not make major life choices because of hormones or her heart or whatever."

"What makes you think I'm offended?"

"I just assumed since I'm always saying the wrong thing around you."

"Lauren, you can say anything to me or around me. You must know—"

"Did you take money from my dad before we got married?" she blurted.

"Who told you that?" Ben didn't sound so relaxed anymore.

Lauren glanced around to make sure her brother wasn't within earshot. "Avah told me my dad tried to bribe her to leave town. He told her he did the same to you when we were together."

Ben stepped closer, crowding her, his gaze intense as he studied her face. "You believe that I would take money from your dad?"

"I know you needed money for your dad's stint in rehab. Truly, it's water under the bridge."

"More like a flood destroying a bridge the two of us were standing on."

"Don't say that," she told him. "Don't be like that."

"You're the one who asked the question," he reminded her as if she didn't realize it.

"Forget I said anything."

"Not a chance. Yes, your dad offered me money."

Lauren sucked in a breath. "You never told me."

"I didn't take it. I wasn't tempted. It was right around Christmas senior year. Before rehab. Before we…"

"Before we got married," she supplied.

"I wouldn't have done that to you, Laur. Not for anything."

She believed his words without question. She'd known the truth in her heart. In many ways, her insecurity and weakness when it came to her father prompted her to ask the question.

She reached a hand out and stroked his cheek, then leaned in to press her mouth to his.

"Oh, for the love of Pete."

They jumped apart as Phil Wainright limped down the aisle toward them.

"Not you, too. I thought I was limited to finding my daughter and son-in-law making out like a couple of teenagers in the back of the store." Phil grimaced. "Are we running a hardware store or a kissing booth here?"

"Don't pretend like you are not a romantic at heart, Dad," Lily Dawes said as she followed her father around the corner. Brody and Hannah appeared next. Lauren rolled her eyes as Brody elbowed his niece.

"Did you know about that?" Brody asked Hannah.

"Why do you think she gave me my phone back?" Hannah made a gagging noise. "She's all *blissed out*. I don't even want to think about the details. I might barf."

"We're going to make her barf," Ben said into Lauren's hair. "I think that means she approves."

Lauren flicked a glance over her shoulder. "I'm not worried about what she thinks either at this point."

But that wasn't true. She was glad her daughter liked Ben. She appreciated that Hannah considered this town her home even though it hadn't been that way for Lauren. They also couldn't stay.

"Did you find more twinkle lights?" Lauren asked Brody.

Avah had complained that the main cabin, which had functioned as a mess hall and makeshift community room when the camp was operational, wasn't pretty enough for her wedding.

It was an understandable sentiment, so Kayla had volunteered to work with Gabe Carlyle, who owned the floral shop in town, to order flowers and candelabras and fabric to drape and make the space look more fit for the bridezilla their soon-to-be sister-in-law was turning out to be. Lauren and Brody were tasked with buying more twinkle lights.

Her brother shook his head and pointed toward Lily, who gave an apologetic nod of agreement.

"No luck on the twinkle lights," she told Lauren. "We're sold out, and I've called around to every locally owned hardware store and big box establishment in a hundred-mile radius. Who would've thought there could be a shortage of white lights at Christmas?"

"It's fine," Brody assured them. "Avah will understand."

Phil let out a snort. "Is Avah the bride?"

"Yep."

Was it Lauren's imagination, or did she detect a hint of hopelessness in her brother's voice?

"If a bride wants something, son, you better figure out how to give it to her. My daddy always said to start as you mean to go on. If you mean to go on by pissing off your wife because you can't give her what she wants…well, that's your choice."

"Dad." Lily smacked his arm gently. "A wedding is one day. What counts is the rest of your life with that person."

"He looks like he's going to faint," Ben whispered.

Brody indeed appeared a bit green around the gills.

"I'll figure it out. We'll find the lights." Lauren nodded and tried to look confident. "Even if I have to drive all the way to the North Pole. We're going to give Avah the wedding of her dreams on a budget that you can afford."

"Go, Lauren Maxwell." Phil chuckled. "If anyone is up to that task, it's you. You've single-handedly revived Camp Blossom—so much so that people around here are wondering why we ever let it close in the first place and questioning the wisdom of building a bunch of McMansions that this community does not need. Now you're gonna save the wedding, too. You, sweetheart, are a force of nature."

Lauren darted a glance at Ben, who looked like he wanted to melt into the ground.

"Dad, I think we're running low on popcorn," Lily said, guiding her father toward the end of the aisle.

"We got plenty of popcorn."

"You can never have too much." Lily patted Lauren's shoulder on the way past. "Let me know if there's anything I can help with."

"More popcorn is perfect," Lauren told the other woman.

"Why can't everyone understand this is going to be a good thing for our community?" Ben asked, and Lauren wasn't sure if he was speaking directly to her or voicing a rhetorical question.

"Hey, Uncle Brody, that popcorn made me thirsty. Want to get an Italian soda at the bakery?"

"More than anything," Lauren's brother answered.

She mouthed the words *cowards* to the two of them as they turned and walked away.

"People like you, Ben," Lauren said. "They trust you."

"That doesn't answer my question."

"Change is hard," she said softly. "Especially when it comes at the cost of losing something precious."

She wondered if he understood she was talking about more than the land.

"What most people don't realize is that Jim was going to lose the camp either way." He ran a hand through his hair, making it stick up in rumpled spikes around the crown of his head, and Lauren wanted to smooth it down. She wanted to smooth over his agitation.

She took his hand, for the moment not caring that he and her father were tearing down their special place, the camp where she'd been the happiest in her life. So many of her best memories involved Ben.

It was silly to think of it as a personal attack. The plans had been well underway before she returned to town and would come to fruition after she left.

"It doesn't matter what other people think. You're doing what makes you happy. You've made the decision you feel is right for you, the community and Jim. No one doubts you, Ben."

She squeezed his hand. "I have faith in you, but maybe the tool aisle in the hardware store isn't the best place to discuss this."

"Right." Ben looked around as if waking from a dream. "I need to do what's right."

Lauren wasn't sure why that sounded vaguely ominous but nodded. "I've got to get lumber for the arch Brody's building."

His shoulders slumped, but he offered her a genuine smile. "I'm sorry to have intruded on your errands."

"I'm glad I saw you. I'm sorry I believed you would've let my dad bribe you. You don't deserve that from me."

He leaned in and kissed her forehead. "I'm sorry about a lot of things, Lauren," he said, then turned and started down the aisle.

Regret pinged through Lauren's head like tiny elves working to have everything ready by Christmas.

She had never expected to return to Magnolia, and she certainly hadn't believed she could feel tied to this town again. Not after everything that had happened.

She shook off her sentimental thoughts and searched for the supplies she needed, reminding herself that the future she wanted more every day was not hers to claim.

CHAPTER EIGHTEEN

BEN STUDIED THE beer sitting on the burnished oak high-top table in front of him two nights later but didn't take a drink.

"What's the problem?" his friend Cam Arlinghaus asked as he slid into the chair across from Ben. Brody plopped down on the remaining chair at the table.

When Ben didn't immediately answer, Scott O'Day, who'd accompanied him to Champions, his favorite local watering hole, leaned in as if revealing a secret. "Our guy has a lot on his mind. Woman trouble mostly."

The bar was lively tonight, with patrons in the back playing pool and darts and a group of what looked to be coworkers out for an office holiday party occupying several booths on one side of the refurbished space. A trio of women in their twenties huddled around the vintage jukebox selecting the music they'd all have to listen to.

Brody clasped his head between his hands. "My sister. She's tying you up in knots again." He'd come from a job site covered with a fine layer of sawdust, which made Ben want to smile. As fastidious as Robert acted, his son was the complete opposite.

Ben caught the eye of Declan Murphy, Champions' owner who was staffing the bar tonight, and motioned for a round of beers for their group.

Brody pointed across the table when Scott chuckled softly. "Don't think you're immune. You get that whipped look whenever Kayla's name comes up. I'm telling you, guys, my sisters are great. I love them. But they are messed up. Big-time."

Ben could only imagine how Lauren and Kayla would react to Brody's assessment of the two of them.

"These are the two sisters who dropped everything to help you plan a wedding, correct?" Cam asked Brody pointedly.

Ben had known Cam Arlinghaus for years. He was another Magnolia native with a troubled past. A few years earlier, he'd gotten roped into helping to renovate a boutique hotel in one of the fancier neighborhoods near downtown. They'd lost touch before that because Cam had stopped being social after his first wife died.

But he'd fallen in love with the proprietress of the Wildflower Inn and gotten a new lease on life because of it.

Cam was a talented carpenter, furniture builder, and a hell of a boat captain who'd carved out a niche for himself around the region.

They'd worked together on a couple of projects and become friends.

Unlike most people in Ben's past, Cam didn't feel the need to remind Ben how shocking it was that he'd managed to revamp the image the town held of his family, particularly the deadbeat men who were part of it. After meeting Scott at camp, the retired tech millionaire had asked Ben for some advice on a few of the renovations he was doing on his beach house, and the two had an easy camaraderie.

"The problem is not your sister," Ben said as a waitress brought a bucket of the happy-hour special beer. The more time he spent with Lauren, the more she felt like the possible solution to his problems—at least the emptiness inside him.

Maybe all his grinding and pushing over the years hadn't been what he needed to feel secure and content in his own skin finally.

It was possible he'd needed the other piece to his heart—the one Lauren had taken with her when she'd left years ago.

"For the record," Scott said after taking a drink of his beer, "I don't get any type of look where Kayla is concerned."

"You get a look," Ben told his new friend. "Don't bother denying it."

"I like both your sisters," Cam said. "But I'm the type of guy secure enough in my masculinity to appreciate strong women."

Ben, Brody and Scott started laughing simultaneously, and Cam's grin widened. "That's what Emma tells me when she's bossing me around, and it makes my life easier to believe her."

"Happy wife, happy life," Ben said, sipping his beer and then toasting Cam.

He noticed Brody cringe slightly.

"Is everything okay?" He wasn't sure the younger man would share, but if it took the spotlight off Ben, he'd at least give it a try.

"Avah really wants more lights." Brody dipped his head and stared at the table like it might be the key to understanding how he'd gotten into this situation. "We're not married yet, and I can't keep her happy. I'm not sure this bodes well for the future. What if the kid wants some special toy for Christmas, and I'm the dad who can't find it?" He straightened and jabbed a finger into the air. "Like that movie with Arnold Schwarzenegger where he went to all those lengths to get his kid a doll for Christmas. I want to be that kind of father and husband. The kind my family can rely on."

"I think you'll give Arnold a run for his money in the good dad department," Scott said slowly.

Ben knew he wasn't the only person at this table who'd dealt with unfounded assumptions. From the time he'd been a kid, Brody had a happy-go-lucky personality, almost aggressively chill in any situation.

Ben hadn't realized until later that part of the reason was that the poor kid was doing his best to keep the peace at the oceanfront mausoleum his father called a home.

It wasn't just issues between Lauren and Kayla, although they had more than their share. Robert treated his only son more like a pet than a person.

Ben was embarrassed to admit he'd believed that Brody was the easygoing but good-for-nothing slacker his father assumed him to be. Did part of embracing marriage and fatherhood involve wanting to be seen as something different?

"It's not too late to change your mind," Ben told Brody after a moment. He had the impression each of them was thinking of Cam's words about his wife and the look of pure adoration that skimmed across his face when he mentioned her.

He wondered if that was the look Brody had been referring to with regard to Scott's face when he looked at Kayla. Did Ben get that kind of a look with Lauren? He wouldn't doubt it.

Brody did not appear close to dreamy when discussing his bride-to-be. It was more like the look the kid sitting next to Ben in fourth grade had before he'd puked all over the row in front of them.

Ben hated that for Brody. He hated it for anyone except perhaps Robert Maxwell. He wouldn't mind if that guy were miserable.

"I'm going to do this," Brody said, his tone resolute. "I'm going to be more than my dad believes I can."

Scott tapped his beer bottle on the table. "I don't know you or your dad well, but I'm getting to know Kayla and watching her jump through hoop after hoop trying to make your father happy and proud." He drew in a long breath. "Take it from somebody with experience in hard-to-please fathers—there's nothing you can do to make him happy. You're only going to drive yourself crazy by trying."

Ben wondered if the same rationale would apply to a wife who was difficult to please, although he certainly wasn't about to compare Brody's fiancée and his father.

He had to admit, at least to himself, that he was partnering with a man he didn't like to build a housing development that—according to Phil Wainright at the hardware store—the community didn't want. The thought had him draining the rest of his beer in one gulp.

"I'm not doing this for my dad," Brody said. "I'm marrying Avah because it's the right thing to do for her and our baby."

As declarations of love went, Brody wouldn't be recruited by any greeting card companies in the near future, but Ben understood and appreciated duty.

"We'll find the twinkle lights," he promised. At least he could make someone happy.

"Having the wedding at the inn is an option," Cam suggested. "Emma and her partners are known for throwing amazing weddings, and I'm positive she'll give you a good rate."

Ben held his breath as he waited for Brody's answer. He knew what hosting her brother's wedding at camp meant to Lauren.

Brody shook his head. "I'm holding fast to Camp Blossom for the venue. I'll get all the twinkle lights and flowers and pretty decorations I can, but that place is special."

"It really is," Scott murmured, "although Kayla told me she didn't love it as a kid."

Ben chuckled. "Kayla went through a bit of a vampire phase. She didn't like going outside."

"At all," Brody confirmed with a grin. "But to be fair, she was a magnet for mosquitos, and her skin burned like crazy. It wasn't a good look."

"Couldn't have been comfortable either," Scott said. "Yet she's putting aside her personal experience to help with the carnival and only speaks positively of the camp. It's adorable."

Ben choked out a laugh. He could imagine Lauren's driven, prickly younger sister being described in various ways. Adorable was not one of them.

"That's what I'm talking about." Brody threw up his hands, although it was obvious from his smile that he also was amused by Scott being so smitten with Kayla. "Mosquitos and sunburn are not adorable, and neither are my sisters."

"I disagree," Scott said without hesitation. "At least in Kayla's case."

Ben wished he could comment casually on Lauren,

but she'd skin him alive if she heard about it. Their connection felt too tenuous. The physical attraction was simple enough to manage, but anything more felt like it could pitch them into uncharted territory.

"I won't deny the camp is special," Cam said. "It's also got a lot of history in the area, and from an ecological perspective, there aren't many parcels of land that can compare in this part of the state."

"Have you considered keeping it a camp instead of building houses on the land?" Scott asked, seemingly out of nowhere, at least as far as Ben was concerned.

It felt as though the noise from the bar crowd swelled at that moment, or maybe it was the roaring in his ears.

"I can't afford that."

He knew that with certainty because he'd considered it as an option after learning how upside down Jim's finances were from Nancy's medical bills.

Ben's guilt for being so consumed with his life that he'd taken his eye off a couple who meant the world to him nearly brought him to his knees. But there was no debating that he didn't have the money to invest in the camp the way it would need. The truth was, he didn't want to run a summer camp.

He liked his work, so the partnership with Robert, flawed is it might be, felt like a solution for all of them. That rationalization had enabled him to ignore his misgivings and concerns about the emotional toll tearing down camp would take.

It had been easy enough to ignore when the place was in disrepair. With just a little love and attention, Lauren had changed everything.

No. Not everything.

Some things could not be altered.

"Even if I wanted to, I signed a partnership deal with Robert." He looked at each of them and tried not to acknowledge the disappointment their gazes reflected. "But I'm going to take care of things in my own way."

Scott acknowledged his words with a nod. "Be careful. Taking care of things shouldn't eat away at your soul so much that it changes who you are. I saw what that can do to a person and the ramifications of it in the end."

"If there's anyone who can suck away a person's soul," Brody added, "it's my dad."

"My soul is safe," Ben assured them with a confidence he wished he truly felt.

"Do you trust your father?"

Kayla felt alarm shoot through her as she considered Scott's question.

They were sitting on the sofa in his living room, her legs stretched across his lap as he traced circles around her jeans-clad kneecap with one finger.

How was it that her whole body felt electric from a simple touch?

"Is that a trick question?"

"It's a question I'd like you to answer without deflecting," Scott said calmly, keeping his gaze steady on her in a way that made her heart fling itself against her rib cage.

She opened her mouth to tell him that, of course, she trusted her dad. Even if he could be dictatorial and manipulative, Robert Maxwell operated with his own sense of honor. But that wasn't the truth, and she couldn't pretend.

"No." The word came out of her mouth before she could stop it.

Scott's hand stilled, although his expression remained neutral. "Yet you are working for him and want me to sell my land to his company?"

Did she still want that? Kayla was embarrassed to admit she did. That making her father happy was always in the back of her mind as a measure of success.

"I want you to make the right decision for you. Adding a portion of your property to the development would make my dad happy. And if you choose to sell, I'll ensure the deal benefits you. I might not implicitly trust my dad, but I trust myself."

"Do you?"

She moved her legs away from him, tucking them under herself and scooting to the far end of the sofa.

"I'm not trying to upset you," Scott said. "I had an interesting conversation with Brody, Ben, and Cam Arlinghaus tonight at Champions."

"You talked about me?" She didn't like the thought of that.

"We talked about a lot of things." He raised a brow. "As friends do when they're hanging out. There was nothing shady about it. The three of them gave me advice on my plans for this house, and we all got some insight into Brody's feelings about his upcoming nuptials."

"Which are?"

"Committed to doing what he feels is right, particularly where the baby is concerned."

Kayla's stomach sank, but she had a feeling Brody's remark wouldn't be the most upsetting thing she heard about their conversation.

"What else?" She knew there was more.

"We discussed the plans for Camp Blossom, and I was curious why Ben decided to partner with your father instead of doing something on his own or trying to reopen the camp in some fashion."

"He partnered with Dad because he needs the money," Kayla answered as if Scott truly needed the explanation.

"Right," he agreed. "Ben needs money. I have money. Money and not a lot of purpose."

"Do you believe your purpose is to run a summer camp?"

He made a face. "I can think of less honorable ways to make a living."

Kayla pressed two fingers to her temple when her head started to pound. She looked around his house, which was more of a home than her father's had ever been, despite what she'd first believed.

It had been easier to assume he was simply another wealthy man without much of a soul, but spending time with him proved that Scott was nothing like her father.

He was a man who wanted to make a positive impact on the world, heal his past and find a place to call home, although Kayla wasn't sure what that word meant to her. Disappointing her father wouldn't help her figure it out.

"It's a done deal. There are investors in addition to my dad. Thousands were spent on plans, inspections and permits. Jim and Ben caved to my sister because she wanted a final holiday hurrah. But Lauren doesn't want to run a summer camp either. She's coordinating the carnival weekends as much to give herself purpose and prove something to her daughter as she is out of a feeling of loyalty or a sense of community. She doesn't need you to be her knight in shining armor."

Kayla swallowed and forced herself to continue. "Neither do I."

No matter how much she wanted it.

Scott frowned. "This isn't about your sister. It isn't about one person. The land and Camp Blossom are bigger than any one person. There's a history there, a tradition that's important to honor. Your father has you backed into a corner working for him. You don't want to make waves but feel the need to keep the peace to make up for the fact that the corporate law firm career he wanted for you wasn't a fit."

"You think you know me so well." Emotion colored her voice, and she tried to swallow it down. "You don't know what I want."

"Kayla."

It was the first time he'd called her by her name and not Max. It made things seem more real and made her feel vulnerable like he did know her—possibly better than she knew herself. At least better than she was willing to admit.

"Is it so wrong to want to make my father proud? I owe him my loyalty. He didn't have to adopt me or treat me like his daughter after my mother died. Do you know what would have happened to me if Robert Maxwell hadn't been part of my life?"

Scott shook his head.

"I had no one. No family to take me in after my grandmother died. I would have gone into foster care or been adopted by strangers. I know my father is flawed, but he's my family, adoptive or not."

"Lauren and Brody are your family, too. I've seen how you try to care for them, even when they don't want your help."

How did she respond to that? She often felt she deserved to be treated as unworthy of carrying the Maxwell name. Her mother had gotten pregnant to have a baby that would tie them to Robert Maxwell, no matter what happened.

Kayla had never repeated what Marcie shared about choosing to become a mother again in her early forties, but the understanding stayed with her. It shaped her like a stream shapes the rocks under it by the everyday wearing away of the surface.

Scott reached out and placed a gentle hand on her knee. She wanted to pull away but didn't. His touch was too comforting, even in this small gesture.

"Max, you shouldn't have to earn a parent's love by jumping through a million arbitrary hoops. A parent's love is the kind that should be offered freely with no strings."

She laughed softly. "Not in my experience. Be honest, Scott. Was that your experience? Does anyone truly receive unconditional love? Because you're throwing out a lot of deep thoughts for a man who has in many ways cut himself off from the world."

"I didn't get it from my father," Scott said, and she hated the pain in his voice. She hated to think that her defensiveness had contributed to it. She knew how much his friend and partner's death had affected him.

Then he surprised her even more by wiping a tear from his cheek, his gaze serene. "But that's how my mother loved me. I know what it's like to be loved unconditionally, and it's a wondrous thing. It took Pete's death to understand how precious of a gift she gave me, and I still struggle to allow myself to feel. You're right about hiding away, but you've helped me see I have more to give. It's time to risk opening myself up again."

To what? she wanted to ask him. *Love...failure... loss?*

Where was her part? Did she deserve a place in this sweet, kind, honorable man's world when her motivations were still conflicted?

"When you love someone," he continued, "it's supposed to be without strings, particularly with children, no matter how old they are."

Kayla blinked back tears as she thought about her mother and the survival instinct that had permeated her actions and most of her thinking.

She wanted to believe her mother had loved her unconditionally, and maybe she had in her own way. But Marcie's fear had left as much of an indelible impression on Kayla as her love.

"I'm not saying you're wrong." Her chin trembled. "But I don't know what that kind of love looks like."

"I'd like to show you if you could find a way to let me in."

Oh, how she wanted to. She wanted to lean into his strength.

"I'm not sure I know how," she said honestly. "I think the only way in is through the broken parts, which aren't the pieces of me I want anyone to see."

He moved closer and held out his hands, palms up. She knew what he was doing, giving her a choice. He wanted her, flawed as his reasoning might be, but he wouldn't force it.

There was no need since her heart had already been captured. How could she resist a man who wanted to do the right thing and be a good person?

Her dad wasn't a good person. Her ex hadn't been either. Brody was in his own way, but like Lauren and Kayla, he had ways of compromising himself because that was easier than standing up to their father. Or facing the potential of failing.

She waited so long, lost in her tumbling thoughts, that Scott started pulling back.

Without worrying about what it might mean or how she could hurt them both, she grabbed his hands and climbed into his lap, wrapping her arms tight around his neck.

"I want to try, too," she said, kissing him.

She normally felt as soft as glass, all jagged edges and sharp corners. But Scott was like a warm blanket around her, making her feel safe and whole.

His kiss was less gentle than before, like he couldn't restrain himself where she was concerned. He made her feel so discombobulated that she reveled in the notion that she might have the same kind of effect on him.

Their tongues melded, and she felt each stroke to her core. Scott gripped her hips, pulling their bodies together until she felt the evidence that he was as aroused as her.

A soft moan slipped out of her mouth, and he deepened the kiss even more like a promise she had no doubt he'd be able to keep.

It was the woman kissing him back just as passionately that Kayla didn't recognize. Scott brought out a side of her she wanted to explore—specifically with him.

She broke the kiss and gazed into his gentle eyes—not so soft at the moment, which made her smile. "I want you," she said, deciding the direct path to what she wanted would be best.

His throat bobbed as he swallowed. "Now?"

"Is that a problem?" Lord, she hoped it wasn't a problem.

As an answer, Scott stood with her in his arms and started toward the back of the house. "That is the opposite of a problem, Max. It's the best thing I've heard in forever."

And despite telling herself that now would be enough, Kayla couldn't deny that the word *forever* might be just what she wanted from Scott O'Day.

CHAPTER NINETEEN

LATER THAT WEEK, Lauren placed the last box of string lights in the back of Ben's truck and stepped back to admire their handiwork.

"Is Brody planning on giving sunglasses to all the guests?" Ben asked with a laugh. "At this point, I'm expecting a call from the local utility company about draining the grid."

They'd driven a hundred miles southwest to a hardware store in a small mountain town that happened to have gotten in a massive supply of string lights.

"Shush, you." Lauren playfully swatted Ben's arm. She knew he was joking, but she'd deal with the utility company even if he weren't.

Nothing could burst her bubble of happiness at getting this task accomplished. She wasn't sure why the twinkle lights had taken on such a monumental meaning for her brother and his fiancée. Still, their lack seemed to represent everything Brody worried about regarding his potential for failure in his bid to become a better father and husband than their dad.

She and Kayla had repeatedly assured him that simply trying to be a decent family man would be a huge accomplishment compared to their father, but nothing could convince him.

"Are twinkle lights the key to a happy marriage?" Ben asked softly.

She turned to find him staring at her with an intensity that stole her breath.

"Because I would have raided Jim's stash back in the day if it meant an opportunity to change our ending."

Lauren forced a lighthearted smile. "I'm not sure there was any other way we could have ended." She sighed. "We were so young."

"It felt like I'd loved you for a thousand years," Ben told her. "It still does sometimes. I remember everything."

Lauren did, too. She remembered the sweetness of his touch and how safe she felt with him. She also remembered how much it hurt when things ended and how she'd left town feeling like her heart would never recover.

Maybe it hadn't healed. How else could she explain that she'd opened herself up to Ben again so quickly? He hadn't been part of her plan to return to her hometown.

As much as she'd promised herself she would keep her walls high around her heart where Ben was concerned, he'd already infiltrated her defenses. She had no way to resist his kindness and how he made her believe in things she'd given up long ago.

Hannah liked him, which counted for a lot in Lauren's world. Practically everything, but she didn't know how to trust him again.

She didn't trust herself either. She knew what happened when she loved someone—they left her or let her down because she was hard to manage and deal with for the long haul, just like her mother.

Maybe she could take a page from her sister's book

and try to get along, but could she manage it? Did she even want to?

"I can almost see the wheels turning in your mind." Ben shut the truck bed, then leaned against it, pulling her between his legs and resting his hands on her hips. "What if we don't overthink this right now?"

"But I'm an overthinking expert." Lauren cringed even as she owned the words. Overthinking was just one of her many deficiencies, and Ben would realize that sooner than later even if he'd allowed time and distance to soften his memory of her.

"What if instead of stewing over the past, we went ice-skating?" he asked.

A laugh bubbled up in her throat. "I'm not an easy woman to surprise, yet you continually manage it." She glanced around the half-empty parking lot of the hardware store. "But we're in North Carolina, not Minnesota, in case you've forgotten. There's not exactly an abundance of ice-skating rinks in the area."

He lifted his hands to cup her face between his palms, pressing a kiss to her lips so gently it made shivers erupt along her spine.

"How about you let me handle it? Can you do that, Lauren? Can you let go and give me control for one afternoon?"

She started to refuse out of habit and her sense of self-preservation. This man had no idea the control he had over her and how she was constantly losing hers when he was around.

Besides, letting someone else take care of things was utterly foreign to her at this point. Lauren was used to dealing with every part of her life, and she liked it that way. If she didn't depend on people, she wouldn't be disappointed by them.

But all that independence and self-reliance could be exhausting and gave her far too many reasons to worry and overthink things.

It was easy to let anxiety rule the day in every area of her life. Was her daughter indeed on the right track, or was this trip to Magnolia a blessedly peaceful detour on the path of teenage rebellion and troubles? Would her brother be okay, or was his marriage as doomed as it appeared on the surface? Would she make it through the holiday season emotionally unscathed from her father's subtle attacks, and could she trust the unexpected bond she felt with Kayla? There was so much to worry about, so much she could not control, no matter her best intentions.

"Would this be considered a date?"

"Do you want it to be?" Ben sounded shocked but didn't release her. She didn't want him to let go.

She gave a noncommittal shrug but couldn't help her smile. "Sadly, it's proven that I am a sure thing where you're concerned. I don't *need* to be taken on a real date."

"I want to," he said and kissed her.

She felt their connection all the way to her toes. But they weren't in their hometown. There were no ghosts from the past or worries about the future right now. They were two people together a week before Christmas, not so young but in—

Oh, no. She wouldn't let herself go there.

But she would go ice-skating.

She pulled away enough to speak against his mouth.

"I'd like to go on a date with you," she said. "Ice-skating or otherwise."

"Definitely ice-skating *and* otherwise," he told her. "I'm going to make giving up control worth your while."

You already have, she wanted to tell him.

They climbed back in the truck, and he punched something into his GPS, then headed out of the hardware store's parking lot.

"I love the beach, but I love the forest around here, too." She gazed out the window. "I hope you'll save some trees when you do the development. I hate those subdivisions that are just wiped bare at the start. The trees around Camp Blossom are special, you know?"

It wasn't easy for her to talk rationally about the planned demolition of the camp, but she would try. There was no use pretending she could stop it, even though she secretly wished Ben would pull out of the partnership with her dad.

She realized that wasn't fair. After talking to Jim about his situation in more detail, she understood how much Ben had done to pull the man they both loved from the brink of irreparable financial ruin.

It was still difficult to believe her dad wouldn't find a way to take advantage of that and dupe both Ben and Jim in the process.

"We're going to keep as many trees as possible," Ben assured her. "And plant new ones. I'm also planning to use some of the lumber we salvage from the cabins in the community clubhouse."

"Good," she murmured, even though her heart ached knowing things would never be the same. "I trust you, Ben."

She had to, because the alternative would drive her mad with worry.

"That means a lot," he answered, and the rough timbre of his voice washed over her senses.

She should tell him she'd changed her mind, and they should return to Magnolia immediately. Heck, she'd been a fool to agree to undertake this errand with him in the first place.

But then he was turning into the half-empty parking lot of a nondescript steel building with a strange amount of inflatables and other holiday decorations adorning the front walk. In some ways, it reminded her of camp. The building wouldn't stand out normally, but dressed up for the season, it felt charming.

"What is this place?"

"It's the local skating rink." He nodded as if confirming for himself. "I checked the town's website. Each Christmas, they have open skating sessions where they turn the rink into a winter wonderland."

"A winter wonderland, huh?" She grinned as happiness spiraled through her. "You've put some thought into this, Donnelly. I'm impressed."

He looked slightly embarrassed by the compliment.

"Well, it's not like I rented out the whole place, although I considered it. They have peewee hockey practice on the schedule today, so it wasn't an option."

Her grin widened as she hopped out of the truck and took his hand. "Thank you," she said, hoping he understood how much his thoughtfulness meant to her.

He lifted her hand and kissed her knuckles. "I know how hard you've been working on making the camp carnival memorable, especially for Jim. So many of his years at camp were spent with Nancy, and now he'll have new happy memories to take with him."

"It's not a big deal," she said automatically. If she acknowledged precisely how much the event had come to mean to her, it would involve admitting that she'd opened her heart again to both her hometown and Ben.

"You deserve something special in return for all you've done, and I happen to know you have a soft spot for ice-skating."

"You do?" she asked. "I'm not sure I knew that."

He didn't seem fazed by her confusion. "I remember how much you loved the scene in *Elf* where Buddy and Jovie skated at Rockefeller Center on their first date. You and I were going to visit New York during the holidays for our first Christmas together as a married couple."

The memory tugged wistfully at her heart.

"That was my plan," she acknowledged. "But a lot of things didn't work out the way I thought."

He squeezed her fingers as they walked toward the building. "Did you ever make it to New York City for ice-skating with Hannah?"

"No. I would normally tell you I didn't have the time or money for that kind of trip." Lauren's wistfulness took on a sharp edge. "Both excuses would be the truth, but they are also just excuses. My daughter, who is wise beyond her years despite her underdeveloped teenage frontal lobe, accused me of playing small in my life. She said I used motherhood, particularly being a single mother, to justify not going after my dreams or what I want in life."

"I think you and Hannah need to cut each other a little slack."

"Maybe," she admitted. "But she's also not wrong."

"It's not too late," Ben said as he held the door to the rink open for her.

Lauren wondered if he was talking about more than just her choices with jobs, but it was too much to consider those possibilities when she'd locked away her big dreams a long time ago.

She was saved from answering when an older man dressed as Santa approached them with a hearty *ho-ho-ho*. Maybe it wasn't too late to believe in second chances, Christmas magic, and becoming more than she believed herself to be.

"Who do we have here?" the old man asked, then began flipping through the old-fashioned notepad he held in his hands. "Are you Lauren Maxwell?"

She choked out a laugh and glanced at Ben.

"What did you do?" she asked.

"I called yesterday and discovered they have a VIP package." He nodded toward Santa Claus. "It includes a skating lesson from the big guy himself, but you don't have to sit on his lap."

Lauren laughed harder. "I'm not sitting on your lap," she told Santa.

The man held up his white-gloved hands, palms facing out. "Fair enough. How about we get the two of you sized for skates, and then we'll start the lesson?"

"You ready for an adventure?" Ben asked, and Lauren was immediately transported back to years earlier when he'd asked the same question each time he picked her up for a day or night spent together.

"Always with you," she told him, which was how she'd always responded. The words rolled off her tongue like the distance between them hadn't spanned almost a decade. She had the scars on her heart to prove it had, but even scars healed.

They followed Santa to the rental counter at the back of the rink, and Lauren felt a little embarrassed at how much she enjoyed the personal attention.

Ben made her feel special, and not just because of a skating lesson from the man in red. It was how he recognized the effort she'd put into the winter carnival, although the fact that he was going ahead with his plans to demolish the camp they both loved put a damper on her merriment.

She wanted to believe they might have another chance at a happy ending, but how could that be possible when his goals were so out of sync with hers?

Except did she even know her goals?

"Overthinking," Ben murmured, and she glanced up from lacing her skates to find him watching her.

"You don't know that," she said, wrinkling her nose. "You aren't a mind reader. I could be simply admiring the stained tile floor and the scent of hot chocolate mixed with the pervading aroma of hockey pads."

He cringed. "I'll never drink hot chocolate again thanks to that association."

She scooted closer to him on the bench. Santa had gone to greet a gaggle of kids while Ben and Lauren got ready for the ice, so they had a quiet moment to themselves. "Or maybe I'm thinking about how much I appreciate you doing this."

Leaning over to kiss his cheek, she savored his warmth and the way he always smelled like the forest. As if he were a part of the natural world all the way to his soul. "You're a good man, Ben. You always have been. This is a perfect day. Thank you."

"Any day is perfect if we're together."

Lauren closed her eyes and smiled as she listened to the sound of the rink around them. For one brief moment, she had the wild thought to grab Ben's hand, lead him out of this place to drive and pick up her daughter and then head to some deserted island—just the three of them. No reality. No past to ruminate about or future to worry over.

Just free and easy for as long as they could manage it.

Only free and easy came with a price as well, and it was one she couldn't afford to pay as a mother trying to be a role model for her daughter.

Still, she took his hand and, on wobbly legs, led him to the skating rink, with Santa coaching them to balance and glide without falling.

It was a lesson Lauren badly needed.

CHAPTER TWENTY

"KAYLA."

Kayla considered ignoring her father's voice as she walked toward the garage through the house she'd thought empty.

He had lunch at the country club on Friday afternoons, a standing date with his cronies, and one she'd counted on to give her time to get in and out of the house without interacting with him.

There was no use pretending she hadn't heard him. If Robert wanted something from her, she might as well figure out what it was.

She veered into the kitchen and plastered on a wide smile. "Hey, Dad. I didn't expect to see you. What happened to lunch?"

"I left early," he said, crossing his arms over his chest as he stared at her from the other side of the massive island. "Where are you going dressed like that?"

She blinked, then glanced down at her sturdy work boots and baggy overalls covering a ribbed turtleneck. "I'm heading to Camp Blossom to do some wedding prep with Brody and Lauren, then staying for the carnival. The ticket sales have been through the roof. We're expecting a huge crowd both nights of the final weekend."

"What a waste of time and energy." Robert scoffed.

"Which part?" she asked, unsure on whose behalf to be offended.

"Both. You can't believe a marriage between your brother and that woman will work out."

Kayla agreed it was most likely doomed to fail, but she wouldn't admit that to her dad.

"It's not my right to judge or decide what's good or bad for Brody. I'm supporting the decision he's made, not trying to take over."

"We coddled him too much when he was younger. I should have been tougher on him. His life has been too easy."

"Mom died when he was barely a year old." Emotion knotted thick and bitter in Kayla's throat. She wanted to believe that her mom would have ensured some of their family's difficulties hadn't been so bad. Marcie would have found a way to keep Robert in line and convince Lauren not to cut ties so abruptly.

For years, she'd blamed herself for being unable to prevent the issues within her family, but she now understood that a child should have never taken on the responsibility. Sadly, her dad had done nothing to alleviate the pressure or reassure her that she wasn't expected to stitch together the frayed pieces of each of them.

"Exactly," Robert agreed. "Your mom was an amazing woman, Kayla. The love of my life. But she wasn't here when you kids needed her the most."

"Do you blame her for dying?" Kayla couldn't believe she was even asking.

"I blame myself for not doing better by my children," he said, and Kayla sucked in a breath. Maybe there was hope for their fractured family yet.

"The three of you are weak. I wanted you to grow

up tough and resilient and to parlay that into successful lives. Each of you has disappointed me greatly."

Her stomach clenched at the admonishment. So much for that hope.

"I've got to go, Dad. Lauren and Brody are expecting me."

"What about my expectations, Kayla?" He stepped forward and stretched out his long arms, planting his palms on the counter. "I thought you left the firm because you wanted to be more involved in the family business. We're not in the business of enabling your brother to make a huge mistake."

Her heart started to beat an uneven tempo, her palms going sweaty, and she recognized the beginnings of a panic attack. *Focus on breathing*, she reminded herself.

"I spent the morning drafting the documents to finalize the county's infrastructure requirements with the zoning department," she reported. "It's been a tangle, to say the least."

"You spent last night at Scott O'Day's house." Her dad spoke like he had every right to comment on her personal life.

"I did," she said, her chest constricting painfully. She needed to extricate herself from this conversation, which could only get worse.

"Is he going to sell the land?"

She shook her head and looked past her father's shoulder, focusing her gaze on one of the oil-rubbed bronze knobs of the counter.

"Then break it off with him," her dad commanded. "I have a dinner tonight at the club with some potential new investors. I want you there."

"Dad, I told you…" She broke off when he sharply stabbed at the air with one hand.

"The wedding nonsense is one thing. At least if you're involved, the event won't be a complete embarrassment, even if the marriage is an exercise in futile stupidity. But I refuse to have all three of my children humiliate me by spending more time at that stupid camp than they do with their father."

"Come out with me," Kayla urged. "You should see what Lauren has done with the place. The crowd of people—"

"—is a joke," he bellowed. "A slap in the face to me when I plan to tear it down in a few weeks. No one around here had given any thought to that throwback property in years. Suddenly, thanks to your sister, I can't go any damn place in town without hearing about how adorable, fun, and cute the carnival is."

"It's all those things," Kayla said softly. "Maybe you could be proud of her."

She hadn't meant the suggestion as a condemnation of her father. Or maybe she had. Perhaps the past few weeks of connecting with her stepsister and getting to know her niece had made Kayla realize that being a pushover where her dad was concerned didn't get her anywhere with him and left her feeling hollow inside.

Laughing with Lauren over silly memories they shared made her appreciate their connection, tenuous as it still felt. Supporting Hannah gave her a purpose that was fulfilling in a far deeper way than any contract case had been.

Then there was Scott, who'd been the initial catalyst for her breaking out of her self-imposed social exile. He was the real surprise. It was as if he saw her ugly parts and found their beauty anyway.

He didn't care if she was perfect, docile, or easygoing, and she didn't want to taint that. Not for security or even her father's love.

Her father glared at her like she was a smudge of dirt on his pristine marble floor. "You have no idea what you're talking about, young lady."

"I'm not that young anymore, Dad." As comebacks went, that was a lame one, and her father took advantage, as she should've expected.

His gaze crawled over her. "What would your mother say to you, Kayla? I know how important it was for her not to make waves. She understood her place in the world and what got her there. Would she appreciate you biting the hand that fed you for all those years?"

"No," Kayla whispered after a moment. "But I hope she'd be proud of me for doing what I think is right. I guess it's too much to think you could find it in your heart to feel the same."

"What exactly is there to be proud of?" Her father's face had darkened several shades of red. "Am I supposed to be proud of my son who has two degrees that I paid for but no career prospects in his areas of study? Or my eldest daughter, barely scraping by and driving that god-awful Jeep that was old back when she first insisted on bringing it home? She's making a public spectacle of herself by championing a summer camp that hasn't been in operation for years when I plan to close it down at the beginning of the new year."

His hands started to tremble slightly. Although he didn't raise his voice, Kayla could tell how agitated he was becoming.

"Dad, these things you're so upset about...they aren't personal attacks on you. All three of us are trying to make our way in the world the best we can. It might not be what you want, but you have to honor our right to make our own choices."

"I don't have to honor a damn thing." He stabbed his hand in the air. Kayla waited for more vitriol to spill out, but instead, Robert's face froze, then his eyes closed, and his mouth compressed into a grimace.

His hand lowered, and he clutched at his heart.

Kayla screamed as he crumpled to the ground.

THREE HOURS LATER, Kayla sat in a nondescript hospital waiting room with Lauren and Brody, pondering—of all things—how many hours of her life had been wasted staring at pale yellow walls. She would have sworn the color the hospital had chosen for the public areas was the same hue on the walls of her office and the conference room at the firm in Charlotte.

If Kayla ended up with an office at the Maxwell Enterprises headquarters—or even out on her own since the thought of working for her father seemed less manageable every day—she would paint her walls a different color. Maybe a soft lavender or even a bright teal blue.

Something cheery and welcoming. Something that gave an indication of her personality, although she had yet to discover which version of herself she wanted to embrace.

She looked up as Lauren thrust a cardboard cup of coffee into her hand. "I dumped a ton of sweetener and creamer in it the way you like. You may be perfect on most fronts, but you should give up sugar. It's not good for you."

"That's right," Brody agreed. "You need to drink that coffee black as night like Lauren does. It'll put hair on your chest."

Despite her upset, Kayla barked out a laugh. "The last thing I need is hair on my chest. Not the last thing," she amended. "The last thing I need is for Dad to die and it to be my fault."

Lauren sank into the chair next to her. "It's not your fault, K. You can believe me when I say that. I loved blaming things on you. The doctor said, based on his arteries, it was a matter of time."

Their father had been taken by ambulance to the level-one trauma center closest to Magnolia, which didn't seem to be crowded this afternoon. After testing in the ER, the cardio-thoracic surgeon on call had him prepped for surgery. Other than staff walking past the door and the woman behind the information desk on the far side of the room, they were the only visitors waiting.

"But it happened when he and I were arguing. I never argue, and the one time I do…"

"You made it count," Brody told her. He sat across from them on an upholstered chair too small to be comfortable for him.

Kayla gaped as Lauren kicked their brother's shin. "Are you trying to be an ass?"

Brody looked immediately chagrined, like a puppy who'd been scolded by his favorite human. "I'm sorry. I didn't mean that. Hell, it sounds like something Dad would say, which is the last thing I want. Who knows what would've happened if you hadn't been there? He could have keeled over on that spin bike he loves so much, and nobody would have called 911. You saved him."

"That might be laying it on a little thick," Lauren said dryly.

Kayla wasn't sure whether to laugh again or burst into tears. Still, one thing she knew for certain was that if she was going through this traumatic experience, she appreciated Lauren and Brody showing up to support her. However, she knew they both had other responsibilities just as important.

"You guys can go if you need to. I know you sold out carnival tickets for tonight. There will be record crowds with the nice weather, and it being not just the final weekend of the holiday activities, but…"

"…of the camp as most people remember it," Lauren murmured.

"Exactly." Kayla nodded. "You should be there. Brody, I'm sure Ben can use your help, and Avah won't be thrilled at you being away for so long."

"Avah might be thrilled to have me out of her hair for a bit. She keeps accusing me of hovering. Like I'm some overprotective mother hen."

"Are you?" Lauren asked.

Brody shrugged. "I don't know. As you can imagine, and Dad would be thrilled to remind everyone, I never gave much thought to being a father or husband before I found out Avah was pregnant. I don't have the best role model for being a successful father. Everything I know about parenting comes from the two of you."

Lauren and Kayla shared a look, then both cracked up over his words.

"It's not funny." Brody leaned forward, placing his

elbows on the knees of his faded jeans and gripping his head like it was about to explode.

Kayla immediately moved to the seat next to him and wrapped an arm around his bulky shoulder. "You're doing great, bro."

"Way better than any of us expected," Lauren added.

"Thanks, I guess." Brody gripped his head more tightly. "I don't want to be like him. I never wanted to be anything like him. I feel terrible about it because he could die, and I spent years wishing it had been him in that car with me at the time of the wreck and not Mom. I thought I didn't care enough about him to give a rip if he lived or died."

His voice shook with emotion. "It turns out, I do. I don't know if that makes me smart or a fool."

"You aren't a fool." Kayla rubbed her hand in circles over his back the way she used to when he'd been sick as a kid. She hated seeing him this way, but at least it gave her purpose beyond wallowing in her own guilt.

"Hold on." Lauren took a deep drink of her coffee and then scooted forward on the chair. "Let's get something clear once and for all. I'm the oldest, and you two have to listen to me. Brody, you were a baby when your mother died. It was a miracle you survived that crash unscathed. You are an actual miracle."

"Maybe she was distracted because I'd been crying in the back seat, and that's why she took her eyes off the road just as the guy in the other lane swerved."

"None of us knows why the accident happened." Lauren shifted her gaze to Kayla. "Although we do know why Dad had a heart attack. His veins look like the Atlanta turnpike during rush hour on a Friday."

"Have you been to LA?" Brody straightened in his

seat. "The traffic out there beats Atlanta any day of the week. If you want to talk about clogged—"

"I think she was making a point." Kayla patted him on the back, then drew her hands into her lap. "And I appreciate it. I appreciate both of you. But really, you can go. I'll call you when they say he's out of surgery. We've already been here a while. Who knows how long it could take?"

"You did the same thing when we were kids," Lauren said, inclining her head. She studied Kayla like she might be seeing her for the first time. "I always thought it was because you wanted Dad's attention for yourself. But that wasn't it at all, was it?"

"I don't know what you're talking about," Kayla lied, even as the little hairs on her neck rose.

She knew exactly what her sister was talking about, which was no good.

"Besides," she continued, "this isn't about me. We're here because of Dad. So if you want to lecture me about how—"

"Do you believe he doesn't consider you his real daughter?" Lauren sounded genuinely curious. "I can't believe all this time I thought you were trying to make me look bad. It was never about me."

"Not everything is about you," Brody said. "Most of it is about me."

Kayla knew he was trying to lighten the mood. There was no denying the tension that had seeped into the room. Two other people started to walk in at that moment but took one look at the Maxwell siblings and backed out of the room like it was on fire.

"Of course it's about Lauren." Kayla stood and walked two paces before returning to face her sister.

"I wanted to be you and to be loved by you. I dreamed of Dad loving me the way he did you. None of those things happened, no matter how hard I tried, and I've been trying for a very long time."

Lauren shook her head. "But he does love you, at least as much as he can love anyone. I'm not saying it's healthy, but seeing how close the two of you were hurt me. You were the perfect daughter with the mom he loved. I could never compete."

Kayla shook her head. "You shouldn't have had to, and I thought you hated me because I had a bigger bedroom."

Lauren laughed. "That was annoying until I took it from you, but I hated you because you were a family. All I wanted my whole life was family, and neither one of my parents cared about me."

"He came for you," Kayla reminded her. "He could have left you in Italy with your mother."

"I didn't see him for years because he didn't care enough to visit. Yes, he brought me back here, but he didn't want to. I didn't fit the mold of his cookie-cutter country club family the way you and your mom did. I was a leftover—a reminder of a mistake he had made. An unwanted pregnancy with a woman he didn't love."

Lauren shifted her gaze to Brody. "You aren't the same as him," she said before returning her attention to Kayla. "You don't need to prove anything because he won't send you away, even now. If he did, he's a fool."

Brody cleared his throat. "I hate to break it to you, but our father might be the biggest fool on the planet. He was a fool for fighting with you and encouraging the two of you to go after each other. He's a fool for underestimating and undervaluing me. He's a selfish jerk to make Ben feel he needs to partner with him to be a legitimate success. As much as I don't want him to die, I wouldn't mind this episode scaring some sense into him."

"We should be so lucky," Kayla murmured.

Brody patted the chair next to him, and Kayla sat back down. "I'm not the oldest, so I don't have as much experience as Lauren at bossing people around." He shrugged when Lauren snorted. "That's not my personality anyway, but it's time you both knock it off. Your relationship has been defined by loss and lack for too many years. Lauren lost her mom when Dad came to take her away, and Kayla lost ours because of the accident. There must be loads of stuff written about the toll of being a motherless daughter, but you two have something many women don't. You have each other. Stop pretending you don't matter to each other."

"I just said how much she matters to me," Kayla whispered. "She's the one—"

"You both contributed to this. Lauren thinks Dad loves Kayla, and Kayla is convinced Dad loves Lauren better. How about the two of you stop worrying about him and start caring for yourselves?"

"You aren't a burden on this family," Lauren told Kayla.

Kayla was surprised at how much it meant to hear the words and realized she might not be the only one who needed to.

She reached across the small space and took her sister's warm hand. "You aren't either. You never were."

"Y'all don't have to say it to me." Brody leaned forward and covered both of their hands with one of his.

"I know I'm not a burden. I am, in fact, a miracle, as Laur pointed out."

Kayla squeezed Lauren's fingers before all three of them sat back. "We created a monster with you," she told her little brother.

"Just so you know, we're going to do it even more with your son or daughter." Lauren wiggled her brows. "Paybacks are hell, Brody."

He grinned, then turned serious. "I'm pretty sure we'll need all the help we can get, even though I'm not saying that to Dad."

Kayla shared a meaningful look with Lauren. Neither of them had confronted Brody about the fact that the baby he claimed wasn't biologically his. She wondered now if Lauren would bring it up.

Kayla had no intention of mentioning it. Despite what she'd believed for many years, sharing DNA didn't guarantee a perfect relationship. Brody's commitment would ensure that he did his best; she knew that would be enough.

"Whatever you need," Lauren said with a decisive nod.

Brody's mouth pulled down at one end. "What if I need you both to stay?"

"Are you Robert Maxwell's family?"

At the question, shock coursed through Kayla like that first jump into the cold sound each summer, but she turned toward the man in scrubs who'd appeared in the doorway without any of them noticing.

Lauren immediately stood. "Yes. We're his children. How is he?"

Brody's hand found Kayla's as they waited for the doctor to speak. "I'm Dr. Blaser. He's in recovery now.

We did a coronary angioplasty to open the main artery. Your dad should be good as new—better, in fact." The man rubbed his hand against the back of his neck. "He's got a strong heart to match his…strong personality."

"Can we see him?" Brody asked.

Dr. Blaser seemed to consider his answer before nodding. "He's being transferred from ICU to the surgical floor so, yes, but I should warn you. He's what I would describe as ornery. Many people come out of an episode like this with a sense of gratitude for a new lease on life, but others—like your father—are frustrated and angry at a perceived loss of control."

Kayla felt her own heart settle. She glanced at Lauren and Brody, who had comically similar expressions on their faces.

"I think that's exactly what we expected to hear," she said. "The three of us can handle this, Doctor."

"Then I'll take you to him," the man answered, and they followed him down the hall.

CHAPTER TWENTY-ONE

BEN SAT BACK in his chair at Over Easy, his dad's favorite breakfast spot in downtown Magnolia, and tried not to gape as his father and Jim shared a laugh about someone they'd both known growing up. The restaurant was decorated like an old-school diner with Formica tables, red-lacquered banquets and framed photos of old movie stars on the walls.

It was a throwback to another era, which suited Ben fine since he felt like he'd landed in an alternate universe watching the scene unfold before him.

"Didn't you teach your son that it's impolite to leave his mouth hanging open like a barn door?" Jim asked, pointing a jam-slathered biscuit in Ben's direction.

"I didn't teach him much of anything other than what not to do," Bart countered. "You took care of the important stuff. I owe you, Jim."

"Are the two of you trying to freak me out?" Ben demanded with a shake of his head.

"What's your problem, Benny?" his dad asked. "I thought you wanted me and ol' Jim here to get along?"

"I did." Ben wondered why witnessing them do just that stupefied him. "However, I didn't expect it to happen in my lifetime."

"Are you starting with the old stuff again?" Jim

laughed like Ben hadn't spoken. "You're the guy with the bad hip."

"Yeah, but that fancy surgeon you recommended is going to take care of that for me. I'm gonna be the bionic man."

"The ladies at Shady Acres will like that. Hardware is sexy."

"Oh, my God," Ben mumbled.

"Don't act like you don't know about sexy," Jim said with a raised brow. "I've seen you sneaking across camp at night to pay a visit to Lauren's cabin when her daughter isn't there. Same as you used to when you were kids."

"Doubtful you're borrowing a cup of sugar," Bart added, earning another chuckle from Jim.

"He's bringing the sugar," Jim said.

"Stop!" Ben held up a hand then waved to the other diners in the restaurant when several turned to stare at him.

His father and Jim had gone silent after sharing a look that Ben couldn't decipher.

"Seriously, what's going on? Why are the two of you suddenly acting like you've been best friends for years?"

"Not years," Jim said. "Although we've known each other for decades."

"And shared a mutual disdain for as long as I can remember." He pinned his father with a stare. "Do you know how many times Nancy and Jim tried to get you to come out to camp for some of the activities?"

"Now, son," Bart began, but Ben cut him off with a sharp flick of his hand.

"I practically had to hog-tie you to agree to Thanksgiving dinner with the Lowerys each year, and you managed to convey how much you hated being there without saying a word."

"Jim makes lumpy potatoes," Bart said, as if that explained everything. "Although Nancy's stuffing was legendary."

"My Nancy-girl was gifted in the kitchen," Jim agreed. "Not sure why she always insisted I whip the potatoes when I couldn't get them smooth to save my life."

"Trying to have a pointed conversation with the two of you is like herding cats," Ben said, exasperation filling him. "What's going on? Is this some fakeout thing to put me on the defensive? Dad, I'm waiting for Jim to say something that sets you off and to have to break up an old geezer fistfight."

"Come on." Bart's voice was placating. "I haven't gotten into a fight since I gave up the brown liquor."

"Yeah, Dad, I get it. You lost your taste for alcohol, but you certainly didn't develop one for Jim."

"Benny." Bart scrubbed a gnarled hand over his face. "There hasn't been a day in the past seventeen years that I haven't craved a drink. Sometimes the need is so overwhelming it takes my breath away. I'm not sure you can understand that kind of ache."

Ben understood because it was how he felt about Lauren—like an addict who'd been on the wagon for years, minding his own business and mistakenly assuming he had things under control. Suddenly he got another taste for the good stuff, and he was back to wanting in a deeper way than he could even fathom.

"One of the things that kept me sober for all these years is you, son. I let you down in many ways. Our whole family let you down, and for too long, I ignored that fact. I was too proud to admit I owed Jim a great debt for his help guiding you to become the amazing man you are."

Ben stilled, uncertain how to react to this kind of honesty from his father.

"Although you may have grown up thinking that I was damn near perfect," Jim said with a wry smile, "I can admit now that I didn't mind the fact that your father struggled to be there for you. It meant I had an opportunity to be a bigger part of your life. You were the son Nancy and I never had. If I could have chosen a child for myself, it would have been you."

Ben's throat clogged with emotion. He didn't know how to respond to either of them, although it seemed like they didn't expect a response, because Jim continued, "Nancy told me that I needed to do more to bridge the distance between the two of you, but I didn't want it. I'm not proud of that, but it's the truth."

"I don't know much," Ben's father said, patting Jim on the hand. "But one thing I know for sure is regrets do nothing but eat away at a person's soul. If I had a nickel for every regret, particularly where it came to my family, I could personally buy that damn camp the two of you love so much. I don't care about my reputation or our family name, Ben. Your happiness matters more."

Before Ben's shock could reverberate any deeper, Jim made a growling sound low in his throat. "If we're talking about regrets, there's one I can't release—selling the camp."

The words were like a knife to Ben's heart.

"You regret selling the camp to me? Jim, you have to know I'm going to honor the legacy of the Camp Blossom land. You agreed that running it again is too much for you. I thought this was what you wanted."

In the midst of all his worries, Ben had held on to that indisputable truth. He was doing what was right for Jim. If that weren't the case and his father didn't care about restoring their family name, had everything he'd worked for been a waste of time and energy?

His gut churned at the thought.

"I need to sell for financial reasons." Jim picked up a piece of bacon and studied the slice as he spoke. "Plus, without Nancy, the magic of running camp is gone for me. There are too many memories of her sprinkled around the property."

He bit the bacon slice in half and chewed. "You and Lauren have helped me remember the good times and left me with happy memories, Ben. That's enough for this old geezer."

Ben lifted a forkful of omelet halfway to his mouth, trying to act normal, then lowered it again. "Then why are you talking about regrets? That doesn't sound happy."

"It's damned Robert Maxwell's involvement," Jim muttered, chomping on the bacon like it had done him a disservice. All three men were silent as the waitress stopped by the table to refill their coffee cups.

"I know you love Lauren," Bart said when she left. "But her dad is a jackass."

"Loved," Ben clarified. "What Lauren I had is in the past."

"So all that trotting around camp in the dark is because she's some casual hookup that doesn't mean anything to you?" His dad quirked a brow. "Jim didn't raise you to treat a woman that way, and I hope you learned something from my mistakes."

Ben wondered if it was possible to grind his teeth to nubs right here at breakfast. "She means something, but it's not love." The lie tasted as bitter as day-old coffee on his tongue.

Bart didn't look convinced. "If that's what you want to tell yourself..."

"I'm not discussing Lauren with you. We're talking about Camp Blossom and Jim's regrets." He took a long breath to calm himself. "I don't want to go forward with the development plans if it's not what you want."

Jim frowned. "Can you honestly tell me that a gated community of cookie-cutter mansions is what's best for the land and this community? Because if you believe it, I trust you."

Ben opened his mouth to say exactly that, but the words wouldn't come. "This deal gives me the money to take care of you, Jim."

He shifted his gaze to his father. "It will make me enough money down the road to take care of you, too. I'm not walking into it blind or without an appreciation of what Jim is giving up. I don't see another way."

"Have you looked for one?" his father asked.

"Or do you like the idea of working with Robert?" Jim inclined his head. "We know you have something to prove, Ben, but what your dad and I don't understand is why you can't see that you've already done it. You're a good man. You make a difference in people's lives. That's success in my book."

"I wanted to make the choices I did," Ben argued. "No one forced me."

"Maybe not," Bart agreed, "But you have other options now."

"You two think success on a level that this development affords isn't a good option." Ben pressed his lips together to keep from shouting out in frustration. "Am I supposed to play small because that's all I'm capable of being? Robert Maxwell isn't the only one with a vision for the land."

"It's not your ability to succeed that worries us." His father held Ben's gaze with a surprising steadiness. "You've already achieved more than I could have dreamed. We want you to honor your own vision."

"Don't let that man convince you otherwise," Jim added. "We trust you to do what's right for everyone involved."

If only Ben had that kind of faith in himself.

As Ben checked the setup for a few of the more popular games later that afternoon in preparation for the final night of the camp's winter carnival, he paused to look around at the scenery so familiar to him.

He knew the cabins like the back of his hand and the thick forest surrounding the property as if it cradled him in a protective embrace.

He remembered the first time he'd walked from his trailer the four miles to Camp Blossom after his peewee football coach had arranged a scholarship to pay his registration and cajoled Bart into agreeing to let him go.

In hindsight, Ben understood he'd received a scholarship because Jim and Nancy had agreed to allow him to attend for free. They offered that to kids who someone told them could benefit from a summer away from home but didn't have the means to pay.

The picturesque property and quaint buildings had seemed like a forest fairy tale come true, and the gentle lapping of water on the shore had soothed a little boy who was used to living in a state of hypervigilance and stress, unsure what might set off his dad.

The fresh air, clean sheets, and the structure of days at camp, not to mention the Lowerys' kindness, made him feel at home in a way he never had while constantly walking on eggshells with his father under their dented aluminum roof.

He also took a moment to imagine what this place would look like once it was filled with houses, sidewalks and paved roads. These high-end residential developments were all the rage on the coast, with companies like Maxwell Enterprises buying up tracts of land wherever they could get a good deal.

Ben had made sure that Jim was well-compensated in this situation, and he was proud of what he'd done to make his dream of being a significant player in the future of his hometown a reality. He was happy. Why had his father and Jim seemed convinced he wasn't?

He'd worked hard for this moment and didn't like the gray cloud that hovered over his plans. He was fulfilled, a key ingredient of happiness.

Having a purpose was like happiness for adults, right? Yet he couldn't seem to step out from under the cloud of doubt that followed him around like a shadow.

As he continued to stare at the sound, he realized a lone figure sat at the end of the dock. He couldn't believe he hadn't noticed Lauren when he first stepped outside.

It felt like his heart was attuned to her, a needle on a compass pointing to its true north. But she'd been so still, it was almost as if she blended into the natural world.

He watched as she stood and lifted her arms wide, gazing up at the pale winter sky. She turned and made her way back toward solid land, dashing her hands over her cheeks as she got closer. Alarm bells went off in his head.

There was no sense worrying about his future if something had upset Lauren enough to make her cry, and he immediately strode toward her.

He couldn't be happy when she was sad.

"Hey," he called as he got closer. She looked up, clearly surprised at not being alone in this moment. Then she smiled, and her eyes grew warm like she was happy to see him, as if he was essential to her joy the way she was to his.

"What's going on?" he asked. "Is it your dad? Did he have a setback? What can I do?"

He took hold of her arms and drew her to him before she had a chance to answer. If nothing else, he could offer her some comfort that way. His heart settled as she relaxed into him, resting her hand against his chest.

"My dad is fine for a man who survived his first heart attack. Kayla and I went to see him this morning. He was cranky, rude and disagreeable. Pretty much back to normal."

"Then what's going on?"

"I'm happy," she said softly.

"You were crying. I don't understand."

She drew back and looked up at him, emotion shimmering in her gaze. "I'm unsure how to explain it, but I'll try. It might take a minute."

"I've got all the time in the world," Ben assured her.

Lauren flashed a grin. "When Hannah was younger, before she decided rebellion fit her, I used to go to all of the school conferences the way parents do."

"Mine never did," he said, shaking his head.

"The way most parents do," she amended. "I always

heard the same things. 'Hannah is smart and creative, a good student and a respectful classmate and friend. A little too talkative.' I cried every single time. It was so embarrassing, especially the year she had the alpha male teacher who seemed to take my tears as a personal affront."

Ben lowered his head to kiss her damp cheek. "There's nothing wrong with tears."

"I don't like them," she said with a watery smile. "But sometimes they come anyway, and for me, it's mostly when the feelings get to be too much. I used to be able to deal with sadness—I was a master at compartmentalizing. But when the emotion overflows, I can't stop the waterworks. Tonight is the last night of carnival and the countdown to the end of camp as we know it."

She smoothed a hand over the soft fabric of his puffer jacket, and the touch was oddly comforting.

"I didn't expect any of this." It sounded as much like she was talking to herself as to him. "I didn't expect a few weeks back here under the guise of helping Brody to help me so much. A lot has changed. My relationship with my daughter and with my sister. Did you notice I'm not calling her my stepsister anymore? That's a big deal, right? A lot has changed, and…"

Her voice trailed off as if she had more to say but couldn't find the right words. *Me*, he wanted to tell her. *Tell me that I'm part of that change.*

He wasn't sure why it was so important to him or what good it would do for either of them, but that didn't change his wanting.

Nothing could touch the yearning he felt when it came to Lauren.

"I definitely hadn't planned on reconnecting with

you in the way we have," she said like she'd heard his silent plea and decided to take pity on him and answer it.

But when her gaze returned his, it wasn't pity swimming in its blue depths. He didn't even dare try to name what he saw there, but it made him realize that two old men had been right over breakfast that morning. Purpose and fulfillment were all well and good, but they weren't happiness, at least where Ben was concerned. Lauren made him happy.

"What if you stayed?" The question popped out before he could stop it.

Her mouth dropped open. "That wasn't the plan."

He kissed her forehead and tried to memorize the feel of her soft skin against his lips. He tried to imagine a world where this woman would belong to him finally and forever the way he'd always thought it would be.

"Plans change. You know that more than anyone."

"I wish it were that simple."

If he told her he loved her, would that make it simple? Would that kind of declaration be enough to make her stay?

She made him happy, and if she gave him a chance, he would do his best to make her happy in return. But he didn't say those three little words because he'd tried that once before. Hell, he'd married her, and it hadn't been enough to make her stay.

He knew himself well enough to understand that if he risked that much of himself now, there would be no coming back from it if she rejected him. Preparing for disappointment felt more familiar to Ben than being happy.

"What have you got to lose?" he asked instead, and immediately realized that was the wrong response. The warmth in her blue eyes cooled considerably. But as much as he wanted more, he also understood what was on the line for him if he put himself out there and Lauren rebuffed him again. She'd walked away once before. What would change?

"I've got nothing. I'm not staying." She stepped away from him. Like the fool he was, he let her go.

"I'm the kind of person who cries when I'm happy, not just because of the emotion but because happiness scares me, Ben."

She wrinkled her nose. "I don't trust it. I don't trust it to last. If I let down my guard, something will bite me in the ass. If I had to choose being safe or happy, I'd pick safe every day."

Ben couldn't even argue, because he understood that feeling. He embodied that feeling. "For the record, I've been happier in the past couple weeks with you, getting to know Hannah and giving Jim this last Christmas at camp, than I can remember since our last summer here. I don't trust it either."

"I guess we make a good pair," Lauren said, her voice taking on a soft tone.

Somehow this moment felt different than the ones that had come before. He'd gotten to know her body over the past couple of weeks, but now he felt he was getting a true glimpse into her soul, not simply the hints he'd seen earlier.

"We always have," he answered, but he wanted to tell her what was in his heart. To say those three words that could change everything for both of them.

Instead, he kept his mouth tightly shut.

CHAPTER TWENTY-TWO

FROM WHERE SHE stood near the edge of the action, Lauren watched the visitors and locals mill about the carnival. The crowd laughed as they enjoyed the activities she'd created, the joy of the event adding to the happiness that had settled in her heart when she'd sat at the end of the dock, appreciating the beauty of the world around her. There'd been something about the quiet moments looking out to the water that conjured memories of the good times she'd had in the past and the unexpected feeling of contentment the past few weeks had given her.

It had been an impulsive decision to return to Magnolia—one motivated by fear of what could have happened to Hannah if the car wreck had been more serious, as well a deep desire to help her brother. Her choice of renting the cabin from the camp's outdated website had been made from self-preservation to avoid her father and all the complications he presented. She was glad she'd made both of those decisions.

Although they had most of the details in place for the Christmas Eve wedding four days from now, she wasn't sure if making certain that event went off without a hitch would truly help Brody. But it was what he wanted, and it had brought Lauren close to her stepsister in ways that still surprised her.

She also couldn't deny that so much of what made her happy during her stay involved Ben. He might not have agreed with her initial plan to revive camp for one last holiday season extravaganza, but he'd pitched in anyway because it meant something to her.

Meaning something and being in love were apparently two different things.

She had no right to ask Ben to consider changing the plans made for the housing development and no idea if he could extricate himself from the partnership deal without risking his financial security and that of both Jim and his own father. Understanding those things in her rational mind was all well and good, but Lauren's heart didn't quite get the message.

As pragmatic and intent on survival as Lauren prided herself on being, she was a romantic at heart. When she'd turned and saw him waiting for her on the shore, she hoped that her happiness would convince him to change his mind. Their future might motivate him to something more.

She reread the letter she'd written all those years ago at least once daily. The dreams she'd had as a wide-eyed teenager weren't too different from those she had now. Only the present-day version of Lauren realized how out of reach they truly were.

"Mom! You aren't going to believe this."

Lauren plastered on a smile as Hannah rushed toward her.

"I'll believe anything right now," she said, brushing her daughter's flyaway hair off her face. "That's the deal with Christmas. You have to believe to receive."

"I got asked out on a date by the cutest boy I've ever seen," Hannah said, her voice filled with wonder. "Then this group of local girls in my grade told me they like my aesthetic."

"I didn't know you had an aesthetic." Lauren tried

not to be alarmed at the comment about the cutest boy in Magnolia.

"I didn't either." Hannah glanced down at her baggy sweatshirt and high-waisted jeans with rips in both knees like she was seeing herself for the first time. "They seem nice, Mom, and they asked me to go downtown for ice cream. I can go, right? Please say yes. We won't be out late. They're just the kind of wholesome teens you always want me to be friends with."

Lauren bit back her smile. "Wholesome teens, huh? You know you're grounded."

"Until when?"

"I don't know. I haven't given it much thought, but we're leaving the day after Christmas."

Hannah's eyes widened with shock. "Were you going to clue me in on that little fact?"

It was difficult for Lauren to answer the question since she'd made the decision at this exact moment.

"Why do we have to leave so soon? I turned in all my assignments and took my finals online. Mom, I'm on track to get an A in every class except environmental science, and that will be a really high B. These are the best grades I've ever gotten. I've helped with the carnival and been nice to Avah. I'm doing good. Don't you trust me?"

How could Lauren explain that Hannah wasn't the real issue? The problem was Lauren's mistrust of herself. If Hannah was thriving, then Lauren had no reason to leave, besides the fact that she was too afraid to risk being hurt again by staying.

She was about to tell her daughter no, but something stopped her. She thought about Nancy and how the camp owner had trusted Lauren to lead the younger campers at a time when it felt like no one else believed in her. Hannah needed Lauren to have that same faith that she was finally making the right choices. Her daughter might be sad when they left, but meanwhile she could experience the simple pleasures this town still offered. It might help her understand she could still claim that happiness once they returned to their regular life.

"You're right, Banana." She pulled her daughter in for a quick hug. "I'm proud of who you've become in these weeks here. I trust you, and I want you to have fun. Wholesome fun is the best. Yes, you can go with your new friends. Be safe and make good choices. Home by eleven."

"Thank you, Mom."

Hannah's smile brought tears to Lauren's eyes. She needed to get a hold of herself in the waterworks department. It was as if once the floodgate of tears opened, she couldn't close it again.

"I'm going to make you proud. I promise."

"I'm proud of you, sweetheart. Even when I'm mad or disappointed in your actions, I know your heart, and it's golden. You are always on my nice list. I'm lucky to be your mother."

"I love you," Hannah whispered, then turned and bounced away toward a group of kids who did indeed look like the picture of Mayberry wholesomeness. Maybe things would've turned out differently for Lauren if she'd had more friends like that.

Except she had. Izzy and Maren had their share of problems, just like she did, but their friendship had been one of the most authentic things in her life, and she wished she hadn't let them go.

Christmas was a time to believe in magic. Looking around at the smiling faces of the people enjoying this final night, she realized that, like her daughter, Lauren wanted to hold on to whatever bits of happiness she could.

So after checking on several of the booths and refreshment stations, then greeting a few more people, she went to find Ben.

He was standing near the edge of the big cabin talking to Malcolm Grimes, Magnolia's mayor.

"Hey there, Miss Maxwell," Mal greeted her as she approached. "You've added something special to Christmas on the Coast this year. And you've made a lot of people around here realize how much they're going to miss this camp when it's gone."

She felt Ben tense at that comment but ignored it. She didn't want another argument. Not tonight.

"I couldn't have done it without Ben's help." She linked her arm with his. "We made a great team this holiday."

The older man smiled. "I didn't know either of you when you were younger, but I've heard stories about you over the years." He inclined his head toward Lauren, his dark chocolate-colored eyes warm with amusement. "Several of them painted you as a bit of hell-raiser."

"I'm not the same person I was back then," she answered, choosing not to imagine what he must have heard.

"I liked that person," Ben said, drawing her closer. Maybe she wasn't the only one who wanted a truce for the night.

"I bet I would have, too," the mayor agreed. "We all change and grow—at least, that's the goal. Otherwise, what's the point of getting out of bed every day?"

"You should mention that changing and growing to my dad." Lauren made a face. "He's determined that life and everyone who's a part of his world fall in step to his arbitrary standards."

"Believe me, I have talked to him until I'm out of words, and that's saying something for me." Mayor Mal shrugged. "Your daddy has an eye for development and is a master at making a deal. I understand the benefit of bringing new tax revenue to this community, but bigger isn't always better. Sometimes more is just more, not an improvement."

He glanced past Lauren and Ben to wave as someone called out a greeting before returning his attention to them. "Sometimes prioritizing a community's character is more important than money and growth."

"Sometimes you can have both," Ben countered.

"I hope you're right." Malcolm tipped his hat and then took a step back. "I'm going to get another cup of hot chocolate."

"Tell Kayla to give you extra marshmallows on the house," Lauren told him with a wink.

"Extra extra," Mal said, and chuckled as he walked away.

"Why does it feel like everyone is suddenly against me?" Ben asked when they were alone again.

"They aren't." Lauren turned to face him and placed her hands on the soft flannel that covered his broad shoulders. "No one is against you. Maybe they realized they didn't value what was important to them when they had it. Like the song says, it feels like you don't always know what you've got 'til it's gone."

"I'm not sure that makes it better or worse," Ben said. "Because I always knew what I had. I couldn't find a way to save it. How is it that on the cusp of what should be the biggest success in my life, I feel like I'm teetering on the edge of utter failure?"

"You aren't a failure. You have never been a failure.

Change is scary for all of us, and you can't have big success without some risk."

"I don't want to risk the wrong things," he told her. "Not anymore. Not again."

Was he also talking about the two of them? She wanted to believe it, but he didn't offer anything more, and she wouldn't ask—not tonight.

"I let Hannah go into town for ice cream with kids I don't know. Am I a fool?"

Ben squeezed her waist. "She's a good kid, Lauren. Even good kids act out, but you have to trust them again. The world is all about second chances."

"People always tell me they see me in my daughter, and that scares the hell out of me," Lauren admitted with a sigh. "I rebelled for the sake of it because thwarting the rules allowed me to feel something—mainly anger, which in the long run got me nowhere. I don't want Hannah to take after me. I want her to do better, to be better. I've played small her whole life because I mistakenly believed that if I didn't risk anything, then I wouldn't fail her."

"She's going to make mistakes no matter what you do or how you try to protect her."

"I'm also trying to protect myself, but it's exhausting. I'm tired of pretending, Ben."

He leaned in and pressed his forehead to hers like they could give each other strength. Maybe he was right—sharing her worries with him made her feel oddly better.

"Adulting is hard," he told her, like that explained everything.

She laughed and turned when applause exploded near the snowball fight game as two teams of friends finished, the winners crowing with pride.

"We have an hour left, and then the carnival closes." She breathed through the tumult of emotions crowding her heart, knowing they would easily overwhelm her if she gave them space. "After Brody's wedding on Christmas Eve, nothing will be left here."

She placed two fingers against his mouth when he started to respond. "I don't want to think about that right now. I don't want to talk about the future or the past. I want to pretend like the mistakes I made didn't have long-lasting repercussions. Can you pretend with me, Ben? Can we be happy for the next couple of minutes, hours, and possibly even days?"

It took him a long time to answer, and Lauren wondered if he would reject her silly request.

Neither one of them could truly ignore reality, escape the past or disregard the future.

"There's a nearly full moon tonight," he said, pointing to the night sky. "Do you want to go out on the sound with me?"

"All the boats are put away. Jim never let people take them out off-season, and definitely not after dark. It's too dangerous if someone ends up in the water."

Ben pulled a small key ring out of his front pocket and jingled it in front of her. "I have access, and I'm in a rebellious mood. Think of it as a challenge, Laur. We can be happy rebels one more time. Are you with me?"

"Oh, Lord. I'm a terrible influence on you, Ben Donnelly. You never broke the rules."

"You're worth it," he whispered, and the intensity of his voice made it feel like the stars were shining in her heart. "You're worth it all."

She glanced over her shoulder at the bustling carnival. "I'm supposed to be in charge here."

Kayla's eyes met Lauren's from across the open

space where the booths had been set up as if it was synchronicity. Her sister held up her hands in question, and Lauren quickly pulled her phone from her jacket to type a text.

Cover for me? Ben and I are going to play hooky.

She watched as Kayla read the message. A smile spread across her sister's face.

You've got it.

"Kayla will take care of things here," Lauren said as she took Ben's hand and followed him toward the shed near the water that held the boating equipment. "I hope Hannah doesn't find out about this. It kind of degrades my street cred as a strict mom if I'm the one breaking the rules."

Ben chuckled. "It probably feels like old times for Kayla."

Lauren paused at Ben's offhand remark. He tugged, so she started walking again, but the question wouldn't leave her mind.

"What are you talking about, old times?"

He laughed softly. "From what she's told me, there were only a couple of instances where your dad noticed you'd left, but in those cases, she covered for you when we used to sneak out. During the times you snuck out with friends, too."

"I didn't know Dad ever realized I wasn't around. Nobody knew. I was a sneaky sneaker-outer."

They made it to the shed, and Ben began to work the lock. "Kayla knew."

"Why didn't she turn me in? It would have been

right up her alley to get me in even bigger trouble than I could manage alone."

"Because she had your back even if you didn't realize it."

Ben shared that news like it wasn't a big deal, but it meant something to Lauren. For years she'd felt like the outsider, as if no one was in her corner. Brody didn't count because he'd been younger, but she'd been wrong then, foolish, and so determined not to let anybody in so she wouldn't get hurt.

She hadn't realized her insistence on the story that she had to take care of herself was the actual thing hurting her. It was one more way she'd screwed up the past, but it wasn't too late. Not for her or for Hannah.

He opened the door. "We're in. You and me against the world, Laur. Or at least against the wind until we get too cold out on the sound."

"Sure."

"Hey, what's going on?" He turned toward her, paddle in hand, his brow puckered with concern. Lauren wished she had a better poker face.

"I already don't want this moment to end." She managed a smile. "I'm not going to cry. I've shed more tears in the past three weeks than I have my whole life. I didn't cry like this when I learned my mom was sending me away. And when she died, I showed no emotion. How pathetic is that?"

"Nothing about you is pathetic." Ben took one of the two-person canoes off the boat rack. "You are probably the least pathetic person I've ever met. It's okay to show emotion. Sometimes the feelings get so big they have to find a way out."

"I'm glad to have this moment with you."

She didn't ask for more, and he didn't offer it, but

there seemed to be a mutual understanding that this evening was precious. Silently, they carried the boat down to the water the way Lauren had done so many times in the past. The air was still, and she could see her breath in a misty cloud. The sound was nearly waveless, moonlight shimmering off its surface.

"Let's get in from the dock," Ben said. "We'll stay dry that way."

"I hope you're going to keep the dock as part of the new community."

Her heart sank when he didn't answer, which was an answer in and of itself.

"It's okay," she said as much to herself as to him. It was all going to be okay.

He took her hand and helped her into the boat, then sat behind her. They began to paddle toward the center of the sound, and she could almost believe things would work out for the best. She could believe anything with Ben there to ground her with his steady presence.

She wished she hadn't let herself fall in love with him again, but there was no denying it. There was also nothing to do that would make it last.

"It looks even prettier from this vantage point," he said and used an oar to point back to camp.

Lauren's breath caught in her throat as she took in the view.

"It really is a winter wonderland," she said in a hushed tone. Although the air was crisp, the wind had died down, so they could hear the sounds of laughter and conversation drifting across the water from the carnival.

The twinkle lights lit up the central area of camp, making it appear like a fairy enclave in the middle of the darkness. The view perfectly represented what Camp

Blossom had meant to her when she was growing up. It was a light in the darkness that had seemed ready to consume her. The shadows were no match for the joy Camp Blossom brought people, and with the magic of Christmas added to the scene tonight, it was the most beautiful thing she'd ever witnessed.

"I'm glad you came back and that the website hadn't been updated." Ben shifted so that his knees supported her from behind. He tipped her head back and kissed her gently. "Although I'm rethinking whether it was a good idea to clean out the cabin for you. Maybe you should have stayed with me the whole time."

"I see how you are, Ben Donnelly. You want to ruin my reputation. I have to tell you, with the mess I made years ago, I'm not sure there's anything left to save."

But it wasn't only her reputation he'd ruined; it was her heart for anyone else. Maybe that had been done decades earlier. Perhaps that was why it had been so easy to keep herself closed off—the only one she'd ever truly wanted to open for was Ben.

"I like everything about you, Lauren Maxwell. Including your reputation."

He wrapped his strong arms around her tightly, and she waited for him to say more. She didn't want to simply be liked by Ben or even cared for or desired. She wanted him to love her the way she did him, with a love so deep it couldn't be measured, and nothing could keep them apart.

She could say those words to him, but she was afraid to take the risk. Not without knowing how he would respond. And when he said nothing else, she knew she was right to keep hold of the few defenses that still guarded her heart when it came to Ben.

KAYLA LET BEN into the Maxwell house the following morning, her smile faltering when she took in his expression.

"Is your dad around?"

"This isn't going to be good, is it?"

"No." Ben didn't bother sugarcoating it. "I know he's still recovering, but I need to talk to him."

"He's in the office. Do you want out of the deal?"

He paused in the massive foyer, which felt like a throwback to another era with its polished marble floors and elaborately wallpapered walls. Silk drapes framed the two-story windows. It did nothing to change his impression that Robert Maxwell's house would have been a better fit in some tony neighborhood in a big-city suburb rather than nestled in a beach community on the Carolina shore.

Would the development they'd partnered to build also stick out like a modern sore thumb? He'd only been in this house one other time, which seemed bizarre given his ties to the Maxwell family. But Lauren had wanted to spend as little time as possible here when they'd been teenagers, and all his business with her father had been conducted at the company's office.

Ben knew Robert regularly entertained at his home but had never received an invitation to the beach house. He should have recognized it for the sign it was—a sign that Robert didn't see him as an equal.

"I should talk to your dad first," Ben said, his voice tight, knowing how badly this could honestly go. "By the way, Lauren doesn't know I'm here today. She and Hannah had already left camp to get breakfast in town before the final dress fitting."

Kayla glanced at her watch and then over her shoulder. "Which is where I'm heading now unless you need me to stay. You might want me to stay, Ben."

"Thanks, K," he said with a genuine smile. "But I've got this. Don't say anything to your sister yet, okay?"

"I can't spill the beans because I don't know what flavor they are," Kayla answered.

"Um…probably something nasty like black licorice." Ben sighed. "Which way to his inner sanctum?"

"Down the hall." She pointed. "Second door on the right. The first door is a powder room in case you want to throw up first."

"I'll be fine," Ben assured her. As much as his gut clenched at the thought of what Robert's reaction to Ben's visit would be, he'd dealt with worse than a rich man's ire.

And all he had to do was to remember the feel of Lauren wrapped in his arms to know that he was making the right choice for his future.

A future he'd never imagined but wanted with his whole heart.

He walked down the hall, his work boots clomping noisily on the gleaming marble. Pausing to take a breath as he came to the half-open door to the study, he gave himself a quick mental pep talk, then knocked and poked in his head.

"Ben, this is a surprise," Robert said from behind the massive desk.

"Do you have a few minutes?"

Robert pushed back in his chair but didn't rise, and Ben had the impression of being granted an audience with a king on his throne. This king looked pale and like he'd lost a few pounds since the heart attack, his starched dress shirt loose on his tall frame. "I've got too much time on my hands since that ridiculous doctor told me I can't work for the next two weeks."

Ben let his gaze stray to the computer monitor as he moved into the office. "Let me guess. You're watching cute cat videos on YouTube to while away the hours?"

"I can't officially work," Robert amended. "My assistant says if I set foot in the office, she'll quit, and she's too valuable to lose. But I can log into email from here. I was responding to a few messages. My contact at Regional Building said he hadn't seen the final plans from you. The title company wants those signed by the county before we close. You're still on track to finalize the sale right after the holidays, correct?"

"That's what I want to talk to you about."

Robert held up a hand. "Don't tell me you are so damned whipped over my daughter once again that you're willing to torpedo your future for her."

"This isn't about Lauren." The hackles on Ben's back rose to sharp points. "Not entirely."

"My ass, it isn't," Robert muttered. "I thought you were smarter than the other men in your family. You might not have gone off the rails with drinks or drugs, but you're a bigger fool. Almost everyone in this town who was speaking to your father at the time your parents got together told him your mother was no good. That's saying something, that people felt the need to warn Bart Donnelly."

"Don't speak about my mother," Ben said with a control he didn't feel.

"Trust me. There's nothing special or worth mentioning about your mother—just another Appalachian hillbilly looking to escape the mountains. Even though your father didn't have two pennies to rub together, he bent over backward to make that woman happy. It was never going to happen, just like it will never work with you and my daughter."

"Not that you have any right to speak for Lauren, but I'll tell you again. This isn't about her. The decision is mine."

"It's bad enough to think you were doing this for love, misguided as that might be, but you and I both know you don't have the money or power to take me on."

Robert pressed a hand to his chest, and alarm zinged through Ben.

"I don't want to upset you. I know this is a complicated time to have this conversation—"

"You aren't upsetting me. You're motivating me and confirming what I already knew. You are too weak, mealymouthed, and swayed by emotion to be a player in the real estate game around here."

Ben tried not to let the words pierce his resolve. He knew that success could be measured by many different markers. Robert's material wealth and influence might be impressive, but they didn't make him the sort of man Ben wanted to emulate on any level.

"That's a chance I'm willing to take based on how I define success."

"I'm only going to say this once." Robert's tone was glacial in its chill. "If you cross me, it will be a mistake you regret your whole life. I've already set up a contingency plan for your cowardice."

"I'm not a coward," Ben said through gritted teeth, then couldn't help his curiosity. "What kind of plan?"

Robert sniffed. "Do you think I'm so stupid that I didn't see what was happening? I came out to that damn carnival."

"Did they skimp on the marshmallows in your hot chocolate?"

Robert's lip curled, but it looked more like a sneer than a smile.

"I saw this coming," he repeated. "I didn't get to where I am today by naivete in business. I've already talked to the bank about options for a new contract when you can't come up with the money for the closing. Part of why you got the deal you did was because of my involvement. I've explained to several of my friends on the bank's board that things might change with our partnership and to think twice about approving your loan to buy the camp. At least without a very hefty down payment, more cash than I imagine you can access."

Ben didn't react outwardly, but inside, the force of Robert's unspoken threat hit like a category four hurricane making landfall. Ben had already leveraged everything from his business to selling his home so that he would have enough money to make the deal go through.

"Does it matter to you how special that place is to your children?"

"It does, in fact," Robert answered, a muscle in his jaw ticking. "My children have prioritized that rundown camp over me for years. It's over. I win."

"You don't win by hurting the people you love." Shock at the absurdity of Robert's statement reverberated through Ben.

"That advice should serve you well when you're alone with nothing to show for years of hard work." Robert leaned forward. "I assume you know Lauren's leaving the day after Christmas, since the two of you are so close."

"This isn't about Lauren," Ben repeated, although he was having trouble continuing to hide his shock as Robert's words continued to hit like shrapnel. He'd known she was leaving but hadn't realized she'd be gone before the new year. She'd be gone unless he did something to stop her.

"Lauren doesn't know I'm here," he told Robert, as if that proved something.

"So you're blowing up your life without a guarantee it will make a difference to her? You might be the biggest idiot the Donnelly line has ever produced, and that's saying something." Robert stood, swaying slightly and appearing paler than when Ben first entered the room. Maybe he wasn't as immune to the potential consequences of this conversation as he acted.

"I'm in a generous mood, Ben, and I understand how appealing my daughter can be. She takes after her mother in that way—a train wreck, but a beautiful one."

Ben shook his head, wondering how he'd ever considered partnering with such a detestable man. Had he thought so little of his own worth as not just a viable business leader in this community, but a person, to believe he needed Robert's validation to feel like he'd finally made it?

Just like Lauren, he deserved more. They both had earned some faith in themselves and each other.

"I'll give you one chance to rethink this folly," Robert continued. "But I'll also take—"

"Nothing," Ben interrupted. "You'll take nothing from me or your daughter anymore. This decision is mine, just like Lauren gets to choose her future. And I will do my best to ensure that future involves me. I'm not afraid of taking you on, Robert. I'm more honorable a man than you could ever hope to be."

"Honor doesn't pay the bills or get deals made."

There was no mistaking the warning in his tone. "You don't want to cross me."

Ben shrugged. "I already have, and I'm still here. Merry Christmas, Robert."

"That's Mr. Maxwell to you, son."

Ben didn't bother replying. He simply walked out the door.

"YOU LOOK BEAUTIFUL," Lauren said, and she didn't have to fake the smile. As promised, Mariella had altered the wedding gown to fit Avah perfectly. The fabric gathered under her bodice and spilled into a classic A-line, and the ivory shade complemented her skin tone.

Mariella had left Lauren and Kayla with Avah while she assisted a customer at the front of the store. But based on the shade of pink infusing Avah's cheeks as she clearly attempted to fight back tears, Lauren wished the dress designer had stayed with them. Mariella's confidence and calming presence could mollify Avah. The Maxwell sisters didn't seem to possess enough of either to suffice in this moment.

"I'm a fat cow. Moo." Avah climbed off the pedestal in the back office of A Second Chance and rummaged around in her purse, eventually pulling out a gargantuan-sized—although half-eaten—chocolate bar.

She took a bite and then let out a screech when another piece broke off and rolled down the front of the wedding gown, leaving a dotted trail of chocolate in its wake.

"Now it's ruined." Avah burst into sloppy tears, her mouth hanging open with its contents exposed. Lauren was momentarily shocked into stillness, but thankfully, Kayla jumped up and grabbed a towel from a nearby desk. She shoved it against Avah's face.

"It's not ruined. We can deal with the stain. But for God's sake, keep your mouth closed. You don't need to drip more down the front."

Lauren wasn't sure she'd ever heard Kayla snap at anyone. Avah stepped back, sinking into the chair next to Lauren. Her pretty mouth trembled as tears streamed down her face.

"Kayla, would you go ask Mariella what she would suggest using to get chocolate off lace and silk? I'll stay here with Avah. We're going to figure this out. All of it."

The words were simple enough to say, but she didn't believe them and doubted her sister or soon-to-be sister-in-law did either.

Kayla glared at Avah, hands on hips for several long moments, then gave a disgusted snort and walked out of the room.

"From everything Brody told me," Avah said, blowing her nose into the towel, "I thought you were the mean one."

"I *am* the mean one." Lauren leaned forward. "Kayla might have lost her temper for a moment, but she's all bark. I'm deadly serious when it comes to protecting the people I love. You are marrying my brother tomorrow, and he's devoted to you and a baby he did not create. I need to know you aren't going to make his life miserable. You better start convincing me real quick, girl, or you will see just how mean I can be."

Avah drew in a shaky breath. "Would you have married Hannah's father if you had to do it over again?"

Lauren blinked. She hadn't expected that question. Her mouth went suddenly dry as she considered her answer. "No."

Avah closed her eyes and nodded.

"I wasn't marrying my brother," Lauren clarified.

The other woman's eyes flew open. "I don't mean that in a creepy way. I wasn't marrying a man who was kind or devoted to me. Brody wants to be a good father and husband. He wants to take care of you."

"I know." Avah dabbed at her cheeks with the towel. "I'm not quite as shallow as you and your sister want to believe. I realize that Brody is a good man. He's the best, which is why he deserves to be with somebody who loves him."

"How can you say that? Everybody loves Brody. It's like loving a golden retriever."

Avah wrinkled her pert nose. "I'm not a fan of dog hair," she said. Strange as the answer was, it made sense.

"You're getting married tomorrow," Lauren repeated, "and you'll learn to love him. It's obvious what an amazing father he's going to be. It sounds strange now, but nothing is sexier than a man who's good with a baby."

Avah seemed to consider that, and Lauren held her breath, waiting for the other woman's answer. "Your daughter is lucky to have you," Avah said. "It's obvious there's nothing in your life more important than her, even if you screw it up a lot of the time."

"Harsh," Lauren whispered.

"And true," Avah insisted, her voice steadier than a few minutes earlier. "I think you're missing part of the equation. A child should see their mother happy. It probably sounds selfish, but people already know that about me, so I'm not concerned."

Lauren's heart began to thump behind her rib cage. "You may be selfish," she agreed, "but you're not wrong. Happiness is hard to trust when you've failed at it more than once. It takes a risk to be happy, and that's scary."

Avah nodded. "At least we can agree on something."

"Take that risk with Brody," Lauren urged. "I promise you won't regret it."

Avah smiled, then swiped the towel over her cheeks once more as Kayla entered the room again.

"I've got it. Chocolate comes out with hydrogen peroxide. The dress is going to be good as new."

"As new as secondhand can be," Avah murmured under her breath. Lauren heard and ignored the comment.

She didn't know whether she'd done the right thing being honest with her brother's fiancée, but as much as she wouldn't do marriage to Tommy over again, the situation with Avah and Brody was different.

At least, that's what she wanted to believe. The alternative was that her brother was about to make the biggest mistake of his life, and she was going to stand by and watch it happen. She had let her relationship with Ben run its course without fighting for it, either in the past or now.

That hadn't made her happy, and if the past few weeks had taught her anything, it was that she longed to find happiness.

CHAPTER TWENTY-THREE

"I'm SURPRISED YOU deigned to grace us with your presence today," Lauren said to her father the following afternoon as they stood together at the back of the camp's main cabin, which had been transformed into a dreamy Christmas scene, no detail too small to be overlooked.

"It's my son's wedding," Robert answered, then added, "even if he is having it at this rinky-dink venue that makes our family look cheap and common."

"You could have stopped at the part about it being Brody's wedding." Lauren crossed her arms over her chest, then uncrossed them and waved as Malcolm Grimes entered the cabin from the kitchen along with Brody. The two took their places in front of the arbor Ben had built, wrapped in strings of lights, greenery and gorgeous flowers in shades of white, ivory and deep red. Gabe, the florist, had come through in a huge way, helping Kayla to fill the cabin with hundreds of winter blooms. Holly, paperwhites, mistletoe, Christmas rose, rosemary, and poinsettias all added to the seasonal beauty.

Brody and Mal both wore dark suits with crisp white shirts underneath. Brody had a tiny red rose pinned to the lapel and looked handsome, if slightly uncomfortable, in his formal garb. The mayor had agreed to officiate the wedding and had arrived at camp early that morning for a pre-wedding hike through the forest with Ben and Brody.

"Men only," Brody had told Lauren and Kayla; neither had argued. Instead, they'd welcomed Avah, who'd shown up with all the joy of someone attending a funeral instead of a wedding.

In all honesty, Lauren had been relieved the bride had decided to go through with the wedding, although she could not muster any enthusiasm for trying to bolster Avah's mood. Clearly reading the tension in the room, Hannah had stepped forward with a cheery smile and some offhand remark about clear skies on a wedding day. She'd offered to help Avah with her makeup while they watched some ridiculous reality show they were both obsessed with in Lauren's cabin.

"He looks nervous," Robert said, watching Brody greet Lily along with her husband and father, all of whom were seated in the front row.

It was a small affair, with only forty or so guests invited. Brody was just as popular around town as he'd always been, so he could have drawn a crowd. But he'd wanted to keep the guest list small, and as far as Lauren knew, Avah had only invited a few friends and her immediate family, none of whom had arrived yet. Lauren had no idea if they'd attend.

"Probably because you're glaring at him," she said, keeping a smile on her face. "How are you feeling?"

"I'll survive, if that's what you're wondering." Robert fiddled with one of the silver cuff links he wore. "The doctor said my heart is good as new, so don't start spending your inheritance just yet."

She barked out a laugh. "Trust me, Dad, I don't expect to be included in the will."

"You're my daughter." He grunted like the words

were painful to say out loud. "Of course I'll provide for you. Hannah, too."

Lauren wasn't sure how to respond. Financial provisions weren't the same as being loved and accepted. But she understood that money meant more to her father than almost anything else, so she supposed it was kind that he'd even consider her in his plans despite everything they'd been through.

She settled on a simple "Thanks, Dad," and then glanced at her watch. "I'm going to check on Avah. It's almost time to start."

"This is a mistake," Robert said, as if his opinion would make a difference.

"It's Brody's choice." She took a step away, then turned back. "I know you don't like this place, but at least you can admit we did a good job with the decorations." Her heart swelled as she watched Brody and Mal admire the garland that lined the cabin's interior. Kayla had used berries and classic red ribbon to encircle the rustic chandeliers, a wreath was affixed to the back of each seat, and two stately Christmas trees flanked the arbor.

"The space is beautiful and perfect for today. You should be happy. Thanks to the process of helping Brody and working together on the carnival, Kayla and I finally have the relationship we should have had years ago."

"It's not your relationship with your sister that concerns me," Robert said, and Lauren frowned. He let out a disgusted snort. "Don't act like you don't know what I'm talking about or that you didn't do all this with an end goal that involved me in mind."

"By *end goal*, are you talking about the wedding, or possibly giving Jim Lowery some happy memories to take with him when he moves into Shady Acres? Despite what you think, the Camp Blossom Winter Wonderland Carnival wasn't intended to be a middle finger to you."

She made a show of examining her hands. "If I wanted to give you the middle finger, I'd just straight-up flip you off."

Robert smiled as if her rudeness pleased him, and Lauren realized how twisted their relationship had become. Or maybe it had always been this way because that's all he knew and it's what she'd learned from him.

She wasn't the lonely, desperate girl of years ago and knew she wanted and deserved something different—something better. "I won't apologize for the success of the event. I'm done being sad or sorry."

"That's fine for now. You can be both when Ben is left with nothing. I know you don't truly care about him. He's just another way to get back at me."

She shook her head. "My relationship with Ben was never about you."

"Right. He thinks he's making some kind of noble choice now, but that never lasts."

Lauren had no idea what her father was talking about, and at this point, she didn't care.

She'd tried as best she could to offer an olive branch, and maybe this feeling of dread in her stomach was her own fault for expecting anything more when he couldn't give it to her.

"Enjoy Brody's wedding, Dad."

"He took the money," Robert said before she had fully turned away.

Although Lauren knew she didn't have to rehash this topic, she couldn't help facing him. Things might not have worked out with Ben the way she thought they would, but he was a good man doing what he thought was right. She wouldn't let her father tarnish her memories along with her future.

"I don't want to talk about this again. Ben told me he didn't take the money, and I believe him. There's no reason—"

Robert shoved his phone into her hands, and she glanced down before she thought better of it, then immediately wished he hadn't when she recognized the image he wanted her to see.

It was a photo of a canceled check dated two weeks before she'd left town the first time.

"Maybe the guy deserves some credit. He probably used the money to pay for his loser dad's stay in the rehab facility. But if he loved you as much as you seem to think he did... I'm sure he could have found another way."

"Why are you showing this to me?" Her voice sounded hollow in her own ears.

"You need to know that he took the money then, just like he's set to make a hefty profit from developing the land now. He can tell you whatever story he wants about doing it for Jim or being loyal to his father. So we are both clear, he's doing this to benefit himself, just like I am. You can hate me all you want, but at least I'm not pretending to be someone else."

She hated that her eyes stung with tears, and she tried to blink them away. "Why, Dad? Why is it so abhorrent to you that I find some happiness in life? You have to take it from me or taint it so it turns ugly."

"I'm not the one who makes things turn ugly," Robert said. "That's just life. It's an ugly world, kid."

"No." Lauren reached up and tugged her earlobe between two fingers, not caring if she gave away how she felt. Hadn't that been part of her problem all along?

She'd been so unwilling to reveal her deeper emotions that she relied on anger for everything.

But anger—although sometimes well-deserved, like the urge to kick her father in the shin—also couldn't fix things.

Being mad at her dad didn't help and wouldn't heal her. She wanted to heal and feel whole. She couldn't do that with Ben if he'd lied and taken the money from her dad. That felt like more than she was capable of forgiving, but it wouldn't stop her from being happy.

She would find happiness without fear of it being taken from her. She'd work until she created contentment inside herself so no one could steal it. Not Ben or her father, and certainly not the fear of not being enough that was wedged deep in her heart.

"I refuse to accept anything less than a good life, because I deserve that. Life is beautiful, not ugly. It's the lesson I want to teach my daughter. No matter how hard you try, you aren't going to take it from me. I won't give you that sort of power. Not anymore."

He stared at her like he was seeing her for the first time, then shrugged. "I don't need to take it from you. It was never yours to begin with."

A lone tear tracked down her cheek, and she didn't bother to wipe it away. There was no use pretending her father's words didn't hurt.

Pretending had gotten her nowhere.

Perhaps Ben would have picked her if she'd been more open with him about how much she loved and needed him when they were younger.

There were so many maybes, but second-guessing the past didn't help. There was only now, and today wasn't about her or her father or Ben. It was about Brody and his choice.

Lauren might not have chosen Avah for him, but she would do whatever she could to see this through and make her brother happy.

She turned again but had only taken one step toward the door when Kayla burst into the back of the cabin and gestured to her.

Not bothering to look at her father again, Lauren followed her sister into the chilly afternoon.

"I need to talk to you." Kayla sounded like she'd just finished running a marathon. "Both you and Brody."

"What's going on? What's wrong?" Lauren asked the question but feared she already knew the answer.

"We need to talk to Brody," Kayla repeated, gasping a little. "I'll go to the kitchen door and meet you there so we don't draw attention."

Lauren shook her head. "Kayla, the wedding is about to start. Where is Avah?"

Kayla pressed her mouth into a thin line. "Go get Brody. There's not going to be a wedding today, Lauren. And like it or not, you played a part in that."

She headed around the side of the cabin before Lauren could reply. She wanted to call after her but saw Ben approaching from across the camp. She could not deal with him right now—not when her sister's vague accusation rang in her ears.

Ignoring his wave and plastering a smile on her face, she reentered the cabin and approached the arbor where Brody and Malcolm stood like everything was normal.

"Brody, I need you in the kitchen for a minute," she said.

He gave her a funny look. "Honestly, Lauren, I don't care what appetizers you serve. Or what kind of food emergency you might think you're having. I'm about to soil my pants from nerves, and I think if I move, it's going to happen. Just let me get married, and then everything will be good, and I can deal with whatever you need me to."

He looked so handsome and uncertain. Lauren wanted to respect his request. She didn't want to take him into the kitchen and certainly didn't want to believe that whatever this mess was had involved her.

She'd done nothing other than assure his fiancée that he was lovable and committed to making her happy. How did that make her the bad guy?

"It has to be now, Brody." She must have infused her tone with the severity the situation warranted, because he stilled for a moment, then gave a tight nod.

Malcolm reached over and clasped a bear-paw-sized hand on Brody's shoulder. "You got this, bro. It's your wedding day. Nothing's going to ruin it."

Famous last words, Lauren thought as she led Brody past the guests already seated and into the cabin's kitchen.

Kayla stood near the industrial size range in the center island, the Wildflower Inn catering staff bustling around her. Cam's wife, Emma, who ran the boutique hotel, had offered to cater the reception. Lauren greatly appreciated the help since Emma typically only handled food for events at the inn.

As she'd said, everybody loved Brody. Everybody except his fiancée.

Brody looked around the kitchen as if he were searching for something, and then his gaze settled on Kayla. "What's wrong? Where's Avah? Is it nerves?" He placed a hand on his stomach. "I get it. I have them, too. Where is she, K? I'll talk to her."

Kayla winced and smoothed a hand over her simple black sheath. It was an appropriate color for the news Lauren imagined her sister was about to deliver. "She's not here. Brody, I'm so sorry. Her parents showed up. I guess she called them after…"

Kayla's gaze went steely as she looked toward Lauren. "If you were going to talk her out of getting married, the least you could have done is mention it or encourage her to make the decision before the guests arrived."

If Lauren had been shocked about the check her father had shown her, she was absolutely dumbfounded by Kayla's words.

"I didn't convince her of anything."

"What did you say?" Brody stepped away from her, moving closer to Kayla.

"Lauren told Avah that she regretted marrying Tommy and that she should find her own happiness at any cost." She handed Brody a slip of paper Lauren hadn't noticed her holding before now. "She left a note."

"Brody, I didn't say at any cost. I told her she couldn't do any better than you. I fought for what you wanted." She held out a pleading hand to her sister. "Tell him, K. You were there for the dress fitting. I was supportive."

"She says I also deserve to be happy, and she can't give that to me." Brody frowned as he read the note, then glanced up at Lauren. "Did you tell her she'd be happier without me?"

"No. It wasn't like that." Lauren stepped forward but stopped when Kayla held up a hand.

The catering crew had stopped their work, and she felt a half-dozen pairs of eyes on her. "You can't blame me for this."

"I don't blame you, Laur." Brody's normally cheerful voice sounded hollow. "I blame myself for not being what she wanted. Never quite enough when things get serious."

"It didn't have to be this way." Kayla narrowed her

eyes at Lauren. "I could have helped handle it better if you'd asked for my input."

"Come on." Lauren held out her hands, feeling desperate to make the situation better but unsure how to make that happen. "Kayla, I don't understand why you're so upset. Neither of us thought this was the right thing for Brody. Hell, the baby wasn't even his."

"You think you know best," Kayla said, "and you must be in control. I might have thought Brody was making a huge mistake, but I also respected him enough to let him make it."

"You thought I was making a huge mistake?"

Lauren focused her gaze on Kayla. "Were you willing to let him make it or too scared about rocking the boat to say anything? There's a difference, you know."

"I might be scared, but at least I didn't run away or encourage Avah to leave."

Before Lauren could respond, Brody let out a guttural snarl and lurched forward, banging into the counter and knocking the trays of appetizers to the floor with a giant clatter.

"Stop hijacking my problems to fuel your dumb little war. I thought you two had made peace." He threw up his hands before either of them could answer. "I don't care. I don't care because this isn't about you. It's about me being left at the altar. The one time I get brave enough to do the right thing, it backfires. Why do I bother?"

"Is everything okay back here?" Ben asked as he entered the kitchen, Hannah following on his heels. "From out there, it sounds like…"

He paused and took in the mess of food and silver platters. "It sounds about like this kitchen looks. You okay?" he asked Brody.

"Not at all. I've got to get out of here. Kayla, will you…" his throat worked as he swallowed "…make the announcement to the guests?"

She nodded. "Of course."

"Brody, you have to believe this wasn't my intention." Lauren knew she sounded desperate but didn't care. She had to make him understand—

"Stop," Brody said again. "I don't want to hear anything more from you. I don't know why you would give Avah advice on marriage. It's not like you've done a bang-up job handling your own problems. That never stopped Dad from hopping on his high horse and acting like he knew what was best for me. You're in fine company there, Laur."

"The conversation wasn't like that," Lauren whispered.

Brody ignored her as he studied Kayla. "Was she telling the truth? Did you think it was a mistake? And don't give me the line about how the baby wasn't mine, because love isn't about DNA. It's about stepping up and being there."

Kayla darted a glance toward Lauren, then nodded. "You're right, and I love and admire you for your commitment. I disagree with how Lauren handled it, but she wasn't wrong to believe it was a mistake."

"I think they're both wrong," Hannah said. "And I think Avah is stupid if she doesn't want to marry you."

Brody flashed a dismal grin. "I appreciate that, sweetheart. So much for the magic of the Christmas cabin," he said, looking up to the ceiling like it held answers to the questions deep in his heart.

He started out of the room, then gave a half-hearted wave to Emma. "Sorry about the mess."

"I've seen worse," she said. "Most messes can be

cleaned up with a little time, elbow grease and patience."

Those words seem to take the edge off his anger. Brody blew out a long breath. "I hope you're right." He walked out the back door of the kitchen, and Kayla cleared her throat.

"I'm going to go talk to everyone."

"I'll go with you," Lauren offered, but her sister shook her head.

"I think you've done enough."

"Oh, my gosh, Mom." Hannah stamped one angry ballerina flat on the floor. "You ruined Uncle Brody's life. Why do you have to be like that?"

"Give your mom a break," Ben said, and Lauren imagined that Hannah's dumbfounded expression mirrored her own.

"Don't talk to my daughter that way."

"I'm sticking up for you." Ben threw up his hands. "When I'm not even sure you deserve it."

"Not the tack I would have taken," Emma said to the woman beside her. "Hey, Hannah. I'm going to grab some boxes out of the truck to pack up the serving trays we're not using. Any chance you want to help me?"

"Gladly...any excuse to get away from here right now."

In under a minute, the kitchen had cleared of everyone except Lauren and Ben. She heard the murmured swell of conversation from the main cabin and could only imagine how her father would react to the news that Avah had jilted Brody.

"That came out wrong," Ben said gently as he walked toward her. "I'm sorry. It's just that I don't know what's going on—"

"Because it's none of your business. I'm none of your business. I should never have let things start between us again. It made me forget my priorities. I spoke to Avah about my past, thinking that you and I had a future. Assuming that she and Brody would as well. Once a fool, always a fool."

"We can have that future." Ben's gray-green eyes were so warm and appealing that Lauren wanted to allow herself to be enveloped in his strong arms. She longed to ignore reality the way she'd been doing for this whole Christmas season.

As Brody had reminded her, sometimes the magic didn't happen. If she let herself believe, that meant she could be hurt all the more. She didn't know how to handle the dull ache that had lodged behind her rib cage from Kayla and Brody blaming her for today. Or how to deal with the sharp stab of pain from knowing that Ben had lied to her.

"Not a chance." Her frustration, lack of control, fear, and heartbreak seeped into every word.

"I was right to leave you in my rearview mirror, Ben Donnelly. I know what you did. My dad showed me the check. You betrayed me when we were kids, and you lied to me now. All that talk about your father needing help. You weren't so noble, and you betrayed me." She practically spat the words, emotion making her voice tremble.

His head snapped back as if she'd smacked him. "What check are you talking about? I told you I didn't take your dad's money. I've proven over and over that you can trust me."

She wanted to trust him, but it was too much to risk. Ben had betrayed her, and if he continued to deny it, she didn't know if she would survive the pain.

"None of it matters," she said, trying to regain control. "We're not so different. This Christmas was about me and what I wanted. I wanted to save the camp and be the hero for Jim and my brother. You were a means to an end, just like when we were teenagers. I married you so I could get out of this town."

His face went ghost white as he dragged a hand through his already rumpled hair. "You're lying, and you're a terrible liar. It was just as real now as it was then. I love you, Lauren. I'm not sure I ever stopped loving you. You are written on my heart, and there is nothing I can do to change that."

"That's a shame for you, but I don't feel the same." The words spilled out of her mouth like they weren't killing her to say them. Ben didn't need to be written on her heart. He was simply a part of it, which was why she had to close it off. It was the only way to save herself from the misery she felt at this moment.

"You won't even fight for us?" he asked, but there was no emotion to the question.

"There's nothing left to fight for," she answered with the same lack of feeling. Numbness was at least better than anguish and shock. "Hannah and I are leaving the day after tomorrow. I'll make other arrangements for where we stay tonight. It's best that you and I don't see each other again."

For a moment, she thought he might argue, and that silly hopeful place inside her wanted him to. But he nodded and walked out of the cabin without another word, leaving the shattered pieces of her heart in his wake.

CHAPTER TWENTY-FOUR

"WE HAVE TO stop meeting like this."

Kayla didn't move as Scott placed a blanket around her shoulders. She was once again sitting alone on one of his lounge chairs, staring at the ocean waves and thinking how different this Christmas season was from what she'd planned.

"Why?" she asked. "Are you looking for an argument or have bad news to break to your friends and family? I'm useful to have around in those situations."

"Rough day, huh?" He took the seat next to her. "You could have gone into the house."

"You weren't home," she muttered.

"Yes, but I gave you the code for the door."

"I still can't. It's not right."

"Won't," he corrected her. "And I wish you would, Kayla. The door code barely scratches the surface of the things I wish where you're concerned."

"Lauren wishes I would fall off the face of the earth," she said, because focusing on her misery seemed easier than parsing the hidden meaning in Scott's words and how they made her feel.

"Brody said you were hard on her," he answered. "Can we go inside to finish this conversation? Come summer, I'll be happy to argue with you outside but—"

"I was defending Brody." She jumped up from the

lounge chair but kept the blanket tight around her shoulders. "Lauren ruined his wedding day."

"You told me you didn't think he and Avah were a good fit. I understand that the timing was less than ideal, but is the wedding not taking place the worst thing that could happen?"

"She doesn't get to control everything," Kayla shot back. "Lauren always thinks she knows best."

"You agree with her in this case." He stood, frowning, and Kayla felt the hot wash of embarrassment over the fact that she sounded like a petulant little sister with an inability to stem the feeling of insecurity when it came to Lauren.

Scott shook his head. "I don't understand why you're fighting so hard for a relationship that everyone except Brody could see was doomed to fail."

"Suddenly you're such an expert on relationships?" She jabbed a finger in the direction of his house. "It must be so effortless to pass judgment when you have the money to hole up in this house and not let anyone in."

"I let you in," he said gently, and despite the darkening sky, she could see the sparks dancing in his gaze, like flecks of gold spinning around a shot of the most potent whiskey. "Hell, I opened the damned door for you. But you refuse to walk through. Maybe I should take the hints you keep dropping at my feet like glacial-size breadcrumbs. I just wish I hadn't fallen in love with you in the process. Merry Christmas, Kayla."

He moved around her toward the house, and she stood in shock for several seconds before his words truly registered. When they did, she quickly turned and ran after him.

"You can't say that," she shouted at his retreating form, but Scott didn't break stride.

She paused again and glanced toward her father's house. Not since her mother had anyone told Kayla they loved her with the tenderness that infused Scott's tone. She believed him wholeheartedly.

It terrified and thrilled her in equal measure.

When the back door to the house clicked shut, she realized she had a choice. She could choose to live in fear or embrace something better for herself. She could choose to be brave.

That thought spurred her forward. She turned the knob and burst into the kitchen a few steps behind him.

"You can't say that and walk away," she announced to his back. It was easier to speak the words she needed to say without looking into his eyes.

"And before I say I love you too, I want you to know that it only counts if you love all of me. I need you to love all of me." Her voice trailed off as her throat clogged with emotion.

Scott turned and took a step toward her. "What makes you think I don't love all of you?"

His gaze hadn't exactly softened. So as good at test-taking as Kayla had always been, she had a feeling she might fail this one. Vulnerability was not a subject with which she had much experience.

But she was getting more comfortable being honest, so figured she'd start there. "I haven't done anything to earn your love," she said quietly. When he began to speak, she shook her head. "I've done the opposite, in fact. I agreed to go out with you because I thought I could convince you to sell your land to my father. I'm not a good person. I'm the evil henchwoman, the ogre's dutiful lackey. I'm the villain in this story, and I'm embarrassed at how far I was willing to go to win my dad's approval."

Scott cocked his head, looking more curious than shocked. "Is that why you slept with me?"

Maybe a normal woman would have been offended by that question, but Kayla had to admit it was legitimate.

"No. Although if you ask my dad, he will tell you I did. He'll have a lot to say about me once he realizes what I've done."

"That sounds ominous and not like you're going to reveal that you've also fallen in love with me, leaving me standing here with my stomach in knots."

"Oh, I've fallen in love with you," she told him. "I tried not to. I tried, but you're kind of irresistible." As declarations went, it was pathetic, but Scott didn't seem to mind as a blush crept into his cheeks.

He chuckled. "Hardly."

"For the record, it has nothing to do with your money."

"What about my offer to buy the camp to prevent your dad from bulldozing it?"

"Not that either, although Lauren mentioned something about the original deed for the land, so I did some investigating. When you're quiet, people forget you're paying attention."

"But you're always paying attention," Scott supplied.

"When it matters, I am. Here's what I discovered. The original land was owned by a couple who included several interesting stipulations when they sold it for a price well below market value to the family who started Camp Blossom. One was that the land would be used in perpetuity to benefit the physical and emotional well-being of the youth of North Carolina."

"Does that mean—"

"—that it can't legally be used for a housing development?" Kayla nodded. "Yes."

"Why don't you sound happier? I think that makes you the hero."

"I've known about this information for twenty-four hours, and you're the first person I've told. Dad will hate me if I ruin his deal, and Lauren would never forgive me if she found out I didn't say anything."

Kayla noticed that Scott had been drawing steadily closer as they spoke. She wanted to reach for him and also push him away. She'd never felt like this before and didn't know how to handle it.

"I'm not the hero, because I've come close to shredding the deed I found at least a dozen times. No one would ever know."

"I know."

"But you have the money to buy the camp. You don't need a deed. There's no reason for me to take a stand now."

"Your father is threatening to sue Ben. I have money and resources—more than Maxwell Enterprises. But it would certainly be easier not to have to employ them. That deed changes everything, and you shared it with me."

She huffed out of breath. "Don't look so satisfied. For all you know, this is me self-sabotaging us. I share this with you and remain my father's dutiful daughter."

"I'll love you anyway," Scott said simply.

"You wouldn't. You couldn't. I don't deserve that."

"I love you whether or not you think you deserve it.

You brought me back to life, Kayla. I was living in this big house but felt dead on the inside. I blame myself for my friend's death. The guilt paralyzed me. I wasn't willing to do or try anything else. You claim to be the villain, but I'm a coward."

"No," she whispered as she closed the distance between them, taking his hands in hers. "You are good and honorable. Look at how you're getting involved to save Camp Blossom. You're the white knight."

"Money doesn't mean much to me because I have a lot of it. Pete's family set up a foundation in his name that provides services for young people dealing with mental health issues. They invited me to partner with them or sit on the board. When I declined both offers, they asked me to attend the annual gala to attract more press coverage. People are interested in me because I'm interested in being alone. But I wouldn't do anything because it felt like my chest might crack open whenever I thought about going near his family. How could they want me in their lives? I'm the reason their son is dead."

"It's not your fault. It was never your fault."

He closed his eyes briefly and nodded as if taking in her words and trying to believe them.

"I see that now," he said, "and I'm sure I would've gotten there eventually, but I believe it because of you. You might not think you deserve love, but you never stop striving for it. You haven't let your sister's resentment or your dad's controlling nature change you. I fell in love with the person you are on the inside, Kayla."

"When we do bad things," she said slowly, "it makes people love us less. I said some awful things to my sister today because I wanted her to be the bad guy. Misery loves company, I suppose. And there are things I haven't said to my father because if I say them out loud, he'll know I believe he's the bad guy."

"Treating someone poorly is not an act of love. It's fear. You and Lauren are twisted in your views of each other because of how your dad treated you both. It's how he made sure he had power over you, but emotional abuse isn't power. It's abuse."

She wanted to balk. She'd never thought of her dad as an abuser. Domineering and mercurial, yes, but he'd taken care of her.

Scott's words shook something loose inside her.

"I don't want to feel like I'm beholden to him any longer," she said. "I want to be a hero."

"Then do it," he told her like he had every confidence in the world that she could. His belief gave her an answering resolve.

"I'm going to give the documents to Ben." For as confident as she felt in her decision, her voice still shook.

"It will change everything," Scott said as if he could read her mind.

She nodded. "It's the right decision. I don't want to be the bad guy," she repeated.

Scott held her face between his hands. "I love you, Kayla—hero, bad guy, or anything in between. All good heroes need a sidekick. I'd like to volunteer for that job."

She shook her head and then placed her hands on top of his. "I'm the kind of hero who wants a partner, not a sidekick. I'd like it to be you, Scott O'Day. I love you for who you are and for loving me for who I am. I don't know what comes next or where life will take us, but I'm up for the adventure if you are."

He kissed her, and it felt like the start of a brand-new

story that was destined to have a happy ending because she would write it that way. She was finally going to take control.

As he kissed her more passionately and then led her through the house toward his bedroom, Kayla was almost overcome with the joy of this moment.

It was a season for miracles, and this was hers.

She had more work to do to fix things with her brother and sister, which she would manage. Heroes took care of things, and right now, she was taking care of Scott, who was the best and biggest part of her heart. With him at her side, she could do anything.

CHAPTER TWENTY-FIVE

"It's Christmas, son," Ben's father announced over a simple holiday lunch of boxed macaroni and cheese and store-bought ham the following afternoon. "You look like jolly old St. Nick put a lump of coal instead of the Red Ryder BB gun you were hoping for under the tree."

Ben listlessly moved his macaroni noodles around the plate. Until this point, Bart and Jim had ignored Ben's sullen attitude. He wasn't sure how much Lauren had told Jim about their final conversation and her reason for leaving Camp Blossom, but he certainly didn't want to discuss it.

"You were right, Dad. Donnelly men have crap luck in love. I should have listened to you a long time ago."

He figured that would shock his dad into silence, and he would have admitted just about anything at the moment if it meant being left alone.

He'd tried to beg off Christmas dinner. There had been plenty of years when first his dad and then Jim, after Nancy's death, hadn't wanted to celebrate. Now Ben could appreciate how annoying it must have been when he'd forced them to partake. All he wanted was to be left alone, but that didn't seem like it was in the cards.

"Sometimes a person has to make their own luck," Jim said, pointing a forkful of ham in Ben's direction. "I would argue you did that, Ben. You are a success with or without Robert Maxwell's approval and partnership."

Ben sat back from the table and scrubbed a hand over his face. He'd barely slept the previous night after the chaos of the canceled wedding and Lauren lashing out at him.

"I had a plan," he said more to himself than the other men. "But I was willing to change everything for her like I did seventeen years ago. It landed me in about as much trouble now as it did then."

The window next to the dining table rattled slightly as the wind kicked up. Although the cabin was warm and cozy, the blustery day outside reflected his mood to a T.

"I want to see this camp saved as much as anyone else," Jim admitted. "I never liked the idea of houses built on land that had always been meant for everyone to enjoy."

"Then why did you agree? I was doing this to help you," Ben insisted.

Jim smiled. "And I was doing it to help you. It's what you thought was right, and I trust you."

"Unlike Lauren," Ben muttered. "I don't know where this leaves me. Scott is willing and interested in investing in Camp Blossom and revamping it to be a world-class summer camp destination, but the vision was going to be hers. That was my plan."

"Do you think you should have made the plan *with* her instead of *for* her?" Bart's voice was uncharacteristically gentle. "You don't have to take everything on by yourself. That's not what a partnership is about."

"Maybe I wasn't supposed to be partners with anyone," Ben said. "I wouldn't work with Robert again, even if he wanted me to. Not with how he lied to Lauren about that check. The worst part is she believed him. I would never have taken his money. How could she believe that about me?"

Jim cleared his throat, and Ben looked up to see a silent communication pass between the two men that he didn't recognize but left a sinking feeling in his gut.

"What?" He leaned forward. "What do you know that I don't?"

His father picked up a salt shaker shaped like a nutcracker that had been Nancy's. Every dish, spoon and napkin on the table was Christmas-themed because that's how she liked it. She'd made the most of the holidays every year.

"Tell him." Jim crossed his arms over his barrel chest. "You should've told him years ago. It was going to come out eventually. There was no way Robert was going to let that lie."

"Speaking of lies," his father said. "You might have taken the money, son."

"Might have," Ben repeated slowly, working the words over on his tongue where they felt like burning acid. "What in the hell is that supposed to mean?"

"Do you remember how an anonymous benefactor ended up paying for my stay in rehab?"

"Yes." The sinking feeling widened into a gaping pit of dread.

"I wanted to get clean. I would have done anything to get clean. Not just for me, Ben. For you, too. You were heartbroken that Lauren left and served you with divorce papers because you committed to stay and help me. If you were willing to give up that much, it was going to happen, but I couldn't do it on my own.

I needed the facility, and we both know there was no money."

"Tell me what you did," Ben repeated.

"I wasn't looking for it, but I found the check in your dresser drawer."

"You happened to stumble across it in the drawer?" Ben scoffed. "Give me a break."

"Point taken, but it was a desperate time, at least for me. I forged your signature, and I cashed it." Bart's eyes shone with unshed tears. Ben had never once seen his father cry.

"I thought about driving away with the money. It was a low point, Benny. That check would have gotten me to a bar on the beach on some tropical island where I could drink myself into oblivion. Maybe that's what I should have done. Maybe that would've been better for everyone in the long run. But I didn't. I took the money and used it to get clean."

"You used dirty money to get clean." Ben stood from the table and paced to the edge of the cabin. He gazed out the window that faced the center of camp. The lights that he and Lauren had hung were on and shone like a bright beacon in the dreariness of the drab day. The twinkling strands and festive decorations they'd lovingly placed around the property couldn't have been more at odds with his mood.

"You had no right," he said, not turning around.

"I know, but I didn't think it mattered. She was already gone. I didn't think her father would ever be a part of your life again. I wanted to tell you when this business about the two of you partnering came up."

"But you didn't."

"I've disappointed you so many times. I couldn't do

it again." He felt his father's hand on his shoulder. "I'm sorry, son. I was wrong. So wrong."

Ben drew in a ragged breath. "Which means Lauren was right to believe her father. It means I'm still beholden to Robert Maxwell. We were never true partners. He always had the upper hand."

"No." Jim slapped a hand on the table. "I'm sick and damn tired of that man lording his money and power over us like he's the only one who matters. I'll use some of my money from the sale to pay him back. You can explain to Lauren—"

"It's too late," Ben whispered. "She's gone again."

"Call her," Jim urged.

"Go after her," his father added. "Not because you've got it all figured out. The two of you need to figure things out together."

"If we were meant to be, it would have happened by now. Lauren would have trusted me."

"Maybe you need to trust yourself first," Bart advised. "I wish you could see yourself the way I do, Ben. You didn't need to partner with Maxwell or have your name associated with some fancy development. You've always been enough. I've made a crap ton of mistakes in my life."

"A permanent place on the naughty list," Jim interjected, and Ben shook his head as his dad smiled and nodded in agreement.

"But you're the one good thing I've done. I don't deserve a son like you, but I'm grateful and proud of you, Ben. It's past time for you to be happy. Is Lauren a part of that?"

"She's all of it," Ben said without hesitation.

"Then don't give up," Jim called from the table with

another hand slap, causing the plates to bounce and rattle.

A gust of wind blew, causing the chimes that hung from the cabin's front porch to tinkle.

"More angels getting their wings," Bart said quietly. "I think it's time to make your own Christmas miracle, son."

Jim nodded. "We didn't raise you to wimp out when the going got tough."

Ben's heart began to race with fear and hope. It was strange how the two could be so tangled together, and he realized this moment wasn't the first time he'd felt the contradictory pull.

In the past, fear had won the day, but as the chimes jingled again, the hope inside him swelled, the light of it casting fear into the shadows, much like those tiny lights around camp brightened the dreariness of the day.

Lauren was the driving force behind his hope. They'd hurt each other, but they could also find healing and a new beginning together if only he could convince her to give him another chance. A future with her would be worth risking anything—even losing his heart all over again.

"Come on, Mom." Hannah tugged on Lauren's hand later that night in their room at the Wildflower Inn. "Get out of bed. You have to come downstairs. You've missed almost all of Christmas Day. You love Christmas."

"We opened presents earlier, and I'm not fit company for anyone, sweetheart. Bah humbug and all that." Lauren burrowed more deeply under the covers. But she left her hand in her daughter's. She needed something to ground her to the world when it felt like she was spinning into oblivion with no safe place to land.

"Aunt Kayla and Uncle Brody are downstairs with Emma and the other guests." Hannah squeezed her fingers, then released them as she climbed off the bed. "Everyone is asking about you."

"So they can yell at me some more," Lauren said. "I'm done, Banana. Done with the holidays and this town. I just want to go…"

"Where, Mom? Back to Atlanta? You weren't happy there either."

"Happiness is an illusion. It's fake, just like Christmas and Santa. Jolly Old St. Nicholas is a big fat phony."

"You don't believe that or you wouldn't have worked so hard to make the carnival special. This is just—"

There was a demanding knock at the door of the room's connected sitting area.

"Do not let anyone in unless it's one of the Hemsworth brothers," Lauren told her daughter. "Or someone with a giant piece of chocolate cake. Take the cake, but don't let them in."

"I left the door propped open," Hannah admitted, and Lauren could hear the smile in her daughter's voice. "No Hemsworths hanging out in the hall, but I'm sure you'd rather see your brother anyway."

Lauren's heart raced at the sound of Brody's voice.

"No," she shouted from underneath the covers, wiping away her tears. She was so sick of trying not to cry. "You blame me for ruining your life. And now my life is ruined, but I'm still the bad guy. I hope you're happy."

"I wouldn't describe my current mood as happy," Brody said with an unexpected laugh. "But I'll get there."

Lauren was starting to sweat under the covers, but she refused to emerge to face her brother and...

"Kayla better not be up here with you. I don't want to see either one of you. We should have never come back here. Hannah and I were fine on our own." She watched as the covers moved up and down with her breath.

"I told you she was in bad shape." Hannah's voice was hushed. "She didn't touch the chocolate croissants I brought up for breakfast, and you know how she is about baked goods."

"I was five when she nearly wrenched my shoulder from the socket when I tried to eat the last doughnut in the box," Brody said.

"You know I can hear you?"

Silence greeted her, and for a moment, she thought Hannah and Brody had left the room again. Then the mattress sagged as someone climbed onto it next to her, and the scent of white musk hit her nostrils.

"Go away, Kayla. I don't want to talk to you either."

"How did you know it was me?"

"I bought you that perfume when you were fifteen, and you're still wearing it. You need a new signature perfume if you want to sneak up on people."

"I love this scent, mostly because my sister introduced me to it. I'm not sneaking, and nobody hates or blames you. I'm sorry I lashed out yesterday, Laur. Come out."

"You seemed pretty sure of your opinion yesterday."

"Yesterday was a lot," Brody said as he hopped onto the bed too.

"Ooof." Lauren finally threw back the covers. "You landed right on my knee, you big oaf."

"There's more spring to this mattress than I anticipated."

Lauren glared at her daughter. "What part of 'don't let anyone come in' confused you?"

Hannah looked unconcerned about her mother's potential wrath. "The part where I know you don't want to fight anymore."

"Yeah, Laur." Brody tapped on her head with one finger the way he used to wake her up on weekend mornings when he was an annoying kid. "We know you love us."

"Did you seriously ever doubt that I loved you?"

Kayla raised her hand. "I did."

"I didn't love you then, and it was a mistake to start now."

"Love is never a mistake," Kayla told her, snuggling closer. "And you always loved me."

"But you loved me best of all." Brody draped a giant leg across her thigh.

"Until I came along," Hannah added with a laugh.

"We all love you best," Kayla assured the girl.

To Lauren's horror, she burst into tears at her sister's words.

"Do not ask if she's on her period," Kayla warned Brody, making Lauren laugh through tears. "That's rude and sexist."

"I was twelve when I asked her that," Brody countered. "I know better now. Besides, I'm not judging anyone's tears. I shed more than my share last night."

"That might have been the half a bottle of Jack Daniels you drank on your own." Kayla reached across Lauren and patted Brody's arm. "Luckily, you're young, so hangovers don't last long."

Lauren gave him a little shove, then patted the mattress next to her.

"Come here, Banana," she told her daughter. "Save me from these two annoying humans."

Hannah scooted in close, and Lauren felt not as hopeless as she had minutes earlier.

"I'm truly sorry, Brody. I did not expect the things I said to Avah to make her leave the way she did. That was never my intention."

"I know. I reread the note, and we talked on the phone last night. The decision to leave was hers. The timing wasn't the greatest, but I suppose it's better that she made it before we were married and the baby came. That would have been an absolute disaster."

"Do you love her?" Lauren asked softly. "Are you heartbroken?"

"Heartbroken might be pushing it," Brody said. "Avah and I weren't the best match, but it felt like the right thing. I would have been a good dad. I love that baby already and hate the idea of not being a part of his or her life. Avah's reached out to her ex. She's willing to give it another go with him for the baby's sake."

"She should have married you," Hannah said. "Once a cheater, always a cheater."

"She wasn't the brightest bulb," Kayla said, then yelped when Lauren smacked her thigh.

"These two are violent," Brody warned Hannah. "Be careful. By the way, you were right with your advice, Laur. I'm sorry I came down hard on you." He shifted onto his elbows and looked over her to Kayla. "Both of you."

"I'm sorry, too," Kayla said softly. "I know you

weren't trying to sabotage Brody or convince Avah not to go through with the wedding."

Lauren had turned the conversation she and Avah'd had at the final fitting over in her mind so many times in the past twenty-four hours. Maybe she'd unconsciously sabotaged her brother because she didn't want him to make the same mistake.

She raised a brow and leaned into Kayla ever so slightly. "Are you sure about that? We all know I can be a bit heavy-handed, although I'm usually right. Probably more like 99 percent of the time."

Hannah snorted. "Don't push it, Mom, or I'm going to share all the times you haven't been right, and there are plenty."

"Don't sass your mother, little one," Brody said as he wrapped Hannah in one of his big bear hugs. Avah truly was a fool. In addition to being handsome, smart and loyal, Brody was a world-class hugger.

Hannah pretended to fight the embrace, but Lauren could feel her happiness at his teasing. Even when they left Magnolia, she would make sure Hannah stayed close to her aunt and uncle. She wanted the girl to know she was surrounded by love from a family that would see her through whatever life threw at her.

"Mom." Hannah pinched her arm.

"Ouch."

"Didn't you hear my question?"

Lauren had been lost in her own thoughts. "Ask me again."

"I asked if you were going to rip into Uncle Brody the way you did Ben when he tried to take your side against my brilliant teenage observations."

"*Brilliant* might be pushing it," Brody said with a dry laugh.

Kayla sat up straighter. "But let's take this opportunity to change the subject and talk about Ben."

"Let's not and say we did." Lauren tried to pull the covers over her head again, but Hannah and Kayla tugged them down just as quickly.

"What's your problem with my boy Ben?" Brody asked. "The guy's a prince among men."

"The problem is I love him." Panic gripped her like a vise at admitting the words out loud.

There was a moment of silence before Kayla asked, "Why is that a problem?"

"Because he lied to me and took money from Dad, and the fact is, I don't care. I love him anyway, which makes me stupid."

"Or forgiving of a mistake," Hannah suggested. "He was eighteen, and his dad was in trouble. Teenagers do stupid things. You forgave me for wrecking the car."

"That's different. I can't let myself fall in love with Ben again."

"Pretty sure that horse has left the barn," Brody said, kicking her leg.

"You all need to stop beating on me." Lauren blew out a breath.

"What's the real problem?" Kayla asked, her gift for understanding Lauren growing more irritating by the second.

"I'm not good at loving people. I mess it up, and then I get hurt. I've already had my heart broken by Ben Donnelly once. Twice if you count yesterday's debacle." She glanced toward Brody. "It wasn't just about you."

"Fair enough," he agreed, "but you aren't giving yourself enough credit."

"You're good at loving me," Hannah agreed.

"And me," Brody added.

Kayla cleared her throat, then said, "Even me, although you tried hard not to be."

Those simple declarations of faith in her warmed her heart, but the cold fingers of fear didn't loosen their grip.

"I'm even worse at letting people love me."

Silence greeted her words.

"Everyone has stuff to work on," Brody told her. "Except me, because from a young age, my sisters made me believe I'm perfect."

"Not quite," Kayla shot back. "But if there's anyone perfect at loving Lauren, it's Ben. He doesn't care about your prickly edges. He loves you for who you are." She sighed. "That's what makes it magical."

"Who are you, and what have you done with my practical, burned-by-romance sister?"

"Aunt Kayla caught feels for the hottie neighbor," Hannah announced.

Lauren turned her head to see Kayla's face going deep pink. "Is that true?"

"Yes, but we're not discussing my happy ending. This is about fixing—"

"Hello?"

Lauren's heart stuttered at the sound of Ben's deep voice from the sitting area.

"Has anyone heard of closing a door behind them?" she demanded, swatting first Brody and then Kayla. "Any lunatic could walk in here."

"But we've got *your* lunatic," Brody answered as Ben appeared in the doorway to the bedroom.

To his credit, Ben didn't react to the unusual scene, although Lauren doubted he would have expected to find her in bed with her daughter and two siblings.

"Am I interrupting?" he asked with a smile that faltered at the edges.

"Not a bit." Brody bounded out of bed like someone had just thrown a tennis ball he needed to chase across the room. "Merry Christmas, Ben."

"Merry Christmas, everyone." He scrubbed a hand over his jaw. "Lauren, could I talk to you for a minute?"

"Yes," she answered automatically.

"Do you want to…um…get out of bed?"

She shook her head. "I'm not wearing pants."

"I think he's seen you without pants, Mom," Hannah stage-whispered.

"Alrighty then." Kayla, who'd popped off the bed at the same time as Brody, crooked a finger at the girl. "Let's go downstairs for a minute. We can raid Emma's dessert table."

"You don't have to leave," Lauren blurted, suddenly terrified of being alone with Ben. There was so much she wanted to tell him, and all of it scared her.

Hannah squeezed her hand. "You've got this, Mom. I believe in you."

"Thanks, Banana," Lauren whispered. She tucked the covers more tightly around her as Kayla, Brody and Hannah exited the room, closing the door behind them.

"You're committed to staying in bed?" Ben drew closer when it was just the two of them.

"I've been here most of the day," she said like that answered his question.

"What about breakfast?" He cocked a brow. "A Christmas morning spread is your favorite."

She bit down on her lower lip and thought about how to answer. "A broken heart ruined my appetite."

They stared at each other for a moment, and then he climbed onto the bed and took her hands in his. "You aren't going to make this easy on me, are you?"

"I wish I did easy," she admitted with a sigh. "I owe you an apology, Ben. I'm sorry about how I reacted to the check. You had a right to do what you needed to for your dad."

"He forged my signature." Ben traced his thumb over her knuckles. "He told me earlier today. I should have guessed it, but I didn't. I'm sorry, too, Lauren."

Her heart knocked against her ribs at the intensity of his tone. "But you didn't do anything."

"I let you go and didn't have the courage to fight for us. Twice, almost."

"Almost?"

"I'm not going to watch you walk away again. I made that mistake once, and losing you almost killed me. I didn't believe I deserved you or how happy I felt when we were together. It seemed easier to let you go than to risk my heart, but that's stupid."

"We were both stupid," she admitted and leaned forward to kiss his cheek. The truth was, she couldn't resist leaning into him. He was her true home.

He released her hands to cup her cheeks and kissed her until she sagged against him.

This was the only Christmas magic she needed.

"I love you, Lauren." He pulled back and then dropped gentle kisses on her tear-stained lashes. "Always have and always will. I don't care what comes next as long as we're together for it. You have given me the best gift of my life—the courage to believe in myself. I want to do the right thing for you and because of you. Letting people love me doesn't come easy—"

"Ditto," she muttered, and his gaze gentled even more.

"But if you give me another chance, I'll fix that. I'll do whatever it takes."

She sniffed and swiped her sleeve across her nose. The tears were coming fast now, and she didn't even care. "I love you, Ben. Always and forever. You don't have to fix a thing because you are perfect for me. There was no chance of you losing me again. I'm stuck to you like glue, buddy. You're going to have to pry me off like a barnacle if you want out."

His gaze lit with amusement.

"I'm even worse at the love thing than you," she said, and pressed her forehead to his. "Love me anyway?"

"With my whole heart. The card companies won't be hiring either of us, but that works for me. I want real and messy and tears and laughter. All of it, Lauren."

"Even an incredibly awful father-in-law?" She lifted her head, afraid she might have gone too far with that question, but Ben's eyes were still filled with that same intensity.

"Even Robert Maxwell. Although I've backed out of partnering with him. It might get rough."

It felt as though a weight had been lifted off her shoulders. "I can take rough, Ben. I'll be at your side for every moment."

He slid a hand to the nape of her neck and kissed her again. And all those shattered pieces of her heart mended together better than before.

After several long moments, he pulled back but continued to cradle her head. She never wanted him to let go.

His brows rose as he studied her, and he smirked. "About those pants..."

She wiggled her shoulders. "You like me with no pants."

"That is true," he conceded. "Although it might be awkward if your family—including your teenage daughter—return, as I fully expect them to. People love you, Lauren. Not just me."

As much as that last part warmed her heart, the first piece had her scrambling off the bed. "I have a teenage daughter. What kind of role model am I? I just spent Christmas Day wallowing in self-pity. We need to get downstairs, Ben. There are carols to be sung. It's not too late."

He stood, then straightened the covers she'd thrown off. "It's never too late," he assured her.

A few minutes later, she and Ben entered the family room at the boutique inn. Emma, Cam and their guests called out Christmas greetings as her family threw their arms around them both.

"It's about time," Brody said, trying to put Lauren in a headlock. "I knew you were smarter than you act."

Kayla choked out a laugh. "We need to work on your ability to give compliments, bro."

"We'll have plenty of time," Lauren said, wrapping an arm around Hannah's shoulders. "If you still want to stay in Magnolia, we can."

"Yes!" Hannah shouted, then yanked her phone from the pocket in her black leggings. "I need to text my friends." She glanced up at Ben. "You make my mom happy, but don't expect me to call you Daddy."

He mock shuddered. "God, no."

"She's teasing you," Lauren whispered as the girl chuckled and walked away, her thumbs working furiously on the phone screen.

"I've got a lot to learn," he said, "including how to revive a summer camp."

"Scott's buying it," Kayla told Lauren. "He went to pick up Jim and Bart to bring them over."

Lauren's heart thudded with wonder and delight. "Camp Blossom is saved."

"Thanks to you," Ben told her, and dropped a kiss on her forehead. "I love you, Lauren. I can't say it enough. I love you with everything I have and all that I am."

"I love you, too, Ben. I never stopped, and I never will." She wrapped her arms around his neck, breathing in his familiar scent and marveling at how much joy this holiday season had brought into her life. She would never again take for granted the magic of Christmas or the power of true love.

EPILOGUE

"Do you think Scott will really go for all of this?" Lauren asked as she studied the hand-drawn plans spread out across the kitchen table in the caretaker's cabin.

Ben came to stand behind her, wrapping his arms around her waist and resting his chin on her shoulder. "He'd be a fool not to see your vision, and Scott O'Day is no fool. But are you sure this is how you want to ring in the new year? We could hold off meeting with him until next week and head into town for the big celebration."

"I can't think of a better way to celebrate fresh beginnings than with a bright future for Camp Blossom." She lifted her head to kiss him gently on the cheek. "Besides, since Hannah is spending the night at one of her new friend's houses tonight, you and I can have a private party later."

He made a growling sound low in his throat. "I like how your mind works, Ms. Maxwell. Although I like everything about you."

"I like how happy you make me, Mr. Donnelly." She turned in his embrace and wrapped her arms around his neck.

Her plans for the camp were forgotten as Ben lowered his mouth to hers. Since Christmas, they'd spent as much time together as possible, and Lauren did her best not to dwell on regrets or the mistakes she'd made that had kept her from living the life she'd wanted.

She'd done her best at the time, and now things would be even better. Hannah was thrilled to be staying in Magnolia, and Lauren was looking forward to her daughter being surrounded by family and friends who loved her.

Lauren's father wasn't speaking to her or Kayla, and although she hoped he'd come to appreciate his daughters working together for something they believed right, she wasn't counting on it. He'd been furious by what he considered their betrayal when the plans for the luxury community on the camp property fell apart.

But his anger was offset by her transformed relationship with Kayla and Brody and the happiness being close to each of them brought to her life.

Kayla had met with a local attorney in town to discuss joining his general practice. She and Scott were committed to each other and building their lives in Magnolia.

Lauren wasn't sure what Brody would do—being abandoned at the altar seemed to leave him more stunned than heartbroken. He'd hopped a flight to visit a friend in Costa Rica for the new year, promising he'd return once he cleared his mind. Her brother was stronger than she'd realized, and she hoped he'd give love another chance.

It had taken a lot of time and effort for Lauren to do just that, but the reward was worth it. Ben drew back and cupped her face in his hands. "There's one thing we must discuss before Kayla and Scott get here."

"Is it whether to start with drinks and appetizers or dive right into my ideas for renovating camp?" she asked, wrinkling her nose. "Because I'm hungry, but I can't wait to see what he thinks about my proposal to reshape the camp mission into one that will encompass outdoor adventures and environmental studies. I think we'll have the opportunity to attract campers from all over the country if we focus on the unique resources of this area. We can do this. I can do this, Ben."

"I have no doubt." He kissed the tip of her nose. "And neither does Scott. That's why he asked you to head up the rebrand." He took a step away from her. "But that's not the topic."

"You look serious," she told him, unsure what emotion she was reading in his gaze.

"I am."

Before she could say more, he pulled a small box from his pocket and dropped to one knee in front of her. "I'm seriously in love with you, Lauren. And I want to spend the rest of our lives showing you how much you mean to me. Will you do me the honor of becoming my wife?" His smile widened, and his eyes sparkled with love. "Again."

Without thinking about it, she dropped to the floor with him. "Yes," she said and hugged him tightly.

He laughed as he kissed her. "I haven't shown you the ring yet."

She drew away, shaking her head. "I don't care about…oh, Ben." He'd opened the velvet box to reveal the exact ring she'd seen in a jewelry store in town all those years ago and immediately adored. He hadn't been able to afford it as an eighteen-year-old, and the princess-cut diamond with tiny emeralds on either side was just as beautiful as she remembered.

"How did you find this?"

He slipped the ring onto her finger. "At the time, it

didn't make sense, but as soon as I could afford this ring, I bought it. It's been in the top drawer of my dresser for nearly fifteen years. I think my heart always knew we'd find our way back to each other."

She sighed, her own heart filled with more happiness than she'd ever imagined. "And now that we have, it's forever."

Ben was her forever, this Christmas and always.

* * * * *

A CAROLINA SONG

CHAPTER ONE

MEGHAN BANKS HADN'T expected the school day to end with her crouched on a toilet seat, knees pulled up against her chest, locked in the bathroom stall outside the main office of Magnolia Elementary.

Wednesdays were typically uneventful, like most of Meghan's days. But unlike some people, she didn't mind. Boring simply meant she was staying in control, an aspect of her life she'd come to value.

It was the middle of October, and the school year so far had been a marked improvement over the previous year when she thought she was going to lose her job and after weathering the blow of her overbearing mother selling her late grandma's house with no warning and displacing Meghan in the process.

The principal who'd fostered so much trouble for her last year had taken a job in a neighboring school district, so she didn't have to deal with Greg Wheeler, or Principal Ferret, as she not so affectionately thought of him.

The new principal, Tally Ridder, was a decade older than Meghan and the best boss she'd ever had—at least until Tally made a fateful decision without consulting her first and changed everything.

The door to the girls' bathroom squeaked as someone opened it, and Meghan drew her knees closer and tried not to make a peep. She could manage a panic attack without her labored breathing giving away her presence.

"Meghan, where are you?" The lilting voice and clip of heels on the linoleum floor were familiar, but Meghan didn't answer. "Come on out now, honey. I know you're in here."

A rap of knuckles on the stall prompted Meghan to climb off the commode and press one hand to the door's cool metal. "I think I ate some bad chicken last night. You need to go away and leave me alone. I'll be out when I can."

"You'll come out now," her friend said, and Meghan recognized the commanding tone. Annalise Haverford had been the undisputed queen of the social bees in their small town on the North Carolina coast, at least before her spectacular fall from grace.

While her ex-husband's conviction for running a Ponzi scheme rocked the close-knit community earlier that year, Annalise had worked tirelessly to reinvent herself and helped Meghan discover a confidence she didn't know she possessed in the process.

She didn't feel confident at the moment.

"Meghan, the first practice for the fall talent show is starting in five—make that three—minutes. You're in charge."

"Not with him involved," Meghan muttered, staring at the ground. "You do it," she said to the stylish leather slingbacks she could see facing the stall door.

"Are you going to let Walker Calloway run your life? Where's your sense of pride, woman?"

"I used it to sweep up the pieces of my broken heart after I was dumb enough to fall for a famous country music star." She blew out an indignant breath. "Even dumber to believe he'd fallen in return."

"Open the door."

Meghan did what she was told because newly found backbone aside, in times of stress, being amenable was her go-to survival mechanism.

"You weren't imagining it," Annalise said as the door swung open. "Walker liked you. The man wrote a song inspired by you that is now a number one chart-topper."

Meghan's heart thudded despite her resolve not to be affected by Walker's rugged good looks, soulful voice or the kindness he'd shown her last spring. "You don't know that."

But indifference wouldn't have her hiding in the girls' bathroom after the announcement that he was back in town for an extended period and volunteering to help coordinate the annual event for the school.

She and Walker had become close—or so she'd thought—after she and Gus, the nephew he was raising in his late brother's stead, had convinced him to volunteer as the music teacher for the final few months of the previous school year.

Now she wondered if she'd created the chemistry and the significance of the kiss they'd shared in her mind. She wouldn't be the first woman to lose her heart to Walker. There were multiple online fan clubs dedicated to him. She was not a member.

"I know," Annalise insisted. "Come out here so I can take thirty seconds to freshen you up. Then you're going to practice."

"How do you know?" Meghan stood dutifully still as Annalise took a few makeup items from her monogrammed purse and began working her Southern magic. "Did Jack tell you?"

Annalise's fiancé, Jack Grainger, was Walker's manager and best friend. He also ran Whimsy Farm, Walker's horse property outside of town. Meghan hadn't been back there since the benefit concert where Walker had debuted the emotional ballad, "*There's a Light.*"

Meghan had been watching from the crowd with the third member of her trio of besties, Shauna Myer, and honestly believed the song might be about her based on her connection with Walker.

Then Danielle Griggs, the country music starlet who also happened to be Walker's ex-girlfriend, sauntered on stage and planted a kiss on him that left no doubt that she was his inspiration.

That was the last time Meghan had seen Walker.

But he was here and…

"I can't do it." She reached up and clutched Annalise's wrist. "No amount of makeup in the world will make me brave enough to face him."

"You'll face him anyway." Annalise dabbed gloss across Meghan's lips. "You don't need to be brave, just resilient, and you are that. You're stronger than you know, and I wouldn't blow sunshine up your skirt. If you can't find faith in yourself, borrow mine."

"I can't believe I thought you were a bitch," Meghan said as she hugged her friend.

"I acted like one often enough," Annalise laughed softly, then pulled back. "People make mistakes. Hurting you was a significant one for Walker, although I wonder if he even realizes how big."

Meghan shrugged. "He texted a couple of times from Nashville over the summer."

"What?" Annalise's doe eyes widened. "You never told us that. This changes things."

"Not for me. They were late-night drunk texts that don't mean anything."

"What did he say?"

Meghan took a step back. "He missed me."

"And how did you respond?"

"I left him on read."

Annalise wrinkled her perfectly pert nose. "Because?"

Meghan turned to gaze at her reflection in the hazy bathroom mirror. Despite the refresh, a familiar face stared back at her. She was what people called a girl next door, a code phrase for boring in all respects. Shoulder-length brown hair with eyes nearly the same color. Average build and average height with nothing remarkable to make her stand out. Only Walker had made her feel special, and when he'd walked away, it hurt more than she'd admitted to her friends.

"He broke my heart," she blurted. There was no point sugarcoating it at this juncture. "We didn't even officially date, and I fell for him. Hard. He was sweet, kind, and I thought he liked me. I thought it might turn into more than like for both of us."

"Oh, honey." Annalise wrapped her in a citrus-scented embrace. "All the more reason for you to face him. Walker Calloway isn't all that and a bag of chips."

"He's kind of a whole truckload of chips," Meghan said, drawing in a breath.

"Chips are overrated," Annalise insisted. "Unless they come with salsa and guacamole. You, my friend, are guacamole."

The absurdity of the statement made Meghan smile. "Smooth and creamy?" she said, then laughed.

"With a little bit of spice. Come on, Megs. Let's show Walker what he missed out on."

Meghan wanted to argue that he probably knew and didn't care, but she wasn't that mealymouthed version of herself anymore.

Instead, she grabbed the lip gloss from Annalise, smoothed on another coat and air-kissed her friend. "You'll back me up, right?" It was easier to be brave with a friend at her side.

"Always," Annalise promised.

Meghan nodded. "Then the show must go on," she declared. "Especially the Magnolia Elementary talent show. Let's do this."

And together, they headed out the door.

CHAPTER TWO

"HEY, UNCLE WALKER. How did me and Trey do? I messed up a couple times, but we'll practice every night until the talent show. Jack said if I get real good, he's gonna let me use one of the barn bunnies for the grand finale."

Walker patted his nephew's head, accustomed to Gus's rapid-fire manner of speaking when he was excited. Sometimes, Walker's heart ached at how much Gus reminded him of his late brother. "I believe Ms. Banks discouraged using live animals in the talent show."

Gus frowned, so Walker quickly added, "You and Trey did a fine job being magicians, although you also have a great singing voice. I've heard you playing your dad's guitar up in your bedroom. I thought you might play a song for the talent show?"

At the way Gus's shoulders deflated, Walker knew he'd messed up.

And it wasn't just with the boy. Meghan not only avoided speaking to him for the whole of the talent show rehearsal, but she'd also refused to make eye contact. Walker was used to feeling off his game while dealing with his late brother's son. He did his best, but as the old song said, his best wasn't good enough—most of the time, anyway

"I understand if you don't want to sing, buddy." Walker searched his brain for suitable parental pearls of wisdom to maneuver through this current emotional mine-field. His brother would have known what to say, but they wouldn't be in the situation if Nash were still alive.

Yet here they were. The past year ten months had been tough on the kid, and with Walker doing a few select shows and spending time in the Nashville recording studio over the summer, he felt disconnected from the boy. He wanted to find a way to reconnect. Gus was a quirky kid with awkward limbs and big owl eyes that sometimes saw too much. Walker loved him with his whole tarnished heart.

"I have a gig booked in Las Vegas in a few weeks, right around your Thanksgiving break. How about you fly out and we can see a couple of magic shows? Jack and Annalise can come and bring Trey and Margo."

"Sure, Uncle Walker." Gus scratched his chin. "That sounds great. I see Ms. Annalise gettin' ready to leave. I'm going over to Trey's so we can practice. She said she'd bring me home for dinner."

"Sure, buddy. I'll see you later."

The back of Walker's neck began to itch as Gus walked away, which he blamed on the moms he could feel staring at him from the far end of the elementary school gym-nasium. Unfortunately, the one woman whose attention he wanted was on the other side of the room, doing her best to ignore his existence.

Walker had a healthy ego—a musician didn't achieve his level of fame, selling out stadium tours and racking up music awards without one—but he was self-aware enough to admit he'd screwed up big-time with Meghan.

His lame text after the benefit concert and the paltry attempts at keeping in touch while he was away over the summer reflected badly on him. He wanted to blame his schedule and the pressure of recording new music for the first time since his brother's death. Writing songs and playing them without Nash at his side, the one constant he'd relied on his entire life, was a shift he didn't know if he'd ever come to accept.

Now he could see that those things had been issues, but the real problem had been his feelings for Meghan. In a span of a few weeks, she captured his heart in a way he hadn't realized anyone could. She seemed to see him for the man he wanted to be, not the mistakes he'd made. They'd spent every day together at school, and he missed talking to her and the way she'd laughed at his corny jokes. But when he'd heard the crowd's reaction to the song Meghan had inspired—the first one he'd written without his brother—it scared the hell out of him.

Walker hadn't believed he could be happy in a world that didn't include his larger-than-life brother. He went through the motions for Gus's sake but felt like his heart had stopped beating in that terrible tour bus accident right along with his brother's.

Meghan made him want things he hadn't for a very long time, and that wouldn't do. He'd run away, but she wasn't that easy to get out of his mind and heart. So he'd started doing the work necessary to heal himself—he'd seen a therapist and now had better tools for handling his grief and survivor's guilt.

He had hope for building a new life and longed for Meghan Banks to be part of it, which was why he'd volunteered to help with the talent show once he knew she was in charge. It would be difficult to convince her to give him a second chance if she refused to talk to him.

He rolled his neck, shoved his hands in his pockets and, with confidence he didn't feel, started across the quickly emptying gym toward her. How was it that he could stand on stage and belt out songs for thousands of fans, but approaching Meghan made his palms sweat like he was a teenager asking his crush to the home-coming dance?

As he got closer, the woman Meghan was talking to, the new permanent music teacher Raina Rauth, took a small step toward him.

"Hi, Walker," she said as she smiled and fidg-eted, looking nervous and enthusiastic. "Nice to see you. Thanks for volunteering your time. Everything's going great with those lesson plans you left to get me up to speed on last spring's curriculum. That was re-ally thoughtful."

Those were also a lot of words strung together in rapid succession. People did that around him sometimes when they were nervous. Meghan used to get charm-ingly shy when they were together. At the moment, she looked irritated.

"My pleasure, Raina," he told his replacement. "Meghan taught me everything I know about lesson planning."

"Raina, you're doing fantastic," Meghan assured the new teacher. "The kids love you, and we need someone dedicated and reliable at the school."

Ouch.

"That's me," Raina chirped, her cheeks bright with color. "I love the new single, Walker."

"Thank you. We're excited about the album drop-ping next month."

"Me, too. So excited. I'll see you both later."

"Dedicated and reliable?" He winked at Meghan. "Sounds like how Jack describes a good working horse."

Meghan did not react to the wink or the smile he'd included. He missed her sweet blush and the moment of breathlessness she'd had every time she looked at him. He knew himself to be a charming man, but it was clearly going to take more than that to soften her sharp edges.

"When you say 'we,' does that refer to you and Danielle Griggs?" Her brown eyes snapped as she mentioned his ex-girlfriend's name.

His smile faded. "Dani and I don't have a relationship, Meghan. We haven't for several years."

"Right." She tapped a finger on her chin as she contemplated his words. "Because you go around kissing lots of women. It doesn't mean anything."

"Sometimes it does," he countered. "You and I—"

"Are nothing to each other," she interrupted, squaring her lovely shoulders. She wore a simple pink cardigan over a white T-shirt paired with ankle-length dress pants. "I'm happy for your success. I wish you more of it and appreciate your help with the talent show. You always add a bit of star power to our little school. But you and I…"

She frowned as if the words were stuck in her throat. "I have a date this Friday!" she exclaimed after a moment.

"Is it serious?" he asked, disliking the way his heart clenched in response to that surprising bit of news.

"Not yet." She crossed her arms over her chest. "It's a first date. But it could be something. I'm an ordinary woman, as you well know."

"There's nothing ordinary about you, Meghan. To me, you are—"

"Please don't feed me a line. I'm not made for bright

lights or drama or…" She flicked a hand up and down in front of him like that explained everything. "My feet are firmly planted on the ground, a safe distance from the stars, because I don't want to get burned." Her gaze shifted away before she looked up into his eyes. "Again."

"I'm sorry," he whispered because what else could he offer her in this moment?

"I am, too," she said quietly, then turned and left him standing alone.

CHAPTER THREE

THE FOLLOWING EVENING, Meghan sat on the porch of her landlord and friend Shauna Myers's painted two-story Victorian home and stared into the golden liquid of her margarita.

"People make mistakes, you know," Shauna said as she topped off Annalise's drink.

Annalise nodded, then squeezed another slice of lime into her glass. "Shauna knows this from firsthand experience. Flynn made plenty of mistakes and praise the Lord for that since it's part of why we became friends."

Flynn Murphy was now Shauna's husband and the father of her twin boys, Timmy and Zach. They'd had a troubled love affair when they were younger but reunited when Flynn returned to town last spring. Their small wedding at Whimsy Farm over the fourth of July weekend had been charming and so sweet. Around the same time, Annalise and Jack bought a house together, although Jack still stayed at the farm when Walker was out of town.

Meghan had figured she'd lose the first two friends she'd ever made. But Annalise and Shauna continued to prioritize their friendship while Jack and Flynn treated her like a little sister, which she loved.

She'd never fit in with her overachieving biological family, so her found family was integral to her happiness. Shauna had also insisted that Meghan keep renting the first floor of the converted carriage house, although she turned the apartment where Annalise had lived into an art studio.

Annalise, who had once lived in one of the most ostentatious houses in Magnolia, had chosen a modest two-story with Jack, a few blocks from where Shauna lived. It had a large wraparound front porch, which, according to Annalise, had been nonnegotiable.

So now the three friends got together once or twice a week as their schedules allowed, either at Shauna's house or Annalise's. If the weather was bad, they would hang out in one of the cozy kitchens but preferred to spend most of their time gathered on a front porch.

"I'm not sure Walker understands how badly he hurt you and how careless he was with your heart," Annalise told her. "Famous men often aren't held to high standards by the women in their lives, which is an issue and not any excuse."

"I'm not in his life any longer." Meghan's voice was steady despite the emotion she felt inside. "I don't want to be either."

"Are you trying to convince yourself or us?" Shauna asked.

Meghan honestly wasn't sure, and there was no point pretending any different with two women who knew her so well.

"Let's not talk about Walker." She stared at her margarita.

"Okay," Shauna agreed. "Let's talk about your date on Friday."

Meghan took a giant drink. "Letting you two convince me to join a dating app was not one of my smarter moves. I don't know why I agreed in the first place."

Annalise inclined her head. "That was the night I

made the pitcher of piña coladas to celebrate the end of summer. I think the coconut rum had something to do with it."

"For sure the rum is to blame," Meghan grumbled. She shook her head. "Nope. That's not true. I'm excited about meeting…"

What was her blind date's name again? She blamed Walker for this lapse in memory, as well. The man left her entirely too senseless.

"Jeremiah…no, Jeremy. Jeremy Blevins. He's an engineer and lives in the town of Smoketree. He's outdoorsy and has a full head of hair. I'm excited." She was definitely trying to convince herself on that one.

"You also have good hair," Annalise said carefully. "Seems like a good match."

There was a beat of silence, then all three women burst into giggles.

"I only agreed to go out with him because he happened to message me the day Gus told me his uncle Walker was back in town for an extended period. I've avoided the confounded man since the start of the school year. I can handle two weeks of working together after school. It's not like I ever have to be alone with him."

Shauna leaned closer. "But do you want to be alone with him?"

"Where Walker is concerned, I stopped wanting when he left town after the concert."

Shauna handed her a basket of chips. "Have something to eat, sweetheart. It makes the lies go down easier."

Meghan took one, dipped it into the guacamole and shoved it into her mouth. Shauna made the best guac she'd ever tasted, but she wasn't sure anything could make forgetting Walker Calloway easier.

Still, she was bound and determined to try. There

was no other way to protect herself. Walker was out of her league, and she needed to remember that.

WALKER WAS GOING to convince Meghan to give him another chance, although he had absolutely no idea how to go about doing it or if he even deserved one.

That last bit wasn't exactly true. He knew he didn't deserve one. Nash would have smacked him upside the head for the way he'd retreated like a coward at the beginning of the summer.

Jack did his best to be stand-in brother figure but preferred to let Walker dig himself out of his own mistakes, and there were plenty.

Topping his list of mistakes waiting so long to finally put a stop to Dani and her gossip leaks to the tabloids about them having rekindled their romance.

He hadn't even remembered her kissing him at the benefit concert when she walked on stage to join him for the chart-topping duet that had added to his fame and made her a household name two summers earlier. He'd been so lost in the moment and grateful beyond belief that he'd been able to perform without Nash next to him.

He'd assumed Meghan knew that. Hell, he'd been singing directly to her, but then he'd been swept up in the adrenaline rush. Jack had been working things out with Annalise at the time so he'd taken his eye off the ball, or in this case, Walker.

Despite the fanfare surrounding his return to the stage, Walker didn't feel like much of a big shot knowing that he'd allowed himself to be carried away—immediately heading into the recording studio to lay down Meghan's song. "Strike while the iron is hot," the record company told him. Without Nash or Jack to assure him he could do things on his own time frame and in his own way, he'd gone along with what other people wanted.

He wanted to change because it was time to be more than what people expected of him. It was time to go after a life that would make him happy.

He'd been traveling back and forth between Magnolia and knew Jack was worried he'd announce he was staying in Music City. He'd preemptively explained that while he respected Walker's ability to choose, Magnolia was Jack's home now.

But Jack was more than a manager and a stand-in big brother. He was Walker's best friend and the man he admired most in the world.

"She's going on a date," he complained the following morning, feeding the horses in the barn. Jack did that deep, knowing chuckle that alerted Walker he was about to be highly annoyed.

"Did you expect her to sit around twiddling her thumbs and darning socks 'til you pulled your head out of your pants?"

"I don't think you can twiddle thumbs and darn simultaneously," Walker countered, tossing a bucket of oats into the feeding trough with more force than necessary. Orion, his late brother's horse, whinnied in agreement.

Walker immediately reached out a hand to soothe the animal. "Sorry, boy."

Orion had fallen into a deep depression without his beloved owner, but he'd eventually accepted the change and found his joy again. It was a lesson Walker desperately needed to learn.

The horse leaned into Walker's touch. "This guy forgives me. Why won't Meghan?"

Jack laughed again. "First off, I don't think I'd go around comparing a woman to a horse."

"I love this horse." Walker cursed under his breath when Jack's eyes widened. "I'm not saying I love Meghan."

"But do you? Could you?"

"I can't do anything if she starts dating another guy."

It wasn't an actual answer to the question because Walker wasn't ready to admit his feelings. But he could no longer deny them to himself. Hell, when the new album came out, it would become apparent. He'd written almost every song for her. But unrequited love was lonely, and he didn't want to be lonely anymore. Was it truly too late?

"I don't know what to do, Jack. I volunteered to help with an elementary school talent show to be near her, and she still manages to ignore me."

"You're not used to being ignored." Jack sounded amused by the concept of it.

"That's not the point."

Jack gave the last of the feed to the horses and then turned to face Walker. "If you want her for the right reasons, don't give up."

"The right reasons?" Walker scrubbed a hand over his jaw. "Are there wrong reasons?"

"Come on, Walker. Don't play dumb. You're many things, but stupid isn't one of them, despite some of your behavior."

"Don't sugarcoat it."

They started to walk back toward the main house. The sun was high in the bluebird sky, and the temperatures had cooled to a level that made Walker want to spend all his time outdoors.

"Meghan isn't a woman to be toyed with. She's got a big heart, and you were careless with it."

Jack held up a hand when Walker would have argued. "I'm not saying I have a lot of advice to give in this area. It took almost losing Annalise to pull my own head out of my shorts, but that's what it's going to take for you, as well. This will be a commitment to her and a life you haven't led before. A life that's stable and filled with hard work and compromise."

Walker swept out his hand. "I own a horse property in a sleepy Southern town." He pointed to the area that had begun to be cleared where he was building a new state-of-the-art recording studio, more extensive than the one they'd created in the small guest quarters behind the house. "I'm raising a kid. I'm stable. I work hard. I may not be Nash, but I'm doing my best."

"Your brother was a good father and friend," Jack said. "Not perfect. You are just as solid of a man as Nash."

"Don't say that," Walker shot back, his chest clenching painfully.

"You need to know it. You need to believe it."

"What if I can't?" What if he needed Meghan to help him?

"I have faith in you, Walker. I have faith that you can work things out with Meghan. I wish I could tell you it would be easy."

"Nothing worth having is," Walker murmured, repeating one of his late brother's favorite sayings.

Jack patted him on the shoulder. "Let's get some coffee and bacon in us, and then we'll devise a plan."

"Thanks, Jack." Walker had to believe he could find a way. He wouldn't accept anything else. Meghan meant too much to him, and he refused to lose another person he…cared about.

CHAPTER FOUR

MEGHAN HAD BEEN on her date for fifty-five minutes, which was fifty-four minutes too long.

The Fall Festival was in full swing with local music performances, a beer garden, food vendors and a children's carnival.

She smiled as Jeremy Blevins told another story about his ex-girlfriend, detailing the year they'd won first prize in a Halloween party costume conference dressing up as a wall socket and plug.

"Denise was so crafty. She could sew, plus she made her own soap and lotion." He gave Meghan a hopeful nod. "I assume you're crafty, too, since you're an art teacher."

"I don't sew," Meghan said slowly.

"Do you compost?"

"Yes," she lied. "Not really. Not at all," she amended, wondering why she felt the need to lie to impress a man she never planned to see again after this night. Getting along was Meghan's superpower, and how she lived before her grandmother's death changed something inside her.

Meeting Shauna and Annalise had given her the courage to be herself—or at least begin to discover that person. Walker had also been part of her transformation. The way he listened to her ideas and treated her like she mattered had bolstered her confidence. Seeing herself through his eyes had made a world of difference in her life.

Jeremy popped a handful of caramel popcorn into his mouth. He chewed with his mouth open, which might not be as egregious a sin as failing to compost, but it was yet another deal-breaker for Meghan.

"I support composting," she said, then cringed at how dumb that sounded. Was there anybody against composting in theory? "I recycle every week."

He gave a brief nod of acknowledgment, although she could feel his disappointment with her.

Not enjoying the date was at least one thing they had in common, or so she assumed.

"Have you thought about trying to work things out with Denise? It sounds like the two of you had a good thing going." This might be a new low.

Meghan wasn't a hugely experienced dater but counseling a man on getting back together with his ex-girlfriend should receive an honorable mention in the Lousy Date Hall of Fame.

"She took the water regulator out of the showerhead when she moved in with me," he said as if Meghan was supposed to understand the significance of that. She didn't have to wait long for him to explain it.

"I thought she and I were on the same page regarding our values." He tipped the popcorn bag up to his mouth and then polished off the final kernels without once offering her a bite.

It was too bad because they'd left the potential for dinner after the Fall Festival open, and now she was sure she would be making an excuse then going home to heat leftovers or have a bowl of cereal in front of the TV.

"Yes, someone who shares your values and respects you is important." Her mind went to an image of Walker before she could stop the blasted thing.

"Denise had both of those," Jeremy said, almost morosely. At the start of the evening, they'd established that this their first match with someone on a dating app.

Meghan wasn't even angry or disappointed. She might not be waxing on about Walker, but she couldn't stop thinking about him and comparing the fun and laughter they'd shared to this night, filled with neither.

"There's give-and-take to relationships," she said, squeezing Jeremy's rather soft arm. No comparing his to Walker's muscles, she silently counseled herself. "It sounds like Denise cared about you. But she also likes powerful water pressure. Maybe you could suggest shorter showers as a trade-off?"

Jeremy seemed to consider that, but before he could answer, Meghan felt someone hug her from behind.

"Hi, Ms. Banks!" Gus Calloway exclaimed.

Meghan turned to smile down at Gus, who remained one of her favorite students with his quirky sense of humor.

"Hi, Gus. Are you enjoying Fall Festival?"

"Uncle Walker and I were talking about you."

"We were talking about the talent show," Walker said, approaching in Gus's wake. "Not exactly about you."

"Yes, we were." Gus wrinkled his nose. "You were just saying—"

"Why don't we head over to the funnel cake booth?" Walker interrupted. "Ms. Banks—" Was it Meghan's imagination or did he emphasize calling her by her last name like they hadn't been friends? "—is on a date," he finished darkly.

Gus snorted. "With you? I thought the two of you—"

"Gus, this is my friend Jeremy." Meghan turned and was almost disappointed to see the man still standing a few feet away. She'd nearly forgotten about him, but he wasn't looking at her. He stared with starstruck wonder at the man looming behind her. It was a look Meghan had seen before on many faces. She certainly hadn't expected Jeremy, who took everything seriously, including the environment and himself, to be a country music fan.

"You're Walker Calloway."

"Guilty as charged." Walker deepened the Southern twang and held up his hands like they were in an old Western shoot-out.

Meghan rolled her eyes even as she smiled. Being recognized was nothing new to him, so she knew he laid it on thick because Jeremy was her date.

"I hope you're showing our Ms. Banks a proper good time. She's awfully special."

Meghan's cheeks colored then heated even more when Jeremy stared at her blankly.

"My last name is Banks," she reminded him.

"You're friends with Walker Calloway? I thought you were just a teacher."

"You know I'm an art teacher," she explained. "His nephew is one of my students."

"Hey, Uncle Walker, grown-up talk is boring." Gus tugged on the sleeve of Walker's Western button-down. "I see Margo and Trey. Can I go say hi?"

Meghan looked to where the boy was pointing and saw Annalise and Jack standing with Annalise's children and Margo's best friend, Violet Atwell.

Annalise gave a half-hearted thumbs-up, then made a face, clearly understanding that standing between Walker and her date for the evening was not the most comfortable position for Meghan to be in. She figured Walker would use Gus's request as an excuse to leave, but no such luck.

"That's fine, Gus. Stay with the group and I'll be right over." He shoved his hands in his pockets and rocked back on the heels of his scuffed work boots. "So Jeremy, tell me what you do to make a living."

"I'm an environmental engineer."

"You must've been real good in school, huh?" A shiver ran the length of Meghan's spine. Something about the casual lilt to Walker's tone gave her pause.

"Yes. I have a master's degree from NC State."

"Then I'm surprised to hear you use the phrase 'just a teacher.' You must understand how important they are in our world. I am not a learned man myself. But I can tell you without a doubt that Meghan has had a considerable impact on my nephew and—" Walker drew in a breath then finished in a tone so sweet it felt like a caress "—me."

If Jeremy realized he'd been schooled, he showed no signs of it.

"Yeah." Jeremy nodded. "Teachers are great—Meghan's great. The reason I clicked on her profile is because she reminded me of my ex-girlfriend. Denise is a high school biology teacher. I've been telling Meghan all about her."

Walker looked genuinely surprised as his gaze darted between Meghan and Jeremy. "That must be fascinating conversation for a first date."

"We've been having a lovely time," Meghan lied.

Walker raised a brow, calling her on it without saying a word, and her skin tingled with awareness. She tried to give herself a break. Before things went wrong, she'd felt he knew her better than anyone. That didn't change overnight, despite how much she wanted it to.

"You know that new song?" Jeremy leaned in like he was sharing a state secret. "The one that's been all over the radio since summer?"

Walker nodded and stopped rocking. Tension shimmered through him before he made an obvious effort to tamp it down. Had she told Jeremy that she suspected he'd written "There's a Light" about her?

"I feel like it's me singing the words to Denise. Like you climbed into my heart and wrote exactly what I felt."

Meghan bit down on the inside of her cheek to stop herself from bursting into hysterical laughter. She couldn't even catch the attention of an average guy—how could she have ever allowed herself to believe she'd captured Walker's?

"My brother taught me everything I know about playing guitar and songwriting," Walker said easily. "That's a compliment to his memory as much as it is to me. You might have been able to relate but let me assure you, I had someone particular in mind when I wrote 'There's a Light.'"

Jeremy nodded. "Someone who made you feel like Denise."

Walker was back to rocking on his heels and appeared to be enjoying this conversation far more than Meghan. "Well, now, Jeremy. I don't rightly know Denise, but the woman who inspired the song…" His voice dropped to that gentle croon again. "She's special."

Meghan registered Jeremy's hand on her arm but couldn't feel his touch, not with the way Walker's gaze made her feel like they were alone instead of standing in the middle of the town's busy central square.

"Would you mind if we cut this evening short?" Jeremy asked. "I need to..."

"Go ahead," she told him with a genuine smile. "I hope you and Denise are happy together."

"You're a peach." Jeremy squeezed her arm, then grabbed Walker's hand and enthusiastically shook it. "You, too."

Then he was gone, and Meghan and Walker were left standing together with the crowd milling around them. Meghan realized she was in big trouble because at Walker's side was the only place she wanted to be.

CHAPTER FIVE

WALKER WATCHED JEREMIAH—or Josiah or whatever the guy's name was—walk away, thinking he must be a colossal fool to ditch Meghan in the middle of a date.

He slowly turned his attention to her, wondering if she would be angry that he'd supplied much of the motivation for the desertion, only to find her surreptitiously wiping her cheeks as she glanced away.

"Don't cry, Megs. I'm sorry. The dude was a loser, but I didn't mean—"

He broke off when she returned her gaze to him and realized she wasn't crying tears of sorrow but of laughter. In fact, she was nearly bent over with it.

His heart did a funny little dance in his chest, and he immediately heard the start of another song in his head—one more inspired by her. He'd always disregarded the notion of a muse, but his feelings for Meghan drove his creativity more than anything ever had.

"I've been on some memorable dates," she told him when she finally seemed to be breathing normally, "but Jeremy and I will go down in the all-time low record book." She shook her head. "You have no reason to apologize, although if he and Denise work things out, I'm pretty sure they'll play your song at the wedding."

"It's your song," he said. "Is there any question about that?"

Her smile faded, but she held his gaze, which was a huge improvement over the past few days.

"I'm happy for your success, Walker. You're talented and deserve every accolade you receive."

"I would trade all of it if you forgave me."

She looked startled, and he wasn't sure if he shocked her with his words or the sentiment behind them.

Success was fine, but it didn't bring happiness. Before Meghan, Walker hadn't considered happiness as a worthy goal to achieve. He'd followed in his brother's footsteps, happy to skate through life while Nash took the lead. His brother had always seemed to be striving for something out of reach. Maybe it had been peace and contentment.

If Walker had it to do over again, he would have asked those questions. He would have paid more attention. There was no do-over with his brother, but he prayed Meghan would give him one.

"There's nothing to forgive. But there's a reason I didn't answer your texts this summer. As I've told you—"

"I was wrong and stupid. Texting wasn't anywhere near what you deserve from me. I should have come back sooner. I should have fought for you. For us."

"Come on, Walker." Her smile looked resigned. "We were never meant to be."

"How can you say that?" He ran a hand through his hair, trying not to panic at the calm finality in her words. "There's something special between us. I couldn't have been the only one to feel it. That kiss we shared meant something."

"It did," she confirmed. "But we come from two different worlds."

He held out his arms wide. "It looks to me like we share this world. Is it Gus? I know a child is a lot to take on, even for an amazing teacher who cares about kids. It's not the same as—"

She cupped his cheek with one soft hand, and his knees almost buckled from the pleasure of her touch. Just as quickly, his heart sank at the look of resignation in her eyes.

"I adore Gus. I…" He hoped she would tell him she adored him as well, but she shook off whatever she'd been about to say. "We were friends, right?"

He momentarily closed his eyes and fought to regain control of his emotions. When she drew back her hand, he reached out and held it. "Other than Nash and Jack, you were the best friend I'd ever had. And those two don't really count. Nash was my brother, so he had to put up with me and Jack is like family. You're the friend I chose, Meghan."

She was so much more than a friend, but he was afraid of saying anything that would widen the distance she seemed determined to put between them. "My feelings haven't changed despite my uncanny ability to be a jackass."

She laughed at his self-deprecating joke as he'd hoped she would then offered him a gentle smile. "I think we can be friends again. I'd like that."

"Me, too," he answered. It was the truth, if not the whole of it.

"Okay." She bit down on her lower lip, and his body went on high alert. "What do you think about two friends getting a funnel cake?"

Walker nodded. "I'd love a funnel cake," he told her, grateful for a second chance, even if it started with baby steps.

CHAPTER SIX

WALKER WAS POURING a cup of coffee into his mug the following Tuesday morning when Jack walked into the kitchen from the back patio door.

"Morning. I didn't expect you here so early," Walker offered as a greeting. "I told you Carl and I could handle the horses for the early feeding. He's already out there and doing a bang-up job. Even you wouldn't be able to find fault with his work ethic."

Carl was the older man Walker had insisted on hiring, so Jack didn't feel he needed to spend so much time at the farm. Now that his friend and manager had Annalise and her children in his life, he should be free to prioritize the things that were most important to him.

That's what Walker planned to do. It had been disappointing when Meghan had friend-zoned him at the festival Friday night, but he had to believe friendship was a step in the right direction. They'd had a great time eating and drinking, playing games and then watching the kids compete in a dance contest.

It was easy to be with her, but he wouldn't make the mistake again of thinking it could be effortless. He would take it as slow as she needed, but he'd also determined he wanted to do a little wooing in his own way.

He'd sent her flowers on Sunday morning, signed "From a friend," and then had her favorite menu items from the bakery in town delivered to the school yesterday. She chided him at the talent show, but she'd smiled and blushed slightly as she told him his efforts were unnecessary. He would take her smile any day of the week.

Jack frowned as he shut the door to the back porch behind him. "I'm not here about Carl." Jack rubbed a hand along the back of his neck. "Have you been on social media this morning?"

Walker gestured to the container of flour, carton of eggs and the mixing bowl in front of him. "I have more important things to do with my morning than scroll the newsfeed. I'm making pancakes. Gus will be down in a few minutes. I like having breakfast with him."

"You know there's a country music showcase at the Ryman Auditorium this weekend."

"I declined to participate in it." Walker picked an egg out of the carton and started cracking it on the side of the mixing bowl.

"You were announced as a special guest star just this morning," Jack told him.

The egg splattered on the counter.

"I said no," he repeated.

Jack nodded. "I called the event organizers this morning, along with the record company. Apparently, they were told by Dani that you would be joining her on stage for your duet and you'd be willing to encore with '*There's a Light.*'"

"Why would anyone believe Danielle when I explicitly said no? I'm not doing it."

"They posted the announcement two hours ago, and it's already gotten a hundred thousand likes. They're going to record a special on the history of country music and want to feature you as one of its brightest stars. I hate to say it because I've told you to do things on your own terms, but this would be a smart move career-wise."

Walker was about to tell Jack that he didn't give a damn about his career, but that wasn't true. He didn't want success only for himself. He wanted to honor his brother's legacy and what they'd created with the Calloway Brothers band.

Two kids from a broken home without enough money for bus fare between them had risen to the top. He didn't want to let that go, but he needed balance.

He sure as hell didn't appreciate his ex-girlfriend manipulating him.

"They also want to do a tribute to Nash during the showcase," Jack added quietly. "It's a big deal."

Walker grabbed a wad of paper towels and began cleaning up the egg that was sitting useless and cracked on the granite counter.

"Next Saturday is the night of the talent show," he said as if Jack didn't realize it.

"You'll be here for the rehearsals, and I'll videotape the show so you can see it."

"Are you saying I have to do the Nashville event?"

"I'm not going to tell you to do anything. As your manager, I recommend it. As your friend, I—"

"You're just like Daddy!" Gus shouted as he entered the room from the hallway, small fists clenched at his sides. "Work always comes first. He didn't want to be a dad, and you're no better."

Walker's mouth dropped open at the vehemence in the kid's voice. Gus thought the sun rose and set by his exuberant and bighearted father. Yes, Gus's upbringing had been out of the ordinary. Before he started school, the kid spent most of his time on tour buses or playing in the makeshift nursery Jack set up at every venue.

But Nash had always made things fun. It had been an adventure and so much better than the childhood the Calloway brothers endured.

"Your daddy loved you," Walker said, and even to his own ears, his tone sounded too forceful. Although he knew Nash was human and made mistakes, it was still difficult to fathom anyone speaking ill of his late brother, especially the son who adored him.

"No one is prioritizing a career over you, Gussie. But as Jack said, this one night would mean a lot to your father's memory. I know it's not what we planned, but sometimes we have to make the best of the circumstances given to us."

"Why am I always the one who has to make the best of it?" Gus demanded, his angry gaze swooping between Walker and Jack. "Jack gets to go off with a new family, and you pop in and out whenever you feel like it. I'm always here. Why don't you just send me to boarding school? It would make things easier. That's probably what my dad would have done if he was still alive."

"Your father never would have sent you away. He loved being with you."

"When I fit in his schedule," Gus muttered, then stomped to the refrigerator, opened it and grabbed a yogurt container and one of the blueberry muffins Annalise had brought over the previous day.

"I'm making pancakes so we can eat breakfast together." Walker tapped a finger on the edge of the mixing bowl. "I'll even put chocolate chips in them."

"I don't have time," Gus said, his eyes flashing.

"I got to keep practicing for the talent show. I'm sure plenty of parents want to watch their kids."

"I'm here, Gus. You know that. It's one night."

"A couple of nights," Jack clarified. "They'll need you in Nashville for a sound check, but I can put them off until Friday."

Walker sighed, feeling torn. He didn't want to disappoint his nephew, but how could he pass up an opportunity to attend an event offering to honor his brother?

One of his biggest fears was that Nash would be forgotten—a gone-too-early footnote in the story of their career. The success of the new song and the buzz his solo album had garnered had added another layer to the guilt he felt over living when Nash had died. This was their dream together, but Walker was the only one reaping the rewards of it. He couldn't turn his back on Nash's memory and his role in Walker's success.

Kids were resilient, right? He had to believe Gus would come to understand his decision.

Gus heaved a similar sigh, then rolled his skinny shoulders. "It's okay, Uncle Walker. You did a lot to help with the talent show, and Daddy is important. I know he loved me, but I wish he were here."

"I do, too, buddy."

"That makes three of us," Jack said and ruffled Gus's hair. "How about you practice in the kitchen while your uncle makes breakfast? I'm a good audience and never say no to pancakes. It's a personal rule I think you should follow as well."

For about the millionth time, Walker felt grateful he wasn't in this parenting thing alone.

"All right." Gus handed the muffin and yogurt to Jack. "Me and Trey are getting a lot better."

"Trey and I," Walker corrected.

"That's what I said." Gus turned and ran down the hall to collect his magic supplies.

"Will missing the talent show scar him forever?" Walker cracked another egg, this one straight into the mixing bowl.

"He'll be fine. You do a good job of trying to balance it all. So you know, Nash struggled with the same kinds of worries. I think all parents do. Even Annalise, who is as confident of a woman as I've ever met, questions herself when it comes to her children."

"Thanks, Jack. I needed to hear that." Even if the other man was blowing sunshine, Walker could use the light to guide him at the moment.

CHAPTER SEVEN

"Gus, is everything okay?" Meghan stared at the boy slumped in his seat, his thin shoulders drooping and his gaze downcast. She was used to him joining her in her classroom for lunch and recess since the timing coordinated with her free period, and he liked to draw more than he liked being with the other kids on the playground.

Gus was working on an original comic book he wanted to give Walker as a Christmas present. She had promised to help him have it bound once he was finished. Most afternoons, he talked while he illustrated, explaining to her the nuances of the characters and storyline, or offering up random tidbits of scientific and music history facts.

Gus in a glum mood was rare and bothered Meghan, especially when she'd been feeling so buoyant the last few days, like she was walking on a bed of champagne bubbles.

Walker was the reason for her mood. He didn't seem bothered by her suggestion of friendship only. But she suspected his thoughtfulness, attentive manner at rehearsals and the flirty texts he was regularly sending meant something more.

A second chance for a deeper connection, which she also longed for, despite her claim to the contrary. Her feelings for the man hadn't changed and allowing him back in her life only reminded her how sweet he could be. He listened and shared his thoughts like she mattered, which made her feel special and valued. Meghan had grown up not feeling like she mattered to anyone in her family, so it was the quickest way back into her heart.

"It's nothing." He frowned at the paper he'd been coloring for the past half hour, wrinkled his nose and then crushed it between his hands.

"I don't believe you, but I'll respect your right to privacy. I'm here if you need to talk, and I know your Uncle Walker would also be happy to listen."

"Too bad he isn't gonna be here to listen or watch me and Trey in the talent show." He paused, then amended, "Trey and me. I don't even want to do the stupid magic act anymore."

Meghan folded herself into the child-sized desk next to Gus's, her heart thudding in her chest. "What do you mean he's not going to be here?"

Yesterday afternoon at rehearsal, Walker had offered to have all the participants and their families back to Whimsy Farm for ice cream after the show.

"That stupid Dani Griggs signed him up for a concert in Nashville Saturday night." Gus crossed his arms over his chest. "I don't like her."

"I don't either," Meghan agreed, "but we don't call people stupid." She would have called Danielle Griggs a bitch, but not out loud.

"Your uncle didn't mention the concert to me." It sounded like he'd just found out, but Meghan still felt disappointment slice through her.

Feeling like she was valued, respected and cared for,

which she wanted from Walker, included him talking to her even when the conversation was difficult. That had been part of the problem in the summer. He'd left when things got complicated, and she'd been stuck dealing with her bruised heart alone.

"They're giving some award to my dad or making a speech about him or something. I wish nobody in my family played music. If Daddy hadn't been on the tour bus, he wouldn't have been in the accident. He'd still be here with me."

Meghan ached for the pain she could feel coming like a wave off the sweet boy. She understood loss and grief but hadn't experienced it at the level Gus and Walker had by losing Nash.

"I wish we could know that were true. It's easy to blame your father's career, and I know it's hard when the demands of the job take your uncle away from you. But there is no way of rewriting the past. You had a daddy who loved you. Your uncle loves you, as well. Even if he can't be here sometimes, that doesn't change. You know other parents can't be around for everything because of their jobs or other circumstances."

"I know. Trey's dad is in the clinker so he can't come either."

She tried not to grimace. "I don't think I'd compare Walker to Trey's dad."

Gus nodded. "Can I tell you a secret?"

"Yes, and I promise to do my best to honor whatever you tell me."

"I like playing guitar and singing. I like it better than drawing or magic or most everything else."

Meghan let out a relieved breath. "That's wonderful, Gus. Musical talent runs in your family."

"But it makes me scared. I want to have a normal life."

"You can have the life you choose, and your uncle and Jack will support you. Have you played for either of them?"

Gus shook his head and pulled out a blank sheet of paper. "Uncle Walker said he's heard me in my bedroom, but I don't want to disappoint him if I'm not as good as Daddy was when he was my age."

Meghan reached out and squeezed the boy's arm. She might be hurt by what she assumed was Walker's disregard for her feelings, but she knew how much he loved his nephew. "There's nothing you can do that will disappoint Walker if it makes you happy. Have a little faith in him."

"Do you have faith in him?"

Meghan's heart started thudding once again. If only she knew how to answer that question. "I have faith that he loves you very much."

Gus seemed to consider that for a moment, then nodded. "He does." He glanced up at her. "I think I'm going to go outside and find Trey to work on our act for the rest of lunch. Is that okay?"

"Of course." Meghan smiled and tried to pretend it wasn't wobbly at the edges.

When she was alone in the room, she grabbed her phone from the desk drawer, wondering if she'd received a text or call from Walker.

Nothing.

She understood what that meant. He didn't care enough to alert her of his plans. Flowers and baked goods were easy enough to order, she supposed. Tricky conversations were part of genuine relationships, the only kind she wanted. If Walker couldn't handle that, it was his loss. At least, that's what she told herself.

She half expected him not to show up to the afternoon rehearsal. Today, they were running through the acts from kindergarten to grade three, so Gus and Trey weren't part of the lineup.

She was speaking with Raina hen Walker entered the auditorium, a fact she knew because of how her body tingled with awareness. As he approached, Raina quickly excused herself to herd a group of kids playing Duck Duck Goose on one side of the stage.

"You don't seem to be having a good day," she said, proud of how steady her voice sounded.

Walker looked like he was coming off the tail end of a monthlong binge, his skin pale and his eyes exhausted. His hair was rumpled like he'd been tugging at the ends, and he nervously shifted from one foot to the other.

"Can I talk to you?" he asked, his tone despondent.

"Is it about missing the talent show for a concert?" she chirped. "It's no biggie." Maybe she was getting the hang of faking it after all.

He looked surprised by her cheery tone but nodded. "They're honoring Nash, but only because I will be there. I don't want to go. I promise I'd rather be here. If you want me to stay, I'll say no."

She wanted him to stay, but more importantly, she wanted him to choose that. To choose her.

"You should go," she answered. "It's fine, Walker. I understand why honoring your brother is important."

"I didn't say yes." He rubbed one hand against his jaw. "I wouldn't have committed to the talent show knowing I couldn't be here for the performance. I don't want to let you down, Meghan. I've done that before."

Maybe they weren't meant to be, despite what her heart longed for. Yet she could see the decision weighed on him and didn't want that.

"Magnolia will still be here when you get back. We're even having the show professionally recorded. It will be like you didn't miss a thing."

That wasn't true, and they both knew it.

"If it wasn't for Nash's tribute…"

"Walker, stop." She placed a hand on his arm. "You're making the best decision for you, and I appreciate you telling me about it instead of simply leaving."

"I wouldn't do that. You mean—"

"Miss Banks, Joey Minner puked backstage!" one of the kids shouted, running toward her.

She immediately turned to deal with Joey and his sick stomach but glanced over her shoulder. "We're *friends*," she told Walker, emphasizing the word. "That won't change."

It seemed that nothing would where Walker was concerned. But as the old saying went, the show must go on. One way or another, she'd remember that.

CHAPTER EIGHT

Meghan arrived at the elementary school early Saturday morning to set up the talent show stage backdrop and ensure all the last-minute details were in place.

This was the biggest student event of the fall semester, and as part of it, she'd arranged to have sixth-grade volunteers at the doors to staff a canned food drive. She hoped they'd be able to help stock the local community center food bank with donations before the upcoming holiday season.

Her principal was excited and grateful for Meghan's leadership. Meghan knew deep in her heart that despite some of the challenges she'd faced, staying in Magnolia after her grandmother's death was the right decision.

She was doing her best to focus on the positive aspects of her life, of which there were so many, and ignore the dull ache of disappointment that Walker wasn't here to share this day.

He'd texted several times from Nashville and asked if she'd consider visiting the city that had been his home for many years over the holidays.

She hadn't answered, which wasn't exactly fair. But it was still difficult to believe that a man like him would choose a woman like her. She was coming to see that even though he hadn't handled things well after the spring benefit concert, she'd also made mistakes. Fear and insecurity kept her from telling him how she felt. It was water under the bridge now, but maybe if she'd had more faith in the connection they shared, things could have been different before now.

"Meghan, are you here?"

"I'm backstage," Meghan called out in response to Annalise's familiar voice.

She straightened some of the props left behind after the dress rehearsal the previous afternoon and turned— only to stop short at the look on her friend's face. "What is it? What happened?"

Annalise shook her head, a few wisps of golden blond hair falling out of her messy bun. Meghan figured something must be terribly wrong because even though Annalise had changed quite a bit about her life, she still dressed to the nines most days. This morning, she wore a baggy UNC sweatshirt and black leggings, with her feet shoved into a pair of sneakers.

"Don't worry. It's nothing horrible. Well, it's horrible for me because my kid is sick. Trey felt a sore throat coming on last night and woke up feeling awful and running a fever. I took him to the pediatrician's after-hours clinic, and he's been diagnosed with strep throat."

"No," Meghan murmured.

"Unfortunately, yes. Jack is staying with Gus while Walker's in Nashville, so I called him on the way over, and he's breaking the news to Gus. You were next on my list, but I passed the school on the way to the pharmacy and saw your car. I figured I'd stop in instead."

"Poor Trey! I feel terrible for Gus, but these things happen."

"I'm sure Jack is calling Walker. I wish he were here. He can always make Gus feel better when he's upset."

"I wish Walker were here, too," Meghan said softly.

Annalise studied her for a moment. "How are you?"

"I've been doing some thinking."

"That sounds ominous."

"Maybe," Meghan sighed. "I've told you my parents were both doctors and worked a lot. I didn't fit the mold they'd created the way my older brother and sister did, and they were both in college by the time I was Gus and Trey's age, so I was left alone. A lot. Whenever my mom and dad chose their careers or social lives over me, it felt like a rejection. I thought that if I'd been more interesting, prettier or smarter, I could have held their attention. I could have earned their love."

"Kids shouldn't have to earn their parents' love," Annalise told her.

Meghan nodded. "But I kept trying anyway." She breathed out a sad laugh. "Trying and failing. Trust is hard for me because I still feel like I'm not enough, especially with someone like Walker. He's not only successful at a level I can barely comprehend, but he's also famous and has women literally throwing themselves at him. How can I compete with that?"

"I don't think he expects you to."

"Exactly. He makes me feel like I'm important just for being me, and that's scary, at least for my heart."

Meghan gestured to the autumn scene behind them on the stage she and Walker had created together, talking and laughing as they worked. She'd painted the canvas backdrop while Walker had used cardboard, PVC pipe and colorful tissue paper to make the trees that brought the fall setting to life. "He tries. He's been trying with me, and I haven't given him a chance. It stinks that he's not here to help Gus feel better, but he's a good man. I think he likes me, but I don't know how to trust him. I'm not sure how to trust myself with him."

Annalise grinned. "Girl, he more than *likes* you. But giving your heart to someone is a risk. You might think it's safer not to try, but you're missing out on the good stuff if you don't."

"I want the good stuff," Meghan murmured. "I want it with Walker."

"So what are you going to do about that?"

Nerves fluttered through Meghan's stomach as she thought about the action she wanted to take. It would leave no question of her feelings for Walker. As much as it scared her, she knew it was time to be brave for herself and him.

"There's an early flight out of Raleigh to Nashville. I'm going to book it and surprise him tomorrow morning." She squeezed her hands together. "I want to see his world there. I want him to know he's important to me."

Annalise gave her a quick hug. "A grand gesture. I love it. I think Walker will, too."

"What if he doesn't?" Doubt bubbled up inside her, trying to suffocate her excitement at the anticipation of finally going after something she wanted.

"You won't know unless you try. You're stronger than you think, my friend. You can handle whatever comes next."

Meghan embraced Annalise once more. "Thank you for that reminder. I might be borrowing your faith in me one more time."

"I've got more than enough," Annalise promised.

CHAPTER NINE

MEGHAN'S NERVOUS THOUGHTS regarding her plan to surprise Walker took a backseat for the rest of the day, as preparations for the talent show kept her blessedly busy.

Thirty minutes before curtain time, the auditorium was nearly standing room only and Raina reported they'd collected over forty boxes of canned goods for the food pantry.

The student performers were gathered backstage in small groups and the excitement shimmered in the air like elementary-school fairy dust. She glanced at her watch and thought about Walker. He'd be at the Ryman getting ready for his big night, and she wondered if the anticipation she felt compared at all to his emotions before a show.

She'd get the chance to ask him tomorrow morning. The uncertainty of her plan still frightened her, but the risk would be worth the potential reward. An ordinary life might be enough to satisfy her, but she wanted something more in her heart. She wanted Walker.

"Miss Banks?"

She turned and smiled as Gus approached her, holding out her arms for a hug. He gave her a tight one, and she realized he was holding a bulky guitar case in one hand. "I'm so sorry about Trey and the magic act, sweetie."

He pulled back and held up the case. "Yeah, but I was wondering if I can still be in the show with a different act? I want to play a song."

"I would love that," she said, emotions making her heart clench. "I think everyone would enjoy hearing you play." She smoothed away a lock of hair that fell over his big brown eyes. "And we're recording the show so your uncle will get to see it, too."

"I think I'd rather watch in person."

The din of the voices surrounding them faded away as Walker approached from the back door of the auditorium. Her heart flung itself against her ribs like it needed to be closer to the man who made it pound.

"Uncle Walker came home," Gus explained as if she didn't realize it, which was fair since Meghan felt like she must be imagining his presence.

Then he was close enough to reach out and take her hand, linking their fingers. "I came home," he repeated, his voice soft and low.

Gus glanced between the two of them. "I just said that. Grown-ups are weird. I'm gonna tune my guitar," he announced, unaware of how overcome with emotion Meghan felt at this moment.

"What about the concert?" she asked.

"It wasn't important," he said with a shrug. "Not like Gus." He lifted her hand and grazed a light kiss across her knuckles. "Or you."

"No."

Pain flashed in his bourbon-hued eyes. "Meghan, please."

She held a finger to his lips. "I don't want you to make yourself smaller for me, Walker. I'm glad you're here, but I know how much music means to you. Honoring your brother is important. I've made myself small for too long. I'm an ordinary schoolteacher—"

He wrapped his free hand around her finger. "There is nothing ordinary about you."

"Because you make me feel special, and I'm trying to believe it. I want to have faith—in both of us. I want to love big, Walker."

"With me?" he asked and the uncertainty in his gaze had her heart melting.

"Fifteen minutes to showtime," Raina announced from the far side of the stage.

Meghan turned, still holding Walker's hand and rushed down the hall that led to the main part of the school. When she got to her classroom, she opened the door, pulled him inside then turned and pressed her mouth to his.

It was different from the kiss they'd shared months earlier because now she was sure—not of the future—but that she could be brave enough to go after the one she wanted.

The kiss flooded her senses, making her nearly delirious with longing, and it took all her willpower to pull away. "I bought a plane ticket," she said, her voice breathless.

Walker blinked then frowned. "Where are you going?"

"I was coming to you." She felt a blush rise to her cheeks at the way he grinned in response. "I was going to surprise you tomorrow morning."

"That would have been a hell of a way to wake up." He leaned down and kissed her again, his lips gentle like he wanted to savor her. As if they had all the time in the world.

"Having you here is better." She wrapped her arms around his neck. "I think I'm falling in love with you, Walker Calloway."

"I know I'm falling for you, Meghan Banks," he answered without hesitation then made a funny face. "The whole world is going to know it, too. I probably should have called the new album Ode to Meghan."

By now, her heart was racing so fast she felt like it would never slow down. Even when things went back to normal, she knew her feelings for Walker would be there, steady and true. She had faith in him—and herself.

She leaned in to kiss him again, but her gaze snagged on her watch. "We need to go," she said, pulling away quickly even though she wanted to stay wrapped in his arms. "It's time."

"Let's put on the best talent show this school has ever seen." He dropped a final kiss on her forehead then they hurried back toward the auditorium. "We've got all the time in the world."

Time for love and to live a life Meghan had only dreamed of—with this man at her side.

THE AFTER-SHOW ICE CREAM celebration was in full swing when Walker realized his nephew had disappeared. He found him standing near the edge of the horse pasture, petting Orion's soft neck.

"Did you need a break from the party?" he asked as he came to stand next to the boy.

"I heard Orion whinny," Gus explained, "and I wanted to tell him about playing guitar. Sometimes talking to him makes me feel closer to Daddy."

"I know what you mean," Walker agreed, his chest

squeezing at the wistfulness in Gus's tone. "Your father would have been so proud of you tonight."

Gus looked up at him, his feathery brows furrowed. "I was worried I wouldn't be good enough, like everyone expected me to be just like him."

Man, could Walker relate to that. "It doesn't matter what other people expect, Gus. You should be the best version of you. That's all your dad would want. Mainly, he'd want you to be happy."

"I'm happy you came back," Gus answered. "Are you upset about missing the concert? I guess they didn't say nice things about Dad since you weren't there."

"They went ahead with the tribute," Walker told his nephew as Orion strolled away toward the rest of the herd. Even Nash's horse seemed to be recovering from the grief of losing his owner. "But I realized your father wouldn't have cared about a bunch of industry people honoring him. You are his legacy, Gus. I know the music pulled him away from you at times, but he loved you with his whole heart. I do, too, buddy."

"I love you, Uncle Walker." A soft breeze kicked up, ruffling the boy's hair the way Nash used to. Memories flooded Walker's mind, but they were sweet instead of filled with sorrow and guilt. "I want another scoop of ice cream. How about you?"

Walker smiled, amazed as always at how blessed he was to have this kid in his life. Gus was a constant reminder of the best parts of Nash, and Walker was determined to finally take Jack's advice and begin living a life that made him happy. One he created on his terms.

Meghan met them halfway back to the house, and Gus ran ahead after giving her a quick hug.

"His performance gave me goosebumps tonight,"

she said, rubbing her bare arms. She wore a long, floral-patterned dress in some silky material that Walker could imagine pooling at her feet as he took it off her.

He looped an arm around her shoulder and kissed the top of her head. "That's how it was with Nash from the start," he revealed. "Gus inherited his father's talent."

"And his uncle's," she added, wrapping her arm around his waist.

He turned to face her. "I'm sorry I was stupid when it came to us."

She nodded. "I'm sorry I was scared."

"I can't promise I won't be stupid again, but I'm going to try like hell to be the man you deserve, Meghan. You mean the world to me, and I'm so damn grateful for another chance to prove it to you."

She kissed him in response, and he knew he'd never take the way she made him feel for granted. He'd found the happiness he'd always wanted and knew without a doubt that love was the most precious gift of all. He'd spend their whole lives making sure she understood that she held his heart in her hands and that he would cherish hers in return.

* * * * *

Do you love romance books?

JOIN

on Facebook by scanning the code below:

A group dedicated to book recommendations, author exclusives, SWOONING and all things romance! A community made for romance readers by romance readers.

Facebook.com/groups/readloverepeat

RLRBPA0323